I dedicate this book to my husband David who enjoyed his twenty two years in the Royal Navy, above and below the ocean waves.

Acknowledgements

A huge thank you to Super Suze for all her hard work on the computer and confidence boosting lectures; to dear Alan Stewart for his wonderful cover, his friendship, kindness and patience; to Sarah, professional and reliable as ever; to Marc for exquisite and exciting drawings; thank you Jim for the photo; to all my family and friends who listened whether they wanted to or not! A big big thank you.

Catherine Bond

Moonglimmer

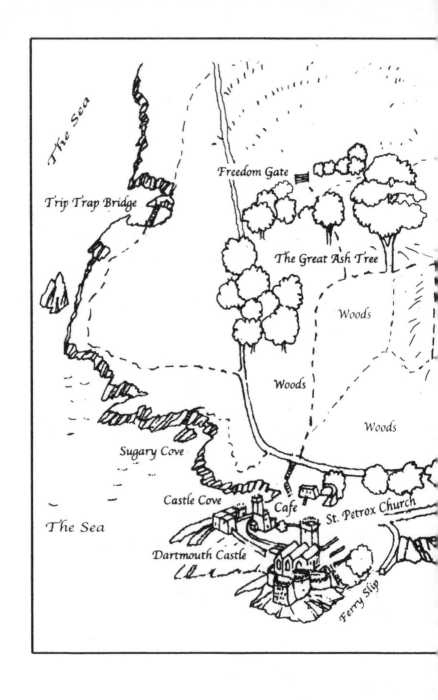

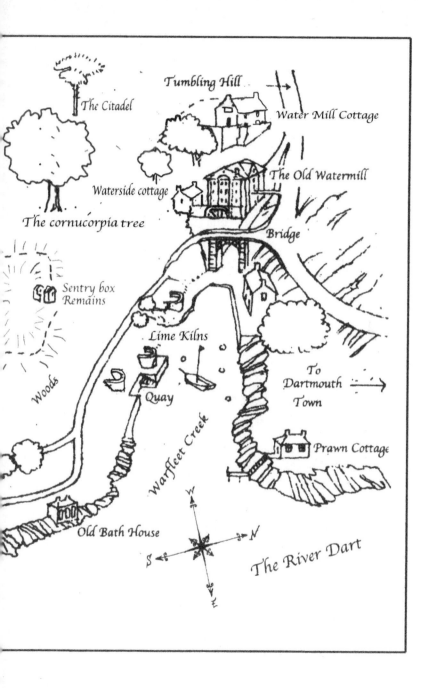

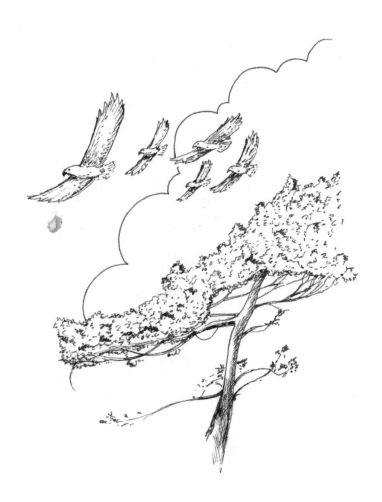

Chapter One
Contact with Patrick

Eddie and Ellie had grown up at Watermill Cottage, just two hundred metres from the water's edge at Warfleet Creek and close to the wooded hillside of Gallants Bower, where the ancient boundaries of the old Seafarers' and Woodlanders' kingdoms had been established centuries ago. During the autumn half term, this brother and sister had experienced a thrilling adventure with their Scottish friend, Patrick McNab and all three had been transported back in time to the end of the English Civil War in 1646. They had all become involved with the strange inhabitants of the woodland and the sea shore.

On his return journey to Paddington station, Patrick decided to rebel against his unhappy life. He got off the train at Newton Abbott and stood alone on the platform, looking vacantly around, wondering what to do. *I'm not going back,* he told himself firmly, even though he was frightened at the prospect of going it alone; he had money in his pocket, a good brain and plenty of spirit. Oh no, he was staying in Devon to be with his great new friends, Eddie and Ellie. *To hell with school!* And he tossed his head and made his way to the nearest bus stop.

His father, Sam, was waiting at the London station for his son and when he did not arrive at the appointed time he rang Bridget and George, Patrick's godparents, to see what had happened. He was rather cross and angry on the phone.

Disturbed and upset by Patrick's disappearance, George and Bridget sat together wondering what on earth could have happened to him. Eddie and Ellie sat at the dining table, surprised, but knowing in their hearts the depths of Patrick's unhappiness, remembering his outbursts before he left. His desperate words came echoing back to them:

"I don't want to go back you know. I'd rather stay here. I really don't want to go back to that school ever again."

How deeply he must have meant it; this time he had done something about it, perhaps finding new self-confidence from his adventure in the Civil War with Eddie.

Eddie and Ellie looked at each other, longing for a private conversation away from the ears of the distraught godparents.

"What do you think? Eddie lad? Where on earth can he be? I just don't understand it," repeated poor George, over and over again.

Eddie wanted to say something to comfort the old man, who genuinely was fond of Patrick, but what? He had a few ideas of his own where Patrick was.

"He'll be in touch, George, you'll see. We all knew he didn't want to go back. Didn't we? His father is the only one he hadn't told," Eddie answered rather grimly.

Ellie said nothing, stunned by the news. As long as he was safe she didn't care. She was extremely fond of Patrick.

The phone rang again. George sprang to his feet to answer it, his face betraying instantly who it was.

"Patrick! Thank God! Where are you?" George blustered on, his face white with anxiety.

"Just tell me where you are and I'll come and get you. You really must ring your father. Have you got some money? Oh no, he's gone!" George looked at the now-buzzing receiver and put it down gently.

"Tell us, George!" cried out Bridget, tears in her eyes, "Where is he?"

"He wouldn't tell me," George said sadly, shaking his head. "Just wanted to let us know he was alright. I blame myself of course. Should have realised how unhappy he was. Having a great time here with you two had made it worse. It's all our fault." And he broke down, sad and guilty, covering his face with his large hands and sighing deeply.

Bridget sprang to her feet and hugged him. Eddie and Ellie sat still, embarrassed and feeling awkward as the two lovely people they adored were lost in grief.

"Come on, Ellie," said Eddie softly. "Let's leave them for a while," and he got up and pulled Ellie after him.

"We've got to talk," he whispered to her surprised face, "come on," and pushed her gently downstairs to one of the bedrooms.

"What do you make of it, Ellie?" he burst out when they had closed the door quietly.

"I just don't know, but he must have got off the train somewhere, and—"

"Headed back here I reckon," interrupted Eddie. "I mean, where else would he go?" He looked at his sister for reassurance, suddenly questioning where Patrick would go.

"He doesn't know anybody but us," reasoned Ellie sensibly. "But surely he knows that George will send him back. I just can't see the point…"

"He's desperate, that's why. He sounded so sad when he said goodbye."

"What about Prawn Cottage? It's empty still isn't it, since Captain Avery left? Does he know where the key is?"

"Yes he does," remembered Eddie. "He saw me get it out of the jam jar by the jetty."

"Or the lime kiln. Don't you remember? All our emergency stuff is there." Ellie was getting excited now. Patrick was a clever boy; he'd have thought all this out on the train before he hopped off, she was sure of it.

They heard the phone ring again and ran up the stairs to hear what was going on.

"Well?" Eddie blurted out, as he saw Bridget holding the phone. She put her finger to her lips to hush them.

"Oh, I'm so glad, Irene," she said, beaming. "We'll wait to hear from you. Thank you for ringing us," and she rang off. "George, cheer up, he's just phoned his mother."

George sat up straight, looked heavenward and said "Thank the Lord."

"I hope she's satisfied. Always gadding off here and there, on some University business. Why, she hasn't phoned him once here, not once, to see how he's getting on, not all the time he's been here. Calls herself a mother. Hmm." Bridget got rid of all her pent-up feelings in one go.

"Aye, Bridget, I reckon you're right," agreed George reluctantly.

"Well," confirmed his sister excitedly," he says that he's not going back to the boarding school. He's staying in Dartmouth somewhere and they can come and meet him if they want to discuss it." And she folded her arms in satisfaction, enjoying the drama now that she knew Patrick was safe.

"It suits them to shove him in that boarding school and send him down here in the holidays for you to look after him. No wonder he feels so unwanted," Eddie said nastily.

"Where is he, do you think?" asked George, and he peered out of the window into the black night sky. "Any ideas?"

Eddie and Ellie had their own ideas but kept very quiet.

"Well anyway, I'll take you back home to your mum and dad in the morning. Goodnight then," said George curtly.

"Goodnight." They kissed Bridget and went off downstairs to their rooms.

"We've got to find him before they do," Eddie told Ellie firmly. "Come on, get ready to go out, we're off on a man hunt."

They dressed in warm outdoor clothes, collected a torch each and a bar of chocolate and sat on the bed in Ellie's room looking out at the glinting, gliding river and the windy trees waving in the winter darkness.

"Do you think we'll find him?" said Ellie, suddenly doubting the wisdom of venturing out into the cold and dark.

"I'll bet you five pounds we do," Eddie replied with utter certainty. "I know Patrick now. He can only be in two places – Prawn Cottage or the lime kiln. I'm certain of it." He smiled with confidence at her.

"Have Bridget and George gone to bed yet? We need to be sure they're asleep first. Bridget might lie awake worrying. Just wait for a bit longer, give it another five minutes."

They sat together, brother and sister, itching to get outside and begin the search for the best friend either of them had ever had, determined not to let him down. They would find him if it was possible, before all the grownups started fighting and arguing over the quiet Scottish boy. They had until dawn.

Chapter Two
Seeking a friend

Out they stepped into the breezy darkness and felt their way along the patio, up the metal staircase and onto the road. Eddie switched his torch on and they followed the welcoming bright circle of light down to the lime kilns, finally arriving at the very last one. With fast-beating hearts, both played their torches into the dark depths of the man-made caves. The lights exposed piles of sailing gear covered with a tarpaulin, but nobody was there. No cheery boy was snuggled down in a pile of blankets, hiding from the rest of the world.

"He's not here," said Ellie disappointed.

"No, and neither is *Sargasso*. Come on, help me lift this up." The determined boy and girl pulled the heavy sheet aside. It was still dry underneath and had protected all the gear they used for sailing their little green Cornish shrimper named *Sargasso*.

"He's been in here!" Eddie announced with mounting excitement. "Some of the stuff is definitely gone. Can you see Ellie?" He beamed at his delighted sister.

"Yes, yes I can, what's he taken?" as she lifted the coats to see. "Help me move the sails."

They pieced together from memory the items they had put there. Food, clothing, blankets, candles, matches, and a plastic container of tools was also missing.

"Put the cover back and then we'll head off to Prawn Cottage. Can you see anything happening over there?" asked Eddie.

Directly across the shimmering water, standing on the rocks at the farthest point of the creek was the tiny pink cottage. The grey shutters were firmly closed and the whole place was pitch black.

"Patrick's not that stupid," replied Ellie sarcastically, helping to cover the hidden stores.

They set off again to the opposite side of the creek and didn't speak until they arrived at the muddy steps leading down to the cottage.

"Go down to the jetty and see if the jam jar's empty," urged Ellie, "then we'll know if he's here."

"OK, stay where you are." He indicated to his impatient sister and disappeared around the side of the cottage into the darkness. As she stood alone waiting, Ellie couldn't help remembering times before, when the ghosts of the sea captain John Avery and his faithful dog Syracuse had secretly stayed in this little cottage for part of the summer. Together, they had sailed the small green boat and enjoyed some thrilling adventures, but now he was gone – catapulted back in time with the two mice Ellie had discovered living in the old church at the castle. She felt sad; she had tried not to think about Ferdinand and Isabella.

"Stop it," she told herself sharply, waiting in the darkness for Eddie to reappear. Several minutes later his face appeared. He was holding up the empty jam jar, grinning from ear to ear and pointing to it.

"We are on your trail, Patrick." Ellie laughed, pleased and excited.

"Come on. We'll have to shout through the letterbox, or bang on the windows."

With Ellie holding on tightly to Eddie's arm in the pitch darkness they found their way round to the front door, pressed open the letter box, and Eddie bent down and called out.

"Patrick! Patrick!" he repeated in a breathless but insistent way. There was no answer.

"You call again. I'll get a stick," Eddie whispered

Suddenly a light shone through the chinks of the shutters and Ellie heard footsteps; a sleepy voice called back from the other side of the door.

"Who's that? Is it you Eddie? Ellie?"

"Yes," hissed Ellie, looking desperately through the narrow slit. Two eyes met hers and then smiled.

"Wait a minute," said the voice they both recognised, as they waited impatiently, listening to keys clinking and mutterings, and finally the old door swung open to reveal a refugee wrapped in one of their blankets from the lime kiln.

"Patrick!" They were so glad to see him and all three hugged each other together briefly.

"How did you find me?" asked the amazed Patrick, whose hair was sticking up and who looked very scruffy and unlike himself.

"Easy," laughed Eddie, "can we come in? It's cold out here."

So at 1.30am on a cold wintry night, the three friends were reunited once again. Shining faces smiled at each other as they sat in the nautical cabin that had been created inside the tiny cottage. Patrick put the kettle on and they drank cups of instant tomato soup, all talking at once.

"You'd better tell us what happened," said Eddie suddenly becoming serious, waiting to hear Patrick's story. Ellie looked up at him, wondering if he would be able to really tell them the truth about his life and his feelings which he had kept very much to himself up until now.

Patrick sat looking awkward in his blanket, quiet for a moment. Then he began in a rush.

"I don't quite know, really. It just sort of crept over me on the train, all these funny feelings. I'd – we'd – had such a fantastic time, and somehow, for the first time I just sort of belonged. I had a… I know this sounds stupid, but… I had people of my own and I didn't have to prove anything. Everybody just liked me for me, and it was so… well, comfortable. I can't think of how else to say it."

He looked down into his empty mug of soup sadly. Ellie opened her mouth to say something, but Eddie put his hand on her arm firmly and said,

"No, Ellie. Go on, Patrick." He nodded to him. "You were on the train, and… go on."

Patrick sighed a big sigh and began again.

"I felt more and more that I was leaving everything behind, that there was nothing in front of me to look forward to, and…" He hesitated, staring into his mug again. Eddie and Ellie waited. He took a deep breath and it all came tumbling out.

"Nobody cared about me anywhere. My mum and dad are too busy to bother with me. I go to school and I'm locked up there and I feel like a parcel shifted around where I'm going to be the least trouble. I mean, I'm sure they love me in their strange way but I'm so lonely and well… alone, most of the time. It wasn't until I met you lot, that I started to see things differently. And now, well… Now I just can't face going back there. That's all. So, I decided to get off the train at Newton Abbott and made my way back here. I knew where the key was and the extra stores and here I am. I've made my decision."

He turned to them both triumphantly, looking pleased and said, "You've proved how much you care about me because you've taken the trouble to come and find me, haven't you?" And they could see the faintest glint of tears in Patrick's eyes.

Eddie and Ellie felt very upset for him and Ellie collected up the mugs and went to the sink to wash them.

Dear me, she thought, *how dreadful, but I'm sure they'll send him back. You can't just leave everything, can you?*

"I bet your dad's here tomorrow morning first thing," said Eddie, "He's been on the phone to George. He was very worried about you. So were Bridget and George," he added.

"I felt terrible about that but I didn't have a choice. It's all your fault you know, I have such a good time when we're altogether. Captain Avery and the medallion and just... everything. So now I want to be part of it, just like you," and they all fell about laughing, feeling better at once. Ellie spied the long red scarf she had knitted, underneath the blanket.

"Kept you warm then?" She pointed to it.

"Could have wrapped myself up like an Egyptian mummy!"

"What shall we tell George and Bridget?" asked Ellie anxiously.

"Tell them the truth," said Patrick finally, "I don't care anymore. I'll take whatever's coming to me."

So the three of them talked for a bit longer and then, yawning, Eddie and Ellie decided they had better return to the Old Bath House. They hugged their friend and crept off into the darkness, finding their way back along the riverbank, down the steps to the open patio door, and slipped inside the quiet house. Only snores from George's bedroom could be heard, as they whispered goodnight to each other.

Nobody knew what the outcome would be. Each could only guess what fate had in store for Patrick McNab, escapee from Burnside College, Edinburgh.

Chapter Three
A joyful reunion

The phone rang very early the next morning, waking everyone up. George got there first, sprinting along in his pyjamas to answer it.

"Don't worry, it's your dad," he called out, but by the time Eddie and Ellie had rushed upstairs, George had hung up.

"Sorry, just a message to say the plane has been delayed and they won't be home until very late this evening, so… you're going to have to stay here just one more night." He smiled sympathetically." I expect you've had enough of us."

"No, no, not at all, George. We've had a great time, you know that," reassured Eddie at once. Many thoughts raced through his mind. It was quite lucky really; he could have the day to give Patrick moral support.

"George, Bridget, come and sit down, we've got something to tell you," announced Eddie. Bridget was now in her tartan dressing gown making tea in the kitchen.

"Just coming," she called, "got a nice cup of tea for you all. Here we are." She set a tray down on the long coffee table.

She looked at Eddie anxiously. "Not bad news I hope?"

"We've found Patrick," blurted out Eddie. "He's safe and well and staying nearby."

"No! Really? Thank goodness," came all the predictable replies. Bridget sat back on the squashy sofa, rather shocked.

George, quick thinking as usual, said to Eddie, "He can't have gone far on that train then, must have got off locally. Fancy making his way back here and he didn't think to come to us. Hmm." He sounded hurt that Patrick hadn't returned to them.

"We'd have understood, wouldn't we, love?" He turned to Bridget, "When did you find him then?"

"Late last night. I had a hunch where he might be."

"Oh yes, and where exactly was that?"

"At the old pink cottage by the creek," Eddie told him uncomfortably. He and Ellie could sense that George was a little angry now.

"I hope he hasn't caused any damage breaking in. It won't look good for him, I can tell you."

The phone rang again making everyone jump. It was Mr and Mrs McNab; they were already part of the way to Devon and would be there at lunchtime.

"We've found the lad," George told him, "please don't worry anymore. We'll see you later."

George sat down. Eddie and Ellie looked at his gloomy face.

"Shall we go and get him?" Ellie asked Bridget.

"Yes, yes," Bridget replied. "Off you go and I'll get breakfast."

The two youngsters quickly returned to the kitchen.

"We won't be long," Eddie told them, heading swiftly for the door, both wishing to escape the sombre atmosphere in the house.

Ellie followed, saying very little. She hoped Patrick wouldn't get into terrible trouble and be dragged back to Scotland unwillingly. As they were now staying for one more night they would meet Mr and Mrs McNab and hear what the verdict was.

Poor Patrick, Ellie thought over and over again as she walked to the pink cottage. Eddie was in front thinking similar thoughts and was upset and morose.

"I don't want him to think there is no hope for him. His dad sounds rather scary, don't you think, Ellie?"

"He certainly does," she agreed.

"Let's wait and see what they're like, we can always go and collect the Moonmirror from the turret room at the tea shop. I want to show it to Dad. He's going to tell us off you know, because we haven't taken the boat out of the water."

"Yes, but we've been using it, haven't we? Sailing around Devon with a seventeenth century ghost, enjoying the end of the Civil War in Dartmouth... we've been much too busy." she laughed.

Reaching the cottage door they knocked rather loudly. It opened at once, Patrick's face greeting them.

"I've been up for ages. I heard you laughing. Come on in. What's everyone saying about me?" Patrick asked.

"Oh you know, the usual sort of things, but your mum and dad will be here by lunch time so better get ready to face them, eh?" Eddie tried to be quite breezy about the whole thing.

Both youngsters looked around the tiny house filled with all the things connected to the sea – ships lights and portholes, a table made from a ships wheel, bits of driftwood and shells, wooden pulley blocks and ropes. A tiny veranda surrounded the cottage with incredible sea views and it had its own iron steps leading to a jetty. It was in fact a perfect holiday hideaway.

They locked up and walked briskly back to the Old Bath House.

"Aren't you going home today?" puzzled Patrick.

"Plane's delayed, they rang last night, so we're staying one more night," explained Eddie.

"That's good," joked Patrick, "you can help me face my dad."

"Oh no, you're on your own for that one."

Arriving back, Patrick succumbed to hugs and kisses from Bridget, a clapping on the back and vigorous hand shaking from

George. It was quite obvious they were thrilled to have him back. No questions were asked and no explanations offered.

"So far so good," whispered Eddie to Ellie. Half an hour later Patrick and his adopted family were sitting at the table enjoying a cooked breakfast of bacon, egg, mushrooms, tomatoes and fat shiny sausages.

"Yumm," said Eddie and looking at Patrick said, "The condemned prisoner ate a hearty breakfast," and the two boys laughed together.

"Eddie!" reproved Bridget and Ellie together, "how could you?"

Patrick smiled. "It's my own fault, got to take what's coming to me."

"Can we fetch the Moonmirror this morning?" asked Eddie.

"Yes, see you all later," replied George and he went off to open the tea shop.

"We've got to get lunch ready haven't we?" Bridget told Ellie and so the morning was mapped out, making sure everybody would be back in the house for the ominous arrival of Mr and Mrs McNab.

Chapter Four
Collecting the Moonmirror

Nobody could stop the ceaseless, silent, movement of the clock slipping round unnoticed that morning. Eddie and Patrick made their way to the café.

George greeted them warmly and gave them the key to the turret room. Many memories came flooding back to them as they climbed the spiral stone steps to the rooftop and found their experiments tucked neatly away in a corner under a plastic cover.

"When is the next full moon anyway?" asked Patrick casually, picking up a box.

"Don't know," Eddie replied, "I'll check later. Ready?" and balancing two boxes in his arms, set off carefully through the café back to the house.

"I must charge them up. Trouble is, we don't get a very good view of the moon at home, the hill at the back is in the way," Eddie told Patrick rather despondently.

"Why don't we set the Moonmirror up on the top of the hill then?" suggested his friend. "We could make a sort of hide for it so it doesn't get wet."

"Now that is a brilliant idea."

The boys were pleased with this plan and of course itching to start, but not today, definitely not today. They staggered in, arms aching, to wonderful smells creeping through the house.

"What is it?" asked Eddie, sniffing. The boys trooped into the kitchen where Ellie told them proudly.

"It's pork fillet with stuffing, roast potatoes, carrots and parsnips and apple sauce; to follow, gooseberry crumble and clotted cream. We're aiming to feed them into submission aren't we, Bridget?" The two cooks laughed together; the meal, wine, with coffees and brandies after, Mr McNab would have to be made of stone not to mellow just a little after all that.

"We're only doing it for you, Patrick dear," added Bridget with a twinkle.

George arrived home having closed the café early; winter was upon them and the afternoons were dark and often quiet.

"All ready then?" he asked, smiling. "I think, Patrick, that you and your parents need some privacy to talk, so I'm going to take us all off to Totnes. Alright?"

"Yes… yes of course," agreed Patrick, suddenly dreading being left alone with his parents.

"Right, we're all set then. You'll be alright, you'll see," and he left them to sit down with Bridget who had poured herself a sherry to steady her nerves before the arrival. Everyone was rather nervous.

Chapter Five
The arrival of Mr and Mrs McNab

A smart car glided along the narrow lane over a carpet of glossy leaves lying in great drifts.

"Just here on the left, isn't it?" pointed the glamorous woman in the passenger seat.

"Well this should be very interesting," remarked Mr McNab dryly. "Let's see what he's got to say for himself. I can't really afford the time for all this nonsense but there it is. Ready Irene?" He looked at his wife. She nodded and took his arm, daintily stepping down the steps in her high-heeled shoes.

"Rather muddy isn't it?" she remarked.

They rang the bell and waited. Soon the door was flung open and George stood there in his red sweater and tartan bow tie to greet them.

"Hello Sam, hello Irene." He kissed her cheek and shook hands with his old friend.

"Good day to you, George. How are you and Bridget and the boy? What a lot of trouble he's caused us all."

George, ignoring this remark, said, "Come in, come in," and took their coats. In the sitting room Eddie and Ellie sat nervously, saying to each other in quiet voices, "They're here," and glanced at Patrick who was looking out of the window. He seemed icily cool and quietly confident. Hearing voices approaching, they all stood up. Bridget smiled at them and whispered,

"I know we can charm them." And she winked at Patrick reassuringly.

Mrs McNab came in first and Ellie looked at her with interest. She was a slim, pretty woman with red hair fastened up into a clip and wore a pink and beige tweed suit and pale beige high-heeled shoes. She was neat and efficient looking with bright light-brown eyes. She went to Patrick first and kissed him lightly, then took both his hands and stepped back to study him.

"How are you Patrick? You look fine, just fine. Are you really alright?" and she gazed into his face. He smiled brightly back, with his head held high.

"Hello, Mum. Yes I'm great, thanks,"

"Dad." He moved to his father and shook hands with him.

"Hello Patrick," said his father coldly. "What have you been up to, eh?"

Eddie saw a short, well-built, balding man with blue eyes dressed in a grey suit and white shirt with a red patterned silk tie. He looked a no-nonsense sort of guy with an air of arrogance about him.

Patrick ignored the question and stared defiantly back at his father. George brought a tray of drinks in and Eddie handed round the little cheese biscuits that Bridget had made so carefully that morning.

"Now, you two must be Eddie and Ellie," smiled Mrs McNab. "How nice to meet you at last. Please call me Irene, won't you?" she was very friendly and charming.

"Come and sit here beside me, Ellie." Catching Bridget's eye, Ellie did as she was told.

"Have you had a good holiday?" Irene questioned her. Mr McNab sat down too but wasn't quite so chatty.

After twenty minutes Bridget invited them to the dining table where they started the delicious lunch. They discussed everything except school and Patrick, but it was pleasant and relaxed and the food was wonderful.

Patrick's parents looked curiously on as their son chatted and laughed happily with his friends and godparents. They began to feel a little left out, like the visitors they were. This was a Patrick they had not seen before. It dawned on Irene that she and her son were in fact polite strangers.

Sam thought how lovely the river looked and how he'd like the time to enjoy racing a fine yacht with his son. He also felt a little left out of Patrick's life. This wasn't how he'd meant the visit to turn out; he'd intended to give his son a good telling off, bundle him back into the car and deliver him straight back to school. But now? He wasn't sure. Everything felt different here in the tranquil, beautiful setting of the river Dart. Somehow he felt his anger seeping out of him. He tried to re-establish his authority once more.

"Now, Patrick, I think we'd better have a wee talk, don't you?"

"Wait just one moment, Sam," interrupted George,

"Bridget and I have planned to take Eddie and Ellie to Totnes this afternoon, How's that?"

Sam and Irene of course agreed. When the coffee was drunk, the brandies placed by their side, George made his move.

"Why don't you stay the night, everything's in order, I'm sure." He glanced at his sister.

"Oh yes, all ready, we insist," she added with her most winning smile, and the four of them left Patrick to his fate.

"I feel such a traitor leaving him," sighed Eddie, getting into the car.

"So do I." agreed Ellie.

"He'll be alright, don't you worry," George told them as they whisked off up the bumpy lane to join the main road.

"They seem very nice but I should think there's a jolly good row brewing don't you?" remarked Eddie.

Back at the house, Patrick wasn't getting on too well. Both his parents were adamant that he was to return to Burnside College and resume his G.C.S.E preparations.

"Well I'm not going back," he said defiantly. "I'll just run away again. I love it down here. There's sailing and freedom and good friends and I feel so happy. You never come and see me or seem interested in me in anyway. I'm just another possession. You don't understand how lonely it is." He sat down, head in hands, feeling bitter and angry.

His mother looked on in an unemotional way.

"You don't seem to have thought this through, Patrick. You can't just abandon life when it suits you or you see something you like better. I agree it is a lovely place – but what do you think the standard of education here is like?"

"Mum, I don't care," repeated Patrick, "I hate Burnside College and all the snobs who go there."

"Patrick!" His father had his turn. "I'm sorry you feel this way, but your mother's right. It must be great to holiday here; why, I'd like to sail here myself." And at that moment a beautiful J-class yacht drifted past the window. "But we must be practical. You're a bright intelligent boy and we only want the best education for you. You've had very good results."

"Yes, but only because I'm locked up there and there's nothing else to do but study," Patrick retorted angrily.

Just then, there was a knock at the door.

"Who's that?" asked Patrick, and raced to open it. Standing in the porch were Mary and Peter.

"Hello, Patrick dear," and the tanned and smiling couple shook his hand. "Where are the kids?"

"Oh dear," said Patrick, a bit overwhelmed and confused. "We didn't think you'd be home until later tonight and they've all gone off to Totnes shopping. My parents are here. You'd better come in." And the two followed him down into the sitting room.

Patrick introduced the two sets of parents. The two men discussed sailing at great length and the ladies talked of houses and holiday cottages.

"There's a nice one just gone on the market here," Mary told Irene brightly.

"Oh, where's that?"

"It's at the bottom of our little creek. It's called Waterside Cottage. It's got a nice garden with a view of the water."

Patrick pounced. "Now that's an idea, Dad. Mum. We could come here for holidays and we could do some sailing, Dad?" He came alive, full of enthusiasm, and everyone began talking at once.

It was eventually agreed that Sam and Irene would take a look at the cottage the following morning.

"We got an RAF flight in the end," Peter told Patrick, "we'd better be off now, perhaps we'll see you tomorrow with the kids." and away they went arm in arm.

Irene made some tea and not long after that, Ellie, Eddie, Bridget and George arrived home.

"We've had a great time," beamed Eddie, looking at Patrick to see how he was. He didn't look too unhappy. Ellie noticed the cups and saucers. So Irene could make a cup of tea then.

"Your parents called round here," Sam told the surprised youngsters. You've to turn up for breakfast tomorrow morning."

Patrick was rather pleased; he could spend his last evening with his friends.

"Right, come on then, let's make some sandwiches for supper – who's helping?" asked Bridget, and the volunteers joined her in the kitchen. Irene, George and Eddie were left alone in the sitting room.

"Now tell me all your plans for the future Eddie?" enquired Irene.

Taken rather aback at her question, Eddie stumbled through an answer.

"I'm not sure yet… haven't made up my mind… but I don't want to leave Dartmouth,"

"Oh really? And why is that?" she asked coolly, raising her eyebrows in a patronising sort of way.

"I love Dartmouth, it's got everything I want right here. The river, the sea, the woods and a busy town, nice people, what else could there be?" he challenged her. She paused.

"I can see, Eddie, how you feel but there's no educational future for you here."

"I know but there's Totnes and Torquay and Kingsbridge. Isn't there?" he persisted, feeling he was losing ground.

"Well I'm sure you'll find your way in your own time," conceded Irene, sensing anger in Eddie's voice. She smiled at him.

Eddie ignored her, got up, looking out at the river with the lights of the town shining out over the place he loved. He gritted his teeth angrily.

"I'm going to help Bridget," he announced abruptly, and left the room.

In the corner George had sat silently, letting the two parry questions. He had listened with interest, aware of the huge gulf between the ambitious woman and the naïve young boy. Wait till he told her about the Moonmirror light they had invented. He might need some extra ammunition later for Patrick's argument.

"It has got a great deal of charm here, I can see that. It might suit me to do a little of my work here, uninterrupted and away from the hubbub. Yes, perhaps?" she mused.

"I rather liked Mary and Peter, he must be away a lot at sea. Still one's career must take priority… don't you think, George?"

"Oh it's not for me to say, Irene. Each to their own, you know. Ah, here's tea. Good."

The others arrived with a lot of chatter and laughter. Sandwiches, cakes, scones, clotted cream and gorgeous raspberry jam embellished the afternoon tea fit for a queen.

"Wonderful. This looks superb," sighed Sam, sinking back to enjoy the luxury of afternoon tea.

"You kids go off downstairs if you want to," suggested George, and in ten seconds they had all leapt up and vanished.

"They are such great friends," confided Bridget to Irene. "Like brothers and sister really."

"I can see that," remarked Sam rather quietly, who had longed for more children, but unluckily none had arrived as Irene had busied herself with advancing her career.

"I shall give some serious thought to looking for a holiday cottage, it would be a good financial investment I'm sure."

Downstairs, Eddie, Ellie and Patrick couldn't wait to tell all.

"What happened?" they begged Patrick. "Did you get into terrible trouble? Was your dad furious?" They fired questions at him.

Patrick remained adamant.

"He wants me to go back of course. They've suddenly got this idea of looking for a holiday cottage. I'm not sure if they're just trying to get round me. You don't know them."

"But that would be fantastic, because you could come here every holiday, just think of that! You can't really stay here, can you… if you're honest?"

Ellie was doubtful. Eddie shot a furious look at her, to shut up. Patrick looked out of the window and then paced the floor, not speaking. His two friends watched him helplessly. At last he spoke quietly.

"You're right of course Ellie, but maybe now they understand how unhappy I am. Maybe if they buy a place I could cope with going back, especially if we buy your boat as well Eddie." and he laughed. Eddie and Ellie felt a lot better to see him laughing.

"Hadn't we better go back upstairs?" asked Ellie.

"Yep, back into the firing line," Patrick joked, and off they went.

***

Upstairs, the three grownups were sipping wine, comfortable in front of the fire. George and Bridget exchanged glances. Things were going quite well.

"Game of Uno?" challenged George.

"Why not?" chorused the three. All reserves and differences were finally erased as a raucous, rowdy, and fun couple of hours followed. It was the first time Patrick could remember enjoying a game with his parents for a very long time. Eventually they all retired to bed with a great deal to think about, put off until the morning.

Lots of noisy laughter came from the twin room the boys were sharing. Ellie smiled to herself. And tomorrow? They would be reunited with their parents, and perhaps Patrick's parents would buy a holiday cottage. That would be so wonderful; it could be the answer to everything.

Chapter Six
A family reunion

Eddie and Patrick crept out of the house just before daybreak. It was 7.30am, freezing cold and cloudy, but they didn't care. They gathered up tools, a ball of string, some odds and ends of wood and the box with the basics. Finally, puffing and hot, the boys reached the top of the hill by the old Civil War earthworks.

"This is the best place," said Eddie. "You'd get a good blast of moonlight here," and pointed to a huge and ancient tree with an enormous thick trunk and many twisted and curved branches spreading out.

"That'll do," agreed Patrick, and they set to work to make a structure with a platform and roof. The whole thing was fastened at the back with four big nails hammered well into the thick grey bark. Then the Moonmirror light's components were gently slid into the back of the box.

"Don't you think it will get wet?" asked Patrick anxiously. "You could do it later couldn't you?"

"I'll sort it out," nodded Eddie. "Maybe Dad will come up too. I've been dying to show it to him anyway."

Pleased with their work, they chased back through the woods to the Old Bath House.

"I've got to get going now with Ellie," said Eddie apologetically. "You will let me know what's going to happen to you, won't you?"

"Thanks, Eddie, for helping me. I'll phone you soon as I can," said Patrick gratefully. "Come on. Ellie will be waiting for you, I bet."

"Where have you been?" she demanded.

"We've set up the Moonmirror in the woods. We had to go early, it was the only chance we had."

George had begun to put their luggage in the car.

"You'd better go and say cheerio to Sam and Irene," he suggested.

They went inside and found them at the breakfast table.

"We're going home now," announced Eddie, "it was nice to meet you."

"Thank you, and give our regards to your parents," replied Sam warmly.

"Yes, do," added Irene without smiling, and returned to her toast and marmalade.

"Bye," said Ellie and left.

Hugging Bridget and George at the doorway they said their goodbyes to Patrick.

"Don't forget, phone me soon as there's any news," insisted Eddie firmly.

"Good luck," called Ellie and George drove them away, back to Watermill Cottage.

As they got nearer, Ellie could see the lights were on and a little tingle of excitement shivered through her. Home again! George swung into the driveway and the front door opened at once.

"Hello, welcome home," greeted the two people on the doorstep and Ellie and Eddie rushed out of the car.

Eddie, gave his mother a hug, while his father ruffled his hair in his usual way and said "Hello, son," warmly. Ellie hugged her father who she had not seen for quite a while and then flung her arms around her mother in happiness.

"Stay and have a cup of tea, George, please," begged Mary. "I want to hear all the news. We called round yesterday and met Mr and Mrs McNab. I gather there's been some sort of trouble with Patrick?"

Ellie and Eddie sat quietly, waiting for the answers. George began.

"Well, it's quite simple really. Patrick's a studious boy, clever and gifted, but he has no home life; suddenly he's met these two, enjoyed freedom, fun and friends and he's realised how lonely he is. Shut up in school, with parents who spend no time with him. I put him on the train to London to meet his father and somehow he made up his mind he didn't want to go back. He got off the train at Newton Abbot and came here and refused to return. So there's been a bit of a rumpus, and… there we are." Loyally glossing over the rest of the details, he seemed a little upset, and then he continued.

"'Course we sort of feel responsible, maybe he's had too good a time! Holidays always have to end. Don't they?"

"Indeed they do," agreed Mary.

"Yes, but rather foolish," added Peter. "It costs a fortune at public school. You can't just leave if you feel like it."

Eddie looked at his father. He began to feel panicky.

"He's got to go straight back hasn't he?"

"I'm not sure," sighed George sadly.

"But it's not fair, it's really not!" burst out Ellie.

"It's not for us to say, Ellie." Mary told them gently.

"His mum and dad are thinking of buying a holiday place, quite seriously I think." Eddie added.

"Well I must be off." George got to his feet, finishing his mug of tea.

"Thank you for looking after my two youngsters," said Peter warmly, looking at his son and daughter. "Bit dull, kids, stuck in Dartmouth, but we'll make it up to you."

If only you knew! thought Eddie and Ellie together.

Chapter Seven
Tolivera gets angry

Outside on the wall by the kitchen a small brown robin had been watching the homecoming. It was Freddie the robin – Faithful Freddie as the children had named him. Since the children's exciting adventure, the robin had retired from his duties on the Woodland Council with honours.

Perched on the weather vane on the garage roof was a grey and white seagull, with only one leg. He was Sargasso, Eddie's long- time companion, who had been saved by the children when they'd found him caught up in some fishing line. He also had been retired with honours by the Seafarers for his services to the children. Both were devoted to the children.

Freddie was disturbed by the arrival of a small long-tailed tit who was rather agitated.

"Hey, Freddie, Oliphant wants to see you urgently."

"But he's usually asleep now," queried Freddie. "Are you sure?"

"No mistake," twittered the long-tailed tit anxiously.

"OK, I'll see to it," agreed the robin. "You can go now, thank you."

Off flew the long-tailed tit to his small group of friends who had taken over a nearby larch tree.

Oliphant, the small white owl, lived in an oval hole in the second ash tree on the right, below them. A rather correct studious type, he was a bit of a loner. He liked to do everything properly and be prepared in advance for all events. No corners were cut and he didn't like surprises. He had received one that morning, unfortunately. Somebody was banging on his door, someone who wouldn't go away. Sleepily he got up and to his surprise found his cousin Tolivera obscuring the light from his doorway.

"My dear fellow!" The large tawny owl looked too large to squeeze in, but he did, not waiting for an invitation.

"Y-y-yes?" stammered Oliphant wearily. "What is the matter, cousin Tolivera?" seeing his angry face and ruffled feathers.

"The matter? I'll tell you what's the matter! Those human boys – those friends whose lives were saved by us Woodlanders – they have desecrated my home, vandalised my tree, ruined my life!" he blustered dramatically.

"Oh… Oh dear no—"

"Oh dear, yes!" snapped Tolivera, interrupting. "They have nailed a box affair to my beloved trunk and left a… a… *contraption* there, fixed very firmly. Now, what is to be done about it? I am extremely displeased."

"I'll try and sort it out." promised the startled owl, his mind blank for a moment.

"I hope so," insisted Tolivera, hissing between his extra-sharp razor beak. "I do hope so." And without even saying goodbye, he squeezed out of the doorway and was gone in two flaps. A small tawny feather swirled down to earth behind him, a token of his visit, leaving poor Oliphant bewildered and befuddled.

The acorn door-knocker went again. Who was it this time? He hardly dared to look. Inching the door open he saw the long-tailed tit again.

"Anything I can do?" he asked inquisitively, twittering and waggling in his nervous way. He'd seen the tawny owl arrive. The great Tolivera didn't often stray down into the lower woodland.

"Yes, there is actually," replied Oliphant quickly. "Go and tell Freddie I need to talk to him urgently, there's a good chap."

Not long after, Freddie arrived. The time was NOONDAY on his Dark Dwellers' clock. It had been a hectic morning, and Oliphant was pleased to see the little robin.

"Come in."

"Now," said Freddie, "how can I help?"

"I've had a visit from Tolivera," began Oliphant. "Early this morning, Eddie and Patrick nailed a box onto the big ash tree. Tolivera is furious and wants me to do something about it, but," he spread out his wings very slightly in despair, "what?"

"That will be Eddie's Moonmirror," said Freddie, very knowingly. He'd learnt a thing or two while he sat by the kitchen window." He'll have put it there to catch the moonlight. When is it full again?"

"Three days from now, of course." Oliphant was a Dark Dweller; the night was his time.

"What does he expect us to do?" asked the robin.

"I don't know," sighed Oliphant. "But I won't get a minute's peace. He's family of course, so one's got to try. Can't you think of anything, Freddie?"

"I expect once the Moonmirror is charged they'll take it away. Maybe it's because of the Mists of Time, the sap and the flow or something like that."

Oliphant listened and was sure the robin was right. Bother Tolivera and his pompousness and his eerie spitefulness. He'd have to learn he couldn't control everything or everybody.

"Sargasso might help," said Freddie. "If Tolivera threatens you again tell me at once." and he reassured the small white owl, who he had become rather fond of, as he left.

Freddie flew towards his spot on the kitchen wall to have a good long think. As he passed the garage roof he saw the seagull perched on the weather vane.

"I've got some news." he called. So Sargasso joined him on top of the wall.

"What's happened, Freddie?" He knew instinctively something was wrong.

"Eddie and Patrick have upset Tolivera. He is hopping mad, and threatened poor old Oliphant."

"What have they done?" puzzled Sargasso.

"They've attached the Moonmirror to the trunk of the Great Ash Tree. He's probably worried it might affect all that spying he does up there."

"I see." Sargasso was thinking. "Those nails may cause internal damage. It is the oldest and most powerful tree in the woodland. What a pity they had to pick that one."

"It's the position of it," pointed out Freddie "They need as much moonlight as possible."

"Do you think I should talk to Eddie again? Maybe I should consult the Spirit of the Sea before I do.When is the next full moon?"

"Three days' time."

"Right, that gives me a short while to make my decision." And the big seabird took off and flew back down to his favourite place at the old lime kiln, where he was warm and dry away from the chilly winds and damp rains of winter. It was time for a good long think. Something would have to be done.

Chapter Eight
A new seaside home

Patrick's parents had got up early and driven down to Dartmouth to visit the estate agents. They were both rather amused by the idea of a holiday home. It was to be their bargaining power with Patrick – he would go back to school and come to Dartmouth for as many of the holidays as he wanted to.

Patrick waited patiently with George and gave him a hand with the morning coffees. Eddie and Ellie were having fun at home opening the various presents their parents had brought home from Portugal. Peter was amusing himself watching the children, with one eye on the morning news. Eddie laughed as he opened a pair of very thick hand-knitted sea socks. Ellie found a warm red-and-blue knitted cardigan with wooden toggles; two boxes of chocolate sardines followed.

"Thank you, Dad," said Ellie. "These are great."

"Yes, thanks very much," agreed Eddie.

"That's alright then." Peter went back to watching the news.

Ellie happened to glance out of the window and saw Irene and Sam walking down the lane with an official- looking man in a suit, a clip board.

Irene and Sam were very pleasantly surprised by the interior of the cottage. Everything came up to their high standards and the views and the proximity of the water's edge made it a desirable spot. Sam was entranced with the creek and Waterside Cottage.

"Let's go back to the office, I'd like to put an offer in…Yes?" he asked Irene, seeking her approval.

"It's alright with me. I like it."

"Do you think Patrick will like it too? Is it enough to get him back to school?" Sam asked, suddenly worrying about his defiant and independent son.

To the delight of the estate agent, an hour later the offer was made; another hour later it had been accepted. Unusually for both of them, normally quiet and reserved and measured in every judgement, they were like excited children.

"It must be the sea air," laughed Irene. "It's gone to our heads!"

"Let's go and tell Patrick," said Sam, and taking her hand he hurried back to his large grand car and drove back to the Old Bath House.

"Let's take everyone out to lunch," said Sam.

"Right," agreed Irene, surprised at this sudden rush of generosity from her normally cautious husband, who managed millions of pounds for corporate companies in the Far East and America.

"I'd better ring Colin McDonald at Burnside College to tell him Patrick is coming back. When shall we say? The day after tomorrow?"

"Plenty of time." said Irene as they rang the doorbell.

Bridget opened the door.

"Guess what? We've bought it!" Sam told her loudly, giving her an unexpected hug.

"Well, well!"

"Waterside was definitely the best, without question," Irene nodded emphatically.

"Quite near to Eddie and Ellie, then." Bridget seemed extra pleased at this news.

"Yes, a stroke of luck," smiled Sam, thinking of how convenient it would be to leave Patrick with two more adults to supervise him.

"Where's Patrick?" asked Irene, looking around.

"He's helping George at the tea shop."

"I was really hoping to take everyone out to lunch, as a sort of celebration…"

"Maybe this evening would be better," suggested Bridget. "Shall we make some phone calls and see?"

And eventually it was organised. They would meet at 7.30pm in the Castle Hotel and dine at 8pm.

***

"Well what do you think?" said Peter to Mary when he put the receiver down. "They've bought Waterside, subject to contract."

"No! Eddie and Ellie will go mad!" and she called the children at once. When they heard the news, they were ecstatic and could hardly believe it.

"Let's go round to the tea shop, I can't wait to see his face!" grinned Eddie. "Do you think he'll go back to school now, Dad? I think I would!"

"It seems a good bargain," agreed his father. "Sam is keen to take up sailing again."

"Oh good, perhaps he'll buy our boat and we can have another one. You did promise!" Ellie reminded him.

"Did I?" Peter looked innocent.

Both the youngsters jumped on him and pinned him to the sofa where he was sitting. After a friendly fight, with cushions, Peter relented.

"OK, OK, I give in. We'll look into it, shall we?"

Satisfied they had made progress, Eddie and Ellie they raced off to the tea shop.

There was only one lonely car in the tea shop car park

"Oh good – it's not very busy," said Ellie.

They peered in through the door. George and Patrick waved from the kitchen and Patrick rushed out to see them.

"Come and have some hot chocolate. We've had a phone call from Sam already, inviting us out to supper. Celebration I think!" smiled George, eyes twinkling.

"Well, what do you think?" asked Eddie, cautiously sitting down beside Ellie and Patrick. All eyes were on the young Scottish lad. George quietly made the frothy drinks, loading chocolate chips and marshmallows and cream on the top, listening intently. The three waited, holding their breath.

"I'm really pleased!" said the boy, with shining eyes. "It's so near to your house and I can come here now whenever I want. I feel so... different. Dad's got the key until 5pm. Shall we go and see it now? Can we, George?" and he turned his happy face to his beloved godfather.

"Be my guest," agreed George.

Gulping down the remainder of the hot, creamy chocolate they couldn't wait to collect the key and rush off to view Waterside Cottage, hopefully, Patrick's new home in Dartmouth.

Chapter Nine
The moles get a shock

The excited youngsters reached the Old Bath House, begged the key from Patrick's delighted parents, and rushed off. The creek waters were dark and angry-looking, white tips skimming the ruffled water. The little green boat bobbed furiously, tugging at its moorings.

"Dad and I had better get her out of the water soon." Eddie pointed anxiously to her from the side path.

"I'll ask my dad about buying her so you'd better look after her!" smiled Patrick staring, his hair ruffling in the breeze, hardly believing what was happening.

"Come on," urged Ellie crossly, "we haven't got long."

They reached the front door of the whitewashed cottage and they peered inside as Patrick fumbled with the keys.

"Come on in," beckoned Patrick and they tiptoed into the large open plan kitchen with beams and an inglenook fireplace, large and wide. Next, the sitting room with glass doors leading to an outside patio area. Patrick unlocked the doors and they followed him up some steep stone steps until they were standing on the steep sides of the small valley overlooking the creek.

"Wow, what a lovely view!" said Ellie, climbing further up the garden towards the trees. In a corner was a stone circular wall, jagged and broken in places, the remnants of an old lime kiln. There was a low boundary wall and the boys of course climbed across it, leaving Ellie looking on disapprovingly as they trampled down the undergrowth and kicked creepers out of the way, noisily disappearing in a few moments.

Ellie went inside to explore the upstairs, which consisted of two bedrooms, a bathroom and a tiny room in the attic. It was all very simple, comfortable, and perfect for holidays. She heard the boys coming back through the undergrowth and went outside to meet them.

"I knew it!" said Eddie triumphantly, and Patrick grinned at her. "It goes right up to your top garden. It's a great shortcut," he said, smiling. "I'm going to put a rope through the woods with knots in it and I can guide myself along it in the dark. Clear a few stones and branches out of the way and it'll be great."

"You boys, you're always making adventures for yourselves. What nonsense."

"It's a short cut Ellie, what's wrong with that?" The boys rolled their eyes at each other.

They locked up and parted company until later that evening and the exciting dinner together.

Their father was in the garden and their mother still ironing and washing after the holiday.

"Well?" she asked, "How's Patrick? All sorted out?"

"He seems very happy now, Patrick likes it. I think he's going back to school," Ellie explained.

"That's good then, it's a reasonable outcome. He's a lucky boy really, you know." Mary nodded approvingly.

Eddie raced up the steps to find his father, who was surveying their small green lawn disapprovingly in the fading afternoon light.

"Just look at this grass, Eddie. It's ruined. Moles have dug channels all over it. It's all spongy and sinking. Come and see." His exasperated father beckoned him over. Eddie stared at the grass. He put his foot on it and it sank immediately beneath him.

"Oh dear, they must have done this while we've been away," Eddie said, quite annoyed at the damage that had been done to their precious lawn – the only piece of grass they had.

Suddenly Eddie saw the grass quiver; he looked hard at it and before his eyes, the ground started to jolt and shudder. He grabbed his dad's arm and they both looked on in astonishment. The grass was swaying as a small pink nose appeared, whiskered, sniffing the air.

"Right," said Peter firmly, "those moles have done enough damage, they've got to go. They're ruining my lawn." And he marched along the garden path and fetched a large spade. Ellie wandered up the steps to see what they were doing. She saw her father swing the spade in the air, and thud it down onto the grass.

"Dad!" she called anxiously, "What are you doing?"

Eddie looked on, not wanting to interfere. Peter looked around as she spoke.

"Those blasted moles have ruined the grass. Just look at it, Ellie!"

Eddie showed her and indicated with his face also how cross their father was.

"But what are you doing with the spade?"

"We've seen the moles moving around, I'm going to give them a good headache," replied Peter grimly and he wasn't joking, as he thumped the spade down flat on the grass again.

"Stop it, stop it, you'll hurt them!" shouted Ellie, and she tried to pull his arm away. "You can get humane mole scarers you know! I won't let you kill them!"

Peter stopped and looked at her in astonishment.

"Have you seen the damage they've done, Ellie? I'll probably have to re-turf the whole lot. I've got to get rid of them."

"Yes, I know but you mustn't kill them, Dad, it's not fair!" and she tried to take the spade away from him. Peter was rather taken aback and looked at his furious, red-faced daughter. He wasn't used to being crossed.

Eddie, not knowing quite what to do, said gently to his angry sister, "Maybe we could get some of those mole scarers tomorrow? Couldn't we try to dig them up and move them, Dad? You know… put them along past the vegetable patch? Ellie's right, Dad, I don't think we should kill them," he added, looking embarrassed.

Peter was silent. He looked at his children. He had been very angry and determined to rid the garden of the pests. Maybe they were right. He felt a little ashamed as he calmed down.

"Well perhaps you've got a point, Eddie." He paused, "I'm just so mad about the garden. Your mother and I have done a lot of work here, don't forget. It's very annoying to see it all destroyed."

"I know, Dad, I can see that," Ellie agreed. She ran to the shed to fetch another spade and they dug in the channels to try to find the moles. Ellie hoped and hoped they were still alive.

"I've got one!" shouted Eddie as he uncovered a black tiny wriggling creature, so small, with little pink hands and feet and a long pink nose. It writhed and twisted on the spade.

"Put it in here," Ellie said quickly and grabbed a large empty flowerpot from the edge.

"I've got the other one!" Peter called with satisfaction, his trophy wriggling on the flat muddy spade. It too went into the terracotta pot to join its friend.

"Got them! I wonder if there are any more?" asked Peter. In fact they could hardly see now, as the winter daylight faded and darkness fell.

"It's too late," said Peter. "Come on, let's just take them as far away as possible for now. First thing tomorrow I will go and get some mole repellents. In fact as you're so keen to save them you go and dig them in somewhere and I'll go and light the fire and get the logs in."

They didn't argue. Ellie and Eddie took the spades and the terrified moles as far as they could along the top garden by the Watermill.

Aren't they sweet?" said Ellie, "How could Dad try to kill them?"

Freddie hopped down beside them. He had been watching helplessly from the apple tree as Peter tried to kill his friends, Maurice and Maudie, two moles from the woodland.

Eddie saw him in the dusky gloomy light. "Hello, Freddie. Look what we've got here."

Ellie dug the earth into loose crumbly pieces. Eddie carefully tipped them up and the moles wriggled and twitched and plopped onto the brown earth. Frantic digging, and twenty seconds later they had vanished, hidden away in the crumbly mound.

"That's good," said Ellie, her face bright with satisfaction, and her lips set, giving an approving nod with her head.

Eddie too was well pleased. "Thank goodness we stopped Dad. They've got a good chance now."

"I expect they've had a bit of a shock. Maybe they have got a headache? I wouldn't be surprised!" and they both laughed.

Hurrying to put the spades and the flowerpot away, they remembered their evening appointment at the Castle Hotel.

"I suppose they'll take Patrick back tomorrow, won't they?" said Eddie.

"Of course they will, but just think, he's only got a few more weeks left."

Reaching the back door they entered the bright warmth.

"I hear you've rescued two moles, Ellie!" greeted her mother. "Well done you!"

"Huhhh." grunted Peter from behind his glasses and his newspaper.

***

Outside in the dark still garden, the two moles were recovering from their shocking ordeal. Maurice and Maudie knew they had trespassed out of the woodland but they found it hard to resist the fresh grass roots and lovely fat worms always present in the humans' garden.

"Oh, my head!" groaned Maurice, trying to sleep.

"There there, dear, try to forget about it, we're lucky to be alive," his soft little wife told him. "It was that girl who saved us – Freddie told me, he's coming to see us tomorrow." And she gave her husband some lemon balm leaves to chew. They snuggled up together for the night, shocked by the whole affair.

Freddie, tucked up by the kitchen wall, worried about the two moles. What if Tolivera, the woodland spy, had seen the commotion? He hoped not, especially as Eddie and Ellie were involved. For now, the two moles had had a lucky escape.

***

The evening at the inn proved to be a pleasant one, everyone in high spirits with plenty to look forward to. Sam told the excited youngsters that provided the survey and searches were satisfactory, they could take possession of the cottage in the second week of December.

"Oh, that's great news, isn't it?" beamed Mary, knowing how much her children were hoping to see Patrick in the Christmas holidays.

"You'll hardly have unpacked and it will be time to come back," Ellie told him.

Patrick nodded in agreement, but said nothing else.

"He's got one or two exams to sort out first, my dear," added Irene in a rather superior way. In no time the evening was finishing in the inn's comfortable lounge with coffee and mints. George and Bridget were rather tired but pleased that the drama with Patrick was over. They sat back and listened, sipping freshly brewed coffee laced with cream and brandy.

"Can we fetch Patrick from the station next time?" Eddie asked his father suddenly.

"Well, yes, if it suits everyone," Peter agreed, and they all exchanged cards and phone numbers.

"Don't forget about the boat, Patrick," added Eddie in a whisper.

At last it was time to go. Mr and Mrs McNab were leaving quite early to drive all the way back to Scotland and they parted company, not so sad this time, knowing Christmas and the holidays were coming soon. They reluctantly waved goodbye from their cars parked in front of the Boat Float.

"Well, I think that's got over that hiccough for now, don't you?" remarked Peter, backing his car out, and setting off for home.

"Hope so," murmured Eddie.

"So do I," Ellie agreed.

"They'll make very nice neighbours," added Mary.

Chapter Ten
The Woodland pharmacy

A few days later Sargasso was determined to find out if he still needed permission to talk to humans. He flew round to the Trip Trap Bridge where the two seals Solomon and Bathsheba lived. They were both beached on the tiny shingle-strewn inlet, only accessible when the tide was low. The seagull hopped up the narrow rocky cove to greet his friends.

"Tell me," asked Sargasso, "how can I reach the Spirit of the Sea again? Is he wintering on foreign shores?"

"He sometimes comes this way on the full moon when the waters run high and stretch up to touch the shore. Fly over the sea until you see the Silver Tinkling Shoals, that's where he'll be."

Sargasso remembered going once before to look for him, sent by the buzzard for a meeting. He was lucky the full moon was nearly here, but he wasn't the only one waiting for its appearance in the sky.

***

Eddie had his eye on it to charge the Moonmirror, waiting patiently so he could use its bright light to make signals with, casting beams far over the sea.

Peter had bought two mole-scaring devices the day after his row with Ellie and inserted them into the ground. They gave off sonic waves which the moles didn't like. He had then worked very hard to flatten and re-turf the lawn and it was looking quite green and smooth again.

Maudie and Maurice recovered after sleeping very soundly for twenty-four hours; they seemed to have suffered little ill-effects from their ordeal.

They were a shy couple, almost blind, whose life's work was tunnelling and exploring. Very infrequently they came to the surface for woodland meetings or special occasions, but both had to wear strongly magnified glasses to see with. These were made at the Cornucopia tree, which was the health centre for the whole woodland.

The buzzards had appointed a pair of pigeons called Dr Dew and Dr Yew Underconstumble to be the woodland physicians and a very dedicated and knowledgeable pair they were too. They both wore spectacles, which they manufactured themselves out of discarded honeycombs and raindrops, set to a hardened shiny finish. The doctors administered to the Woodlanders from a tall elderberry tree on the flat windy top of the hill, not far from the Citadel. It was an exciting and mysterious place.

There was a spiral staircase leading up inside. Jars and bottles were stored on shelves all the way up: elixirs and powders, liquids and strange rocky lumps, pills and potions, stood curiously waiting to be dispensed. At the top a large room opened out. All the windows were covered in a tangle of tree ivy and from the ground it looked like an enormous bird's nest.

Freddie, who had visited the moles the morning after their ordeal, had advised them both to go and have a check-up at the doctors'. Dutifully they washed and groomed their smooth silky black fur, put on their glasses and hand in hand made the long journey up the woodland path to the Cornucopia tree. An icy wind was blowing that morning and the two little creatures were buffeted and blown, the headwind making the climb difficult. Maurice had to help Maudie along.

"What they need is a good tunnel," grumbled Maudie. "Stands to reason. Dry, no obstacles, no wind, what could be better?" as a gale of dried leaves assaulted them.

After a long struggle, they arrived at the foot of the tree. They pulled on the long twisted ivy rope which gave the signal to the doctors that somebody wanted their attention. The two moles clearly heard the jangle of empty conker shells above them and then the door slowly swung open.

Up they climbed on polished wooden treads round the spiral staircase, past all the glinting glass jars, puffing and panting, until they reached the top floor. The pigeons had decided that if creatures really did need them, they would make the effort to walk to the centre and climb up the fifty stairs to reach them. It cut out all those who made illness a pastime and who imagined all their ailments. It seemed to work.

A room spread out before them where two bespectacled grey pigeons were sitting behind a large partner's desk – that is to say, a desk for two persons, joined in the middle, one sitting on either side, facing each other.

"Good morning," spoke Dr Dew, "Maurice and Maudie mole, what can we doooooo for youooooooo today?" They always cooed to everyone in their gentle way.

The moles went to sit down on a circular window seat and a small, quiet white dove fetched them some nettle tea. The two doctors came out from behind their desks and sat beside them.

"Now, tell me everything," cooed Dr Yew. So the moles related their tale with lots of drama and claw waving. When they had finished the pigeons said both together:

"Dear, dear, what a todoooooo! No ill-effects? No headaches, dizziness, blurring of vision, nightmares, hallucinations or vivid lights of bluooooo?" They cooed in their soft voices, perfectly in time.

"No, no," repeated the moles, shaking their heads.

"Good," smiled Dr Dew, and both pigeons spoke together again.

"Two camomile petals three times a day for one week, and an hour of moonshine on the full moon. Come back if you don't feel better soon. Collect your medication as you leave. Good luck to you-oooooo."

They returned to their desk to write in the large ledger while the moles finished their tea. The doctors filled their details in the page carefully in blue-black elderberry ink. The white dove prepared the petals, dropped them into a parchment envelope and presented it to them when Maurice and Maudie reached the bottom of the stairs.

"Toodle-oooooo," she cooed, and closed the door.

"That's over," sighed Maudie. "I always feel better when I've seen Dr Dew and Dr Yew, don't you, Maurice?" Maurice agreed that he did.

As they left, unfortunately they were captured in the Mists of Time, by the long branches of the huge ash tree right on the top of the hill, not far from the Citadel.

All the happenings around this tree were recorded; every tip of every swaying branch could see and the happenings ran down the branches in the sap, into the trunk to the root system. Turning a tap, the sap poured into a silver dish in which the recordings could be viewed. The old sap was distilled and turned into a flavoured liquor called the Mists of Time.

The vantage point where the tree grew was superb. It perched overlooking the river, the sea and a great deal of the woodland.

Tolivera, the large tawny owl, was in charge of the Mists of Time and he had some plans.

He was aware of a blind spot in his viewings; the old horse chestnut tree would be a good additional place. The full moon would be the time to visit the Citadel to persuade the Buzzard

The eve of the full moon had a lot of events depending on it; Eddie to charge his Moonmirror, Sargasso seeking the Spirit of the Sea, and now Tolivera for his permission to set up some more observation positions. Maurice and Maudie were to sit in the moon's healing rays for one hour to complete their recovery. The clarity of this winter moon and the weather would play its part; it could be cloudy or even raining, couldn't it?

Chapter Eleven
The power of moonshine

Peter and Eddie had to work fast to get their boat out of the water. They had left it very late, for with the full moon came the spring tides, and if accompanied by a strong easterly wind, havoc could be created on the river.

Ellie and Mary were going to have a morning cooking to make Christmas cakes and puddings. It was all waiting in the larder to be assembled as thoughts turned towards Christmas. The days were short now and daylight scarce and it had begun to look Christmassy in the town, as trees and sparkling decorations, chocolates, toys and cards filled the shops.

Eddie and his father dressed up warmly in their waterproofs and they reversed the car and trailer down to the bottom of the slipway. Eddie scrambled down onto the rocks where the boat sat forlornly, full of rainwater. He baled furiously and then, slipping the ropes and placing the oars in the rowlocks, rowed across the full and churning creek to the slipway. Then he got out into the water and he and his father wrestled the boat onto the trolley and finally eased her out of the water.

"Well done, Eddie, we've got her now. Hop in and we'll take her up home."

So the beloved and much used Cornish shrimper came to a well-earned rest in the corner of the car park back at Watermill Cottage

"Will you come up and look at my invention now?" Eddie asked his father.

"Yes, why not. How far is it?"

"It's right at the top by the earthworks I'm afraid," replied Eddie.

"Good! That will keep us fit. Come on then." Peter strode out to the narrow entrance on the hill with Eddie beside him.

"Any sign of the moles, Dad?"

"I should hope not!" exploded Peter. "I expect those scarers to last at least a couple of months. How did you come by this idea, Eddie anyway, you know, for these lights of yours?"

"It was a mixture of things really. The solar powered light George gave me, your Francis searchlight in the garage, looking at the moon; it all just seemed to fit together somehow."

"Well it sounds very good, I can't wait to see it," said his father.

Eddie was pleased. It had taken a lot of work by him, George and Patrick to finally make their invention work.

The man and his son climbed the steep path in a steady companionable uphill stride. On and on they went, silently observed by the inhabitants of the woodland.

Peter and Eddie reached the Citadel, passing the Cornucopia tree on the way. Then finally, at the very top of the hill, Eddie reached the old ash tree, running up to it eagerly to find his Moonmirror in its curious shelter. Fortunately it had not rained for a few days, and he remembered his eager promise to Patrick to cover the front up – so very quickly forgotten. He showed his dad the ingenious mechanism for charging the battery power with a small solar glass plate and then magnifying and reflecting the light.

"I think it's a marvellous piece of kit," exclaimed Peter, quite impressed and full of admiration. "What a great idea! Well done, Eddie."

"Oh, George and Patrick helped too," added Eddie loyally.

"It should charge up tonight then – it's a full moon," said Peter. "I wonder what the weather forecast is? You need a really clear sky for a night or two."

Inside the ash tree Tolivera was trying to sleep in his comfortable dwelling. He was disturbed by the voices and got up grumbling to see who it was; he was even crosser when he saw that it was Eddie and that he had not come to take his contraption away.

"Dang and blink!" he swore in Woodlander language, very, very cross. Soon Peter and Eddie disappeared, taking a circular route back down the hill to Watermill Cottage.

I am most certainly going to see the buzzards tonight and I shall mention this, Tolivera thought, making a mental note. He was going to run through the week's happenings in the Mists of Time before visiting the royal family.

The princes listened to everything now. The three sons of the buzzards were growing up, keen and alert. The buzzards, longing to retire, were grooming their sons to take over from them as soon as they reached the age of responsibility.

Tolivera would soon rub off their sharp corners, he decided rather venomously. Silly young pups – he'd show them. Guile and cunning were his weapons – whispers, suggestions and veiled threats, that's what Tolivera traded on to unsettle and frighten. There was nothing like the hint of rumour in a community.

***

As the eve of the full moon approached, the wind seemed to invisibly draw strength from the lunar influence and gradually increased in intensity until it could be seen whipping the branches of the trees and frothing the surface of sea. Every gap in windows or doors whistled, as darkness approached. Broken clouds quickly shunted across the sky in a hurry to be gone.

Sargasso, restless in his dry retreat at the lime kiln, chose the early dusk to make his journey out to sea, when the strange pinkish close of day had an eerie feel to it.

He spread his wings and took off with a flap out across the creek, turned right and headed out between the two castles to face the strong easterly wind over the open sea.

The ocean was dark and grey, stormy and heavy, with a plunging swell and white-topped short-lived waves. Few ships were making way along the Channel coast and no yachtsmen had ventured out. He was quite alone.

He flew on towards the horizon, scanning the darkening waters for the shoals of tinkling silver fish that always accompanied the Great Spirit of the Sea in his travels. He caught sight of a flash of shiny white and descended until he was hovering over the jagged sea and could feel the spray on his feathers. All at once, the shoals arched up from the depths of the water and twisted and rolled on the surface, hundreds of silvery fishes following each other.

"Come to us!" they tinkled like wind chimes. "Come to us, us, us!" echoed their tiny voices, and as they darted through the grey water Sargasso tried to follow them. The slivers of brightness shone like polished teaspoons and danced in the waters, round and round, leading him back to the coast and to the curved rocky inlet of Compass Cove, where the waters crashed onto the rocks.

It was sheltered here from the wind and Sargasso perched on the wooden struts of the bridge spanning the cove and watched. The fish fanned out in the water, resting and waiting. Far out on the horizon he could see a dark shape approaching, a high grey wall of water, which rolled nearer and nearer gaining height until a huge swell came closer and finally curved over.

The break of the wave caused four white horses to rear up out of the foaming white froth, pulling a chariot made of shells. Driving it was the Spirit of the Sea, fierce and fearless, with white ringlets and a crown of seaweed, holding the reins of the rearing horses up high to halt them. As the full moon rose up in the sky behind him, everything was captured in black and white. At his command the sea around him flattened and the horses pawed the water, snorting, finally coming to rest.

"You seek my counsel, Sargasso the Seagull?"

"I ask your advice in the matter of speaking in the human's tongue to them. I have good reason to wish it, for my young master may be in conflict with the Woodlanders and I cannot help him without the spoken word."

The Spirit of the Sea considered his request. "We must try to maintain peace amongst us for as long as possible. If it will contribute to this, then you have my permission to use your human language in the most discreet of circumstances. You and he alone may make such exchanges. I would not have had you written in the Great Scrolls of Time if you were not worthy, Sargasso. The decision is yours; you will not invoke my displeasure."

He paused.

"I have brought a gift for you," he suddenly announced and opening a pouch on the back of one of the horses he removed an object and beckoned Sargasso to him.

Quite taken aback, Sargasso flew forward and perched on the side of the barnacle-encrusted carriage, while the impressive figure placed a necklace over his head. It was a hermit crab shell, covered with mother of pearl and fastened with fine plaited twine

which was made of the strong tail hairs groomed from the horse called Aquarius.

"He who calls into the mouth of this shell, I will hear him. You need not search me out, Sargasso, for always I am travelling through my oceans often far away."

"Thank you my lord," nodded the seagull, overcome with gratitude. "I did not expect this."

"He who seeks no honour shall surely find it, for he is the most deserving of all," smiled the Spirit of the Sea. "And now I have a question for you, Sargasso. You can do something for me."

"Yes lord, anything," agreed the seagull, eagerly listening.

"My people in these waters have told me of strange things, of noises and sounds from creatures they do not recognise. There is a ripple of fear amongst them. Have you heard anything of this?"

"No, my lord, nothing," replied Sargasso truthfully.

"Keep watch and listen, for the tidings will reach you surely from your brothers and sisters in the deep. You have the means now to communicate with me, I shall rest easy. You will not fail me, of this I am certain. You and your young Master Edmond, I wish you luck. Come Aquarius, Neptune, Triton and Aquamarine."

Then he reined in the beautiful white horses who reared up and swung the carriage round. It cut a channel through the water, which closed at once behind it. The Spirit of the Sea plunged through the water illuminated by the brightness of the moon and disappeared. The black waters had engulfed him.

The shiny shoals of tinkling fish leapt into the air, catching the moonlight on their scales as they splashed and swam after him… gone in a flash of sparkling, glittery silver.

The seagull was overwhelmed. He tried to take in what had happened. It had all been so exciting. Now he was alone and it was dark; he should return to the lime kiln to think over all the things that the Spirit of the Sea, his own special master, had said. He looked down at the pearly glistening shell around his chest and felt immensely proud and somehow very reassured, knowing that he could make contact now whenever he needed to. It was a very comforting thought.

***

Above the dark woodland, thick black clots of cloud crossed the moon, strung out in lumps, thick and thin, sometimes blotting it out. Then suddenly and excitingly the revealed moon shone out through the brown, blue and black patches. For a moment it was full face on in all its bright mystery. The trees, like black brushes, stretched to reach upwards, swaying and in the gardens at the foot of the hill, wind chimes made furious music.

Maurice and Maudie put on their crystal raindrop glasses and hand in hand they emerged from their woodland burrow just above Waterside Cottage. They sniffed the air and shivered. Oliphant, the white owl watched them, unseen from his ash tree. As his clock said MOONSHINE, he had looked out into the now illuminated darkness. The moles climbed up the steep slopes to reach the National Trust path, finding the trodden earth easier to walk on. It was a long way for the little Woodlanders and eventually they made it to the top of the hill where they rested in the full light of the splendid moon on a leafy mossy bank not far from the huge ash tree.

"Where does that white path go to?" asked Maudie, pointing to the moon's reflection that cast a long white gleam over the surface of the sea, ending at the horizon.

"I don't know, dear," replied Maurice, "it's a pathway to somewhere far away, that's for sure. Probably over the edge into the next world I think, Maudie."

A flapping in the pine trees not far away was Tolivera arriving at the Citadel to visit the buzzards. He didn't notice the two black moles; they were well camouflaged in the darkness and at least one hundred metres away.

The buzzard princes were alert in the moonlit branches.

"Large tawny owl incoming, Father, from the left, obviously for you."

The Lord of the Woodland stirred from a short nap.

"Whatsat? What did you say, boy? Aha, good evening, Tolivera, welcome," waking up instantly.

"Let's go," whispered the three cheeky young buzzards, "he's such a bore," and sneaked off to steal dried rats tails from their mother's larder.

"Lovely night to be out, is it not?" asked Tolivera politely.

"Why yes," the buzzard replied. "And to what do we owe the honour, Tolly? Something on your mind?" asked the wise woodland lord, knowing his second-in-command of old.

"I'll come straight to the point," continued Tolivera. "That boy, that human changeling that's always poking his nose into things that don't concern him, he's gone too far this time."

"Oh yes?" queried the buzzard, rather intrigued, "and why is that?"

"He's had the audacity to hammer nails into my trunk and to put one of his contraptions up in my tree. If it's not removed, I'll…"

"You'll what?" queried the lord buzzard gently.

"I'll be forced to take steps. I can manage this myself….or maybe you could do it for me, my lord," smiled the old owl slyly.

"Yes, yes, leave it to me. I'm much more used to handling this sort of situation than you. Leave it to me," the buzzard blustered.

Tolivera smiled inwardly. He had got his way.

"Just make sure you do, my lord," he added nastily, with a lazy blink of his large cat-like eyes.

"One more thing, I'd like to add another viewing position and would ask your gracious lord's permission to install it. We have at the moment a blind spot in our surveillance – an important site I feel, lord. It will be a simple procedure. Do you have any objections?" Tolivera asked casually.

"Which site have you chosen?"

"The old chestnut tree by the castle lord. It is the second largest tree in the woodland. A very worthy choice I feel, with an immense spread."

"Hmm, I don't think I have any objections but I shall let you know our decision shortly, and now for the Mists of Time, Tolly. Anything interesting happened this week, eh?"

The local gossip was always the best bit. In his small community, the buzzard always liked to know what was going on.

"Well, my lord, I did happen to notice the two moles leaving the doctors' together. You can check the ledger if you like, but Dr Dew is always rather touchy about us reading it. I'll leave that one in your capable hands, eh?" Tolivera really had no interest in the moles, who were too small, too insignificant, and much too shy to bother him.

"Fine, fine," nodded the buzzard.

"Oh, and that boy and his contraption on my tree, you won't forget, Sire, will you?" he reminded him, getting angry at the mere thought of it.

"Leave it with me, Tolly. It will be on my action list, never fear," replied the buzzard, fearing a ruffling of feathers coming on. With that the moon strayed behind a cloud and the hilltop landscape was plunged into darkness, punctuating their conversation.

"I'll be off now," decided Tolivera, and nodding politely to his superior he spread his large bulk and flew the short distance to his luxurious home.

Three missions had been accomplished by the light of the moon: Sargasso, the moles, and Tolivera had made their important journeys, bathed in the calm, bright light.

Chapter Twelve
Eddie and Peter both have a surprise

"Can we go back up to the woods later on and see if the Moonmirror has charged up?" Eddie asked. It was 8pm and the whole family, full up with a tasty shepherds pie, were lolling about in the sitting room.

"What, now?" said Peter, already comfortably placed on the sofa in front of the fire. Ellie looked up from the dining table where she was making Christmas lists, engrossed in thought. Mary was searching her needlework box for a wool thread in a particular shade of green before sitting down to an hour's tapestry. Eddie, of course, was fidgeting and anxious to be outside.

"Please, Dad, you'll love it! I'll get some torches, shall I?" and he raced off without waiting for an answer. Peter looked at Mary.

"I don't want to disappoint the boy. Shall I go?" He gazed longingly at the glowing fire casting shadows around his warm haven.

"It'll be pretty bleak up there at this time of night," and she laughed at him. "Go on, you know you want to. Why ask me?"

"I think I'd better go," grinned Peter. "Coming, Ellie?"

Ellie was torn between the cosy warm room and an exciting trip out in the dark with her father and brother. "OK, I'll come." And having made her swift decision she too raced upstairs for hat, gloves, scarf and jacket.

"Ah an hour's peace. How lovely," sighed Mary, an amused look on her face, as her whole family galvanised themselves into action.

Five minutes later, armed with torches and a bag of toffees, the little group were mustered for their night time escapade.

"'Bye, Mum," they called from the hallway. The open front door sent cold gusts into the sitting room, making the flames dance in the fire.

The three figures headed purposefully up Gallants Bower, circles of white light from their torches guiding their footsteps up the narrow rutted path.

"Isn't this exciting?" beamed Ellie, holding onto her father's arm when the width of the track permitted. Peter just gave a low laugh, enjoying her childish pleasure. Eddie was the leader, striding out, making the pace. All was quiet and through the criss-crossed branches they could glimpse the blue-white light of the moon in the navy blue sky. Finally they reached the top, their breathing eased and they felt the chill breeze cooling them.

They rounded a corner and the ash tree came into full view, holding up its thick branches almost in an act of adoration to the moon. Peter and the two youngsters stood on the top of the hill looking all around in awe of the wonderful sight before them; the moon's light playing on the water and sending a hundred bright shimmers back.

"Isn't it fabulous to be up here alone? It's like being the only people left in the world," said Eddie, rather surprising himself.

"Yes," agreed the other two, exactly understanding what he meant.......but they were not alone. All the Dark Dwellers in the woodland kingdom were awake and watching them. Oliphant had followed their progress up the daunting hill unseen. When they reached the upper regions of the woodland where the rulers dwelt, the hawkish piercing eyes of the buzzards silently observed, followed by the hooded yellow eyes of Tolivera, malevolent and intense, registering their every move and spoken word.

Moonbathing, resting against the mossy bank just over the hill from the strange group, Maurice and Maudie sniffed the air, disturbed and anxious.

"It's humans," Maurice confirmed. "Strange they're out tonight, isn't it?"

"Shall we go and look?" suggested a brave Maudie.

Maudie took his hand and slowly and quietly they crept along the edge of the woodland, silent and unobserved. For all other attention was riveted on the humans. As they came into view, Maurice clutched Maudie's arm.

"It's the one who tried to kill us!" Fear was gripping him.

"Yes, but there's the one who saved us, too – that girl," said Maudie. "Let's just watch for one minute and then we'll go home. I promise, really."

Eddie switched on the Moonmirror and at once the light shone out over the hillside and over the sea like a bright beacon. The owl and the buzzards were astounded and their eyes blinded by the strange light. They blinked and looked away.

"Good heavens, how bright it is." Peter was amazed.

"Good isn't it?" laughed Eddie as Ellie watched happily. She hadn't been up so close to the Moonmirror before.

Maudie and Maurice were entranced. With their very blind eyes and their necessity to wear glasses, this new light helped them to see everything a great deal better.

"Well done, Eddie, it's simply terrific!" and Peter again expressed his praise for the new device.

Maurice tapped Maudie's shoulder and they crept away, excited that they had witnessed the strange light. The healing effect of the moon had been beneficial. They both felt well and recharged with energy. Skipping home downhill in very good humour (for moles are subject to depression on account of their dark surroundings) they reached home down the steep ivy-covered track and tumbled into dry, earthy beds and fell asleep.

The chilly wind blowing off the sea increased in slow gusts and Ellie shivered and felt suddenly cold and tired. She longed for the warmth she had left.

"Can we go back now, Dad? I'm cold," she complained, yawning.

"Yes, Ellie, I think that's a very good idea," Peter agreed, much to their surprise. Eddie however was disappointed.

"I'm not quite finished yet. Why don't you two go on? I'll make my own way back. Yes really," he nodded to an astonished Ellie.

"What in the dark? All by yourself?" she questioned slowly.

"Of course, silly! I'll be alright, I've got my torch," he scoffed.

"Well, if you're sure," said Peter, and he took Ellie's arm. "Ellie's cold, don't be too long now. Bye, son," and he patted his shoulder, rather pleased he wasn't afraid of the eerie darkness of the woods at night. They soon disappeared, Ellie taking one last lingering look over her shoulder to make sure he was all right, and giving him a wave. He waved back and they vanished into the swaying blackness of the trees.

All went very quiet, very quiet indeed, and Eddie switched his Moonmirror off to charge. He had used up all the lunar power in showing off his experiment so he sat down on the dry leaves under the tree to wait for a while. Just one more quick blast of light and he would go. He took another toffee out of the bag and leant back against the tree to wait. He switched off his torch to save the battery and began to think, idly chewing away.

For a long time he had been unable to even look at the Moonmirror again, since Captain Avery and all the friends on the *Fancy* had vanished that sunny morning in October. He had tried so hard to move on and had had a long period of feeling unmotivated and uninterested in everything.

He looked up. It was dark and starry now, crisp and cold. The night sky showed the odd occasional flashes of light, which were a passing aeroplane or a steady, moving satellite tracking across the heavens. As the strong moonlight charged the battery, its strength grew. When there was sufficient energy he switched it to transmit, activating the beam and up into the darkness pierced the soft and silvery white light. It amused Eddie so much to have produced his very own power.

Eddie gazed skyward and noticed a blue twinkle. He stared at it… He strained his eyes… on, off... on, off. Just like that. Then it stopped. Excited, he turned the Moonmirror on again and back went the beam heavenward, pale and beautiful, for several minutes, until the battery gave out and went flat.

"Blast!" cursed Eddie, "Needs a longer charge." And then there it was again, the intermittent blue twinkle.

Now, what could that be? he mused. Then little by little it dawned on Eddie that the blue light could be answering his light. Could it be? Was it possible?

He packed up the box for the evening. Maybe he would try again tomorrow if the moon was visible. He looked up for the last time as he wedged the Moonmirror box back into its hide and stared at the black sky. The stars were beautiful, but no blue light could be seen. He shrugged his shoulders. *Oh well, maybe my eyes have gone funny from staring at the moon!* and he gave a chuckle and headed back down the path on the circular route, home.

***

Unknown to Eddie there was a great deal of consternation at the Citadel and in the Great Ash Tree above his head. The brilliant lights had terrified the birds and they too had seen the strange blue twinkle repeated in the sky. Tolivera had retired with a headache to the depths of his fur-covered bed, feeling too ill to think up revengeful plans to punish Eddie. The buzzards had closed their ivy-covered shutters to block out the light and tried not to think what it could mean.

"I shall have to consult my *Chronicles of Woodland Wisdom and Folklore*," muttered the buzzard King, and promptly fell asleep.

***

Eddie whistled to himself and ate another toffee as he made his way home in the darkness, glad of the comforting light of his torch. He steeled himself to see and hear nothing that could frighten him and soon arrived home safe and well on the doorstep of Watermill Cottage. Inside, his father was browsing through *Yachting Monthly* with a pen and paper at his side.

That looks promising. Eddie thought to himself. "Anything interesting?" he asked his Father.

"Umm, one or two, all a bit pricey though."

"Eddie?" called his mother from the kitchen. He went in to see her.

"You've missed a phone call from Patrick, it was such a shame you weren't here. He's going to ring you tomorrow night

66

at 7 o'clock. Will that be alright?" She looked anxiously at him. Disappointment registered at once on Eddie's face.

"I was so looking forward to speaking to him and hearing his news. Blast! What did he say? Is he alright?"

"Yes, yes he seemed fine. Do you want to ring him back? Just a short call now, Eddie, its long distance. Go on then."

"Oh thanks, Mum!" and he ran upstairs to fetch Patrick's school number with his common room extension. He'd just catch him before bedtime at 9.30pm. He chose the phone beside his parents' bed for extra privacy and shut the door. Sitting on the bed, he quickly dialled the number and waited.

A Scottish voice answered: "Burnside College," and Eddie asked politely for the Junior Common Room 106.

"Robin Elliot speaking. Who do you want?"

"Patrick McNab, please."

There was a silence and then he heard somebody shout, "Nabbers, it's for you!" Soon he heard the familiar voice,

"Hello? Patrick McNab here."

Eddie was delighted, "Hi it's me, Eddie. Sorry I missed you, how's things?"

"Oh, it's all fine, fine thanks. They didn't give me detention or anything. I was really lucky. Just had a bit of a lecture. You know the sort of thing… responsibility, parents, future, blah blah blah. But it wasn't too bad. I wanted you to be the first to know – I'm coming down on the train on the second Monday in December. Mum and Dad are coming later but they are going to give me a key and some money to buy things and stock up the larder for them."

"Oh, that will be fun."

"We'll have two weeks before they arrive, that's what's fun! Will you come and meet me from the train?"

"Leave it to us. That's great."

"And Dad wants to buy the boat so he'll ring your dad about that; I've given him the number."

"Even better. We've just taken her out of the water. Look, Patrick, I've really got to go now. Glad everything's OK. We'll see you very soon. In fact we'll see you in thirteen days! Bye for now."

"Bye, Eddie. Thanks for ringing back." And they both put the receivers down.

Eddie sat quietly for a moment, taking it all in and trying to remember everything to tell Ellie. He was full of happiness and excitement and got up to go downstairs and tell everyone.

The phone suddenly rang beside him, making him jump. Just as quickly it stopped. Somebody had picked it up in the kitchen. He made his way downstairs, listening. He heard his father's voice speaking. He found Ellie in the sitting room and began to tell her all Patrick's news. She of course was delighted too.

"That's not long, it's…"

"Thirteen days!" they both said together and laughed.

"Let's go and tell Mum." And they burst into the kitchen, each one anxious to be the first. However, when they opened the door, their mother put her finger to her mouth to silence them, as their father talked on the phone, looking serious. Mary ushered them both back to the cosy sitting room, a hand on each shoulder.

"Come on; let's leave him in peace to talk. Sit down and I'll get my chocolates out." And she brought out the tempting gold-and-red box with the tassels on the corners.

"Now Ellie, choose one, and you, Eddie. Tell me all about Patrick. How is he?" she coaxed Eddie, keen to change the subject and keep the children occupied. Eddie began at once.

"He sounds great, Mum, and he's coming down here on the—

"Second Monday in December!" chimed in Ellie.

"And he's getting the key and he's got to stock the larder and buy things!" Eddie added.

"Really? Well, that's good," nodded an interested Mary, "and when do Irene and Sam move in?"

"They're coming sometime later."

"So, it's all turned out well for Patrick. I'm thrilled," beamed Mary.

"Can we go and fetch him and can he stay here?" begged Eddie.

"Oh please, Mum, please!" begged Ellie even harder.

"I don't know. We'll have to consult Bridget and George on that one." And there were cries of "That's not fair" and "Why not?" which she silenced.

"No, no, it is fair."

At that moment Peter appeared in the doorway looking very unhappy.

"Sorry everyone, I've got to go. Car's picking me up in a few minutes. Rush job, can't say what," and he made a face.

Eddie and Ellie turned round in horror.

"But you've only just come back, Dad!"

"That's not fair, can't somebody else go?"

"Are you going to be away for Christmas?"

Peter held his hands up.

"Whoa, whoa! Look, I just don't know. Could be all over in a couple of days, I just can't say. Now, where's my number two suit, Mary? And I'll need my thick sea socks this time."

Mary sighed, and putting the chocolates away resigned herself to sorting out all of Peter's kit, as only she knew where it was all stored.

"Come on, then." She pushed Peter gently through the door in front of her. "Let's go and find it all," leaving the two bewildered children alone on the sofa. They sat together staring at the flickering red fire absolutely silent, not wanting to believe what had happened. One minute their father was looking for a boat and the next he was packing up his kit and disappearing, maybe not even going to be home for Christmas. Ellie began to cry softly and Eddie felt a huge heavy lump in his throat.

"There is nothing we can do, Ellie, you only make it worse by crying," he said to her in a strange voice, through gritted teeth.

"I know," she sobbed quietly, "But I can't help it. It's all so unfair and he's only just come back. We've got so many things we wanted to do and now it's all ruined!" and she turned her face into the cushions.

Eddie didn't look at her. Somehow he couldn't find any comfort for Ellie; he was too upset himself, trying to control his emotions. He clenched his fists and said to himself, *I won't cry, I won't!*

Suddenly a car crunched by the window and into the car park. Eddie rushed to the door as a man in uniform got out, smiling. Eddie spoke first.

"I'll get my dad, he's just coming," as Peter and Mary came downstairs carrying bags.

"Righto, son, I'm off now. Look after your mother and sister for me, won't you? I'll be back soon I promise, Eddie." He put his arm around his son and pressed two ten pound notes into his hand.

"To help out with the Christmas shopping," he explained. "Ellie? Where are you?" and she appeared in a moment, eyes wiped and sniffing, trying to smile.

"'Bye Dad, see you soon," was all she could manage. He hugged her, "'Bye Ellie."

"'Bye, be in touch." He kissed his wife and they exchanged meaningful glances and a touch of hands.

The waiting companion was tactfully sitting back in the car listening to the radio.

"Ready, Chris?" Peter said and joined him in the front seat after throwing his bags in the back. He waved as the black car turned around and crunching on the gravel, was gone in a moment. The three left behind slowly turned and went back inside with a heavy miserable feeling and closed the door.

"What's so important, Mum, that Dad's had to go?" asked Eddie insistently in a harsh voice. Mary refused to answer, but caught his face in both her hands, smoothing his hair and looking into his hurt blue eyes.

She decided to tell him the truth.

"All leave has been cancelled for everyone and the ships companies brought back on board. It's in the interests of national security I'm afraid and is very serious. So you see, every father in the Navy has been recalled tonight. There are lots of families like us, dear." Mary was watching their young faces."You're not to worry, it's just a precaution. And now, hot chocolate seems appropriate I think."

The children followed her into the kitchen.

"Tell me all about this evening, Eddie. You were very brave to walk all the way home on your own. Dad was most impressed."

"Yes, it did work again," he told her proudly. "It was very bright and that's a good place for it up there on that tree."

"Will Patrick's holiday coincide with a full moon?" Mary asked, stirring the chocolate drinks.

"I hope so. By my calculations we should have a full moon again on the 27th December but cloudy skies will ruin it."

"Come on; let's go back to the fire. You get some logs, Eddie, and Ellie, shut the curtains across the front door. We'll be nice and snug then." Soon they were sipping hot chocolate feeling just a little better.

"But what about Patrick?" Ellie asked impatiently.

"Yes I know, Ellie, but we've got to consider everyone in this equation," Mary said firmly. "George and Bridget have no family and so Patrick is very special."

"Oh, Mum!" they both protested loudly.

"Yes, I think that's how it should be, because once the cottage is the Mc Nabs, Patrick probably won't go to stay with them that often. So you do see how important it is for them to look after him for just a little longer. I might let you sleep there one night. If you're very, very good," and she raised a finger at them as a warning.

"Mum!" they replied furiously and then laughed. They had broken the gloomy despondency and their spirits lifted.

While they laughed, Peter was halfway on his journey to Plymouth to pick up a ship that would take him far out into the Bay of Biscay that night.

Chapter Thirteen
Tolivera misbehaves

During that night, under the strong influence of the full moon, when Man and Nature are at one, there was a frenzy of activity. The ancient primordial rhythm of the lunar cycle exerted its power on the creatures on Earth, the moon being relatively close to it, a mere 240,000 miles away.

Maudie and Maurice awoke refreshed and revitalised and felt a great urge to dig and explore. Deterred by the sonic mole scarers they discovered wonderful soft leafy mould that took them in the direction of Waterside Cottage's garden. Left undisturbed for many years it was full of plump worms and woodlice, fat leatherjackets and crunchy black beetles. By the time the sun rose in a pink and turquoise dawn, they had made good progress down the slope.

"I feel so much better now," said Maurice, wiping his face on a red spotted handkerchief.

"That's good, nothing like a bit of exercise," agreed Maudie. "Shall we go back for a rest now?"

"Good idea." In no time at all they raced back through the new network of tunnels to their cosy den under the tree roots.

***

Out by the Skerries the tide rose higher and higher under the influence of the Atlantic moon swell. Beneath the sea the water surged in, creating strong currents, while drifts of seaweed, plankton, and bubbles of oxygen swirled. Charged with this new energy, shoals of fish met together forming huge groups and seals, excited by this extra food before their eyes, were caught in the frenzy. Dolphins joined in the exhilaration and unable to stop themselves were full of high spirits, leaping and diving to great heights and depths. Doryana and Diadem, the leaders of the group, swam joyfully leading the acrobatic dance. While these two dolphins pushed themselves to the limits of their endurance, they were suddenly assaulted by some strange and weird noises echoing through the water. Few creatures of the deep communicated in this way. They clicked in dolphin language to each other and agreed they had both heard something unusual. Fearing a predator from a different ocean, a killer whale or another whale species, they returned to a safer depth and led their school back to the coast around Brixham.

"The moon does strange things to some creatures," Doryana told her mate as they lazed and drifted in restful play.

"Who knows what the tide brings under its strong pull?" and they discussed it no more. Unknown to them, the lobsters and prawns, mussels and limpets taking refuge in the rocky edges had also heard the deep wails from under the sea. Nothing much ever frightened these hard-shelled crustaceans, but this was disturbing and the mussels had loosened their grip in fear. The strange noises had now ceased but the effects upon the Seafarers had not. Many had become disorientated and lost their way; others had suffered distortion of vision as the strange sounds had vibrated through the water. Nothing like it had been experienced before so no one knew how long the effects would last.

The following morning dawned clear and bright and Sargasso, looking for food around the sheltered coves, saw his two friends, Solomon and Bathsheba, bobbing in the swell just off Sugary Cove. He swooped down and landed on the sea close by them with a splash. They exchanged greetings and Solomon told him of the strange noises the underwater creatures had been hearing and of general unrest and fear spreading amongst them. Sargasso listened intently.

"What do you think it can be?" he asked the two kindly and gentle creatures who swam quietly around him.

"Who knows? A dark giant from another ocean lost his way. Many fear it may not be alone, but nothing can be done. We must wait. The Spirit of the Sea would help us if we ask him, but he has gone far, far, away to the land of snow and ice to winter," Bathsheba told him sadly.

Sargasso looked down at the pearly shell strung around his neck, half hidden in his feathers and felt glad. If necessary he could reach their spiritual leader. Their talk concluded and bidding each other farewell, the seals disappeared in a plop and a swish, leaving ripples spreading over the water.

Sargasso flew back to Watermill Cottage to see what Eddie was up to. He met Freddie on the garage roof.

"Bad news I'm afraid," said Freddie gloomily, "their father's gone away again and everyone's really fed up. Nobody's even put any crumbs out today. They've forgotten me."

"Any news from higher up?" asked Sargasso.

"I expect they'll be sending for me again," Freddie gloomily predicted. "Tolivera won't give up. Do you think you'll be able to tell Eddie about it? It's the only way."

"I have permission to use the power of speech, yes. Thinking carefully about this, as the Moonmirror is dependent on the light of the moon he will never go up there in the daytime, so I can't see what all the fuss is about."

"I know," sighed the robin in agreement. "Tolivera is so spiteful, he might think up something horrible to pay Eddie back. It all depends on the Mists of Time. If the recall of the past is still clear, then he might forget about it eventually."

"Let's change the subject shall we?" suggested Sargasso, wishing to dispel the sad mood of the robin – his advancing years meant he was often grumpy and difficult. He didn't even bother to tell him about the Seafarers' problem.

***

After school that day Eddie and Ellie felt a bit lonely so they walked round to the teashop to see George and Bridget, to talk about Patrick and discuss their father's departure. There were plenty of people there, lured by a bright winter's afternoon walk, treating themselves to tea.

George was delighted to see them. "Come on in. You'll have to come into the kitchen as we're full up in here."

They all squashed into the back and immediately Ellie rolled her sleeves up, put on an apron and began the washing-up.

"Come on, Eddie, you can dry up," she told him, and to everyone's surprise, he did.

In half an hour it was done and the people began to filter away.

"Let's have a cup of tea now," insisted Bridget and they sat together by the window with fluffy mince pies and teacakes oozing hot butter, smelling spicy and delicious. They looked out to sea as the afternoon's light began to fade. It was only 3.30pm.

"Dad's had to go off again," Ellie announced, munching her teacake.

"What, so soon?" queried George. "I thought he had lots of leave left?"

"It's an emergency," Eddie told them, "The entire Navy's on alert."

"Really?" Bridget looked quite shocked. "What can it be?"

"It'll be on the news this evening I bet," said George knowingly.

"Oh dear! What a shame for Mary," sighed Bridget, shaking her head, "but I expect your poor mother is used to it."

"Patrick phoned us last night as well."

"How is the dear boy?"

"Sounds really good and he's coming here for Christmas!"

"I know," said Bridget triumphantly, "I had a thank you letter from him this morning." She fished it out of her apron skirt pocket.

"He says when he's coming back, the time of the train, even the platform number. I expect he's counting the days, don't you?" She smiled at the two faces eager for news of their favourite friend.

"He'll stay with you of course – won't he?" asked Eddie, in a carefully phrased question.

"We do hope so, until Irene and Sam move in, but he'll be nice and handy down at Waterside Cottage," beamed George. "Everything has a funny way of smoothing itself out, doesn't it? Who'd have thought it? Buying a cottage. Sam needs to get out sailing, it will be really good for him. He's got such a stressful job. Seems to have lost himself in all the tangles and knots of business life, eh lad?"

He addressed himself to Eddie who suddenly thought about his own father, sent away from them in such a hurry, suddenly just gone. He felt sad inside.

"We shall have a Christmas party," announced George. "We'll start planning it, won't we, Bridget?" and he smiled to himself, just thinking of it.

"Yes, why not?" agreed Bridget.

"And you're all invited, of course," added George, patting Ellie's hand trying to cheer them up a bit.

"Oh good, I love parties," she replied.

"I suppose we'd better get home," Eddie said, not feeling at all like a party, getting up and clearing the table as he went. Ellie followed and the teashop was soon bedded down for the night.

The four walked home together down the old stone steps by the castle wall and along the grassy verge past St Petrox church. Ellie looked into the dark windows and the firmly closed door, thinking about her beloved mice Ferdinand and Isabella who used to live there, tucked away in the flower arranging cupboard.

Reaching the gate of the Old Bath House, they said goodbye and the two youngsters walked on home along the darkening lane, scuffing through the carpet of fallen leaves, suddenly alone. The air was cold and their mood rapidly dropped. They fell into silence, their thoughts broken only by a screech from a rook and the cries of a few homecoming seagulls. The trees loomed large and black and the shadows in between felt dark and unfriendly. A twig cracked and a few leaves rustled; the wind pulled at their clothes. The faintest twinkle of a tiny star broke the darkness of the navy blue sky.

They both shivered.

"Come on, let's get home. It's so cold isn't it?" said Ellie, feeling just a little anxious.

"The moon will be up soon." said Eddie, glancing through the trees. "Do you fancy coming up into the woods again tonight?"

"No I don't," she replied in no uncertain terms. "I'm not going again, it's much too cold and I don't like it in the dark, especially now Dad's not here anymore."

A slight movement on the side of the path caught their eye, then another. It was Freddie; he had come to see where they were and to escort them home. The red breast of the robin was puffed out and fluffy and was a bright contrast to the dull winter greys and browns.

"Hello, Freddie," they both called out in delight.

Out of the darkness a large shape approached over their heads and swooped suddenly in front of them, making them jump.

"Oh! What's that?" Ellie clutched Eddie's arm in alarm. Eddie was watching the sky to see where it went, as the black shape turned and made another approach, wide wings outspread, silent and menacing. Its great eyes were visible as it came closer and closer, legs down and talons hooked.

"It's an owl!" Eddie whispered and pushed Ellie down towards the ground, quickly realising the bird looked intent on attacking them. At the last minute they could feel the gust of wind created as it swooped at great speed, its fierce talons grazing Eddie's hair; then it swung up sharply and flapping its wings, retreated into the darkness.

"Are you alright?" Eddie helped to pick up his frightened sister.

"What was it?" she gasped, brushing off the dirt from her clothes as she tried to regain her composure.

"An owl. Stupid thing, what was it doing? It was so close it touched my hair. "Once again the large menacing bird swooped down and flew across their path and over their heads, with a strange and frightening howl.

Ellie screamed loudly. Get away you horrible thing!"

Beside them, on the pathway, Freddie was hopping from one spot to another, chattering in agitation. He was not frightened, he was furious, with a rising anger in his tiny chest. It was Tolivera. He knew it now – that cruel, cunning, conniving old warlord, who would not tolerate Eddie's tinkering on his special tree and had come down to lower ground to prove it.

The robin had never been so angry. How dare he try to attack his beloved children! He wouldn't stand for it.

"Eddie, I'm really frightened! Let's get home!" Ellie was almost crying.

"It's OK, he's gone now I'm sure," Eddie lied to her. "But I'm getting a stick just in case. Come on," and he grabbed her arm. The furious robin accompanied the frightened pair home. Thankfully, they burst through the back doorway. Freddie returned to his place on the garden wall, tucked under the shrubs. He was still very angry.

As usual, their mother was preparing supper and they were very pleased to see her.

"Hi there you two, let's get the fire lit shall we? Then you won't have to go outside again tonight. There's going to be a hard frost."

So Eddie and Ellie were quickly diverted and set about their chores, rolling newspaper into balls and laying the kindling sticks, carefully piling a couple of logs on top; Ellie struck a match and set the whole thing alight. Replacing the fireguard, they sat back in satisfaction.

"There! Do you think it will go?" asked Ellie anxiously, watching the crackling sparks burst into noisy flames.

"'Course it will," replied Eddie and they looked on with enjoyment. There was nothing so comforting as sitting next to the fire, watching it get bigger and bigger.

"I don't think I'll bother going up into the woods after all," decided Eddie. "That owl might be about again."

"Wasn't he awful? Why do you think he did that?"

"Don't know. Just wait till I tell Sargasso. He'll be a match for him don't you think?" grinning at his sister, picturing the large seagull fighting with the tawny owl. Mother called them and they sat down to supper.

"Shall we watch the news? See if there's any news of Dad?"

Ellie leapt up to switch on the television. They all watched the 6 o'clock news bulletin intently but to their surprise there was nothing on the London news and nothing on the local South West programme either. They were very disappointed.

Outside, Freddie was thinking hard. Even he had been taken by surprise at Tolivera's appalling actions. He decided to report him to the buzzards at the earliest opportunity, and snuggled down for the night in his dry shelter, thinking up punishments for the owl. When it came to his beloved children, he would stop at nothing. Now he was an Exalted Woodlander and on the Roll of Honour he had a great deal more power. The buzzards would have to listen to him; it was their duty.

Chapter Fourteen
Patrick gets good news and Eddie makes a discovery

Eddie and Ellie spent the evening with their mother. Ellie got out her knitting needles and the one ball of red wool she had left.

"What can I make with this?" she asked Mary.

"Let me see," replied her mother. "What about a Christmas stocking? You can hang it up at the end of your bed on Christmas Eve!"

"How many stitches shall I cast on?" and at this point Eddie rolled his eyes and went to find his dad's yachting magazine, so he too could browse through the boats for sale. It was tucked down the side of the sofa.

"Ah, got it. Good," he said and sat down contented at last. He noticed several pen marks that his father had made. Eddie was so engrossed in the magazine that he was quite startled when the phone rang. They all looked at each other thinking the same thing. Mary got up at once to answer it. The two listened intently. Then with great relief they heard their mother say,

"Oh hello, Patrick, how are you? Yes I'll get him. Eddie!" She called from the kitchen, and handed him the phone. She went back into the sitting room and sat down heavily, looking rather disappointed.

"I thought it was your father."

Ellie, who had been gripped with anxiety, jumped to her feet. "I'll make the drinks tonight," and rushed off to the kitchen, wool and needles spilling over the floor in her hurry to hear what Eddie was saying.

"That's so lucky! What a thing to happen!" and he chuckled. "Bad luck for them of course, but still, it couldn't be better. When are you coming? That's fantastic!" He grinned at Ellie who was putting the kettle on and getting out the mugs.

She was very curious; it sounded as if Patrick must be coming home early. What could be the matter? She hoped he hadn't been expelled this time and she looked around impatiently, waiting for Eddie to hang up.

"OK then, George will ring us in the morning. See you then. Bye!" He put the receiver down and laughed to himself.

"Do tell me!" insisted Ellie at once.

"Wait till you hear this!" laughed Eddie. "There's been an outbreak of Asian flu and twenty boys are in the sanatorium, so they've decided to send home those pupils whose families are able to have them. Of course some are going abroad for Christmas and have flights booked so they can't leave, and some are being quarantined. Patrick's so lucky because his dormitory are OK, so they're packing up now and catching the first trains tomorrow. He'll be here by the evening, 10pm at Totnes station."

"Wow!" said Ellie, laughing too, "What a bit of luck! You don't think he'll get it later?"

"Who knows? But I bet he'd rather be ill in Dartmouth, don't you?" He raced off to tell his mother the good news, and Ellie followed with the tray.

"Well?" Mary looked up, intrigued to know what all the laughing was about. When Eddie told her she smiled too.

"That's nice for you two, except you will still have to go to school, don't forget. It's not the end of term yet."

They both made a face.

"Yes, but we don't do much work now and there's the parties and carol service so it's not too bad," consoled Ellie.

Eddie wasn't so keen.

"Never mind," said his mother. "He'll be here every afternoon and evening, and weekends. You'll have plenty of time for mischief, Eddie, I'm sure!" They drank their hot chocolate in quiet excitement.

"We've got Christmas to think about too," Mary told them. "That's coming on really well, Ellie," looking at her red strip of knitting growing.

"I see you've made it very large at the top. Expecting lots of presents are you?" Eddie chuckled.

Ellie frowned. "Well there's no point having a small one, is there?" she told them snootily.

Eventually the evening drew to a close; all were in bed by 10 o'clock. They called goodnight to each other and closed their doors.

Eddie was too excited to sleep and leant on the windowsill, staring out between the empty trees into the black beyond. He glimpsed the moon through the branches, clear and white, and many tiny pinpricks of stars dotted across the sky. He sighed. How far away it all was, miles and miles of empty sky, so much space with just the winking, twinkling lights in that lonely expanse of nothing. He thought with satisfaction of his Moonmirror charging up, absorbing all that energy and brightness, high up on the hilltop. What about his Crystal Signaller? He had forgotten all about that.

He looked inside the back of his wardrobe and sure enough, packed into a cardboard box was the crystal signalling light, another of their lunar inventions. He pulled it out carefully and opened it. He was seized by overwhelming excitement as the ideas all came flooding back to him; he couldn't stop himself beginning to piece it together. But – would it work through his bedroom window? He would have to wait for a decent gap between the trees for the best complete view of the moon's face.

He pulled a small table over to the window to balance the experiment on, except that it wasn't an experiment anymore; he *knew* that it worked! He lined up the magnifying glass and the crystal hedgehog that acted as a prism and the mirror with the glass plate, batteries, wire and small bulb, and knelt down by the window, looking at the angle of the moon.

As he watched, the white round circle moved almost imperceptibly behind the branches, one by one, slowly, slowly. Eddie remained still, patiently watching the fascinating, silent progress of the moon until it emerged from the other side of the trees and struck the prism through the magnifying glass. At once, colours danced before his eyes and, repeated by the mirror, were sent back through the window into the starry night. Eddie was delighted. The rainbow colours rippled across his ceiling illuminating his room. After a short while the moon crossed behind the next clump of trees and the light was obscured again. Eddie realised that for this night anyway, the display was over. He was also very, very tired and began wearily to put the pieces back into the box. It was darker now, the moon having slid behind a cloud.

That's it then. Eddie decided to go to bed. He put his pyjamas on, shivered once or twice, and crossed the floor to pull the curtains. As he grasped the edges to draw them together, he glanced up into the darkness. The moon appeared, and he gasped sharply as a blue light glittered brilliantly, flashing on and off right before his eyes. He put his hand up to shield them for a moment, and then opened the window for a clearer view. The cold air rushed in and Eddie grabbed his woolly dressing gown off the bed and flung it around him like a shawl. He stared into the sky… Nothing. Nothing at all. Just the little stars as always, twinkling at him.

But I did see it, he told himself. *I know I did.* It came again. Definitely blue, larger than starlight, flashing on…off…, on…off, just like the rhythm of a lighthouse beam. It was most definitely signalling to someone. Could it have been in answer to his Crystal Signaller? It came from the moon's face, he was sure. He waited. It was too cold to keep the window open. Then it came. A blinding blue flash, so strong it sent Eddie reeling across the room as the windowpane cracked and splintered.

God! What's happening? as Eddie tried to get to his feet. He rushed to look out, but the light had gone and the moon with it. All was black and silent.

Eddie sat on his bed, gathering himself together, shocked and rather frightened.

That was like lightning, he thought, as he pulled the curtains and looked at the broken window. Fortunately the glass had not fallen out. Now, what was he going to tell his mother? Blast! He would worry about that tomorrow. He climbed into his bed and fished around with his feet for his hot water bottle. It was not very hot. He kept his dressing gown on and curled up into a tight ball, too tired to think, and fell asleep in seconds.

***

The Dark Dwellers on Gallants Bower cowered in fear. They too had had an uninterrupted view of the strange blue flashing light, which disturbed and terrified them. The last brilliant flash had caused those who saw it to pass out and fall asleep for several seconds.

Poor Tolivera couldn't understand it because the wretched contraption hidden in his tree trunk had been inactive during the whole thing, so it couldn't have been responsible. He was very puzzled and uncharacteristically fearful. Oliphant, however, being much nearer to Watermill Cottage, had seen the coloured lights from Eddie's window. He had thought them perfectly glorious and had sat mesmerised by the beautiful colours. Being a Dark Dweller, he was not used to seeing the beauty of a rainbow in daylight hours as other animals were.

When the bright flash came he slammed his door closed, his heart thumping and his eyes dazzled, blinded for a while, lights in his head and pain in his eyes. He was very afraid. What powers did the boy possess? What had answered from the sky? It was like lightning without the thunder. All most puzzling. Oliphant was not brave enough to open his door again and he nestled down in his musty dry treetop shelter to try to sleep.

***

Travelling through the night sky, passing through the well-lit expanses of outer space, came the celestial mystery, lights extinguished now, as it made its journey onward to its goal, the last bright beam of reconnaissance necessary to pinpoint its target completed. Reassured of its position, it gathered speed and continued through the heavens, excited and full of anticipation at the thought of making contact with the Signaller of moonlight it had observed.

Chapter Fifteen
Sargasso visits the Spirit of the Sea

Unknown to Eddie, there were two travellers speeding towards him that morning. One was celestial, crossing space, and one terrestrial, rattling along the railway network. When he awoke, the pane of glass, splintered into rather artistic patterns, was staring at him. He tried to remember what had happened. Lying and concocting silly untrue stories were not in Eddie's nature. At first light he tiptoed into his mother's bedroom. Her bedside light was visible beneath the door, so he knew she was awake.

"Mum," he began, as he gently opened the door.

"Yes, dear, what is it?" Mary answered at once.

Eddie ventured in. His mother was sitting up in bed with a cup of tea, reading. She glanced up at him. "What's the matter, Eddie?"

"I'm sorry, Mum," he began, "but my bedroom window is broken. I'm not sure how it happened, but it's all cracked into pieces." He sat down on the bed feeling rather foolish. The truth was he didn't know what had happened.

"What were you doing, Eddie? How could you break the window?" Mary asked him, rather surprised.

"I don't know. I was using my Crystal Signaller and there was a flash and suddenly the window all sort of shattered, but it's not broken everywhere. It's quite alright."

"You'd better let me see." Mary got up, put on her dressing gown and followed Eddie to his room. Everything he had told her was true. The window was cracked beyond repair.

"Oh dear. What shall we do?" Mary asked herself out loud. "It will have to be boarded up until it can be replaced. I'll have to get on the phone to someone. What's the name of that nice builder that our neighbours had?"

Eddie replied at once, glad he could be of some help

"Mr Abrahams. He lives up Tumbling Hill."

"That's good, we can find his number later on." Mary was relieved. All these household disasters always happened when Peter was away. Always.

"I'm sorry, Mum." Eddie said again, looking sad and feeling worse. Mary took a deep breath and pursed her lips trying not to be too cross.

"Don't worry, it was an accident. As long as we can get it fixed, it's not too bad. Only a pane of glass. Now, tell me again how it happened."

They discussed what could have caused the bright flash, but could not decide on a satisfactory answer. It was a real mystery. They both went downstairs to the kitchen and made some more tea, dunking their gingernut biscuits into the large steaming mugs. Ellie, hearing noises downstairs, soon joined them yawning and rubbing her eyes.

"You two are up early," she commented, finding the teapot hot, and pouring herself a mug full.

"Yes," nodded Mary. "You tell her, Eddie."

"What?" Ellie spun round at once.

"My window's broken; all shattered into big cracks."

"What? How did you do that?"

"I didn't do it," Eddie insisted. "A big flash of light came and broke it."

"Oh yes?" Ellie replied sarcastically, grabbing several biscuits and sitting down too.

"I was using my signalling gadget, but it wasn't from the inside, it was from outside." Eddie protested.

"Hmm." Ellie looked at her mother. "Can I see it?"

"Of course, just don't touch it, the glass is very sharp and we don't want it to fall out." And with that Ellie went upstairs followed by Eddie.

"What really happened, Eddie? You can tell me surely?" she told him crossly.

"I have told you," insisted Eddie as they gazed at the cracked window, "but I will tell you this, Ellie. I'm sure something is signalling to me. I've seen it twice now. Something blue is flashing from the moon or somewhere. When I used my Moonmirror that night up in the woods, I saw it after you and Dad had gone home. I'm not making it up, Ellie; I really think something's happening!" He sat down on his bed and said no more.

Ellie bit her lip. "Ummmm, sounds a bit scary to me. You're not going to find somebody else are you? And whisk us off into outer space? Please say you aren't, Eddie, because I don't think I can stand it again." And she too sat on the bed, concerned and worried.

"Well it's not my fault! I haven't done anything except turn the light things on a couple of times! Don't blame me, Ellie!" Eddie retorted.

"At least Patrick's coming home. You can tell him all about it, not me!" and right on cue the phone rang making them jump.

"That will be George I bet," said Eddie, jumping up. Mary took the call downstairs and then shouted up to them,

"George is picking you up at 9 o'clock tonight to go to the station. Is that alright?"

"Fine thanks, Mum," he shouted back, and they both went off to wash and dress.

***

Freddie the robin had slept through it all, sheltered by the evergreen shrubs. When he woke at dawn he headed straight down to the creek to have a serious talk with Sargasso and then to bravely confront the buzzards and lodge a formal complaint against Tolivera.

Sargasso had been down on the shore for a while. He was aware of new anxieties amongst the Seafarers; rumours and strange fears were rippling backward and forward, making everyone nervous around the creek.

"Hello, Freddie," he greeted the small brown bird.

"Have you heard the news?"

"No, what news?"

"There are strange creatures in the seas around our shores. I'm hearing more reports of them every day. Nobody's ever seen them, but they can hear them; noises and strong forces in the water. We think it might be huge sea monsters from the deep, released by underground explosions far away. Some of our friends have been ill, their sight and sound systems affected by the creatures wails."

"What can you do?" Freddie was concerned for his friend.

"I shall have to seek advice from the Spirit of the Sea again. He gave me this silvered shell for just such an occasion." He showed the robin the precious necklace, half hidden in his feathers. Freddie was very impressed.

"I wish you had the same powers over Tolivera," he sighed, eyeing the shell. "He swooped down last night in the twilight as the children were coming home and tried to attack them. He was vicious and frightening. I'm off to the Citadel to complain.

Coming with me?" He wished with all his heart that the brave seagull would, as his old fears of the buzzard returned.

Suspecting the robin needed his moral support and furious at the thought of the owl attacking Eddie and Ellie, Sargasso agreed to go with him, pushing his own worries for the Seafarers into the back of his mind for the time being. Sargasso had been frightened of the Woodlanders' world before he met Freddie. He rarely ventured into their territory, dark and mysterious, and felt uneasy away from the sea and the shore, but for Freddie, his friend, he would do it.

They flew up through the bare trees together, strangely shaped broken branches looking menacing in the sharp, grey light. The sky was heavy and overcast with great black patches of cloud passing overhead and a strong cold wind. No one was out of doors today. They reached the huge pine tree surrounded and protected by thick heavy brambles and tree ivy. The buzzards had seen them approach and the two black rooks, the guardians of the Citadel, had cawed to announce the arrival of the strangers.

Five buzzards peered over the entrance – the three young princes growing fast into manhood and the rapidly ageing almighty buzzard and his consort. She blinked nervously, sensing trouble. They welcomed the visitors politely and due to the extra cold weather invited them into the panelled State room. Sargasso, feeling claustrophobic and trapped, swallowed his fear and followed.

"Your business, Robin and Seagull? Please state your reasons for this visit," officiously demanded the buzzard, ignoring any further polite conversation.

"Yes I shall, lord," bravely announced the robin, taking a deep breath and fluffing out his chest importantly.

"I have come to lodge a complaint against Tolivera, the Deputy Council Leader." Gasps sounded from the three young princes, but their father silenced them with a steely glare of his piercing eyes. Freddie continued courageously, encouraged by Sargasso's faint nod of his yellow beak.

"He has, against our Woodlanders' Law, attacked the boy and the girl from Watermill Cottage. I believe the cause of this unprovoked anger was a wooden box nailed to the Great Ash Tree by the boy. I wish you to investigate this matter and take the necessary steps to admonish the culprit. I have grave fears that to start any enmity between dwellers of the woodland and humans could prove disastrous. That is all, my lord." And the robin bowed and retreated back next to Sargasso.

"Very well done, my friend," whispered the seagull.

The buzzard digested this information and remained silent. He didn't like upsetting Tolivera, who was too smart by half. He had seen the Moonmirror and the bright light that had shone from it and had not known what to do. He had been prepared to just ignore it. However, a formal complaint had been lodged now by this interfering little bird who had always irritated him. Now he would be forced to act. What should he do? He wasn't sure.

"Thank you for bringing this to my attention, Robin. Be assured I shall prepare some action when I have carefully considered it. I do not advocate aggression towards humans and Tolivera must abide by our rules. The Great Ash Tree which is the dwelling place of our respected Deputy has been tampered with and as a result there have been strange lights frightening the Dark Dwellers, so… some action must be taken. I shall think on it, Robin." He paused. "And you, Seagull, what brings you out of your territory into mine? Something of importance must have prompted this?"

Sargasso raised his head and stared into the buzzard's eyes.

"My concern, lord, is for the boy, he is my chosen master. Anybody who harms him, in turn harms me. Do I make myself understood?" and his eyes glittered with intention.

The buzzard did indeed understand. This was more serious. Woodlander and Seafarer had never been set against each other. It was unthinkable. That wretched Tolivera taking matters into his own hands; he'd caused all this, but now it couldn't be ignored.

"I shall of course settle this matter, Seagull. Tolivera answers to me and has perhaps been a little hasty in his actions. However, the lights and the brightness have inconvenienced us, but I gather it is only powerful at the time of the full moon. Is that so?"

"I believe so, my lord," replied Sargasso.

"We do not wish to make enemies with any Seafarers, I can assure you," continued the buzzard. "Let us keep peace between us a priority." He nodded graciously to the two birds standing before him. "You may go now if you are satisfied with my decision," and he beckoned to the three princes who stood in line to acknowledge the departure of the Woodlanders. Their father was teaching them the duties of office, grooming them for an eventual takeover.

Reluctantly, and still not sure of what action, (if any) would be taken, the robin and the seagull left and flew back down to Watermill Cottage, to find a strange man up a ladder outside Eddie's window. It was John Abrahams, the builder from Tumbling Hill, repairing the broken glass. Mary and Eddie were standing outside, dressed for the cold – one holding the ladder and one a bucket of putty.

"Any chance of a cuppa?" called Mr Abrahams, smiling, and Mary went inside at once to make one. Eddie continued to hold the ladder. It was cold work, the easterly wind blowing cruelly across the patio, numbing his hands.

"I've never seen glass break like this before," Mr Abrahams told Eddie. "The stress lines are all wrong and the cracks all go in funny directions. Must be a type of old glass I'm not used to. Strange, very strange." Eddie kept quiet; he knew what was coming next.

"How did it break?"

"It was a freak flash of lightning," said Eddie, and left it at that.

"Really? That's a new one on me," replied the surprised man and with that Mary appeared upstairs and passed the tea out of the window to him. The whole job was finished in an hour and Eddie helped pack up the tools and stow them in the van.

"Thanks, lad," he said gratefully to Eddie, who was carrying the last of the glass carefully into the back.

"I'll be off then."

Soon the garden was deserted and peace descended again. Sargasso and Freddie sat together to discuss the events at the Citadel.

"I don't believe he'll do anything. He's scared of Tolivera if you ask my opinion," said the robin. "I'm going to see Oliphant again. We might have to do this ourselves," he decided with satisfaction.

"I'm going to speak to Eddie and then I will turn my attentions to the mystery of the sea creatures. I'm duty bound now to contact the Spirit of the Sea. Perhaps I'll need your help soon."

"It's willingly given," nodded his loyal friend. "Just send for me." So the two parted to pursue their own urgent business.

Sargasso spied around the house to find Eddie. He was upstairs in his room. The large seagull hardly fitted onto the windowsill, but he perched precariously there and tapped on the new glass with his yellow beak. Eddie opened the window at once.

"What's the matter?" he said, alarmed and not expecting a reply.

"I have come to warn you of the cruel intentions of the tawny owl who lives at the top of the hill. You have nailed a box to his tree and he is out to get you. I have permission from the Spirit of the Sea, my master, to speak. I wish only for your safety."

Eddie was astonished, and knew it was true. It all became clear to him, the strange behaviour of the owl earlier.

"Sargasso! You can talk again. What shall I do? You see we've... Patrick and I have moved the Moonmirror because it's such a great place to charge it up. I don't see enough moonlight from here. It's not doing him any harm is it?"

Sargasso tried to explain.

"That's his tree of residence, a badge of his office as Deputy, and he hates humans interfering in the woodland. I hope you will heed the warning. He may attack again. I only wish for your safety, Eddie." He nodded wisely.

"Thank you, thank you Sargasso, you are a true friend. Eddie stroked him gently. "I'm not scared of an old owl. Let me worry about that."

"As you wish." If only the buzzard would keep Tolivera in check then these things wouldn't be necessary. He hopped to the edge of the windowsill.

"I'll look out for him in future, but I don't know a better place for the Moonmirror." Eddie added defiantly. The gull looked at him rather sadly and took off. He'd done his best to warn him.

Chapter Sixteen
Preparations for an invasion

Sargasso returned to the creek to find he had two visitors bobbing up and down on the high tide by the old steps at the end of the quay. It was Solomon and Bathsheba and they were in a state of high agitation.

"Sargasso, Sargasso," they called when they saw him land. "Thank goodness you're back. We've seen them; we've seen them in the water!"

The seagull joined them to listen. "Tell me, tell me."

"We have been to the far edge of our seas on a journey to catch the shoals of herring and we have seen them! The sea monsters! They are huge and black, swimming through the water faster than any creature we have ever seen. The noise they make is terrifying and the sounds are strange and hurt our ears. We swam away as fast as we could. It was so frightening!" Solomon told him, very badly shaken and upset.

"Yes, there were two of them, great huge things, they just appeared out of nowhere, black and shining, and so fast! No creature we know can swim like that. We're all doomed; we could never get away if they chased us," Bathsheba added, terrified at the thought.

Sargasso listened, his fears growing. It was no good; he knew now he would have to act at once.

"I'm going to call upon the Spirit of the Sea for his advice; it has become too serious now, and we may all be in danger." He pulled the silvered shell from around his neck and tried to remember the words of the Spirit of the Sea when he had presented him with it. They echoed from the dark places in the hidden corners of his mind.

"He who calls into the mouth of this shell, I will hear him," were the instructions he recalled.

"I shall do it now. Trust me. I shall have news soon. Go back to your own gully and I will bring you the answer from the Spirit of the Sea." But Solomon and Bathsheba refused to go; they were too afraid to venture into the waters of the open sea again.

"Stay with me then on the tiny beach under the oak trees. It is calm and quiet here in the creek," relented Sargasso. He nuzzled the shell with his beak to turn it around until the open end of the spiral faced him. Into the dark space he called, "Hear me, Great one, Ruler of the Seas. We have intruders in our waters here on Devon's shores. Great black creatures have been seen by the seals, their speed is frightening, their noise deafening. Help us, Spirit of the Sea. Help your people. I await your reply."

The seals were comforted hearing Sargasso's words and managed to bump and shuffle up to the old shelter and joined the seagull in his hidden cave. They were scared and did not want to be alone on the beach. Sargasso fetched some dried mackerel from his store and fed the seals a few titbits. Gradually they began to settle down but their shock and fears did not subside.

"What will he do to help us?" asked the seals, "What can he do?" They seemed doubtful again but Sargasso was very firm.

"Now, now, we shall not speculate. Let us just rest and wait. Try to think of it no more." And he ruffled up the dry leaves and tried to make them a cosy bed to sleep in.

"You are so kind," sighed the weary seals and sure enough, the lapping waters and the cries of distant seabirds lulled them eventually to doze in the warm shelter while the wind blew past the entrance, unable to get in.

***

Far, far away, in the rolling, churning, grey seas of America's North Atlantic coast, the Spirit of the Sea heard the faint echoing call from the spiralled mother of pearl shell he wore deep in his flowing robes. He frowned as he heard the message from Sargasso roaring like the boom of the sea.

"Trouble, I should think. Great black mysterious strangers, eh? Sounds like a task for my two beached heroes, Hector and Hercules. They've had a long rest so now it's time to wake them up. I'll be interested to see how they deal with this." Deciding not to interfere unless it was really necessary, he began to put his plan into action and his subjects to the test.

Accompanied wherever he went by a huge number of a minute species of herring, he despatched one-quarter of them to the distant shore of Sugary Cove. By spreading his open hands over the water, they were empowered. Hundreds of tiny fish, their bodies filled with quivering excitement, changed direction at once and called to their master in their tiny high-pitched voices in unison.

"We shall go-go-go, Lord of the Ocean, and not return until your will is done!" With a sparkle of their silver scales they sped through the cold water, thrilled to be off, chasing each other in undulating waves. The Spirit of the Sea nodded and his four white horses stretched their necks to watch the silver cloud leave.

It was a long journey across miles of open sea, unbroken by land until the shores of the west of Ireland appeared on the horizon. They took no rest, charged with the power of the sea and skirted Ireland, sharply turned along the coast of Cornwall and headed for south Devon's rocky inlets and golden beaches. Slowing their incredible speed now and nearing the end of their journey, the Silver Tinkling Shoals spread out and glided around

Start Point, carefully avoiding the deadly nets of the trawler men. At a signal from the leaders, they timed their arrival at Sugary Cove to when the tide was at its highest, for otherwise the two whales could not escape from the beach.

Turned into black rocks, they lay on the shingle unknown to any man or creature. They had been de-petrified once before to help save Eddie and Patrick and then had been replaced there by the Spirit of the Sea to rest and await his next command.

On the highest swell of the incoming tide, the Silver Tinkling Shoals arrived, leaping and dancing, thrilled to have reached their designated destination. Their shrill and excited voices drifted over to the two black rocks, soon to be whales again.

"You are called great creatures of the deep, called to duty once again, hear us and wake! Wake! Wake! Come to us, us, us!" was their special alluring and irresistible plea. The two black rocks, whose eyes were fixed in a stare, felt life flood into their heavy bodies, their heads moved and they could see again. Their leaden hulks gave a shudder and the shingle holding them slid away with a sucking noise as the water filled the gap beneath them and floated them onto the next huge incoming wave. The Silver Tinkling Shoals encircled them and pushed them further out into deeper water where they filled their lungs with oxygen. With a flick of their great tails and blowing a spout of water, their return to the world of the Seafarers was complete.

"Come with us, us, us!" appealed the small fishes and the whales followed to receive their instructions sent from the Lord of the Deep.

"You are to seek out the mysterious intruders here in the waters of Devon. They are disturbing and terrifying our people. We shall wait for your answer here in these southern waters. Go now and find the truth, great Hector and Hercules." And the hundreds of tinkling fish surrounded them, encouraging them off on their travels.

"We are proud to be chosen, our work will begin. We shall go now," boomed the voices of the whales and together they slid beneath the waves and disappeared from view. The silver stream of swirling fish spread out over the water, their task partially completed, and they rested at last, satisfied.

Out in the cold, cruel waters of a December afternoon, a small naval patrol boat marked in its ship's log that an unusual sighting had been made – two hump-backed whales, slowly tracking across Start Bay; the positions of latitude and longitude were carefully recorded.

Chapter Seventeen
Action against Tolivera

Back at Watermill Cottage there was a great deal of excitement that afternoon. Patrick's arrival was imminent and the two waiting to collect him got more and more impatient as the afternoon slowly dragged by. It was interrupted however, by a phone call. Eddie and Ellie looked in horror at each other; maybe Patrick had succumbed to the flu virus? Maybe he wasn't coming after all? Two hearts sank as they listened to the shrill insistence of the telephone.

"Well, answer it, somebody!" called their mother from the garden where she was planting snowdrop bulbs. Eddie jumped up at once and ran to the kitchen, grabbed the receiver and breathlessly repeated the number. It was Peter.

"Hi, Dad!" said Eddie, surprised and pleased. "Where are you? Oh, really? Mum! Mum!" he shouted out through the back door. "It's Dad!"

Ellie, hurrying into the kitchen, wanted to speak to him too.

"Yes, OK we will. Tonight, you say? We're fine. Take care, Dad. Here's Ellie," and he passed the phone on to his sister, jumping up and down excitedly.

"Hello? When are you coming home? Oh right, OK. No, Dad, no more mole hills in the grass! Yes, I'm sure!" she sucked her teeth and rolled her eyes at Eddie, laughing. "Here's Mum, 'bye Dad." She relinquished the phone to her mother, now inside and ready to speak to him. She waved them away impatiently.

Reluctantly they trooped off into the sitting room.

"What did he say?" questioned Ellie at once.

"He's just off Norway, its freezing and he said to watch the TV tonight, there's going to be an announcement."

"Oh, that sounds a bit serious, doesn't it?"

Eddie shrugged his shoulders in his uncommunicative way, and closing down his emotions just said, "Don't know," and would say no more. Ellie knew better than to proceed any further, Eddie's fixed face said it all. They waited for their mother to appear and eventually she came and sat down beside them on the sofa.

"It's not bad news," she said to them. "I'll tell you now, because it's going to be on the news tonight anyway. The Russians are accusing us of sinking two of their ships. Two Russian submarines have vanished – of course they shouldn't have been in our waters in the first place, but it's still become what's called an international incident. The Navy has been searching for them but, as yet, no luck. They are nuclear powered, so of course pose a certain threat. That's all I can tell you, kids." She smiled a not very convincing, worried smile.

"Our Navy's better than theirs. We'll find them!" Eddie announced suddenly and defiantly.

"Anyway, don't worry, you've got exciting and nice things to think about – Patrick's arrival tonight and shopping for the cottage, Christmas presents, and soon we'll put the tree up," reassured Mary, not wanting to depress her children any more.

"Do you think Dad will be home by Christmas, Mum?" asked Ellie anxiously.

"I'm sure he will," answered Mary confidently, betraying nothing of her feelings. She went back into the kitchen and put the kettle on. She gazed out into the garden and saw the robin pecking at some stale cake on the windowsill. She stood quietly watching him, and something in her heart told her that everything would be all right. Somehow, watching the robin, a symbol of Christmas, meant it would be.

The robin ate his fill and flew away. He found the second ash tree on the right where Oliphant lived, and knocked gingerly on the door. Presently the oval, greeny-grey door opened and a sleepy, yawning, white owl appeared in polka dot pyjamas. He peered out groggily.

"Who is it?"

"It's me, Freddie," the robin replied. "Sorry to wake you up, Oliphant, but it's time for action!"

"Oh is it? You'd better come in, dear chap, right away," invited Oliphant, waking up at once. He sprang into life and produced some squashed flies he had cut into neat squares.

"Lovely!" they both agreed, pecking greedily.

"Now then, begin," the owl told the robin crisply and so Freddie started.

"Sargasso and I have been to the Citadel – he won't do anything, I'm sure. It's up to us now. Let's think hard," he urged.

In his heart Oliphant had known all along that Tolivera would never be persuaded, even by the mighty buzzard; he was too territorial and fiercely guarded what was his.

Why, when his own mother had been made homeless in the great storm of '87, when the trees were flattened like dominoes, Tolivera had shut his door and pretended to be out. His mother had been forced to move across the valley to Dipsey Wood to find an empty tree. Oh no, Tolivera had no heart or compassion for others; he admired power, power and wealth, and he kept the finest home in Gallants Bower. He had the best view, the most expensive hand crafted furniture, the finest of everything.

Oliphant sat quietly delving deep into the logical thought section in his superior bird brain. There must be a way. Freddie, trying to wait patiently, ate three juicy squashed-fly squares to pass the time. Oliphant looked across his simple country home and noticed a small bunch of camomile flowers tied with string, hanging from the hook by the door. It was to help him sleep and had been kindly issued to him by Dr Dew and Dr Yew Underconstumble. He suddenly jumped up and down, startling Freddie who almost choked on a bluebottle.

"I've got it! I think I've found the answer!" twittered Oliphant, "Oh yes! Have you been to the Cornucopia tree? You haven't?" as Freddie shook his head. "The walls are lined with bottle after bottle of elixirs. If we could get one and give Tolivera a few drops, why we could change him into somebody nice. They've got the Elixir of Happiness, the Elixir of Dreams, the Elixir of Peace…" He looked up at the robin, "What do you think of that?"

Freddie didn't quite know what to think. "It's an idea," he replied, trying to be positive. "But it won't last forever; it's only a temporary measure, isn't it?"

Oliphant agreed. "Oh yes, but it would give us some time wouldn't it? And save Eddie from any more trouble."

"A distinct possibility," nodded the robin; but how would he persuade the doctors to give him the elixir? A firm believer in the old saying that honesty is the best policy, Freddie seized his opportunity.

"Let's both go up to the doctors and get some right now. Shall we Oliphant? Right now?"

Oliphant, opening his large eyes even wider, looked for a moment at the robin and then agreed.

"Right-oo! I'll just put my coat on." Pulling a long fur coat (made from unfortunate voles eaten long ago) over his polka dot pyjamas, they were ready.

There was no time to lose once they had decided on their mission. Showing wisdom and patience, they had reached what could be a satisfactory answer without revenge or spitefulness. Tolivera might be taught a lesson in sociable behaviour, quietly and with restraint.

They flew to the huge old elderberry tree, pulled on the long strong bell-rope and listened for the jangling clanging of the conker shells. The bark-covered door opened, the spiral staircase was revealed and up they hopped.

Constantly on duty, committed to their patients, the two gentle bespectacled pigeons sat at their large desk.

"Welcome, my dears. Come along doooooo!" encouraged both the doctors talking together in perfect time.

Freddie falteringly explained, telling the truth, leaving no detail out, as was his way. The pigeons nodded constantly to each other and to the visitors; small coos now and again could be heard from them.

"And that you see is why we've come for your help," finished Freddie. "Maybe you have an elixir that could help us…, um…, help him, if you see what I mean."

Oliphant and the robin waited desperately for an answer. Verity, the white dove, wearing a gauzy apron, tiptoed in with a tray of nettle tea and laid it down gently in front of them. She poured graciously and tiptoed out again, closing the door quietly. The two doctors sat tapping their pencils and thinking together. The visitors drank their tea and waited.

At last Dr Dew and Dr Yew spoke,

"After careful consideration we have decided that a few drops of Humility would be an admirable addition to Mr Tolivera's diet. Some supplements are occasionally necessary to us all. In his case, I think you'll find this is a very satisfactory one, for all his friends."

The white dove was summoned.

"Now, Verity, please make up a small phial of the Elixir of Humility and enclose a glass dropper to administer it."

Off she went to fetch it.

The doctors went to look out of the ivy-clad windows and were silent for a few moments. Then they both turned around and spoke to the robin and the small white owl.

"You have acted wisely and responsibly in this matter which required a certain amount of careful handling. There is, we fear, a current of disquiet and dissatisfaction in the woodland at the moment. Petty fears, jealousies and an unwillingness to accept change and new things. Bright lights and new stars have been observed and this has caused unrest and fear. We must all learn to accept change, because some of it is better than we could ever have dreamed of, if we just stop being afraid of everything. Mr Tolivera will see this soon. Perhaps he can look forward to a happy and fulfilled retirement," they concluded, clasping their wingtips together.

"We hope so." As Verity entered the room again holding the precious package, the doctors escorted the two birds to the top of the stairs.

"Goodbye and good luck to you-oooooo," they called.

The white dove gave them their parcel, and cooed, "Toodle-ooo dear friends, toodle-ooo!" and carefully the birds negotiated the narrow staircase and out into the cold, grey and lifeless wood, now getting darker. They flew back to the second ash tree on the right above Watermill Cottage, and sat resting in two chairs to discuss their achievement. Oliphant was anxious not to break the bottle and placed it in a corner wrapped in moths' wings. He wondered how he was going to administer the drops, but the robin had worked it all out.

"Don't worry," he told his friend confidently, "I'm going to pour it all into the Mists of Time down in the cellar. Then everybody who drinks it will get a few drops! It won't do anyone any harm will it? And Tolivera sips a glass or two every day, I'd swear to it."

"What a marvellous idea!" Oliphant thumped the solid arm of his country carver chair. "Brilliant, Freddie, brilliant! Why didn't I think of that? Let's celebrate" and he rummaged in his cupboard for a bottle of dew-drop wine. They toasted each other and enjoyed a relaxing acorn cup of the crystal clear wine.

"I feel so much better now," admitted Freddie.

"So do I, my dear friend," agreed Oliphant, and they promptly fell fast asleep in the dimpsey light of the winters' afternoon, warmed by the glow of their friendship and the wine. The elixir which held the key to their success glowed quietly in the dark.

Chapter Eighteen
International affairs

The 6 o'clock news time drew close and the small family gathered around the table in the kitchen. Supper was prepared, so there would be no unnecessary to-ing and fro-ing in front of the television. Ellie and Eddie had been in their rooms finishing homework so that nothing could stand in the way of Patrick's return. The familiar tune that heralded the news began and Mary ladled beef casserole and vegetables exactly on time. But they hesitated to eat, excitement and dread in equal measures stifling their appetites.

The announcer began by explaining the recall of naval personnel to ships from the naval bases of Plymouth and Portsmouth, and mentioned six ships, HMS *Kirkliston*, Peter's ship, being one of them.

"Dad's ship!" Ellie and Eddie whispered together proudly. Mary smiled and nodded, a forkful of carrots not quite reaching its destination. The Russian Minister of Defence was then shown with an angry voice and face to match. The translation was that two new nuclear powered submarines from the naval base at Riga had disappeared, each with 130 men on board. The *Tengiz* and the *Onega* had entered the North Sea from the Baltic on sea trials and all contact had been lost. He accused the British Navy of destroying them, as they had mistakenly entered their international waters, perhaps due to a fault on board with the reactor. This was then strenuously denied by the Prime Minister, Sir Dougal Walters, who had sent the Navy out to try to help locate the missing submarines.

"Oh dear," said Mary, "he seems very convinced they've been destroyed. I don't know how he can be so sure."

The news soon changed to economic affairs, which interested no one. They ate supper slowly, tasting nothing, and sat thinking about HMS *Kirkliston* out at sea, just off the coast of Norway.

"I bet Dad's ship finds them first! I hope so," decided Eddie. "It's quite exciting really – hunting for submarines don't you think, Mum? I wish I was there."

Ellie and Mary exchanged glances and rolled their eyes. Typical. Boys! Their spirits were fairly high however, due to the fact that Peter had phoned and they knew he was safe and well. There was Patrick's arrival to cheer them up and very soon they would be leaving with George to collect him. The children finished supper, helped their mother clear up and went upstairs yet again to mess about on their own. Eddie carefully packed the Crystal Signaller box away, tidied up his paperwork into a folder for school and sat down in the green rocking chair that had been in the corner of his bedroom for so long. As he rocked gently backward and forward it reminded him of Captain John Avery who had returned from the past to share a secret life with him.

It was pitch dark outside now, with the moon waning in size and bright clusters of stars glinting and fading in the velvety sky.

The mysterious celestial body from the dark side of the moon was almost ready to enter the Earth's atmosphere, travelling at great speed, having accurately pinpointed Warfleet and the cottage with its piercing brightly lit blue eyes the night before. It was the vibrating light waves at full intensity from this remarkable little creature that had been responsible for shattering the pane of glass. This Moonglimmer was on its way to Earth.

***

Beneath the turbulent ocean, Hector and Hercules silently roamed, searching and listening, alert to every strange sound, asking fellow creatures if they had seen the black intruders who had been terrifying the Seafarers. Many refused to answer, too scared to get involved, and others nodded, admitting to having heard the sinister wails. A large conger eel, so vicious himself and who was not easily frightened, directed them towards deeper water, just over the continental shelf. Here the water depth plunged from 100 fathoms to over 1000, and gradually increased, deeper and deeper towards the Bay of Biscay. This would make sense, reasoned the whales, if these strange sea monsters had strayed into the shallow coastal waters and become lost; then, realising their mistake, had tried to reposition themselves. On and on they swam, huge and black, streaking and sinewing gracefully through the deep sea, resurfacing to blow spouts of water and fill their lungs with precious air every three-quarters of an hour or so.

The two Russian submarines, whose navigating officers had no idea where they were, were circling around while trying to make contact with their home base in Russia. Their underwater communications systems kept them in constant touch with each other and gave the crew reassurance that eventually they would reach home. Every now and again they launched a buoy to the surface to send signals to Riga, but no contact had yet been made.

Faintly in the distance the whales heard a droning noise and called to each other in excitement. Louder and nearer it came, until into their line of sight loomed the black cigar-shaped hulls of the Russian submarines advancing at great speed, huge and menacing. At once the sonar in the submarines picked up a signal; it was the same one which they had tried to fix on earlier and failed.

Terrified by the strange whirring noise and the unknown and unrecognisable shape of these monsters, the whales dived and backtracked in a northerly direction towards the south coast of Britain. They increased their speed, not realising that two young Russian communicators were following them on their green sonar screens – two dots clearly visible.

"Is this our enemy? Are these mini-subs searching for us?" they asked their captain as the senior officers had gathered in the communications room.

"It's possible. We may now be in foreign waters. Our compass and direction-finding equipment have failed. Order the men to full alert and standby," ordered Captain Grigor Ranoffski, the senior officer. "Keep tracking them. They may lead us into safety, or… it may be a trap, I don't know which yet."

So the chase began, the two beautiful creatures of the deep, each 45 feet long and weighing 35 tons swam swiftly; they could make ten miles distance before having to resurface for air. At full speed, their compressed air would only last thirty minutes. Behind them chugged the sister submarines, *Tengiz* and *Onega*, also progressing north, keeping a reasonable distance between them, unaware of what they were following.

Sargasso the seagull sat on top of the tower of St Petrox church anxiously looking out to the endless grey sea under a cloudy sky. He had heard nothing from the Spirit of the Sea in answer to his urgent plea for help. He had expected some sort of reply or sign of his intentions. Darkness fell and still nothing.

Down below him, by the old church door, car headlights appeared and soon a row of lamps were lit, guiding the way to the entrance. Something was happening. The candles inside the beautiful church were also lit and the colours of the stained glass shone out, illuminating the faces and clothes of the figures glowing in the soft bright light. Suddenly a loud *Dong!* broke through the air and the seagull jumped violently. The bells! One after the other the dinging and donging pealed successive notes and rung out loud and clear, echoing across the woods and valleys.

It was the Advent carol service. Many were making their way from the town, walking briskly, hatted and gloved against the cold air. This, for some of Dartmouth's faithful parishioners, was the exciting beginning of the Christmas celebrations.

At Watermill Cottage, Mary put the rubbish out into the dustbin by the gate and paused, looking up into the night sky. She had heard something. It was niggling at her brain. There was no wind and the air was still and cold. She heard it again; a faint melody carried through the night's darkness to her. The bells! It was the bells of St Petrox ringing out!

"Oh no!" she breathed out anxiously. "The Advent carols, I've completely forgotten!"

She dashed inside, pulled off her apron and rushed upstairs. Comb, lipstick, shoes, downstairs again, purse, gloves, fur hat, and coat, keys and torch.

"Got to go, kids! Forgotten the carol service! Lock up, Eddie, before you go out, won't you? Sorry I've got to rush. See you later!" and the two bewildered children stood in the hallway as she frantically kissed them goodbye and left. Her shoes tap, tap, tapped on the driveway, then the road, and were gone.

"Well," said Ellie, "that was a rush, but at least we didn't have to go!" She laughed and went back to put the television on and wait for George.

***

Up in the bell tower of St Petrox church the bells had been in full voice, the bell-ringers below enjoying their rhythmical exercise, concentrating carefully. The inhabitants of the ancient tower stirred. Hibernating in the peaceful darkness, hanging upside down, were the family of bats – Belvedere, Boadicea his wife and their two small offspring, Theo and Cleo. They yawned and stretched, the thundering clangs of the bells disturbing them. Belvedere, now awake and alert, left his family to search for food. He flew out of the tower through the side vents and bumped straight into Sargasso who was sitting in the darkness.

They greeted each other and Sargasso explained his vigil: "I'm waiting for an answer, a signal or a sign from the sea," and he continued relating the story of the sea monsters, the strange noises and the fear that had spread far into the ocean.

Belvedere listened. "We'll probably stay awake for a week or so now," he told the seagull, and he grinned his devilish toothy smile. Off he went to search the night air for insects, scarce at this time of the year, for his hungry mate and children. As he returned, the glorious strains of the many voices could be heard, singing the timeless words of old carols, echoing around the isolated fortification perched on the precipice looking out to sea. He hoped his wife and children were enjoying the unexpected musical evening. *It's much more exciting here than it was at Tintern Abbey*, he decided with a grin, as he squeezed through the side vent.

Mary, down in the congregation, was engrossed in the comforting atmosphere created by the candle glow, the music and the accomplished singing of several small choirboys. She smiled at some of her acquaintances, who smiled back. She felt

115

cheered and encouraged and was glad she had made the effort. The church brasses twinkled and shone and lavender polish scented the air. It was all very reassuring and she felt God's presence fleetingly, like a hand resting on her shoulder. She must be brave for the children... and Peter. Where was he tonight? She returned to the words of the carol and tried to concentrate.

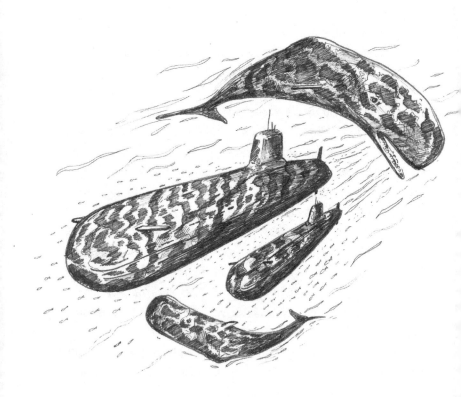

Chapter Nineteen
Two arrivals at Warfleet

While Mary was singing, George's car rolled into the driveway of the cottage and at once two eager young people launched themselves down the steps and into the car.

"Hi, George," they happily greeted him as they took their seats and fastened their seat belts.

"Righty ho, we're off!" George backed out onto the main road and shot off up Tumbling Hill.

"Did you see the news?" Eddie asked, pride in his voice.

"I did indeed lad, bit of a to-do about nothing I reckon. Those Ruskies couldn't find their way out of a paper bag. Probably turned right instead of left if you ask me," and he chuckled. George felt the wheels of the car spin a little and the engine revved.

"Whoa! Ice on the road up here." He carefully dropped his speed and paid a lot more attention to his driving. They sped on, through fairy tale villages and silhouetted woods as the sky cleared and became full of stars. Eddie stared intently up. No blue flashing lights winked back at him. The moon was getting smaller now, waning in size. He sank back thankfully in his seat.

They turned carefully into the station yard, pulling to a halt where they had a good view of the track. There was no point getting out and freezing on the platform, so they sat in the warm car, heater running, and stared and stared into the darkness, excited and impatient. The children fell silent and George turned the radio on. It was the 10 o'clock news.

"No sign of the two Russian submarines has been found yet. They have been missing now for two weeks and their disappearance has sparked an international crisis. Six ships from the Navy's southern task force have been deployed in the hunt for the *Tengiz* and the *Onega*."

Ellie and Eddie looked at each other and George said,

"They'll soon find 'em, don't you worry. They've just been built and are on sea trials. I expect they've joined a red wire to a blue one and the lights have gone out!" and everybody laughed. Ellie pointed out of the window,

"Look! Look! It's coming!" Sure enough, the lights of an oncoming train could be seen approaching and then the hoot of a whistle was heard.

"Oh good, it's on time," said George, who had been worrying about icy tracks and frozen points and waiting around for hours.

They all got out of the car into the frosty air, blowing steaming breath before them. As they entered the white wicket gate the guard waved them through to the platform. Stamping and blowing on their fingers they watched the train slide in beside them, filling the darkness with bright lights, noise, chattering, and doors being opened and slammed closed. Patrick was not last this time and he leapt out of a carriage near to them, pulling on a red knitted ski hat against the cold night air, backpack slung over his shoulder. Three excited faces fastened onto his and his blue eyes smiled back. They became a little huddle hugging each other and arm in arm they made the short journey to the car. Ellie's eyes were alight and happy. Patrick was back! She had to admit she was very pleased to see him. She sat in the front this time and the two boys shared the back seat, after Patrick had thrown his luggage into the boot. Then they were off, leaving the crowded station behind and speeding through the countryside towards Dartmouth.

"Do you feel alright?" questioned Ellie anxiously, turning her head around.

"Amazingly I do, Ellie!" Patrick replied. "I keep waiting to feel ill – sore throat and headache, but no, it hasn't hit me yet."

"Oh, you're too healthy for that," Eddie told him. "Look at all the sea air you've had. That's what keeps you healthy."

"You're right, lad," agreed George. "Cold water, fresh air and no heating! Can't beat it."

"There's hardly anyone left at school," Patrick told them. "I was lucky to get away today. Matron's disinfected us all and practically everything we own."

"That's what the funny smell is then," said Eddie, sniffing. Patrick punched him and they all laughed. It was great to be back together again. At last they reached Dartmouth and dropped Eddie and Ellie off.

"I'll see you tomorrow," Patrick promised and because it was so late they all accepted that a proper reunion would have to be delayed until tomorrow and they ran up the steps to their front door shouting goodbye. The car disappeared into the darkness. Mary opened the door, pleased to see them back.

"Well?"

"He's grand! Pleased to be out of that place, I'm sure!" Eddie told her, throwing off his padded jacket. "Anything to eat, Mum? I'm starving!" Ellie followed him into the kitchen, her eyes shining and cheeks pink with the cold air.

"What shall we have?"

Eddie fell back onto his old favourite – toasted cheese and marmite sandwiches, just a little burnt.

"Can we get you anything?" Ellie called to her mother.

"A cup of coffee would be nice," came the reply. Mary sat stitching a few rows of her tapestry kneeler. Everyone else at the church had finished theirs and she was trying hard to find the time. The youngsters brought in the coffee and they settled down to munch their way through the toasted sandwiches.

"I'm sure I fed you this evening, didn't I?" Mary questioned.

"Yes, but we're starving again. Patrick's coming round after school tomorrow." Eddie told her with his mouth full.

"Eddie dear, I didn't hear a word you said," Mary said crossly. Ellie sniggered.

"I hope you've cleared up the kitchen, young lady." Ellie's face fell.

"Why should I have to do it?"

"Because I know very well that Eddie made the sandwiches. Now, did you?"

"No," was the sullen reply.

"Well, you can go straight out there and tidy up the minute you've finished those sandwiches, my girl." It was Eddie's turn to snigger.

"Stop it, Eddie!" Mary sharply told him. It was a bit of a fraught evening but then it had been a difficult day.

"Sorry, Mum." Eddie looked up at Mary and then at Ellie, realising suddenly that his mother was probably upset and not herself.

"Come on, Ellie, let's go and clear up." And taking the lead, he collected the dirty plates and his mother's cup and went off to the kitchen. Ellie followed in surprise.

"What's got into you?"

"I'm trying to think of Mum for a minute, she must be worried about Dad. I don't want to annoy her tonight."

Ellie nodded, feeling rather guilty and soon the kitchen was tidy and clean. "All done," she called sweetly to Mary. "I think I'm going to bed now." And she went to hug her mother and kiss her goodnight. "Don't worry, Dad will be OK."

Eddie followed. He too kissed and hugged her. "Night, Mum," and off he went.

Mary continued to sew mechanically, strangely unmoved by her children's sudden kindness. It was all bottled up, too far away to reach.

***

At the top of Gallants Bower, the creature from outer space had got into difficulties as soon as he entered the gravitational pull of the Earth. He found he could hardly fly, he felt so heavy, and he made a very clumsy and precarious landing into the trees and then fell into a deep valley of dead beech leaves. He tried to rise but his star-shaped body felt like lead and he overbalanced in the brown bracken. Gradually he moved awkwardly towards the hillside leading down to Watermill Cottage and fell, rolling over in the twisted tree roots, bracken and dead leaves, hurtling down the steep slope. He was exhausted. He curled up to sleep for a while, only comforted by the knowledge that he had almost arrived at his destination.

He was a two-eyed, star-shaped shadow from the dark side of the moon, where powerful eyes, like light-emitting diodes, were essential. No one on Earth has ever seen what is there on the dark side. The Moonglimmer had ventured around one night and he had been captivated by the bright lights from Earth – Eddie's Moonmirror's reflected light being one of the many visible to him. So he had left his grey world, determined to be the first of his kind to travel into the light. His name was Umbraluna.

As dawn approached, the temperature lifted slightly to just above freezing and a westerly wind blew a deep depression across the South West of England. The moisture held in the clouds rapidly cooled and as it gently descended to the ground was turned into miraculous flakes of snow, large and fluffy. Silence followed as the grey clouds settled and the whole of the western world was transformed.

Ugly places became beautiful and trees wore a garnish of soft white. Hollows and crevices filled with snow and the landscape became smoothed out like icing spread thickly with a knife. The Moonglimmer slept on as the comfortable hollow he had rested in became obliterated with the falling flakes. The white world was reflected in the strengthening daylight and an unusual brightness filtered through the bedroom curtains of Watermill Cottage.

It had been at least six years since snow had fallen in Dartmouth. Because of its location at sea level, in a deep valley, the only way out of town was up two very steep hills. Once these became icy and treacherous all traffic was halted and few people could enter or leave the town. Only the river crossing was left. Dartmouth was in fact cut off.

So it was that the inhabitants awoke that morning to find a very changed world.

Eddie and Ellie were overjoyed as the realisation dawned on them that school was out of the question that day.

"Fantastic! Isn't it brilliant? Have we still got a sledge in the garage?" Eddie bombarded his mother and Ellie sat up in the balcony room, gazing, hands on chin, at the breathtaking beauty of the snowy scenery.

"There's more snow on the way, I'm sure. Just look at that sky," their mother told them.

***

Umbraluna stirred in his snowy hollow, his senses alert now to strange lights, new smells, and a sort of whistling noise. He opened his bright circular eyes and was dazzled by what he saw. Gradually his eyes came into focus and he blinked to turn the strength of their beam down; he didn't need his strong light here. Used to the cold, he was quite comfortable but he couldn't believe the amount of new things filling the landscape, all so bright with white soft stuff lying all around him.

The lunar landscape he had left was grey, all grey, rocks and hills and valleys, barren and empty. His people lived under the ground in a city of tunnels opening into squares. Their eyes were blue, strong intense beams so that they could see in the grey dullness. They had no bodies, just a clear glimmering outline and could change into any shape... just like a shadow. Umbraluna had propelled himself from one of the charging stations dotted all around his city, determined to follow the light he had seen. When Eddie had switched on the Crystal Signaller on, the rainbow lights had enticed him utterly. He was going to find where they were coming from, wherever it took him, danger or not.

The soft whistling noises he had heard were coming from some funny little creatures darting about. Colours were unknown to him and he watched fascinated as they bobbed and flitted all around him. A patch of sky appeared just as two heavy grey clouds parted and he gasped at the pale blue colour. There were upright imposing figures covered in the white soft stuff standing very still. They didn't seem to move or talk so even though he was surrounded by them, he decided there was nothing to fear.

He pinpointed Eddie's window with his inbuilt navigation system stored just behind his eyes, and he stared through the trees. That was the centre of the light source, he was quite sure.

He watched and waited, content to lie and observe the new world he had arrived in.

Chapter Twenty
Fun in the snow

As Mary had predicted, the wispy clouds vanished and heavy-duty black ones superseded them as an eerie darkened sky presented itself. Slowly, one by one, tiny crystal flakes began their descent, twirling and dancing their way to earth. Soon clusters of them raced from the sky and the snow fell in earnest, heavy and relentless, stinging eyes, creeping down collars, and blotting out the contours of the ground. Ellie and Eddie, on Mary's instructions, lit the fire in the sitting room. From a store outside the back door Eddie hurriedly filled the log basket and soon a magnificent blaze warmed the room and cheered it up. The whiteness from outside cast a strange new light. The two of them stood by the window watching the road and the top of the creek to see if Patrick was coming yet.

Mary decided it was definitely an indoor day.

"Put the kettle on Eddie, Patrick's here!" Sure enough a white hooded figure thumped his feet outside and knocked on the door. They rushed to open it as Patrick stood there, snowflakes melting on his face. Eddie hung up the coat on a coat hanger by the Rayburn to dry and propped the boots upside down beside it.

"Come on, the fire's lit," and they went at once to sit and warm up. Mary brought coffee in and sat down as Patrick explained the flu epidemic, the new cottage and Christmas arrangements. With a smile he pulled a key from his pocket.

"Here it is!" he said proudly, "the key to freedom!" and Eddie laughed loudly.

"Mother's organised some people from the town to come and deliver carpets, curtains and some furniture. She's bringing the bed linen, clothes and towels and a television man is coming too," he added.

"You're going to be busy," said Mary, rather amused, and took the tray and returned to the kitchen.

"We're off upstairs for a minute, just to look at the Signaller." Eddie and Patrick disappeared quickly. Ellie went to the kitchen and stared out of the window at the unusual scene before her.

"Look, Mum," and they both looked at the tiny arrow-like marks in the snow. The birds' footprints were quickly covered up with new fresh flakes.

"Can I give Freddie some currants?" begged Ellie, "Just as a treat," and she opened the window and poured some out as the icy air blew in. Two robins hopped onto the window sill and greedily pecked them up.

"He's brought a friend today," laughed Ellie, watching them fascinated.

Upstairs, Eddie lost no time in telling Patrick his exciting news of the distant blue flashing light, the broken window, and his certainty that it did answer to his own lights.

"Is the Moonmirror still on the tree?" Patrick asked.

"Oh yes, it works well up there, but the moon's waxing now and won't charge it. Next full moon is the 27th December but it will be almost full for a few days before and after."

"We can use the Crystal Signaller up there too but I won't be able to see this blue flash of yours yet, will I?" Patrick was disappointed.

"No, I don't think so" Eddie agreed, shaking his head. As they looked out of the window over the wooded hills, they noticed the snow gradually lessening and the sky just beginning to lighten. One small brief ray of sunshine found a chink in the clouds.

"Great, it's stopping now, we can go out. I must look for a sledge in the garage. Coming?" and they bounded down the stairs to get ready. The three kitted themselves up for the cold and went outside. The sun was struggling through the gaps and the world looked clean and new. Their footsteps creaked in the dry powdery snow and steamy breath billowed out from their mouths.

Eddie opened the garage door and they went inside. High up on the crossbeams Peter had lashed the sledge – the only one, but it took two people.

"You have a couple of turns, Ellie, and then Patrick and I will go together. OK?" The boys looked at her to see her reaction.

"Alright, I'll have a go."

The creek lane spread out before them, long and white and untouched. No footprints yet had marred its perfect surface. The sledge was placed perfectly for the first run.

"It shouldn't go too fast on this snow, not until it gets packed down a bit." Patrick knew a thing or two about snow, living in Scotland.

"Well, that's comforting!" replied Ellie, feeling just a little scared now, looking down the steep hill in front of her. She pulled her hat down over her ears.

"Got your gloves on? You'll need them to protect your hands. Can you touch the ground with your feet? You might have to use them to steer," Eddie told her and with that Mary clumped round the corner in her wellingtons, red hat and scarf, and thick coat.

"All ready?" she asked her brave daughter, who wasn't feeling so brave.

"She'll be OK, it'll be a good run, you'll see!" reassured Patrick. "I'll go half way down to meet you. You keep her straight, Eddie."

"Right, ready. One, two, three, GO!" and he pushed quite hard to get it going. Ellie clung on, teeth gritted, trying not to laugh, as she picked up speed, and gently at first, slid down the hill, Eddie running beside her shouting encouragement. At the first bend Patrick caught her,

"OK?"

"Yeah fine, give me another push," and steering her away from the wall, the two boys gave her an almighty push and off she went, faster this time. Mary lost sight of her and laughing, hurried down the slippery path to find her.

At the bottom, the snow sledge which had been travelling quite fast, hit a brick and tumbled Ellie out, where she lay in a heap of snow. Eddie and Patrick tried to pull her up but didn't make a very good job of it, as they were laughing too much. Mary found them all thrilled with its success, and planning the next run with no stops.

"You'll have to help pull it up, Ellie." Patrick told her, "It's a long way back."

"Shall I wait here to catch you?" Mary asked, laughing. "That is if I can!"

"Yes please," nodded Ellie. "We won't be long," and off they went, plodding up the white and slippery hill. Ellie climbed on again, more confident this time, and the boys sent her off with a tremendous shove and away she went careering downwards, shrieking and swaying from side to side. The boys ran after her and could see Mary poised at the bottom, but Ellie was going too fast and her mother couldn't catch her, so unfortunately poor Ellie ran off the end of the slipway and into the water, with an enormous scream and a huge splash! The two boys were doubled up with hoots of laughter. Floundering in the water she screamed at them,

"Stop laughing! It isn't funny!" as she struggled to pull the sledge out behind her, and fell over again.

"Shut up!" She burst into tears.

"Sorry, Ellie, it's just so funny!" Both boys made a face at each other and went to help her, trying to stop laughing. Ellie abandoned the sledge and stalked off up the hill.

"You can keep your stupid sledge! I've had enough!"

Patrick and Eddie smothered their giggles and pulled the sledge up the hill after her.

Back home, Ellie stripped off in the kitchen and went upstairs wrapped in a blanket. She wanted a hot bath. She felt really stupid as she stood waiting for the water to be deep enough. Why had it all gone wrong? She had been enjoying herself so much.

What I should have done was fall off. Or I should have put my feet down to try and brake with them. How silly I am. And she plunged into the hot scented bubbles and descended beneath the water, head, hair, and all. Up she came. *That's better*, washing the creek water out of her hair. Picturing herself, Ellie began to giggle and then to roar with laughter at the thought of her hurtling towards the creek.

"How funny!" she chuckled.

"Are you alright Ellie?" she heard her mother call upstairs. "You've not hurt yourself?"

"No, Mum, I'm fine, just thinking what a silly ass I am!"

The back door opened and Patrick and Eddie stood sheepishly on the doorstep.

"Well come in, it's freezing with the door open," scolded Mary.

"We've only come to make sure Ellie is alright, and then we're going down together."

The bathroom window was just above the back door. "I'm fine now," Ellie shouted down to him. "I'm coming out again after lunch."

"Great! That's the spirit, Ellie!" Patrick shouted back. "We'll only be an hour or so."

In fact Ellie could then see them from her bedroom window and she watched her brother and Patrick for a while. She got bored after ten minutes and went to read by the fire, enjoying the quietness to concentrate.

As Eddie and Patrick reached the bottom of the hill for probably the tenth time, Sargasso, tiring of his endless vigil watching the ocean for a sign, came back to the creek side. He was amused by the sight of Eddie and Patrick careering down on their sliding machine, and the laughter they burst into as they fell was infectious. He waddled over for a better look. Eddie, spotting him, went at once to stroke and pet him, talking gently to him.

"How are you, Sargasso? I've not seen you for a while. Dad's gone away to sea, gone to look for some submarines lost by the Russians. They're prowling under the sea somewhere and Dad's squadron is helping to find them. Everyone thinks there will be a war. The Russians think we've blown them up, but I know we haven't... What's the matter, Sargasso?" The gull was ready to speak as Eddie stroked him kindly.

"Come on, Eddie! One more run before lunch! We've got time!" shouted Patrick impatiently, beckoning to him.

"OK!" Eddie shouted back. "Just coming!" and he turned to the seagull, "Got to go now, old fellow," and off he ran back to the toboggan.

Sargasso was disappointed. He had nearly plucked up the courage to ask Eddie several things. Maybe he would know what the frightening sea monsters were. Dejectedly he flew back to the church tower determined to wait for news from the Spirit of the Sea.

***

Much later, returning home wet and cold, the boys took a break.

"Gosh it's cold," complained Eddie, "my hands are dead. Do you think I'll get frostbite?"

"Oh yes," grinned Patrick. "Coming out again, Ellie?" and he raised his eyebrows at her.

"Yes! I think I will," she said, "but… only if you don't laugh."

"Would we?" asked Eddie innocently, blue eyes wide open.

"Maybe we should walk along towards Sugary Cove. There are some gentler hills round that way."

"That's a very good idea," encouraged Mary, glimpsing peace at last. "Yes, you go on off now," and they disappeared at great speed.

Mary was glad to be on her own. She had a few phone calls to make, Christmas cards to write, trying to keep on top of it all. She had to arrange who was decorating the tree, doing the flowers, putting up the Nativity scene at St Petrox, all to be completed by Christmas Eve. This year of course, with the added worry of Peter away for an unknown time, her mind was not quite so focused.

Sugary Cove proved to be just the perfect gradient for tobogganing, not too steep and quite long. Ellie managed to do a couple of very good runs and Eddie and Patrick hurtled down together, fearless and exhilarated. Eventually, even they had had enough and weariness came over them all.

"Shall we go home?" Ellie asked Eddie, who scarcely had the energy to pull the sledge.

"I think so," he agreed, surprisingly giving in. The sun gradually lost its warmth and the crunch of ice could be heard under the snow.

"It's going to freeze again," Eddie remarked as he put the sledge in the garage and happily went inside, unaware of the visitor sleeping in the woods who had travelled over 240,000 to meet him.

Chapter Twenty-one
Searching for Sargasso

The buzzard, snug inside the Citadel during the snowstorm, had done a lot of thinking. He had decided to bargain with Tolivera. He would offer him the exclusive rights to the old chestnut tree, which he knew he keenly desired, in exchange for an assurance that he would no longer persecute the boy, or have any more complaints about the box nailed to his precious ash tree.

He went to his smooth circular bookshelves containing the Chronicles of the Woodland Kingdom and looked for the right volume to help him uncover the mystery of the bright blue flashing light seen in the night sky which had so disturbed his subjects. Which one was it? He finally selected a volume bound in peeling leather, called *Woodland Wisdom and Folklore*, and opening the metal clasp which held it together, blew the dust from beneath the yellowing fragile pages and consulted the index under U.

Unknown objects appearing from the sky

Unusual lights appearing in the North, South, East or West

Unexpected coloured light appearing in the night sky

That seemed to cover it, and turning the heavy pages he read aloud, "Astral bodies may burn out, alter orbit, or hurtle towards Earth, changing colour as they lose their heat and chemical composition. Sun showers may occur and cause sparks or clusters of bright lights to be seen. New stars may be created, as pieces break off larger astral bodies, due to explosions in space, and will appear as intense and brightly lit objects. Electric storms may interrupt light travel and cause intense flashing lights."

"Aha!" he said to himself, pleased with what he had read, "That seems to explain it all perfectly." And he closed the book with an altogether satisfied clunk. He carefully did up the metal clasp and replaced the book on the shelf. He called his three sons to him and they sat intently listening as he explained the mystery of the flashing lights to them.

"We must make our people understand that their fears are unfounded, the lights will disappear and calm will be restored. There is no need for unrest and panic. We shall post a notice up and *you* will compose it."

The three young princes looked at each other uncomfortably.

"Yes, with my help you shall do it," smiled the great buzzard, and he sent them away.

As soon as the snow stopped the buzzard ventured out and flew to the Great Ash Tree which was cloaked in snow. He tapped on the door and waited. Eventually the door slowly creaked open and the buzzard stepped inside. There, reclining on a grey fur-covered couch, was Tolivera, smoking a walnut pipe and sipping from a large frosted glass. He was wrapped up in a crimson dressing gown with white fur-tailed trimmings and a hat to match. He looked magnificent.

"Ah, my lord," he drawled. "What brings you out in this inclement weather? Do have a seat and I'll get you a glass," and he waved imperiously at his master to be seated. The buzzard fumed, but obeyed.

"Just want a word, Tolly, that's all, while it's on my mind, don't you know. Please don't get up on my account." So the aggravating and insulting owl didn't.

They were unaware that at that precise moment, down in the underground workings of the Mists of Time, deep below the same ash tree, things were happening. Freddie and Oliphant had made a decision to add the Elixir of Humility that very afternoon, as few would venture up the hill that day in the cold. Freddie, fortified with currants from the windowsill, flew to rouse Oliphant from his usual daytime sleep. He was full of enthusiasm, determined to make Tolivera pay for his unkindness towards Eddie and Ellie.

"Come on, Olly, stir yourself." he yelled through the door.

"Alright, alright, a chap can't get any peace nowadays," grumbled Oliphant, opening his door.

"Ready?"

"I suppose so. Let's do it, one, two, three, off we go-o-o-o-o-o-o-o!" and the white owl and the robin soared off, straight up to the top of the wood over the white, strangely quiet, landscape. Reaching the ash tree they stopped, carefully looking around to be sure they couldn't be seen. Pecking about, they found the venting pipe concealed in the snow which led down to the workings underground.

"Got the elixir?" checked the owl.

"Yep," nodded the robin.

"OK, here we go-o-o-o-o!" and they both squeezed into the cold pipe and slid down, disappearing at once with a whoosh! Both the birds splashed into a vat at the bottom, and struggling and coughing emerged with very wet feathers, over the side. Shaking themselves dry, they looked around the system of pipes leading into and around the tree roots. Taps, gauges, measures and wheels confused them utterly. A separate pipe led up from the vat they had fallen into, through the roof and disappeared.

"That's Tolivera's personal supply I bet," said the robin firmly. Many tree roots stood with polished taps sunk into them. A large silver dish was propped up on an elaborate table.

"Shall I?" asked the robin, poised with the bottle uncorked.

"Alright, I suppose you'd better," nodded the owl, still uncertain, as brave Freddie tipped the red liquid in. There was a gurgle and a popping noise. Bubbles appeared, and then settled down, the liquid silently spreading smooth and flat again.

"That's it, done," announced the robin confidently. "That's him sorted out for a while."

"I hope you're right," said Oliphant, still a little anxious. "And now, how do we get out?" looking all around. With that, there was a whirr and a clunk and the liquid, amber and clear, was sucked up a pipe from the vat and disappeared.

"He's drawn some off upstairs!" The robin was jubilant, "He'll be drinking it any minute! Yippee!" and he jumped up and down in excitement. "We've done it!"

"Let's get out of here," beckoned the owl with his head, and perched on the edge of the black vat, peering up the venting pipe. There was only the smallest gap.

"Lucky he left the lid off," said Freddie, noticing it lying on the floor. "We'd never have got out." They squeezed into the pipe and hugging their wet wings close to them, headed upwards, bursting into the snowy cold darkening daylight, gasping for air.

"Well done Oliphant, well done!" spluttered the robin, getting to his tiny feet. "I must go and find Sargasso. He's a bit worried at the moment. Got things on his mind."

Oliphant was happy to go back to bed. He flew to the foot of the hill, noticing a strange pale light glowing from under the snow, very gently flickering like the softest candlelight. He looked again with his wings outspread and saw two circles under the snow covering. Being a timid sort of bird and anxious to get home, he ignored it and hurried thankfully indoors.

Freddie searched for Sargasso fruitlessly. He just couldn't find him. The lime kiln was empty, the path snow-covered, criss-crossed with many footprints of birds and animals. He flew to the church rooftop, but the flag pole was empty too.

That's strange, mused the robin, wondering where Sargasso could be. He decided to try the cottage, but the weathervane, the rooftops and the chimney were deserted too. He was beginning to get worried.

He's gone to look for a sign. He's not heard from the Spirit of the Sea and he's taken himself off out to sea to look. I bet that's where he is. Oh dear, I wish he hadn't gone without telling me. The weather is sure to get worse. Freddie felt very anxious now. What could he do?

He was too small to track the ocean in flight, he knew it would be certain death for him, but he could fly round the coast to the Trip Trap bridge and tell Solomon and Bathsheba. Freddie was tired; it had been a long and exciting day, but it had to be done. He told himself firmly that he had to do it for Sargasso's sake, and he set off bravely.

Half an hour later he arrived at the rocky inlet and searched for the seals. They were sheltering on the narrow shingle beach, and were very surprised to hear the robin calling their names.

"Have you seen Sargasso?" he chirruped, and he told them the story.

"We know he has been waiting for an answer. The Spirit of the Sea is on the other side of the world, but he's sent Hector and Hercules off to find the sea monsters; the Silver Tinkling Shoals are waiting for their return. We've seen them," Bathsheba told him.

"They are many miles off the coast, a long way for the seagull, my friend." Solomon added wisely.

"Leave it to us, we will see what we can do. Do not worry, Robin, patience is a great virtue, one that Sargasso does not have in large measure, I know that now. Go home and rest, you have been wise to alert us. A cold night will soon be upon us; get back to your night time roost, little bird." Solomon told him kindly but firmly. "Be off now, no time to lose."

Freddie, happy at last that he had alerted them to Sargasso's potential plight, obeyed thankfully. He shivered, and it was all he could do to fly home in the chill air. He arrived exhausted at Watermill Cottage and sat on the central heating outlet to warm himself up, fluffing out his feathers as he perched on the wire framework, home at last.

Solomon and Bathsheba set off at once, darting through the cold waters in the direction of Land's End, where the edge of the world as they knew it met the sea. It took them several hours to find the Silver Tinkling Shoals, who were lazing around, awaiting the return of Hector and Hercules. The whales had gone far into deeper water and the silver fish did not want to follow.

"Have you seen the seagull called Sargasso?" asked the two seals anxiously, scanning the cloudy threatening sky which was beginning to darken.

"We have seen many birds on our travels," lilted the fish together.

"But you know this one, he is chosen by the Spirit of the Sea," persisted Bathsheba.

"Many are chosen; few are memorable," replied the fish who were vain and unhelpful, bored with waiting and wishing to return to their master. "We are his favourites, we are so beautiful. Look," and they put on their most dazzling display of breathtaking, synchronised swimming. They certainly were beautiful to watch, of that there was no doubt.

"Indeed you are," agreed the seals, "but please keep watch for the seagull, he may be lost; this is too far for him to stray, ice is coming tonight, many will freeze to death. We can smell it in the air."

"We will, we will," replied the Silver Tinkling Shoals but Solomon and Bathsheba were unsure of their good intentions. They parted company from the fish, but were not satisfied.

"Let's go right to the edge of the land and look just once," persuaded Solomon and together they swam to the tip of Land's End, to the rocky sweeps that fall into the sea itself.

"There he is!" Bathsheba mewed, and in front of them, standing proudly on a seaweed-covered rock, on the point where ocean and earth meet, was Sargasso. Cold and tired, his feathers jagged and ruffled, ice was beginning to frost over him.

He would not leave; he had called into his silvered shell as a last resort to reach the Spirit, but hearing nothing, had given up in despair.

"The Spirit of the Sea has abandoned me. Where are you, master?" he cried wearily into the wind. "What am I to do?"

He looked around wildly and saw Solomon and Bathsheba. He stared at them. "Is it you? Can it be you, Solomon and Bathsheba? Are you the sign?" he croaked, exhausted.

"No, my friend. Hector and Hercules have been sent to search out the sea monsters. The Silver Tinkling Shoals are waiting for their return. Do not upset yourself. The Spirit of the Sea has not left you. You must be patient. Everything will happen in its proper sequence. All will be well. Come into the water to melt the ice, come now, join us." The seal coaxed the almost unconscious and exhausted bird into the sea. He swam with them, wearily, and gradually his blood circulated freely again. Very slowly he began to recover and the seals, one on each side to assist him, swam onwards. It was getting dark now.

"We shall have to find a place to rest for the night," insisted Solomon. "Keep your eye out for a suitable spot." They rounded the Lizard and Bathsheba saw a sheltered cove close by, sensing Sargasso's exhaustion and depression. He said little and the seals helped him up the beach. The three settled together under a dry overhang, protected from the wind and frost. They slept soundly – it had been an ordeal for them all.

Chapter Twenty-two
Whales at work and the Moonglimmer wakes up

During that long, cold night Hector and Hercules passed Land's End, swimming endlessly, never tiring, discussing the black creatures they had seen, going over and over the possibilities of what they were, describing exactly what they had looked like and the noise they had made, to report to the Spirit of the Sea. As they entered the busy seaway of the English Channel a huge cruise liner passed them by, the passengers all waving excitedly, telling each other of the sighting of the whales. The captain took his binoculars and went to the bridge window.

"Very unusual in these waters, and at this time of the year. How strange." He took a compass reading and noted it in his log. Then he sent out a signal to all vessels in the area of their presence, and the ships hunting the submarines all received it.

How interesting, Peter thought, as the message was announced to the ship's company on HMS *Kirkliston*. *Whales in the coastal waters? Probably lost in migration. Wouldn't Eddie love to see them! We'll be chugging down the Channel again for the fourth time; I could ask the skipper if I can send him a ship-to-shore message."* And the idea grew in Peter's mind until he decided to do it. Lt.Com. Adrian Scott was a gentle family man and strictly speaking he shouldn't let Peter use the phone, it was kept for urgent messages only, but he had two sons of his own in Portsmouth and frankly the crew were getting bored with the constant and fruitless searching.

"Alright. Go on, Peter," he told him.

In the communications room the call was set up and back in Dartmouth the phone rang. Eddie was the first to reach it as he was in the kitchen taking his torch to pieces and replacing the batteries. Sighing heavily, annoyed at the interruption, he went wearily to the phone.

"Hello?" There was a silence. "Hello?" he repeated.

"Hi Eddie, it's Dad here."

Eddie's face broke into an expression of excited pleasure.

"Dad –I never expected it to be you!" and then suddenly as fear and doubts flickered into focus, "What's wrong, Dad?" he asked in a desperate voice.

"Nothing, nothing, Eddie," his father reassured him quickly, "just a really quick call to tell you there are two whales around, huge ones, you might see them passing if you keep a look out, you never know."

"Really? How fantastic. Where are you?"

"Oh, we're in the Channel now, in fact we'll be coming by Berry Head and Start Point tomorrow night between 8 and 9 o'clock. Sorry I'm so close, but I can't come home yet. Give my love to Mum and Ellie. I'm really sorry but I've got to go now. Take care. See you soon, won't be long now, 'bye son, 'bye," and he was gone.

It had all been over in a flash. He hadn't even had time to call his mother.

A warm feeling of excitement started to creep over him. Whales! How he and Ellie would love to see them! He was reminded of the two whales who had come to his rescue, instructed by the Spirit of the Sea to save his life during his desperate escape from the Royalist soldiers when he had been catapulted back in time.

Mary and Ellie called him from the sitting room.

"Who was it, Eddie?"

He hurried to tell them. "It was Dad! Yes, he rang very quickly to tell us there are two whales about and to keep a close look out at sea."

"Really?" Mary looked very surprised.

"Yes really, and he's in the Channel and will be passing by Dartmouth; well, into Start Bay tomorrow night."

"Oh, what a shame! He's so close," complained Ellie.

Mary took up her tapestry again. *Typical.* She sighed and said nothing. She hadn't even had the chance to say hello. Eddie was extremely excited and was making plans with Ellie to go whale watching tomorrow. She had to smile at him. His enthusiasm was infectious.

"Well, I'm coming too," she told them.

"We're all going, and Patrick," Ellie said emphatically. "What about school?" A sudden panic swept over her.

"Well, unless there's a quick thaw I can't see either of you making it to Kingsbridge or Churston tomorrow," Mary told them. "There'll be a frost tonight and I think you'll find the whale watch is on, cold though it might be."

"Oh good!" Eddie said with feeling. "I'm going to phone Patrick." And off he went back into the kitchen.

They heard Eddie's excited voice on the phone and then the kettle being filled, tin lids and cupboard doors banged. Ellie and Mary looked at each other, Eddie was making the drinks! He must be feeling very happy. Sure enough, he came in proudly carrying the tray piled with chocolate biscuits and shortbread and mugs of tea.

"Thank you, Eddie." Mary praised her smiling son, grateful for the gesture, and he plonked the tray on the coffee table, the tea lurching in the mugs and slopping onto the biscuits.

"Oh sorry! Never mind, we'll have to eat them all now!" grinned Eddie, munching one.

***

Far off in the dark ocean, Hector and Hercules were forced to rest at last. One question had been nagging Hector. He voiced his concern to his friend.

"The large ship the humans passed us by in, it made a noise, a loud noise and the white foam churned as it moved through the water. Why does it do that?" he puzzled.

"All their big ships move that way, it's an invention they've made. It makes them go faster. A wheel turns at the back and spins in the water, moving the whole ship forward. Only the small boats now have sails, I think," answered Hercules, his knowledge limited.

"But the noise, I'm sure it's similar to the noise the black monsters made that we saw in the deep. Maybe they've got the same wheels and that is why they can travel so fast."

It's surely not possible, thought Hector. Weary now, they tried to sleep, lapped by the cold sea and the strong tide. As they slept, the two submarines maintained their slow and steady speed, catching up with them, mile by mile.

Only a short distance away on the shore, secure in a dry narrow cave, slept the seagull and the two seals, warming each other with their resting bodies.

***

Gradually the lights went out at Watermill Cottage, the sky cleared, starry and bright and Umbraluna switched on his luminous blue eyes to low intensity as he awoke in his snow-filled hollow. He had reset his biorhythms and his fatigue had left him. Waking and sleeping, content to observe, he had absorbed all the visual knowledge he could: birds, trees, houses, clouds, plants, people, cars and lorries. He had heard birdsongs, music, voices talking, engines, water, the wind, doorbells, doors banging and a postman whistling. What a strange world it all was, so different from his dull dreary life of grey on the dark side of the moon, and so much more exciting. He longed to be part of it.

He rose from his bed of leaves, and taking on his own invisible star shape he wafted across the hillside and down to the cottage. He perched on the window sill outside the kitchen and shone his eyes in. What a mystery it was!

What can these humans possibly do with all these things? he wondered. *Where is the light, the wonderful light that I saw beaming out to me from this planet? I must find it soon. I shall have to shadow the humans more closely now*, and wafted around the house. When he got to Eddie's window he knew at once where he was. This was the light source, he was convinced of it. He had navigated himself thousands of miles to reach this spot. His inbuilt system told him it was so. He stared at the sleeping boy and glimmered himself inside the house, melting through the edge of the window pane, eyes turned down very low. He could hear Eddie breathing gently. The rhythm was hypnotic and it lulled him. He lay weightless. Contented that he had achieved his mission, he closed his systems down and slept like Eddie.

In the morning the world was still white, cold and frosty, but the magical purity of the untouched snow had gone. School was definitely cancelled and excitement filled the house again. Mary decided they would all make the trek to the top of Coastguard hill with a flask of hot soup and sandwiches, and so preparations began. It felt like a holiday. Eddie yawned and got out of bed.

"Brr, it's cold," he said and rubbed the window pane. All was still snowy. Umbraluna woke up in the brightly lit room and gazed around. It was colourful, with blue and turquoise walls, bright posters, and objects he didn't understand – a radio and cassette player, books, tennis racquet and a camera. As Eddie returned he dressed and went off downstairs. The Moonglimmer followed, intrigued by everything, wafting gently down too, totally invisible.

After breakfast, Ellie made the sandwiches and Mary heated the tomato soup and poured it into the flask. Binoculars, notebooks and something to sit on were gathered up. The Moonglimmer watched curiously. What were they doing? Then they put on hats, coats and gloves, Mary chose a walking stick, and they were off, crunching down the driveway in their Wellington boots. Freddie watched them go, unaware of the Moonglimmer shadowing them, content to stay by the kitchen window, breakfasting on their leftover toast crumbs.

Umbraluna, the Moonglimmer's name, took on Eddie's shape, becoming his shadow, copying silently his every move. He liked this new world, it was so interesting and these humans were amusing him very much. He had never seen clothes or food before, requiring neither himself. Walking, slipping, or sometimes sliding, they made their way to the Old Bath House. Bridget opened it, delighted to see them, and invited them in. They took off their boots and padded into the warm room. Umbraluna followed and was astonished to see the glinting, gliding water of the river Dart, slowly and constantly slinking by, through the wonderful picture window.

"Any news of the submarines?" asked George.

"Not really," replied Mary unhappily, "they're still looking; in fact the squadron is in the Channel today not far from here, just passing through."

"Yes, Dad phoned us last night to say they had seen a pair of whales and told us to look out for them!" Eddie told him with excitement.

"Well, lad," chuckled George, "sure it's not those Russian subs instead?" Mary laughed politely, not finding that funny at all. Patrick arrived, carrying his boots, rushing to be ready.

"Sorry! I slept in a bit this morning."

"Let's go then shall we?" and Mary ushered them out in front of her, carrying her stick."Bye."

Bridget smiled, watching her beloved godson chatting and laughing.

Umbraluna glimmered along behind the children and as the sun managed to find its way out of the clouds the whole scene took on a totally different appearance. It was dazzling. The clouds melted away and crystal clear light showed sky, sea and land in a beautiful panorama. Umbraluna was thrilled. He could be a proper shadow now and he danced from person to person, taking their shape and walking along beside them, an exact mirror image. He found he couldn't look at the sun, it was just too bright. He didn't know about this shining ball in the sky, he had never seen it before, during his existence in permanent dark gloom in the shadows of the other side of the moon.

Why do none of our people know about this place? he wondered. *This place of light and brightness and all the colours of a different life.*

The journey up the hill was not easy; slipping and sliding, and catching hold of each other they giggled and screamed, falling over and getting rather wet, but it was all part of the fun of a day off school.

At the top they entered the National Trust land and choosing a bank on the right with a panoramic view, sat down, puffing; snatching off their hats which were making them hot and sweaty. The air was cold but the sun was warm on their faces. It had been truly worth the climb. Content to rest, they sat in silence gazing across the steep snow-covered hillside to the sea stretching out far into the distance. They could make out Start Point curving round. A container ship was plain to see on the horizon. The binoculars were found and they took it in turns to scan the endless rippled sea for anything unusual, each hoping that they would be the one to spot the whales. Umbraluna squeezed between them, enjoying himself immensely.

Chapter Twenty-three
An amazing discovery

Far down the coast in one of Cornwall's remote bays, two seals and a seagull awoke at dawn, refreshed by a good night's sleep.

"We must begin our journey home now," Solomon told Sargasso. "We will wait at the wide waters of Start Bay to meet the whales on their return. You shall be the first to hear their news, Sargasso," he promised. Agreeing without question, the seagull flew above the seals as they swam mercurially through the wintry waters. He had regained the strength of his body and mind during his sleep, kept warm by the two caring sea creatures.

They continued on at a good speed, swimming close together. Once or twice they heard a mournful echo under the sea and when it became louder and more persistent, they stopped and listened carefully. The seagull dropped down to sit on the water's ruffled surface, and he listened too.

"It's the whales! Hector and Hercules are close by! It is them!" Bathsheba told her mate with certainty and excitement. The three turned to the direction they thought the echoes were coming from and followed the beautiful musical sounds that were magnified as they travelled through the sea water.

Suddenly Sargasso saw a water spout being expelled through a blowhole and the distant dark shape of a whale's hump broke the surface.

"It's them! It's them!" he cawed loudly. The second whale appeared soon after. How huge they were, rolling over in the sea, black and shiny with white barnacles attached to them, tails upright and visible. The three Seafarers swam quickly towards them. The whales' huge eyes soon spotted the seals. Solomon called their names out to show he was a friend and they circled each other, churning up the water as they met at last.

"We're so glad to have found you!" Bathsheba told them joyfully.

"What news from the deep, my friends?" Solomon asked at once. Sargasso hovered overhead, wings beating, anxious to hear everything.

"We have travelled far over the edge of the coastal shallows and we have found the black sea monsters that trespassed into our waters. They are unknown to us; we have never seen anything like them before. They swim at great speed, make a frightening noise and speak in a voice we do not understand that travels in the water and pains our eyes and ears. We left in fear. We can only hope they return to their home in the deep places in the ocean where we cannot go, nor do we want to." Hector and Hercules were sad to admit they didn't know the answers, they only knew the questions.

The two seals and the seagull tactfully nodded and as the whales beckoned to them with a nod of their huge heads, they followed in their wake, being drawn along at great speed with very little effort.

"Travel with us, we must rejoin the Silver Tinkling Shoals who are waiting and will guide us back."

Hector stopped swimming abruptly and dived down into the blue-grey water. The others halted too and waited. What was wrong? Where had he gone? He reappeared with a torrent of water breaking over him.

"They're coming!" he called anxiously in his deep sonorous voice. "They're coming after us! I can hear their noise and they are talking to each other! Listen!" Sure enough the persistent drone of the submarines' engines and their underwater communications made its strange echoes through the water, getting louder and louder.

"It's too late to get away now," Hercules told the frightened seals and the seagull. "They're almost upon us."

"Shall I call the Spirit of the Sea?" Sargasso asked desperately. "I've got my sacred shell."

"Too late, my friend, too late," Hector replied grimly, resigned to his fate.

"We shall have to stand and face them. We'll put up a good fight, you'll see!"

***

In the submarines the crews were on full alert, their sonar screens now showing the whales close by. They loaded warheads into their firing position.

"Let them attack first," advised the weapons officer. "We cannot be seen to be the aggressors. We may be in NATO waters."

Captain Ranoffski took his advice and the two submarines fell silent. They reduced speed and purred through the dimly lit water.

"Take action to avoid collision! We're closing fast!" shouted the navigation officer. "Steer 20 degrees east!"

Paralysed with fear, the whales and seals trod water on the surface, hardly moving, and Sargasso, eager to see what was going on, ducked under for a few seconds, searching frantically with his yellow eyes.

What he saw amazed him. Two long black cigar-shaped objects passed far beneath him with propellers whirring, churning the sea water as they sped by. Strange letters and numbers were painted on the bodies. Sargasso was alerted by the propellers and then by the white writing and something familiar clicked in his small bird's brain. These were not terrifying sea monsters! They were some kind of human sea-travelling machine. They must be – hadn't Eddie's boat got an outboard engine with just such a propeller? And didn't his little green boat have writing on it just like this? As he jolted his head up, the submarines passed harmlessly by, just under a hundred feet below them, visible in the clear water.

He flapped excitedly on the surface as the seals and the whales circled anxiously.

"I know what they are! They aren't sea monsters! They're some sort of machine the humans have made to travel under the sea. Eddie's boat has a propeller like they have, on the back. It's called an engine."

The other Seafarers just stared at him, unable to say a word.

"You don't mean there are humans inside that black monster, do you?" asked Hector and Hercules together in complete amazement.

"Yes, yes I think so," squawked Sargasso in excitement. "There is human writing on the sides as well. I know writing you see," he added very proudly. What a lot he had learnt while he had been at Eddie's side and become his friend. Thinking of his beloved Eddie, Sargasso was filled with the urge to fly home at once and tell him about the dreadful sea monsters. They didn't exist! Nobody need be afraid of them anymore.

"Are you quite sure?" asked the whales and the seals, "because you must tell the Spirit of the Sea at once; we can send the Silver Tinkling Shoals back to meet him. Where are they? We should have found them by now." Hector and Hercules were puzzled; and indeed, where were they?

Bored with waiting, the tiny fishes had resorted to making mischief. They were amusing themselves by leading a fleet of fishing trawlers from Mavegissey a very merry dance. They were so swift and agile they could never be caught. The fishermen were all amazed.

"Never seen anything like it in our lives, they're like jet propelled rockets!" They scratched their heads, not knowing where to put the nets down.

"We can't wait to find them, this is too important," urged Hector and Hercules.

"Those black things are heading back into our home waters, our Seafarers will all be disturbed again; the spawning season will soon be with us and many will not find their way with the weird noises and confusion."

Sargasso pulled his silvered shell from under the feathers around his neck and called to the Great Spirit of the Sea.

"Master, I beg you to hear me. Your whales have discovered the secrets of the black sea monsters. They are human ships, fashioned out of metal that swim under the water. They speak to each other with piercing echoes and sounds that have been affecting all your subjects. We await your instructions, Mighty Spirit, from Sargasso your faithful servant."

As the words entered the shell they travelled at the speed of sound over the oceans and across the world until the Spirit of the Sea received them in his own shell that he too wore around his neck. He listened carefully. He thought for a long time about the consequences of what Sargasso had told him. The humans had entered his undersea domain and there would be peace and freedom no longer. The Seafarers had enjoyed their own special world since the beginning of time. Were they never to be free of the tiresome interference of man? He sent back his answer, his booming voice deafening Sargasso when it came.

"If this is the real truth and all my chosen ones agree, then lead the sea craft into a safe harbour, for I fear they must be lost, wandering aimlessly in the ocean. When you have done so, I wish my great cetaceans to return to find sanctuary on the shores of Sugary Cove once more, to await my instructions. When the task is completed, the Silver Tinkling Shoals must return to me. You have performed well and deserve much praise. I salute you." The voice stopped abruptly, but far off on the horizon a silver sparkle came dazzling and flashing towards them, moving at great speed. The whales turned and spoke.

"They have heard the voice of their great sea lord."

With unbelievable rapidity, the tiny silver fish shot through the water aware of their misbehaviour and irresponsibility and raced to be back at the side of the large black whales before they got into trouble.

"We have come, come, come!" they chimed together. "Our master bids us lead you to a safe harbour, follow us, us, us!" and with a swirl of silver brightness, they dived and chased after the two Russian submarines, making up the miles in seconds. Empowered by the Spirit of the Sea with a strong magnetic field all around their metallic scales, they surrounded the black sea craft. At once, the submarines were locked onto the strong magnetic pull and their instrumentation became useless. They were being dragged along by the intense strength of the smallest of fish. The crew were baffled.

"Captain, what has happened to us?"

Not knowing the answer and not wishing to show lack of leadership, he reassured them all confidently. "We are heading to safety now, men. Our country has rescued us and is towing us to the motherland. Stand down. Return to normal stations and let us celebrate our rescue." The crew cheered and the captain sent up a silent prayer to any God who would listen to save his valiant men. He wanted to go home.

The whales and seals followed and then overtook the submarines as the fish headed towards the Devon coast. Sargasso bade them all farewell and Seafarers' good fortune and flew homeward, elated and full of hope. He too was desperate to reach home and tell Eddie the wonderful news.

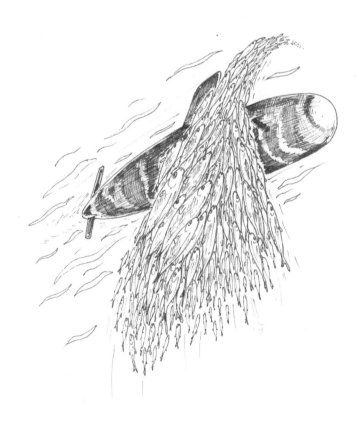

Chapter Twenty-four
Tolivera feels better

The buzzard couldn't believe his luck; his interview with Tolivera had gone so extremely well. Why, the wily old devil had practically been, well – nice! It was extraordinary. Refusing a glass of the Mists of Time on the grounds that it might cloud his judgement, the buzzard explained the purpose of his visit.

"Just a little plan to put to you, dear fellow. Your idea for the great chestnut tree. Remember?"

"Indeed I do," was the solemn reply, as Tolivera sipped gently at yet another frosty glass of liquor, savouring its taste.

"I have given the matter due consideration and have reached the conclusion that if you ignore the rather trivial inconvenience of the boy's wooden contraption on your tree, I am prepared to not only give my wholehearted approval of your new scheme, but to actively assist in its construction and development. In fact, I shall send my sons to help you; good training, I thought. Now, how does that sound to you, eh?"

The owl, who the buzzard feared deep down in his heart, puffed gently on his pipe, gazing around his comfortable home as contentment strangely seeped over him, his memory of recent events fading. Why was he angry about the boy? It was only a childish toy, what did it matter? And did he really want to go to all the trouble of setting up yet another observation post? Was it all worth the considerable effort to spy on a few misdemeanours? The Woodlanders were generally nice folk after all; simple but well meaning. Perhaps he'd take it easy for a while, reconsider and think about it. He hoped he hadn't upset the buzzard or been sharp with him.

"Well, my lord, I appreciate your very kind offer, but just for the moment I have one or two other things in my diary and feel I may postpone my proposed chestnut tree venture until the spring. I don't want to rush into it, do you see? Or inconvenience you in any way."

The buzzard speechless, nodded in agreement, listening incredulously.

The owl continued, "I think I may take a little time off, have a rest during the quiet winter season, prepare for spring, the council meeting, and get my affairs in order. I'll always be here if you wish to consult me, my lord, of course, but you do such a good job of ruling the kingdom, and you're rather busy shaping up your three fine sons to take over one day. I might take a bit of a back seat for just a little while."

"Are you quite well, Tolly, dear chap?" asked the buzzard, unable to believe that he had heard correctly. "You don't think you should have a check-up at the Cornucopia tree? Let Dr Underconstumble take a look at you, eh?"

"No, no, dear fellow, feeling fine, fine. In fact I'm thinking of throwing a Christmas party for us. Get us all together, invite all the Woodlanders and give them a really good time. What do you think? Good idea?" He leaned forward and stared into the buzzard's face intently.

The buzzard, disconcerted, backed away with a start. *He'd gone mad, he must have, he doesn't do things like this!* he thought wildly. What had happened to him?

"Um, good idea, it certainly is, Tolly. Very nice idea." He paused nervously. "Well, must be going now – things to do, things to do," he blustered, getting up. "Is that the time?" and he glanced at Tolivera's magnificent Dark Dwellers' grandfather clock, carved out of black ash with a petrified toadstool pendulum. It pointed to NOONDAY. Tolivera rose out of his chair and wrapped his warm crimson gown around himself.

"Don't worry about the boy, he's not doing much harm. He's only a human after all," nodded the owl mechanically with a glazed look in his eye and an eerie fixed smile. The buzzard took one look at him and fled, mumbling goodbye as he tripped over the thick flower-woven rug in his haste to leave.

"Bye! I'll send you an invitation to the party," promised the syrupy voice of the most feared bird in the whole of the Woodlander kingdom. "Bye now." And he shut his door.

The buzzard was so convinced that either Tolivera had lost his mind or he had lost his, that he decided to walk home for some fresh air. He'd get his wife to call in and make sure the owl was alright. It didn't seem possible that Tolivera could have said those things and he puzzled over it as he strolled through the beautiful woodland back to his home at the Citadel. He hoped his sons had prepared the declaration about the flashing lights – the notice needed to go up soon. Sighing, the weight of office once more weighing him down, he prepared to tutor them once again.

Passing the ivy-clustered Cornucopia tree, which looked for all the world like a huge birds' nest, the buzzard saw the two doctors, Dr Dew and Dr Yew, gathering cupfuls of snow with tiny shovels. They were engrossed in this pursuit, cooing gently to each other, wrapped up in grey and white striped woolly hats with long tails and fluffy white scarves that looked like ruffles.

"Helloooooo!" cooed the pigeons as they saw the buzzard approaching.

"Good day to you, dear doctors," greeted the buzzard with a nod. "Whatever are you doing?"

"We're collecting snowflakes, lord. They have heavenly healing properties and divine powers. Why, haven't they come from heaven themselves? Each one is different and has a special secret. We have almost run out of Heavenly Healing Flakes, there has been no snow for such a long time. We are so lucky today; there are plenty for us to gather." They spoke together like one person made from two people, joined forever.

"Indeed, I didn't know that," remarked the buzzard.

"How is your friend Tolivera today? Is he renewed?" cooed the birds inquiringly.

"He is… quite changed today. I found him – well, as you say, – renewed," was the reply, as the Lord of the Woodland struggled, not quite understanding.

"Probably the snow, you know," nodded Dr Dew. "Perhaps a snowflake or two have drifted into his doorway. We must get on now my lord. Toodle-oooooo!" cooed the two pretty birds, and continued to shovel snow into their containers.

Ummmm, mused the buzzard as he walked on to the Citadel thinking over what the doctors had said. *How lucky we are to have them. They do seem to have a cornucopia of knowledge stored up there.* As he entered the panelled hall of his official residence, his sons were just coming down the spiral staircase with the folded parchment, four nails and a hammer.

"We've done it, Father, Mother's had a look at it and says it's absolutely wonderful. We're just off to put it up for all your subjects to see. Can they all read?" the keen young buzzards asked eagerly. The buzzard was taken aback. He really didn't know, he'd never even thought about it before.

"Just put it up, word will soon get around. The wise will tell the foolish and so it spreads. Well done, my sons, well done," and he let them go, eager to tell his wife about the strange behaviour of their second-in-command.

The sons went off proudly on their first official task. They squabbled over who would carry the document, who would hammer the nails in, and where it was to go. When they reached the old ash tree and saw the wooden bird box hide already there, they decided that it must be a good place as somebody else had chosen it and so the three of them began to try to bang their proclamation into place. One broken talon and one lost nail later, the parchment official document was hanging by its torn corner from three nails.

"There!" said the three princes with satisfaction, just as the door further up the tree opened with a slow creak. The smoke of Tolivera's pipe appeared first, followed by his head and brilliant piercing eyes.

"Aha! The three Princes of the Woodland; chosen my tree for your poster, eh?"

"It wasn't me, it was him!" they all three started accusing each other, frightened of the owl. Tolivera held up one wing to silence them.

"I am honoured you have selected my home to be so favoured. Thank you, boys, thank you!" he beamed at them. The princes bowed politely and hopped away, one limping.

"Let's go home, hurry!" hissed one to the others and they flew off in great haste. Tolivera watched them go. Usually so territorial and unwilling to have his privacy invaded, he felt strangely benevolent.

"What harm will it do?" He shrugged his shoulders, admired the view and closed the door.

Chapter Twenty-five
Whale watching and some very important news

On the steep hillside, just beyond Lighthouse Cottages, the whale watching was being taken very seriously. Sitting on the bank four people in turn searched the horizon for unusual happenings. Umbraluna had sunk to the snowy ground, watching everything that went on, fascinated by the glinting, rippling sea and the huge expanse of sky. He loved the sun. How he loved the sun! He felt warm and drowsy and settled down between Eddie and Ellie, invisible and unseen. Today the sea was flat and the visibility stretched for at least twenty miles. It was a perfect day to watch. However it was cold and the picnic was unpacked and the hot soup happily drunk long before lunchtime. They spent several happy hours while ardent walkers armed with ski poles passed them by with curiosity.

"We're whale watching!" the youngsters informed them.

"Oh really?" replied the surprised hikers, amused and disbelieving.

Eventually disappointment began to creep over them, as a westerly wind brought clouds the thaw started. As the temperature rose, the snow slowly started its drip, drip, dripping and the gradual melt began.

"Back to school tomorrow, I'd say," Mary told them gently.

"How much longer do you want to stay here and keep watch?" she asked sensing the excitement and elation evaporating and reality setting in.

"I think I'd like to go now," replied Patrick, accepting the situation and facing the disappointment.

"Do we have to?" complained Eddie and Ellie together.

"Just remember it gets dark early at this time in December so be home in plenty of time." Mary said.

"I'd like to stay a bit longer I think," decided Eddie. "It might be the only chance I get to ever see a whale; I'd hate to miss it." Ellie wavered,

"What are you doing, Patrick?"

"I've really got to go to the cottage get things organised," he told them apologetically. "Why don't you come and help me, Ellie?" And he turned his young earnest face towards her, blue eyes searching. That did it, Ellie was persuaded and Mary watched, amused at his powers.

"Right, that's settled." Mary began to gather up her things.

"Any food left?" asked Eddie hopefully.

"Just one sandwich and a bottle of mineral water, I'm afraid," as Mary handed the precious leftovers to her eager son. Eddie was left on his own, as the three figures disappeared over the hill, turning to wave a last goodbye to him.

Umbraluna woke up and, sad that the sun had gone behind the clouds, set off to follow Ellie and Patrick, taking their shape and glimmering along beside them. Just for one brief moment the sun's late afternoon gold brightness shone through and Ellie noticed a shadow walking beside her, dark on the road's white and grey slushy surface. It occurred to her that there shouldn't be any shadows at all now, but this one was still bobbing along beside her.

Just the light, she thought.

On the hill, Eddie sat back happily, enjoying the peace and solitude of being alone. Sargasso, returning from his long flight from Cornwall, was nearing his beloved estuary, wearied by his journey. He was pleased with himself for being able to help so powerful a team sent by the Spirit of the Sea. Below him swam

Solomon and Bathsheba, whose loyalty and persistence in finding him he would never forget. They slowed down as they sighted the Trip Trap bridge, by their own rocky inlet.

"Keep watch for them," Sargasso called, "they can't be far behind us."

Eddie stood up to search the sea again, his red sailing jacket bright against the thawing snow. Sargasso noticed the red outline and flew towards it to see what it was. He was overjoyed to find that it was Eddie. Eddie caught sight of him in the binoculars. Could it be Sargasso? He took the binoculars away from his eyes and almost immediately the seagull landed gracefully beside him.

"Sargasso, where have you been? You look a bit bedraggled and tired, you poor thing." He bent down and stroked the gull, his feathers frayed slightly in places.

"Here, eat my sandwich, come on," and the boy fished in his pocket, breaking the brown bread slices in small pieces for him. Gradually the bird felt a little less exhausted, and collecting his courage together decided to break his silence; he was not afraid, he had been granted permission. Sargasso finished eating and Eddie continued to stroke him.

"That's better, isn't it?" he repeated quietly, smoothing the white and grey feathers. The seagull struggled to stand on his one strong leg and faced Eddie.

"I have important news to tell you, my young master," he told him firmly.

"You're talking to me again! What's happened?" The boy was suddenly afraid and he moved away, frightened.

"I have always understood your human language, Eddie, but it is breaking the Seafarers' code to speak it. I have special permission from my master to tell you these things." Eddie listened, rooted to the spot. The seagull continued,

"I was granted the power to warn you of the great owl's anger at your Moonmirror being fastened to his mighty ash tree in the woodland."

Eddie remembered the attempted attack by the owl that evening with Ellie.

Sargasso, feeling guilty, went on,

"I failed to protect you because of even worse things happening to our people. There have been sea monsters from faraway places trespassing in our ocean, frightening many with their piercing echoes and alien voices. They send shock waves under the water which give pain to the eyes and ears of the sea dwellers. They have infiltrated our peaceful home and many are too frightened and confused to venture to their spawning grounds."

Eddie listened fascinated, but with growing alarm.

"The Spirit if the Sea sent some of his swiftest and strongest subjects to investigate. The whales Hector and Hercules have tracked and discovered the sea monsters."

"Whales? Whales in the seas here?"

"Yes, they spend their lives resting on the shores of Sugary Cove, turned into black stones, awaiting a signal from our master to assist in any tasks."

"And.... they have been searching the seas for these monsters?"

"Yes, for days now," nodded Sargasso.

"But my father rang to tell me of their appearance; they have been sighted by many ships crossing the Channel. That's why I'm here looking for them. Where are they?" he asked, excited and thrilled.

"They will be here very soon now. They have found the monsters that have been lost, looking for a way home," Sargasso told him. Eddie laughed loudly.

"What sort of sea monsters? They don't exist. Well, as far as I know," he added, not wanting to offend the bird.

"I have seen them and wish for your opinion because I do not think they are sea creatures at all."

"What?"

"No, they are long and black, huge and shiny with writing I do not understand painted on them. They have a propeller which churns the water white, and make echoes and loud wails which travel through the ocean like the song of the whales," Sargasso confirmed with confidence.

"What!" Eddie jumped up, eyes wide and mouth open. "It can't be, it just can't be! Tell me again, Sargasso, everything, every single little thing you saw. It's very important!"

Proudly the seagull repeated what he and the whales had seen and Eddie was convinced that they could only be the missing Russian submarines. Everything fell into place. It had to be them. Probably lost, their sonar equipment faulty, they had strayed into international waters, unable to contact their base in Russia. Their superiors, with no likely explanation for their disappearance, had presumed them to have been destroyed secretly by the NATO forces. It had all been a huge mistake.

"I've got to tell somebody!" Eddie looked around wildly. "This is terribly important!"

Sargasso was surprised at Eddie's reaction. He had felt so pleased with himself, understanding that these black monsters were man-made, but Eddie seemed very upset by it all. He felt uneasy. Had he done something wrong? He looked out across the bay. The day was closing now and soon it would be dark. The seagull saw a familiar spout of water rising from the surface, then another one joined it; it was the unmistakable sign of the whales. They were here!

"Look, Eddie, look! They're coming, out there, see?" he squawked, and as the distraught boy gazed across the horizon he saw a rising arc of water splashing the surface, followed by a black island which increased in size, spreading through the water, creating white wavelets. He grabbed his binoculars and could clearly see the barnacle-encrusted hide rearing up, followed by the giant flukes of its tail stretching twenty feet above the surface.

"Oh, how wonderful!" he shouted, and the second whale appeared not far off, rising to fill its lungs and preparing to dive again. It rolled from side to side, black and huge and shiny. Eddie was mesmerised as it too lifted its huge tail and crashed down into the water with a great splash.

"Are you sure the submarines are there too?" asked Eddie, scanning across the expanse of sea and all around the now-disappearing whales. He could see nothing; just a circle of seagulls feeding on the water disturbed by the huge bulk of the whales. Scanning carefully and refocusing the binoculars, about 200 metres behind the whales he spotted the faintest black in the sea, standing up above the waves. He followed it closely. It was the periscope of a submarine.

"You're right, Sargasso, it's them!" He checked again, but it disappeared almost immediately. He was in no doubt, he *had* seen it.

"Come on, Sargasso, we must get home and I'll try to telephone my father," he said, as he quickly collected his things together and chased off down the now very slippery hill, which was melting continuously in the warmer westerly air.

***

At Waterside Cottage, Ellie and Patrick were trying to get to grips with the arrival of the furniture and appliances. The electricity and gas were on, the phone line connected, and the central heating just needed to be switched on at the boiler. Umbraluna had followed them round, looking at everything, pleased when the lights went on. Patrick was on the phone and went down the list ensuring the next deliveries were all booked for the next day.

"I need some food now. Let's go down to town, they can deliver it tomorrow." Ellie phoned her mother and told her where they were going, and closing the door, set off up the old stone steps beside the bridge to the main road that led to town.

The Moonglimmer followed, pleased at the idea of exploring yet more new places. He bounced along beside them, first taking Ellie's silhouette and then Patrick's.

When Umbraluna saw the town he was totally amazed. *So this is how they live, in these square linkages, but the links are broken, some stand on their own.*

When they reached the town with its Christmas lights the main Christmas tree came into view, he stopped and stared. He stared and stared, delighted with what he saw.

How lovely this is, so many lights! and he sat beneath the Christmas tree and just smiled. He lost Ellie and Patrick, so engrossed was he in enjoying the wonders around him. Silvers and golds, sparkles and shimmers, shiny paper and coloured foils, winked and blinked at him from everywhere. It was the most wonderful hour he had ever spent, bathed in colour and brightness. The carol singers arrived and sat around the tree on wooden chairs beside the unknown invisible creature. The music was set up and they began; the strains of Silent Night crossing the town, the park and the river. Umbraluna was bewitched. He swayed to the music as they continued the performance, singing many old favourites. A crowd gathered and money was collected for charity.

Eventually it was over, everybody clapped and slowly people wished each other good night and drifted off home. The townsfolk closed their businesses, some of the lights went out, and then quietness descended. It was time to go home. Umbraluna didn't know the way home, so he switched on his navigation equipment situated behind his eyes, set it for the light source he originally travelled to, and lit up his intense blue eyebeams. Then he glimmered gently up into the air and across the rooftops, all the way over the hill and across the valley to Watermill Cottage. He landed in the woods and bounced back to Eddie's windowsill where he squeezed himself through the window frame and sank onto the striped bedcover.

He was very satisfied with his visit to the strange, sprawling, unplanned centre of habitation – quite different from the mathematically calculated tunnels and squares he had come from. Several people had noticed the strange blue lights in the sky and assumed it was bright car headlights, badly adjusted, or some new trendy Christmas light display for outside. Nobody was too bothered about it… It was Christmas, after all.

Patrick and Ellie had long completed their shopping, ordered the delivery for the next morning and hurried back to Warfleet.

"See you tomorrow," they promised, and went their different ways.

"Thanks, Ellie," called Patrick in the darkness, and she smiled to herself, not looking back.

Chapter Twenty-six
Brave actions

Ellie arrived home, pleased after her shopping trip with Patrick, to find Eddie in a state of high excitement and her mother sitting drinking tea, trying to understand him. He was so agitated he could hardly talk. Sargasso was sitting on the weathervane with Freddie beside him, waiting in the darkness to see what was going to happen next.

"Now, slow down, Eddie and go through it all again," Mary persuaded him.

"Hello, dear, come and listen to this." She beckoned Ellie to sit down beside her. Seeing her face, Ellie obeyed at once without commenting and poured herself a cup of tea from the large green pot on the table. Whatever had happened, she wondered, looking at her brother, who would not sit down and was pacing the kitchen floor biting his nails and shaking his head. Oh dear, something was very wrong and she started to worry.

"But I've just told you, Mum, why won't you listen to me?" Eddie blurted out.

"Alright dear, calm down. I just want to be sure you've got this right before we contact anybody in authority. That's all."

"What's happened?" Ellie couldn't help herself.

"Start at the beginning, Eddie," coaxed his mother. So Eddie heaved a great sigh of frustration and began again.

"I was on the hill watching and Sargasso flew back from the sea. He came and sat next to me and kept making me look over and over again, right across the water." Eddie knew he couldn't tell his mother that it was the seagull who had told him, because nobody would believe him, but he would tell Ellie later. "Then I saw the whales, two of them, rise up out of the water, like huge black domes. Water spouted first, and then they rolled over and flipped up their tails. It was fantastic."

"Lucky you!" chimed in Ellie, enviously.

"And then I saw it with the binoculars: the periscope of a submarine poking up in the water! I know I saw it. The whales are actually leading the submarines into the river to safety. I reckon they've been lost. But we must tell Dad! We must!" He was frantic and pulled his hands through his hair desperately.

"Yes dear, OK," soothed his mother, wondering what she should do, just in case it wasn't quite what Eddie was convinced of. She didn't want either herself or Peter to look foolish or …ridiculous. It could have been something else floating on the surface of the sea… a branch of a tree, some plastic rubbish… anything.

"Just let me speak to Dad," begged Eddie. "He won't mind, I know he won't!"

"He won't mind, Mum, I'm sure," reinforced Ellie, munching on a flapjack square. Eddie shot her a grateful glance for her support.

"Well, alright," agreed Mary reluctantly and got up to find the number, knowing Eddie would give her no peace. Eddie sat down at last, exhausted. Ellie pushed the plate of flapjacks towards him. He ate two, one after the other, mechanically. It was not to be, however, as all the phone lines were unavailable and Mary was asked to try again when it was not so busy. They were all very disappointed.

"Oh no!" groaned Eddie, running his fingers through his hair again in despair. "What will we do now?"

"Hang on a minute," said Ellie suddenly. "Didn't Dad say he was going to be near Berry Head sometime tonight, patrolling in the Channel?"

"Yes, but we can't get through, Ellie, we've just tried. It doesn't matter how near he is," Mary told her.

"Ah, but... we could signal to him. Go up to the Moonmirror and flash at him. He'd know it was us, wouldn't he, Eddie?"

Eddie sat still, brain racing, trying to think quickly. Would the Moonmirror's light travel that far? Was it charged up enough? He'd need some help – George or Patrick. If he took the Crystal Signaller too, maybe there would be enough charge stored between them. It was worth a try.

"Yes Ellie, I'm sure we could." He jumped up. "That's it. Ring George Mum, and get Patrick too, I'll need them!" and so the three started getting the plan into action. Mary felt quite idiotic trying to imagine what Peter would think if he knew what they were doing.

Eddie went upstairs to get the Signaller. He turned it towards the window and switched it on. A ray of colours shone out through the glass. He quickly turned it off again, but Umbraluna had seen it and was filled with unexpected joy and elation. He'd found the light he had been searching for! He'd got it right! It had been worth the 24,000 mile journey to reach this place. He attached himself to Eddie as his shadow and wouldn't leave his side for a second, he decided.

Ellie phoned George and begged the surprised man to come with Patrick to make the Moonmirror signal.

"I'll tell you about it later. Please hurry! We're going up through the woods. We'll meet you at the top."

"Well, give me a clue," laughed George. "It's a big wrench leaving my fireside and my supper, lass."

"OK... Eddie thinks he's found the submarines. He thinks they're lost and they're following a pair of whales into the Dart estuary!" she told him breathlessly.

"Really?" George was lost for words and didn't quite believe her. "Righty oh, we'll be there," and he rang off at once.

"What's the time?" Eddie looked anxiously at his watch.

"7.15." Ellie told him. "Dad said they would be passing by between 8 and 9 o'clock, so what should we do? Will it work, Eddie? Do you think it will?" She felt unsure now.

"Dad was always pretty impressed with it."

Mary, not knowing what to think, went along with the plans. *If it doesn't work out it won't matter,* she told herself, feeling not quite as confident as Eddie. "Ready?"

She marshalled the troops, and closing the door and venturing into the dark night, they set off, around the now very squelchy and muddy path, up Gallants Bower. Remnants of the snow were evident, shining white, piled up in melting corners and although no longer freezing and icy, it was still chilly. It was a long hard climb at last they completed the steep section and hurried to the huge ash tree overlooking the whole area. They shivered at the windy summit. The elusive Umbraluna clung to Eddie's side, wafting easily up the path. Nobody noticed the persistent shadow in the darkness.

Two figures loomed up towards them. It was George and Patrick, puffing madly and breathing heavily. "Phew! That takes it out of you!" complained George. "Have to sit down for a minute, get my breath back,"

It was a strange feeling standing on the windy hill, surrounded by bare-branched trees and the glinting blackness of the sea. High above them stretched the dark sky and the odd twinkling pinpoint of a star.

Umbraluna sat in the cleft of a tree so that he could see everything. It did not seem unusual to him that this group of people were out in the darkness.

Mary had never seen the Moonmirror working before and was fascinated to watch. Eddie lined all up the main components while George and Patrick put the Crystal Signaller together on the flat ground and then chose a stone on the wall in front of them to secure it on. There was sadly no moon and Eddie began to doubt if the lights would work without it if the charge ran out. After the lights were set up they checked their watches and sat down to wait for the minutes to tick around to 9 o'clock.

They made a very unusual sight, huddled together under the Great Ash Tree in the dark, with the invisible Moonglimmer wrapped around the tree branches above, watching them. Everyone waited.

Chapter Twenty-seven
Vital information for the Navy

As the evening wore on, the crew of HMS *Kirkliston* were alerted by the radar operator, Jim, who noticed four blips on his screen. He looked closely again before asking Captain Scott to verify what he saw.

"About 20 miles sir, that's all," he answered the captain's rapid questions.

"Looks like four contacts, sir, not two. What do you think?"

Several officers gazed at the four unmistakable objects on the screen.

"They're in Start Bay, sir," said the navigator, "we'll be there in three-quarters of an hour. They're moving very slowly, we'll soon catch them up."

Peter and the other crew members soon sent the news around the ship, all becoming tense and excited. What would they find when they reached them?

The Russians were convinced they were being guided home and hoped they could get out of the Channel and into the North Sea without detection. Feeling their speed slow down, they tried to remain calm and patient, leaving the responsibility of their return to Riga to their supposed rescuers. Captain Ranoffski ordered the cook to prepare a really good meal for the crew and then toasted their safe return with a shot of expensive vodka, alone in his cabin.

***

Fortified with hot coffee, the brave group on the hill overlooking the Dart estuary, set to work. Eddie manned the

Moonmirror and George and Patrick the Crystal Signaller. Checking the time again, Eddie took a deep breath as Ellie counted 1, 2, 3, switch on. At once the pale creamy white light shone out from the mirrored surface, illuminating the sea in front of them with a long shining path.

"Good, it's working." Eddie was so relieved. The Crystal Signaller, whose light caught the prism and the magnifier, shot out a rainbow ray, flashing the colours of the spectrum in its brightest possible light.

"It is wonderful!" a surprised Mary exclaimed. "I didn't realise how clever it all is, it's fantastic!" They were all very pleased and proud. Ellie held on to her mother's hand, glad she was with them. Unmbraluna nearly slipped off his branch. The lights, the beautiful lights were here, right in front of him, flashing their incredible brilliance. He looked and looked in an ecstatic daze... It was what he had longed for, dreamed of, watching from the darkness of his planet, never seeing the light. But now he was here! He looked at the components making up their machines but he had never seen anything like them. Nothing existed even vaguely similar in the tunnels of his world, Obscuraluna. They had progressed far beyond these humans.

***

Now several miles closer, HMS *Kirkliston* turned to round Craggy Head, speeding at around twenty-five knots. Peter and two other sailors stood on the deck on watch. He wanted to be there as they sailed through familiar waters, so close to home, thinking about his family safe at the cottage. The men stamped their feet to keep warm and were brought mugs of tea which they drank gratefully. The ship sliced on and on through the black rippled sea as the contacts on the radar screen closed nearer and nearer. Peter scanned the sea with the powerful binoculars but saw nothing. He put them down and finished his tea.

"Chief, take a look at this," suddenly one of the watch keepers said, eyes fixed through his binos and Peter at once raised his to look.

"Odd," he murmured, "very odd. Flashing one white and one... well, not red, not green... a sort of a mixture, can't quite tell. Do you see it, Scouse? Just verify will you? Just in case the tea was too strong!"

"I see it too, Chief, one's a coloured twinkle and one's a white light. Is it code, do you think?" They counted the white flashes but there was no set pattern. Then, just as quickly as it had come, it went. Darkness clamped down and the sky and sea merged into obscurity.

Disaster has struck on the lonely hillside. The Moonmirror and the Crystal Signaller went out.

"Oh, blast, blast!" cursed Eddie, and George and Patrick agreed wholeheartedly. The invisible Moonglimmer was disappointed; he had been enjoying the light show so much. He thought for a moment and concentrated hard. He could feel no energy from the light source and knew at once that the charge supply had failed.

Simple, he told himself, they *have no charging station here.* And he switched on his eyes to half power and shone a bluish beam onto the dimmed lights, one eye directed at each mirror. The children and George were illuminated in a strange light, similar to those kept for nightclubs and discos.

"What's happened?" they asked each other, looking around. "Where is that light coming from?" George and Mary were quite frightened, but the three youngsters thought it was great.

"Look, look! It's powered the Moonmirror again! We can go on signalling!"

"Is anyone there?" called George, thinking somebody was playing a trick on them, perhaps hiding with a powerful flash light, but only a draughty whistle whispered through the trees. Umbraluna turned his lights off as the hefty light-emitting diode charged up Eddie's lights, a hundred times more powerful. He chuckled to himself.

On the ship, Peter and Scouse saw the lights return even brighter. There was no mistaking it. Peter had a strange feeling and it grew inside him and became a conscious thought. Eddie? Could it be Eddie? His Moonmirror and his Crystal Signaller gave exactly that light.

He had chills all over and felt rather shaky. He had told his son on the phone of their intended course and ETA in Start Bay. Something was wrong. It must be.

"Hang on a minute, Scouse, I'm going to see the skipper." He clambered down the hatchway to the wardroom. Convincing Andrew of the strange happenings and getting permission to use the bridge searchlight, he went back on deck. Swinging the big chrome framework around, he directed the beam hopefully towards the river mouth and the cliffs, and switched it on. At once a blinding shaft of light shone out and with the lever on the side, Peter closed and opened the shutters to make them interrupt the beam.

Looking seaward, the amazed group recognised the signalling light. Not understanding Morse code, they were unable to decipher the flashes, which said:

HMS KIRKLISTON ANSWERING. GET TO THE PHONE AND WAIT. DAD.

But nobody knew what it said.

"It's Dad! It's got to be! He's seen us. Look, look Mum! He's answering us!"

"Sure it's not the lighthouse?" said Mary in disbelief.

"No, of course not! Start Bay's right over there to the right, see?" Eddie pointed in exasperation.

"OK, OK, just checking," Mary replied quickly. "What do you think, George?"

"It's Peter I reckon, but you can't speak to him unless you go home to be by a telephone," reasoned George calmly. "So if you have made contact with him and hopefully it *is* him, and not some fishing trawler, maybe we should all go home right now."

"You're right!" burst out Ellie, "Dad will try to phone us. Come on, Mum!"

Eddie and Patrick scrambled about, putting the Moonmirror back in its woodland hide and collecting the other Signaller into its lidded container. Umbraluna watched in amazement.

Looks like we're off again. Disappointed all the lights had gone off, he drifted upwards off the tree branch, where above him, Tolivera had been disturbed.

Visitors in the night? How extraordinary," and the owl got up from his lunch and looked out. He saw five humans, three of which he recognised: Ellie, Eddie and Patrick.

It's them again, what are they doing up in Dark Dwellers' time?" he wondered. He felt a gentle shudder as Umbraluna left the branch, but of course he couldn't see him.

"Strange creatures, humans," he said to himself, and decided to look tomorrow in the Mists of Time to see what they were doing, before going back to his meal of vole chops and primrose sauce, which was one of his favourites.

Everyone hurried down the narrow muddy paths twisting down the steep Bower.

"Can we come too?" begged Patrick, anxious not to miss out on any of the excitement.

"Oh yes, please come back with us." Mary was grateful at the thought of kind old George being there to steady her already quavering nerves.

The three youngsters hurried on with the door key, talking excitedly to each other.

"What was that strange light?" puzzled Patrick, unaware that Umbraluna was steadily tracking alongside them.

"I'm not sure," said Eddie, carefully stepping over roots and boulders on the slippery path. He had a butterfly feeling creeping into his stomach, because he thought he recognised the light, especially the colour, and he really couldn't work out how it was possible. He concentrated on getting down the hill and at last saw the lamppost lights shining their yellowish tinge onto the road. He heaved a sigh of relief and turned to smile at Patrick and Ellie, close behind him.

"Nearly there," he sighed with relief.

Shedding their clothes inside in the welcome warmth of the kitchen, they all sat down to wait for that important sound, the first ring of the telephone. Peter had allowed them three-quarters of an hour to get home from the steep hill. It was about right, by the time they had put the lights away and made rather slow progress in the dark.

Nervous and excited, anxious and uncertain, the unlikely group sat round the old kitchen table discussing the experiences of the evening. Eddie was rather quieter than expected, because he was desperately trying to understand what had happened.

The blue light had charged his Moonmirror, he was now certain of that. It had somehow been up there, beside them or above them… but how could it be? he asked himself, little knowing that Umbraluna was sitting on the draining board beside the sink. Everyone jumped as the phone rang out, so loud and shrill.

"Who's going to answer it?" said Ellie.

"I'll go," Mary told them firmly, getting up from her chair, heart beating and legs wobbling. Umbraluna was curious. What was this device? When he heard Mary speak into it, he laughed his whistly draughty laugh. Couldn't these humans make their voices travel? Hadn't they got an integral personal voice transmitter? Dear, dear, he was surprised. He laughed again.

"The wind's got up," remarked Patrick, "there's a draft coming through the door." He went to check it was closed properly. It was.

In the communications room on board the minehunter Peter had connected the ship-to-shore telephone. He waited nervously as the number began to ring. He heard Mary's the familiar voice.

"Hello? Is that you, Mary? Peter here. What's the problem? It was Eddie, wasn't it, signalling with the Moonmirror?" He tried not to sound too worried.

"Hello, Peter, yes it was, I'm not sure what's going on but I'm so glad you saw the signal. Eddie wants to talk to you, I'll put him on," as Eddie jumped up and rushed to her side. She handed him the receiver, pleased to have spoken to her husband. He sounded so close.

"Hi Dad, you saw the lights then?" and he chuckled, suddenly feeling that what he was about to say was utterly ridiculous and maybe he'd got it all wrong. He hesitated.

"What's happened, Eddie? I hope it's really, really, important," his father said rather sternly, wondering now what his son was going to say .Eddie continued nervously, fingers running in his hair.

"Yes, Dad, I think it might be. The two Russian submarines you've been searching for, I think we've found them. I'm sure they're in Start Bay, being led into the harbour by..." he hesitated, "two whales. You see they're lost and the whales are piloting them in. I saw the whales yesterday quite clearly and behind them, I'm almost positive I saw a submarine periscope. Do you think it's possible?" and he stopped, waiting for his father to take in this unbelievable and impossible information.

Peter thought seriously for a few moments, stunned....It sounded like madness, stuff from boys' magazines, films, and television, but not reality. Surely not! Then he remembered the four blips on the radar screen. Four? Two whales and two subs? They *were* in Start Bay and they *were* on course for the Dart estuary. Maybe, just maybe. It was so fantastic but... Was it really possible?

"How can you be so sure, son? I'll have to inform the Admiralty and the other boats in the squadron; it's too important to delay if it's really true. Can you be certain, Eddie?"

Eddie searched madly for the answer. He couldn't tell his father a seagull had identified them and given him this vital information!

"Can't you follow them in? You'll see the whales... And can't you send a message to the submarines – they've got underwater communications, haven't they?" Eddie persuaded him desperately.

"I'll talk to the skipper and we'll do something, don't worry. I hope you're right, Eddie, because we've been working so hard to find them. I can't tell you how important this is, we've nearly gone to war over this incident you know," he added confidentially. "You've done well, Eddie, to reach me. I've just got to check it all out now. Don't worry, got to go now, love to Ellie and Mum. Bye son, bye!" and he was gone with a click and a crackle.

"He's gone." Eddie was left holding the empty telephone, wondering now what was going to happen.

"Did he believe you?" asked Mary gently, proud of her courageous Eddie.

"I'm not sure, I think so," he replied sitting down, suddenly exhausted. They were all tired. The excitement melted away, nobody said much, and Mary made some hot chocolate, her recipe for all calamities, which they drank, sipping thoughtfully.

"Well, I think we did a grand job and if it is those Ruski subs lost or disabled, you've done a great service to your country, lad," suddenly announced George. "Aye, and we all helped, and proud I was to do it." He slapped the table loudly. "I think we should have a toast. To peace and freedom!" And he stood up.

"To peace and freedom!" they all repeated, standing up and clinking their mugs together.

George knew the consequences of some of these international incidents and in the past some of them had led to war, as history has shown. He could hardly believe what Eddie had discovered.

"Of course, we couldn't have done it without the Moonmirror," said Ellie thoughtfully.

"No, and we three invented it." Eddie looked at Patrick and George who smiled, agreeing.

"It was a joint effort, lad," said George happily, and he beckoned to the sleepy Patrick. "We'd better get off home to bed."

They dressed again and set off home wearily.

"Thanks for helping," called Eddie from the dark doorway.

"Right, bed!" Mary told her children. They went without a fuss and she sat in the kitchen thinking over the extraordinary night and hoped for Eddie's sake that it was the Russian submarines.

Umbraluna wafted upstairs too and landed on Eddie's bedspread. With his acute auditory sensing powers he could hear the dull drone of the submarines and the faint song of the whales. Everything would be alright, he was sure, even though he didn't quite understand what was going on.

Chapter Twenty-eight
Foreign ships in port

The bats living in the bell tower of St Petrox church stirred. Belevedere and Boadicea woke up, their little hearts beating madly. Their two children did not stir, thankfully, so deep were they in winter's hibernating sleep.

"What did you hear?" the bats asked each other carefully, not wishing to alarm the other.

"I think I heard an underwater echo coming from the sea… But it's getting quite close, it's a frequency seldom used." Belevedere was thoughtful.

"I heard it too," agreed Boadicea, "but I know what it was. It was the call of a humpback whale, echoing through the sea to the river. The sound waves carry a long way and they're bouncing off the rocky underwater edges."

"I'm sure my noise was different," said Belevedere. "It was a powerful high-frequency piercing noise. It has made me feel quite strange." He shook his head to get the ringing out of his ears. He could still hear the faint vibrations. "I'm going outside to look," he told his wife. "I might as well, now I'm awake," and he flitted through the vent in the side of the wall of the tower. It was still dark, dawn had not yet arrived.

Other creatures from the Seafarers' world had also detected the strange sounds from the sea coming closer and closer. Sleep was abandoned. Lobsters climbed out of crevices, crabs collected together for comfort, small fishes congregated in a huge shoal for safety and the jellyfish made one mat of floating gelatinous deterrent, impenetrable and protecting them all. Together, as one, they were drawn to the mouth of the river, gathering along the rocky edges, seeking reassurance from the solid faces of timeless rock that had sheltered the river and the town for centuries. Dolphins and deep-sea fish joined the migration to stand firm against the strange forces of the ocean about to invade the coast around Dartmouth. The whole area was becoming congested with hundreds of fish, crustaceans and sea mammals determined to protect their homes. They would fight to the end.

Sargasso, sensing alarm, flew first to the creek, but it was empty. Every creature had abandoned their tranquil territory and was carefully, slowly, inching towards the castle's rocky inclines. He flew in haste to the church tower for a better view where he spotted Belevedere flying unsteadily around, still slightly disorientated by the vibrations he had detected.

The Silver Tinkling Shoals had created such a strong magnetic field around the submarines that when the crew tried to launch a reconnaissance buoy to discover where they were, the signals became distorted and bounced in all the wrong directions, hitting the magnetic barrier, unable to travel.

The radar screen on the minehunter went blank and the four blips disappeared

"Oh no!" groaned Jim, the radar operator. "Power failure, sir."

"We'll wait till dawn," decided the captain. "A few more hours won't make any difference. Get the Electrical Officer up to the bridge at once," he ordered.

By the time Solomon and Bathsheba and the stalwart, tireless whales, Hector and Hercules, reached the shores of Dartmouth, they were already aware of hundreds of other Seafarers congregating around them. Dolphins clicked and chattered to each other, but the magnetic waves emitted from the submarine meant their language was unintelligible. Solomon and Bathsheba couldn't understand what was happening.

"Why are all these Seafarers travelling here? Have they come to meet us?"

Hector and Hercules knew they should go no further than their homes at Sugary Cove, for fear of being trapped in the narrow confines of the river. They watched in amazement as the sea became crowded with all manner of sea creatures, who seemed to be lining up across the river's entrance, blocking their passage into the harbour.

The Silver Tinkling Shoals came to a halt, sensing something was wrong, and slowing the submarines, still enveloped in the strong shroud of powerful magnetism, to a virtual stop

Sargasso and Belvedere, high on the tower of the church, scanned the sea, unable to comprehend what was happening. Their fellow Seafarers were all migrating to the river mouth and lining up, row upon row, like warriors about to commence battle. In a way they were, determined to repel the strange sea monsters. Each had made up his own mind to prevent the invaders entering their territory. They were all intent on the same action, massing together, joining forces.

Sargasso soon realised their intentions. *They are determined the sea monsters shall not come enter the harbour. This is all unnecessary.* He became frightened. What should he do? He could prevent this. He told the anxious Belvedere to go home to his family. There were no monsters, only ships travelling under the water that the humans had made; every echo, wail and vibration was from them. Puzzled, and hardly believing him, the tired and weary Belvedere squeaked his thanks.

"Thank you, Sargasso, see you in the spring. Good luck." And off he flew back to his children and to sleep in the dark and quiet bell tower.

Sargasso flew over the thronging masses congregated between the two ancient castles of Dartmouth and Kingswear and reached the whales and the seals who were unable to proceed, unsure of their next action.

"What's happening?" they asked him anxiously.

"The Seafarers have risen up against the invasion of the sea monsters and are determined to prevent their passage into the harbour. The human ships must stop, they cannot enter the river," advised Sargasso. The Silver Tinkling Shoals were very angry.

"They should not act without the authority of the Spirit of the Sea. We have had our instructions from him. We will not release the black ships from our power. We must lead them to a safe harbour, those were our instructions."

"Then I must speak with him, and ask his advice" decided Sargasso bravely.

"As you wish, wish, wish," tinkled the glinting darting shoal. "You are a chosen one; we will listen, but only to him, to him, to him!"

Sargasso plucked his silvered hermit shell from around his neck and blew into it gently: "We have urgent need of your counsel, Lord of the Ocean, before a disaster befalls us. I speak for Hector and Hercules and the Silver Tinkling Shoals. Guide us, Great Spirit of the Sea."

As he looked up, as far as the eye could see bright scales sparkled, shot with blues and greens, pearly whites and greys, a quiet glistening swirl in the clear cold swell. The cliffs were thick with seabirds perched high above the shiny crustaceans, who were locked together creating a threatening barrier to the river Dart.

Everyone waited for something to happen, and when it did the seabirds with their keen eyesight saw it first. Two dolphins,

Doryana and Diadem, led the Spirit of the Sea. He balanced in a coral basket, shiny and pink, holding the reins of plaited seaweed harnessed to the dolphins. Waves frothed at the speed of the travelling vehicle and a misty rainbow spray surrounded them. The dolphins halted at the small rocky island called Dancing Beggars and the sea became a glassy mirrored flatness.

Silence fell, and the Spirit of the Sea called the Silver Tinkling Shoals to him.

"My brothers and sisters, return to me." And from the sea where they had trapped the submarines, the brilliant dazzling fish shot into the air and arced over the water to surround the coral basket.

"Sargasso, guardian of the sacred shell, where are you?" echoed the voice, and from the cliffs overlooking the castle flew the grey gull, who perched at the foot of the robes of his great master.

"Here I am, my lord."

The imposing figure stroked the seagull's head.

"Tell me the news, Sargasso. You have been troubled and sought my advice once more. I have travelled at great speed to be here. What has happened?"

Sargasso, so nervous in front of the huge numbers of Seafarers, lost his voice and could only croak.

"Speak up, do not be afraid," encouraged the Spirit of the Sea, and Sargasso tried again.

"Sire, the sea monsters are here beyond the Dancing Beggars but I tell you with certainty, humans have crafted them to travel under the water. They were lost and, following your instructions, the whales and the Silver Shoals have led them to safe waters. The Seafarers have gathered together in a great army to defend our shores from invasion. They could hear them echoing in the ocean, travelling slowly towards our river. Please, please, tell the Seafarers to disperse." And the Gull looked up into the kind face of the Ruler of the Oceans, who smiled at him.

"You have excelled yourself Sargasso, but first I wish to see these machines for myself. Come, show me."

Bathsheba and Solomon, waiting close by, swam forward and led the two dolphins to the stranded submarines, accompanied by the seagull. The whales were waiting and at the request of their ruler swam beneath the two submarines, now freed from the magnetic field of the fish. Slowly and carefully they pushed and lifted each one to the surface where their black hulls and twin conning towers were clearly visible. There were loud gasps as the amazed Seafarers looked on, unable to believe that these strange long shapes had been underwater.

The crews inside the submarines felt themselves rise out of the water and were terrified, but Captain Ranoffski calmed them, and seated at the periscope he raised it, hoping to see the shores of snowy Russia in front of his eyes. It was quite a shock to see the green slopes of Kingswear and Dartmouth, and even more of a shock to see the multitude of dolphins and seals surrounding him. He thought he saw an old man riding in a strange boat, but turning the periscope round again for a better look he lost sight of him.

From his misty cloud, the Spirit of the Sea addressed everyone.

"Seafarers all, you may go home in peace but mark these crafts well, for you may hear and see many more in our oceans in future. They will not harm you. For your loyalty and bravery in assembling here today, I honour you all." He held out his arms to thank them.

From the river a cheer went up which echoed all along the banks and the shore. The danger was over and the invasion thwarted. Movement started at once as each sea creature plummeted back into the ocean. The seabirds blackened the sky as their flocks took to the air. Fish churned the water into a raging whirlpool and the lobsters and crabs crawled away to find rocky crevices. They were going home! Peace again.

Hector and Hercules, at a whisper from their great lord, slipped quietly away to the solitary beach of Sugary Cove where they crept slowly up the shingle, tired and thankful their task was completed, sighed and sank to rest, their great heads looking up. Gradually, inch by inch as their blood stopped flowing and their lungs ceased breathing, they turned to black and solid stone once more. One last call of the humpback whale was heard spreading like a rippled echo into the green ocean beyond – their farewell song. Tears sprang into the eyes of the Great Spirit; their devotion to him and their tireless obedience overwhelming him.

"Sleep now my most precious and faithful friends. I salute you. Rest in your quiet solitude. I shall return soon."

With that, he turned his coral basket around and standing up, flicked the seaweed cords that harnessed Doryana and Diadem and he was off, riding through the white froth of a wave top, that had emerged from nowhere, out of a now emptying sea…But not quite empty, because steaming steadily into view came HMS *Kirkliston* with several sailors standing on deck watching for signs of the submarines.

"Submarines surfacing, sir!" called a junior seaman and as they all looked over the sea the black hulls were clearly visible, stationary in the water. The ship soon reached them and fastened a heaving line to each one. *Tengiz* and *Onega* were towed carefully by the squadron of ships which arrived within the hour, into the harbour of Dartmouth, while frantic messages went backward and forward to the Admiralty, MOD, and Number 10, Downing Street.

Captain Scott was immensely proud and delighted that his ship had been the first one to find them. Arriving at the harbour wall, the forward and aft hatches were opened and for the first time for many weeks, the Russian sailors breathed fresh air and were glad to see the world again. Their home base in Riga had been told of their safe arrival in Britain, and the Russian prime minister telephoned his apologies to the English government.

Sitting in the wardroom, waiting for instructions from the admiral, Andrew Scott and Peter had a quiet hour together, going over the incredible events of the last 24 hours. They confirmed the story that had been authorised by their superiors in the Ministry of Defence, which they would release to the press and television crews who would undoubtedly be thronging the small town. They only had a short time before the news broke all over the world. The two men found it hard to believe that it was Peter's family who had discovered the whereabouts of the submarines. Peter was bursting with pride but tried very hard not to show it.

"Now tell me again, how come he saw them and what is this wonderful light of his?" Andrew urged Peter one more time, and Peter did his best to explain.

Meanwhile the Russians were being examined by a naval doctor for any signs of ill health or stress. They seemed a fairly healthy bunch and after a shower, a meal and a good sleep they were very curious to explore Dartmouth. None of them had ever been to England before. After a briefing by the Russian ambassador, who had been flown by helicopter to see them, they were told exactly what to say and exactly what had happened and were given special permission to visit this foreign town.

It was a version of the story and quite removed from the truth. The truth? Only Sargasso and Eddie knew the real truth. The boy and the seagull, their friendship forged all those years ago by an act of kindness on a tiny beach, had sown a small seed of goodness that had grown into greatness and benefited so many people. No one would ever know how important that afternoon had been.

Chapter Twenty-nine
Peter's return

Sargasso returned to the lime kiln exhausted but very satisfied with himself. Waiting anxiously was the little brown robin, who had wondered why the whole creek was so quiet. His black eyes lit up when he was told the unfolding story and he was more and more surprised with every new bit of news.

"So everybody's safe? The two seals, Eddie's dad, the strange black ships, you, me?" Sargasso nodded happily, almost too tired to tell any more, his eyes heavy and wanting to close. The robin's heart filled with happiness and relief.

"Well done, old friend, well done. Perhaps now we can all have a bit of peace and look forward to a happy Christmas, eh?"

The seagull agreed silently, just able to nod his beak and he tucked his head under his wing and slept at once. The robin looked at him gratefully for a few moments and then flew off back to Watermill Cottage. He was excited with the prospect of an interesting day at home. Eddie's dad would surely be back and all his adopted family would be celebrating. The house would be ringing with laughter and voices, lights on, people coming and going and maybe, just maybe, some nice interesting leftovers on his window sill. Lovely! He rejoiced at the happy prospect and winged off home, back to his favourite stone wall.

The cottage was silent, the curtains still drawn, the inhabitants lost in drowsy sleep, warm under the duvets, resting after an exciting and exhausting day and night. The phone rang but nobody heard it; they were all too far away, dreaming pleasantly.

Peter replaced the telephone in disappointment. It had been decided by the 'powers that be' in the Ministry of Defence and the Admiralty that the news they would release would be as follows:

The Russian submarines, due to an equipment failure, had strayed into British waters. After fruitless searching for several days they had discovered the south coast of Devon on their charts and were proceeding towards it when the squadron had spotted them surfacing for reconnaissance. They had been escorted into Dartmouth where the crew would recover for several days and make repairs to their vessels with the able assistance of the Royal Navy.

A very private meeting would take place on board HMS *Kirkliston* between the Admiral of the Fleet, the Minister of Defence and Peter's entire family. There would be a discreet celebration and they would receive a special thank you. It was, of course, too embarrassing for the government to be seen to have been helped out by the children of Watermill Cottage.

Peter was bursting to see them all again. Andrew Scott gave him the day off and sent him home. Peter raced to his cabin, packed a small bag, changed into civilian clothes and was off down the gangway in minutes, pushing through the reporters crowding the quay, saying he was only the captain's steward and knew nothing. Many were gathered from all the papers and television channels, waiting for an interview with Captain Scott.

Peter walked along Dartmouth's embankment where the boats tied up, enjoying the hubbub and the feel of solid ground beneath his feet. He stopped for flowers, chocolates and the newspapers and strode on home through the town to his house, feeling elated and on top of the world. The last ten days seemed like a far off dream. He still puzzled over how Eddie could possibly have known. He was eager to hear every detail.

Patrick got up to the call of his alarm clock and dragged himself out of his warm snug bed. Bridget gave him porridge and toast in the kitchen and he told her all the news of the discovery of the submarines.

"My, my." She was very impressed. "You youngsters, what you get up to is nobody's business. Dartmouth will be busy today then. Better get that café open!"

"I must go round to Waterside and be there for the deliveries," Patrick told her. "Now the snow's gone they'll be bringing all the stuff, won't they? I'd better phone and double-check." And he got himself organised and collected his notebook and pen, yawning occasionally, feeling tired. George was still asleep.

"Ring me if you need any help," he called to Bridget, as he wrapped the long red scarf that Ellie had given him round his neck.

"I will," she promised. "Now, where's that brother of mine? Work is calling!" She went upstairs balancing a cup of tea for George.

Patrick closed the door and walked along the castle road. He peered over the wall and looked towards the town embankment. He could make out the grey outline of several naval vessels.

Maybe it's Peter's ship, he told himself. *I wonder where the submarines are? I can't wait to hear the news.* And he perked up and was suddenly cheerful again. There certainly hadn't been a dull moment since he'd arrived, and with the prospect of the whole spring and summer holidays before him here in this wonderful place he felt truly happy. First, however, he had to do these important tasks for his parents who would soon be phoning and asking questions.

He arrived at the creek just at the same time as Peter reached the bridge on the top road. Recognising each other at once, they both waved. Patrick ran up the old steps to meet him. Peter put his gifts down by the side of the road and embraced Patrick in a huge bear hug.

"I'm so pleased to see you." Peter clapped him on the back.

"How are you?" Patrick broke away, looking a little embarrassed. "Did you find them? Are they safe? Can you come home now? Wasn't the Moonmirror fantastic?" All these questions came jumbling out one after the other.

"Hang on a minute," asked the confused Peter. "How do you know all about this?"

"I was there! So was George! We helped make the signals!" said Patrick quietly and rather shyly.

"You've all been just, well… just amazing." Peter stumbled over his words, so sincerely spoken. "You've no idea what it means all this. No idea." He bit his lips together and said no more as the horrors of what might have happened to them all rushed through his mind for a few seconds.

"Where were you going? Were you coming to our house?" Peter recovered himself quickly.

"No, well I was there last night when you phoned. We were all very late. I've got to wait for some deliveries to the cottage for Mum and Dad because the snow's delayed everything."

"I see. Look Patrick, it's great to see you but I must get on home now." And he picked up his precious presents, and thanking him again, strode on past the old Watermill anxious to glimpse his cottage once more. Patrick watched him go, feeling very alone, and he dawdled back down the steps and up by the creek to the empty white cottage. He sighed, fished in his pocket for the key and gently opened the door. He was very lucky to have such good friends and to share in their lives. Even if they weren't his family, he felt as if they were.

He made several phone calls and the first delivery was scheduled for half an hour. It wasn't long to wait. In the meantime he opened the white French doors from the sitting room where steps went upwards into the steep garden. He decided to explore outside.

***

Peter, reaching his home, saw the windows with their curtains still drawn and understood why his phone call had been unanswered. After his conversation with Patrick he realised they had gone to bed very late. He opened the front door, balancing all his bags on the doorstep and walked into the hall. A copper jug full of bright holly and berries greeted him. Everything was just the same. He felt the comfort and security of his own home wrap around him like a blanket, and he felt himself relax after the awful tensions of the last weeks. Putting his gifts down on the kitchen table, he opened the curtains, unlocked the back door, and stepped outside into the garden. Freddie flew down at once from the wall to greet him and chirruped and sang, hopping around him.

"Hello, little robin, you still here? Wait a minute, I'll get you something nice to eat," and he went back inside and fetched some ginger biscuits which he crumbled onto the window sill. "We won't tell Mary, eh? It'll be our secret," he told Freddie confidentially, watching the pretty little bird peck up the crumbs. He strolled around looking at the wintry garden and then went back inside to prepare a surprise breakfast before waking his beloved family.

Upstairs, Umbraluna listened to the new person moving about downstairs. He could hear everything; the slightest vibration registered in his audio centre. He was very happy in this new place, having found the light source he had wanted to visit for so long. He knew that Eddie was still sleeping, and feeling restless and inquisitive he went to the window where he glimmered through the window frame and wafted out into the daylight. He was off for an adventure, and decided to take the shadow of the first thing that came by, and to go… well, he would wait and see.

Chapter Thirty
The end of a drama

Gradually, the irresistible smell of bacon crept up the stairs and Eddie, Ellie and Mary opened their eyes. Exciting memories of the previous day filtered into all their conscious thoughts. Mary was the first up, smelling the curious cooking aroma coming from downstairs. She hurriedly put on her dressing gown and went to investigate. Peter sat at the kitchen table in his usual chair, reading the paper in a nonchalant way, toast and coffee stacked up beside him.

"Well!" she exclaimed. "Where's my tea?" and they rushed to hug each other. Eddie and Ellie, hearing voices downstairs, not daring to hope that it was Dad, jumped out of bed to find their parents breakfasting together. Mary's roses were already in a jug on the table.

"Dad! I hoped it was you," Ellie squealed happily.

"Who else, my girl?" said Peter, kissing her and putting his arm around Eddie.

"Hi, Dad." He greeted his father in a more restrained and boyish way. "Any bacon sandwiches?"

It was a very happy reunion, munching and talking and telling the amazing stories to each other, while Freddie sat on the windowsill enjoying the ginger nut treats and joining in. The anxieties of the last few days seemed to evaporate away as they listened to the unbelievable outcome of their chance discovery. Peter pushed several newspapers across the table to Eddie. "Have a look at the headlines."

There in bold, black letters was written dramatically:

RUSSIAN SUBMARINES SAFE AT DARTMOUTH

And another one:

ROYAL NAVY FINDS SUBS SAFE AND SOUND

And one more:

RUSSIAN PM APOLOGISES AS MISSING SUBS FOUND

Eddie and Ellie couldn't believe their eyes.

"Really? All because of us?" They were lost for words, open mouthed.

"You should see it down in town, kids! Reporters, TV cameras, the whole place is crammed with news media people."

"I must tell Patrick." Eddie rushed to the phone.

"Hang on a minute, son," Peter said, "I met Patrick on the way home. He was going to wait for some deliveries to the cottage."

"Of course," nodded Eddie.

"Sit down again, Eddie, I've got something really important to say to you both." Peter became very serious all at once. "This incident has been a glimpse for all of us into how quickly events can overtake us and bring us to the brink of war. The Ministry of Defence cannot be seen to have had this vital information from you lot. So your part in this story will have to be kept secret from the papers and TV. However a special and private thank you will be given on board tomorrow night and some very important people will be there. It is a great honour and we are all invited. Patrick, George, Bridget, all of us, but... it *must* be kept a secret.

You do understand that, don't you? You have played a very, very important part in the peaceful outcome of this whole disaster. I am so very proud of you all. I can't tell you how much…" He couldn't carry on, he was choked for words.

They sat together, taking in for perhaps the first time the enormity of the situation. Peter got up and went off into the garden alone.

"OK, kids, showers and get dressed," said Mary brightly," then we'll all go down and see Patrick. Yes?"

"Yes, Mum," said the two bemused children, quiet for once, and went off upstairs whispering to each other.

"Can you believe it? Isn't it thrilling? I'm nervous already. Wait till I tell Patrick, he simply won't believe it either. Do you think we really helped that much?"

They were still unable to quite take it in. Eddie knew that Sargasso had made the whole thing happen; he had found the submarines, it was he who should have the praise.

When they were both dressed Eddie rescued the bacon rinds left over from breakfast.

"These are a treat for Sargasso," he told Ellie.

"Good idea and I must feed poor Freddie. He's been neglected. Let's give him a treat too," and she fetched two ginger nut biscuits from the tin and crumbled them onto the windowsill.

"Can we go and see Patrick now?" Eddie asked, eager to see his friend.

"Please, Mum?" Ellie begged.

"Alright, alright. Anything for a bit of peace," and with that they shot off down by the creek. Freddie followed them to their first stop, the lime kiln. As usual, Sargasso was sitting in the stone cave, resting. Another small gull was beside him and at their approach it squawked and flew off.

"Hello, you clever old thing!" greeted Eddie. "Look what I've got for you." and he dangled the bacon rinds in front of him. Cawing gratefully, the large bird got up awkwardly on his one leg and hopped over to eat them.

"Can you still talk to me?" the boy asked anxiously.

"I'm not supposed to," came the strange reply, making Eddie and Ellie gasp in surprise.

"Oh!" was all they could manage to say.

"I don't know what will happen to me if the Spirit of the Sea finds out," Sargasso added quietly and almost sadly. "I have to get special permission and only in emergencies."

"But nobody will know," said Ellie.

"We won't tell anyone!" assured Eddie.

"Somebody will," said Sargasso.

"But you're special, very special." Eddie stroked his head, looking quickly around.

"Now I'm old I might be given a Decree of All Transcending Language. Only a very few have been given it. It is a great and important honour."

"Well, you deserve it."

"Who's to say?" modestly sighed the gull.

"My dad," replied Eddie at once. "He says we nearly went to war over the Russian submarines. The Navy have been searching for them for two weeks. The Russians thought we'd destroyed them and now, all because of you, they've found them. Surely that's worth the Decree?"

"It was not only me," replied Sargasso patiently. "Hector and Hercules and the Silver Tinkling Shoals were sent to find them. They located them and led them here to Dartmouth, not I."

"Yes, but you recognised them, they thought they were sea monsters or some other creatures from the deep. Only you knew they were human ships, so you deserve the honour for being so clever," Eddie persisted.

"You've been around us so long you know about boats and engines and talking and words." Ellie hadn't heard the full story yet but she was cleverly piecing the bits together.

Sargasso was merely pleased that he had in some way contributed to Eddie's happiness and was glad the whole thing was over. During the exodus of the Seafarers to the mouth of the river Dart he had made the acquaintance of a pretty young gull, who had been separated from her flock from Brixham. She had returned that morning to thank him and they had sat together in the lime kiln sharing their stories. Sargasso had felt very comfortable with her - he had not had time for a Seafarer's family life, so bound up was he in the children's lives. They were older now. Eddie would be fourteen this summer. Maybe it was time to settle down.

"Let's go and see Patrick now," said Ellie, "before Mum and Dad get here. I want to hear everything." And she pulled Eddie away from Sargasso, calling goodbye to him. Reluctantly Eddie did the same and they walked the short distance to the doorway of the white cottage. They knocked on the door, which was opened swiftly by a grinning Patrick, hair sticking up, munching biscuits.

"Hi, you two, feeling strong?" as two delivery men appeared, coming down the stairs, puffing.

"Tea up, mate, is it?" one of them asked Patrick cheekily.

Another white delivery van pulled up, the local supermarket logo painted on the side. A woman looked out of the driver's window.

"Waterside? Got a delivery for you."

Eddie, Ellie and Patrick helped her unload, and what with the furniture and kitchen appliances, plus the arrival of the television man, for the next hour they didn't stop. Finally it was all in and the vans disappeared.

"Right, let's have a look at it all," said Ellie and proceeded to point to places as the boys shifted the various items to her satisfaction, heaving and lifting, pushing and sliding until she was pleased with it all.

"Do you think—" she began, sucking the end of the pen and holding the clipboard, from which she had been ticking the items off.

"No, Ellie, we don't!" shouted the boys. "No more! We're done in." She knew she was beaten and they all collapsed on the brand new sofa for a rest. Eddie told Patrick about the exciting invitation to the ship, even though it was a secret.

"Wow! I'm so excited. Bridget and George will love it. Are you sure he means us too? We didn't do much."

"Course you did! But actually it was Sargasso."

"What?"

"He came flying along that afternoon when you'd gone and told me about the whales, who thought the submarines were sea monsters. Sargasso had tried to find them and when he saw the propellers and the names painted on the sides he knew they were some sort of ship. He's so clever," he said proudly "So, it's really *him* the country has to thank. Incredible isn't it?" Patrick sat quietly, taking it all in.

"He spoke to me once, during the Civil War, but he hasn't done it again until today," said Ellie.

"I wonder why?" asked Patrick thoughtfully.

"He's not allowed to, that's why. Not unless he gets some special decree."

"Well, I hope he gets it now, he's earned it, don't you think?"

"He really has, this time." agreed Eddie.

A knock at the door disturbed them and Ellie rushed to open it. Peter and Mary stood outside. "Come in, look what we've done."

Patrick stood up and welcomed them in. They explored the cottage, admiring everything, happy for him that now he had his own family base in Dartmouth, down at the creek he had come to love.

"Just need a boat and you're all set," laughed Peter. Eddie and Patrick winked at each other.

"We're off the invite George and Bridget to the get-together, we'll see you later. Bye."

So the three were left by themselves to enjoy the new cottage.

Chapter Thirty-one
The Moonglimmer explores

Umbraluna sat on the highest branch of the tallest tree overlooking the estuary, admiring the sparkling sun on a thousand ripples, the brightness of the sky, and the many musical sounds he could hear from the woodland. He couldn't utter any noise at all, merely the echoing soft whistle of the wind. How he would like a voice.

All the creatures in this place seemed to have a sound of their own, especially the humans. He'd like to talk as they did. Equipped with his special auditory centre of advanced technology, he could hear a great deal. He could hear Tolivera busying about inside the tree he was resting on. The old tawny owl had decided to give a party for the Woodlanders and was urgently making preparations. It was to be *the* Christmas event.

Umbraluna could hear him asking the blue tits if they would make a special illuminated string of lights from long trails of bryony berries to adorn his tree for the evening. He heard him ordering the squirrels to prepare him a feast from their winter stores, a carefully chosen menu of chestnut soup, roasted nut rissoles and hot mushroom pies, piles of sautéed pine kernels, and to finish, his favourite rosehip jelly with nectar topping. He was most specific in what they would drink – half a gallon of last year's sloe syrup, elderflower champagne, and of course, plenty of matured Mists of Time from the under root chamber.

The Moonglimmer heard tiny steps approaching in the undergrowth and trained his eyes to see who would appear.

Maudie and Maurice, the two tiny black moles, scurried through the damp grass, their crystal spectacles glinting in the sunlight.

"We're almost there," puffed Maurice, "I can see the Cornucopia tree now."

Maudie had wrapped a tartan shawl around herself as an extra protection. "Let me just sit here for one minute, Maurice, to catch my breath and to look at the lovely view. We see it so seldom, dear."

Maurice agreed, and adjusted his checked trilby hat which had slid over his eyes during the long trudge up the hill. He was watched curiously by the visitor reclining in the branches above.

"We're not late for our appointment, are we?" fussed Maurice.

"No, dear, Doctor told us when the light pierced through the trees above our new burrow, it would be the right time. This week it is just as she said."

"That's alright, then."

Umbraluna listened attentively to the two small black creatures who had sat down, backs against the old stone wall to take in the view on such a cold morning. When they had rested enough they got up to start the short journey to the surgery of the Doctor Unconstumbles. The Moonglimmer followed, intrigued. When they pulled on the long bell-pull rope, it could be heard clonking and clanging somewhere high up in the ivy-clad tree top. The door opened and the light from inside was cast across the ground. It was warm and welcoming, faintly scented with the elusive smell of wild flowers. Up, up, he followed, wafting around the spiral staircase cut into the tree trunk. Umbraluna stared at the exciting assortment of neatly labelled jars and bottles lining the walls – remedies and cure-alls for those suffering from an assortment of maladies.

Not for Maurice and Maudie however; they had come for some new glasses, as moles have a reputation for very poor eyesight, due to living mostly underground in the darkness. The raindrop crystal glasses made a huge difference to their lives. Verity the white dove brought them out to the moles carefully wrapped in moss and tied with a honeysuckle bow.

Umbraluna reset his language de-coding machine and fastened his intense blue twinkle onto the labels so that he could understand them. The images flashed to his receiving centre and the writing all became clear. One in particular interested him:

FULFILMENT OF DREAMS. POTENCY: EXTRA STRONG. *THREE DROPS ONLY.*

The bottles were all rather lovely shades of blue and green, made of ribbed glass, corked firmly.

"Who's there?" suddenly cooed Dr Dew gently. "Tell us, dooooooo." Umbraluna stopped dead in his tracks. She was the first person who had detected his presence since he had landed on planet Earth. How had she done it?

Having completed their visit the two moles wrapped themselves up again and prepared to leave.

"Shall we see you at the Christmas doooooo?" cooed Dr Dew, "Up at the Great Ash Tree with the wonderful view?"

"I hope so!" squealed Maurice. "But it is a long way to go for an evening out."

"Get a lift you two, any passing bird will dooooooo," suggested Dr Dew kindly.

"Toodle-ooooo! And whooooooo are yuooooooo?" she cooed to the space on the stairs just below the elixir shelf where she could sense the presence of the Moonglimmer. She knew he had come for an elixir and was curious to find out more. "Seen something to tempt you?"

He tried to say something in reply but only the haunting whistle of the wind answered. He put out one of his floating arms and jostled the bottle on the shelf he wanted and it rattled, chinking into its neighbour.

"Ah, that one. Only one dose of that is allowed," she explained crisply. "Of course, no one ever needs another prescription. Is that clear to you?" The draughty wind echoed around the stairs again, ghostlike and chilly.

"Will that one dooooooo for youoooooo? Sure? Very well." And off she went to arrange for her assistant to dispense the precious drops. They were distilled from the pink clouds that the sun shines through at dawn which give the hope and promise of a new day.

He followed her curiously further upstairs into the consulting room and saw the other doctor writing in a ledger at a huge desk. A gentle white dove was measuring carefully from the bottle that Dr Dew had lifted from the shelf.

"I need to know your name to write in the special book we keep because you can never have these particular drops again," she repeated, looking over the top of her glasses calmly, but only the slight rush of a subtle breeze sighed through the room.

"Very well, wait here while you take the drops and then you will be able to tell us your name, but think very carefully before you do. This is a once-in-a-lifetime elixir and each drop only lasts one day. Now, we suspect that you are a being from the dark side of the moon, aren't you-oooooo?"

At this the Moonglimmer was frightened and started to rise, seeing the window above him as a means of escape.

"Do not leave us yet, we wish to help youooooooo!" gently cooed the Doctor Underconstumbles together.

"Come," and both pigeons beckoned him to a soft couch covered in an eiderdown of white feathers of incredible downy softness. Cautiously Umbraluna followed and rested on the most comfortable bed imaginable. The white dove was summoned and rose-coloured drops were slowly squeezed out of the long glass dropper and fell like three stars onto the invisible creature that they knew was there; intuition, an acquired gift of many dedicated doctors, the only reassurance they needed of his presence.

"Make your dreams come true," she cooed softly.

The drops' elusive energy ran like engine oil into the complicated and highly technical components unknown to mankind and produced strange pink twinkles as the different levels of electricity met at the junctions. The auditory powers met the new energy of a temporary oratory system. Umbraluna had been given the power of speech and could now communicate with anything and everything on Earth. He could share a conversation with a passing butterfly, a crawling toad, a drifting seagull or a scurrying mouse, and best of all, Eddie, Ellie, and the boy down at the cottage by the waterside. He felt a little dizzy as he lay back on the Cloud of Ease.

"Remember, three days only and your dream will drift and fade. Go and be happy before you return to the moon," smiled Dr Dew, Dr Yew, and their gentle assistant, Verity.

Umbraluna slowly felt a shiver travel through his celestial body and a grey shadowy face appeared on him, just as if someone had shaded it in from a soft lead pencil. It was hardly visible, but there all the same. He had two eyes, a strong nose and a smiling mouth, and the face was that of a man of strong character, quite stern but kindly. The shape of his body was just apparent, and took the likeness of a five pointed star. It was possible to see the central workings of his electrically charged body – a small flat disc with tiny black holes in it. This insignificant thing was the hub of his mind, the power of the incredible light and the core of all his actions. His thoughts whizzed through connections of various colours and the central disc of control took over. He was recognised by the learned doctors as a simple form of Moonglimmer from the dark side of the moon; never seen here before, but written of in their dusty ledgers of Astronomy and Alternative Life Forces.

"How exciting! Can it be trueooooooo?" They clapped their wing tips together and marvelled at their visitor from far outer space. Umbraluna blinked his new eyes to try them out. So much more advanced than the electrical sockets he'd had before with the strong blue glimmer glass in them. To try out his new mouth, he twisted it all around. It felt strange.

"Say helloooooo," encouraged the two pigeons. "Try, doooooo!"

Slowly at first, whispering softly, then louder, Umbraluna tried his first words.

"Hello! My name is Umbraluna and I have come from the dark side of the moon." The words came out quite well but all in the same breathless tone, gradually getting louder.

"We know, we know," the birds told him excitedly. "Now sit up, you're nearly ready to goooooo!"

Feeling quite himself again he got off the feather bed.

"Thank you, thank you. I know I have only three days, I shall not waste them," he told them with growing confidence.

"Whatever you shadow, you will assume their voice, no matter who or what it is," the doctors reminded him. "You will hear many strange things. Come back and tell us and we will learn what is true-oooooo. But be back before the sun dries the dew on the third sunrise. Toodle-oooooo!"

Umbraluna's face and central operating disc disappeared and they felt a slight draft as he wafted out of the room and down the stairs. He didn't wish to be anyone else in particular, merely to have the power of conversation. He enjoyed shadowing because in his way he became those things, just for a while. As he left the Cornucopia tree a large brown mottled bird, wings outspread, passed over his head.

Here goes, thought the Moonglimmer, and launched himself upwards to follow the shadow of the bird. It was the Lord of the Woodland, the buzzard. He and his new shadow circled the trees in slow motion and then, gliding out across the sea, spiralled upwards in gentle arches, drifting higher and higher on the wind currents, and then gracefully and gradually returned to the land in the same way; down, down, to perch on a dead tree on the edge of the old earthworks. Spying a small grey mouse about its business in the tufty grass, the buzzard blinked. There were too many mice around now, they needed to be reduced in numbers. The odd one wouldn't be missed. He launched himself off the branch with both talons outstretched, his powerful legs pushing him up into the air. Umbraluna was forced to follow, horrified, realising the mouse was facing instant death.

Just as the sharp talons were about to encircle the tiny body, the Moonglimmer shouted out, "No, no, no!" and he pulled away, forcing the buzzard to follow him, their roles reversed, the shadow leading the bird across the grassy heath. The buzzard didn't understand what was happening to him, as the shadow of himself drew him back to the tall pines of the Citadel.

He heard a bird's voice calling to him,

"You must not kill these earth creatures; they have done you no harm." He was alarmed and frightened; it was his own voice he could hear. Umbraluna detached himself from the buzzard, not wishing to follow him any longer, and he left the perturbed Lord of the Woodland to ponder on what had happened.

Upset by the unprovoked attack on the mouse the invisible creature sat quietly to recover. He bathed himself in the warmth of the sun and admired its brilliant light. *Perhaps it will charge up my power centre*, he thought, but very soon he realised that the light of the sun was too powerful and would blow his connections to pieces. He was used to the gentler power of the moon and hoped he had enough energy to last the three days still to go. He had made up his mind to return home then, as the two wise doctors had suggested to him.

A small bee buzzed by, drawn out by the warm sun even though it was still the depths of winter. It was tiny and fascinating.

Why not? thought Umbraluna, and he followed the bee, turning into a small speck as its shadow, zigzagging over the woodland to the gardens of several large houses situated on the top of the hill. Nestled against the wall were some beautiful winter flowers; winter honeysuckle, witch hazel and delicate blue irises stood poised and beautiful against the dreary, dull, brown garden.

How lovely they are, thought the Moonglimmer as the bee touched down on each one. Umbraluna followed the bee's weaving and twisting journey until he found himself squeezing through the white-painted slats of an old-fashioned beehive situated in a quiet corner. Inside were many compartments. Sleeping grubs, fat and creamy, lay together in little rows. Large sheets of sticky clear honey stood untouched in their waxy hexagonal slots. Bees of various sizes were tucked into corners and crevices, sleeping, some snoring loudly.

"Welcome back, your Majesty," greeted a small brown bee, bringing a tiny cup and plate over at once. "Did you have a good flight today? Seems quite nice out there?"

"Yes, Gervaise, I did, thank you." The queen sighed and settled down on her yellow velvety throne, carved out of wax. She sipped the bee tea and ate the small blossom cakes daintily.

"Could I have one, please?" asked the voice of Umbraluna, sounding exactly like the queen bee.

"Of course your Majesty, I'll get another," replied Gervaise, the queen's personal servant, who was suddenly just a little puzzled.

The queen sighed loudly. "How boring I find the long winter. I long for the sunny flower-filled days of summer. I hate this garden now, I want to move again," she buzzed petulantly.

"Do you?" came the voice again.

"Who's that?" asked the queen, looking around angrily.

"I am Umbraluna, from the dark side of the moon," he buzzed, and began to appear, his face becoming clearer and clearer.

"What exactly are you doing here?" the bee asked curiously.

"I have come to visit your world for a while. I was drawn by its bright lights and colour. You see, my home is dark and grey with no beauty. You are so very lucky to live amongst the flowers." The queen bee felt a stab of guilt.

"Yes, but its winter now and the flowers are so few."

Gervaise appeared holding another cup and a plateful of blossom cakes. He noticed the star-shaped person with the face but said nothing, and went quietly away.

"Eat and drink, then I will show you a special place that I visit on the darkest days of winter to cheer myself up," the queen told him. Tasting the delicious cakes and sipping the floral honeyed tea, Umbraluna discovered the pleasures of eating and understood why humans spend so much time sitting together enjoying the delights of food.

The queen waited impatiently; she was anxious to be off out again. Licking his new lips to collect any stray crumbs the small grey shadow hurried after the queen, following her closely out of the beehive and into a walled garden where there were several glasshouses. The bee slotted into a ventilation window and was followed by her shadow into the humid perfumed heaven.

Exotic plants towered to the roof, butterflies fluttered excitedly and small jewelled hummingbirds beat their wings frantically as they extracted nectar from some trumpet-shaped flowers with their long thin beaks. Jasmines and orchids, heady climbers and tropical creepers competed for space.

"Well?" the queen bee asked the small grey shadow, "Is this colourful enough for you?" and she laughed in her buzzing way. It was all fascinating to the creature used to dust and boulders and he was utterly delighted with the exotic tropical hothouse. Huge banana plants, ginger lilies and hanging bulbous fruits mingled with vanilla pods, frangipani flowers and morning glory. The bee and her shadow stayed for a while watching the butterflies and the humming birds until the queen eventually became bored and wanted to go home.

"I've had a wonderful time, thank you," buzzed Umbraluna. "I'll try and remember this when I'm back home in the dark shadows." The queen bee felt guilty for complaining. In future she was going to try to appreciate the beautiful places she could visit whenever she wanted.

"Goodbye, Umbraluna," she buzzed sweetly.

"I won't ever forget the taste of your blossom cakes," he told her wistfully, and returned at once to his own invisible body. She flew off in the direction of her beehive and vanished.

I'm going back to find those other little black furry creatures with the special eyes, Umbraluna decided, and wafted off to locate them, wherever they lived.

Chapter Thirty-two
A hero's welcome

The great day arrived. Bridget, George, Mary, Peter and the three excited young people all met up at the Castle Hotel in the middle of town. They were dressed to impress and admired each other resplendent in clean ironed shirts, pressed trousers, polished shoes, pretty dresses and beautifully washed and curled hair.

"Ready?" Peter asked nervously, smoothing his uniform and adjusting his tie.

"I reckon we are," replied George, shiny and red-faced, smelling of Old Joe's cologne. They trooped out and headed for the main embankment where a small dark-blue launch was waiting for them by the steps. Ellie got the giggles when she saw the smart young sailors waiting to help them into the boat and eventually, all seated, they were expertly ferried across the river to the waiting naval ship moored in the centre of the river.

The Minister of Defence and the Admiral of the Fleet had arrived by car and had been piped onboard one hour before the family were due. It was a great honour for the small ship and Andrew Scott and his wife Lydia had been very nervous indeed. They were now all chatting away merrily with glasses of champagne as the guests of honour arrived.

Shyly they all fell behind Peter and Mary in a line, embarrassed and wondering what they were going to say. Eddie, Ellie and Patrick raised their eyes at each other as a signal, knowing that there was no escape. Eventually their turn came as they moved up the reception line and shook hands with the Minister of Defence, Vincent Naples, and the Admiral of the Fleet, Lord James Beverley. Praise was heaped upon them and glasses were filled and the three youngsters drank champagne mixed with fruit juice as a special treat, at Lord Beverley's insistence.

"Once in a lifetime, m'dear, only happens once," he persuaded Mary, who gave in immediately, not daring to argue. They sat down to a private lunch in the wardroom. The eleven of them just squeezed in and ate smoked salmon, roast venison and French fruit pastries, cheese, coffee and several plates of chocolate mints, which the children demolished heartily.

After lunch, Vincent Naples stood up and thanked the three heroes personally by awarding them each a special medal for bravery and endeavour with a purple and red ribbon on it.

"You have served your country well," he told them, "and we are all very proud of you. We are only sorry that you will not receive the publicity you deserve, due to the delicate nature of the circumstances. You understand I'm sure."

Peter had already explained over coffee that morning that for political reasons the government had to hush the whole thing up.

"Now tell me," he smiled at Eddie and Ellie, "all about the Moonmirror, I am fascinated to hear." And he sat and listened as everyone chipped in here and there, interrupting each other as gradually its invention was revealed.

"I'd love to see it sometime," he told them when at last the story ended.

"Then you shall, sir!" Peter told him triumphantly, looking at Eddie. The admiral sighed. "I'm afraid I'm leaving shortly." He glanced at his watch as his personal assistant, coughing politely, put his head around the wardroom door.

"Sorry to interrupt, sir, launch will be here in ten minutes."

"Very good, Dobson, I shall keep you to your promise, young Eddie, I shall be back in the West Country sometime soon on a private holiday and I might just pay you a call. Would that be alright, Mary?" he asked charmingly.

"I'm quite sure it would, sir." She was blushing at the very thought of it. The minister and the admiral wished them a very happy Christmas and said their goodbyes and then went with Captain Scott into his cabin for a final word in private .They were visiting the Russian captain, Grigor Ranoffski, next for a very short diplomatic call, with an interpreter. The Russian crew were fully recovered and enjoying the freedom of Dartmouth town; they marvelled at the shops with shelves full of food, electrical goods, clothes and luxuries they never saw and admired the standard of living the British people enjoyed. Russian shops were not so well stocked and often the people had to queue to collect a few basics. The sailors spent all their money on presents to take home and were experiencing hospitality and kindness from the good people of Dartmouth, who were anxious to welcome them. In fact the whole episode had turned out well for international relations and the patience of the British Navy had been rewarded by good press all around the world. Everyone was thankful there had been a happy ending to the unfortunate incident.

At last the guests were ready to go home after visiting the engine room, the galley, the ship's bridge and the communications room, hardly believing at the small space and compactness of life on board.

"There's not much room, is there?" remarked Ellie. "Everything is so small."

"You'll never make a sailor!" laughed Peter, patting her head.

"No, Ellie's going to be an Olympic bobsleigh champion aren't you?" laughed Patrick, and Eddie joined him in hearty chuckles.

"Don't be so mean!" Ellie replied angrily, and then remembering her icy plunge, laughed too. They were helped onto the launch again and ferried back to the quayside where they hailed taxis and went back to George and Bridget's house for a party to celebrate properly. Peter was now on extended leave and happiness spilled over – they were all together again.

As darkness crept into the riverside house, the telephone's shrill tones pierced the air and George ambled cheerfully over to answer it. His face gave away his surprise as he listened to the voice at the other end. All the others, sitting comfortably on the squashy sofas, watched with interest.

"Yes, yes of course. We'll see you soon then. Cheerio." and he put the phone down with a click.

"Well, well! We are having a day aren't we?" He smiled an interesting sort of meaningful smile, almost to himself.

"Come on George, tell us!" begged Bridget, "You are a tease!"

George looked at Patrick and said, "Your parents are on the way, just this side of Exeter. I hope you've got that cottage into some sort of shape or you'll be for it, my lad."

"Why, it's practically perfect!" Ellie answered indignantly. "We've worked very hard to make it look nice." She seemed rather downcast all of a sudden.

"It is lovely," agreed Mary, "Sam and Irene will love it, I'm sure."

"If they don't, they can change everything again, can't they?" added Peter, wondering what all the fuss was about.

"Better get them a bite to eat," said Bridget, getting up and heading for the kitchen. Mary and Ellie followed soon afterwards.

"Hmm, what is the best thing to tell them?" Patrick asked Peter, "Because they don't know anything about today, or the Moonmirror or the submarines."

"I expect they've read about it in the papers, surely." Peter replied, thinking for a few moments.

"We'll say nothing, nothing at all. This little party is because I'm home on leave again. Keep your medal safe and well hidden. I really do think it's for the best. I'm sure your parents would be so proud that they couldn't resist telling just *somebody* and that's how these things get around. Are we agreed?"

The two men and the boys did all agree: the excitement was all over, but the praise and thanks they had received would stay with them forever; a very special secret. The publicity would soon die down and it was best forgotten. None of them were looking for glory, they were just happy to have helped.

Out in the kitchen Bridget put together some dainty savoury fingers of sardines on toast and a small tossed salad with olives and parmesan cheese, baby tomatoes and parsley. She arranged everything on a tray and left the toast in a very slow oven.

"There!" she said with satisfaction, wiping her hands. "That should do for a snack."

Ellie was rather disappointed that Patrick's parents were arriving. She had enjoyed having the run of the cottage and making it look cosy, sharing the organisation with Patrick, and now it was all over. She couldn't quite understand why she felt that way, it was very odd, in fact she felt quite cross, and went back to join Eddie and Patrick.

"I suppose we'd better be heading home," sighed Peter from the comfort of the sofa, not really wishing to move.

"OK, Dad," agreed Eddie hoping to avoid Irene, to whom he felt a social and academic failure.

"Yes, let's go," also chimed in Ellie, who didn't want to share Patrick with anyone outside this house. Reluctantly George got up and fetched their coats.

"Ready, Mary?" asked Peter.

"It was a wonderful day, I shall tuck it away in my memory box forever," beamed George. "I felt right proud I can tell you."

Patrick stood back quietly waiting. For him, the magical spell of the day was now broken, and he'd have to face the questioning of his parents whose arrival was now imminent. He felt suddenly anxious – would they be pleased with everything? It was impossible to tell. The two men shook hands and out of the front door stepped the family, from the warmth and brightness into the cold and dark of the night.

"Goodbye!" called Bridget and George.

"See you tomorrow," was Patrick's hopeful farewell and then they were gone, disappearing up the path into the shadows of the trees. An owl hooted not far away.

"Well, that really was a day to remember, wasn't it?" Peter said as they walked along the river's edge, trying to get used to the darkness.

"Do you think they'll go to the cottage tonight?" asked Ellie, holding her father's arm.

"Not for one minute. They're happy to let Bridget run around after them. I'd bet my last penny on it!"

Mary laughed too, rather agreeing with her husband's perceptive remark.

"Right, we've got a lot to do now, it's nearly Christmas and we've no tree, no lights, no turkey and no presents. Better get cracking tomorrow," announced Peter, "or shall we cancel the whole thing for this year?"

"You dare!" squealed Ellie happily, squeezing his arm.

Eddie was quiet, thinking about Sargasso, his long standing friend, and of how he had saved them all from the threat of war. It had happened once before in history when geese had saved the city of Troy from attack by raising the alarm when they heard approaching soldiers. Eddie smiled to himself in satisfaction. Yes, Sargasso was the real hero – what a pity nobody knew it.

Chapter Thirty-three
The Moonglimmer makes some woodland friends

That night not far away, behind Waterside Cottage, Umbraluna had located the moles in their underground burrow of interconnecting tunnels, their tiny scrabblings and earthmovings detected by him. He entered their underground world through a mound of earth, seeping invisibly between the crumbles of soil. In the tunnels he was forced to switch his eyes on; it was like being back home on the moon, everything was dark and colourless. He felt anxious. Maybe this was a mistake?

Travelling along the tunnel he suddenly found himself in a small sitting room which had opened out from the narrow darkness. It was dimly lit with pine cone lights in holders around the walls. Two little figures sat beside the fire in red-checked armchairs, one quietly reading and the other asleep. A clock on the wall ticked rhythmically, made from odd-shaped pieces of wood, its pendulum a snail shell. The clock's face was rather strange. It was a saucepan lid with a knife and fork for hands. The scented smoke from the fire went up into a long pipe and disappeared up the dried hollow stem of a hollyhock plant and emerged out in the overgrown garden at Waterside.

Looking round the room Umbraluna noticed tucked in the corner were two neat beds covered in patchwork quilts, made from small squares cut from flower petals and stitched together with a thick black thread, unravelled from the twists of a poison ivy. The little underground cottage was sparse but all easily packed into a small cart for removals, because the moles moved often. Their home was liable to flooding, subsidence, and human investigation, which meant they had to pack up and go at a moment's notice. The moles were used to their itinerant lifestyle, but it did cause Maurice a certain amount of stress and worry.

He was a keen observer of the weather, always checking for rain storms or hot dry spells. He had hung a piece of seaweed outside on the makeshift bark door of their entrance, checking it every day, and also fastened a sycamore key to the chimney to keep an eye on the wind, spinning like the blades of a helicopter in the breeze. Their adopted garden was steep and wild, joining the woodland in an overgrown tangle. Uninhabited when they arrived, their chimney and windmill lay undiscovered as yet.

Inside, the Moonglimmer was fascinated. These little creatures had the same sort of comforts at home as the human family he had attached himself to – chairs, a table, lights, beds, all in miniature.

I could have a home like this in one of my link tunnels he thought, happy at the idea. A rustle and a sound of falling earth were heard above him in the damp earth of the roof and a small pink tail dropped into sight.

"Quick, here's another one!" shouted one of the moles and in a flash they were up and both hauling on the pink wriggling thing, yanking it into the room below, gripping fiercely to the poor unfortunate worm they had caught.

"Nice fat one!" they both agreed, dragging it breathlessly through a door marked LARDER and slamming it quickly behind them.

"Good heavens, you're not going to eat that, are you?" asked Umbraluna, in his mole voice, unable to keep quiet any longer.

"Who's there?" "Who said that?" the moles both asked in alarm.

"It's only me." And the shadow began to show himself, faintly grey at first, and then his face appeared in the centre of the star shape. The moles didn't know what to make of him and stood transfixed in amazement.

"I have you to thank for my voice," said Umbraluna. "I am a visitor from the dark side of the moon, a place we call Obscuraluna. I came to seek the bright light shining from the house by the woods and I followed you to the Cornucopia tree. It was there I saw the elixirs that the two pigeons have to offer, and now because of you I have fulfilled my dream. I have two days left to talk to the creatures here on planet Earth. Let me thank you and please let me talk to you. Don't be afraid, I shall not harm you," he pleaded.

The moles said nothing, just peered at him through their crystal raindrop glasses in an interested sort of way. The Moonglimmer continued, trying to make them less frightened.

"We do not eat or drink on my planet and have no light or colour, no trees or flowers, no water or bees; this place is all so interesting and full of brightness."

They said nothing, just continued to stare at him. In the background, sobbing could be heard coming from the door marked LARDER. The silence became awkward and uncomfortable.

"But, we like it in the darkness. It's so peaceful and quiet and we have no neighbours to disturb us. We don't like bright colours and noisy places; black is our chosen colour for our clothes, it… it doesn't show the dirt," burst out Maudie bravely.

"Not everyone wants to be cheerful and be seen all the time; we like to go about our business under the ground unnoticed, and… we like to be dull." Maurice told him.

This was certainly a different view of life that Umbraluna hadn't considered, and he found it strange they could turn their back on all the glories to be admired above ground.

227

"What will you do with that long pink wriggling creature in the larder?" he asked, hearing again the sad snuffling of the tearful captive worm.

"We'll chop him up and eat him for dinner!" said Maurice with satisfaction, whiskers twitching at the very thought.

"Oh."

The Moonglimmer didn't know what else to say. It seemed rather cruel to him. The moles seemed so quiet and gentle and a peaceful sort of couple, who worked tirelessly digging tunnels all day, then ate their meals, read their few books, and quietly went to bed. Rather a dull life it seemed to Umbraluna. However he did envy them their cosy little home which seemed to be everything he would like.

"But I could never get any of this sort of thing where I live." He spoke his thoughts out loud, rather sadly.

"If you like the light, why don't you move round to the bright side of the moon?" asked Maudie inquisitively. "We're always moving, aren't we Maurice?"

"Yes, my dear, we are. Sometimes of course we don't want to, circumstances, you know, but I'd quite like to move up to the top of the Bower one day – think of all those new tunnels and hills we could make. We're actually running out of space down here. Too many humans, you know. They get everywhere now," he told Umbraluna.

"What do you do?" he asked suddenly, wondering what on earth somebody from the other side of the moon did.

"Do? Do?" replied the Moonglimmer, "I don't think I do anything. Should I?"

"Of course, everybody does something don't they, Maudie?"

"I'm quite sure of it," she replied. "Why, how else would you pass the day?"

Just at that moment a black spider emerged from a corner and began frantically spinning a large web.

"About time, Lucinda," scolded Maudie, "I've been waiting for you to hang my washing up." She fetched the tablecloth, the two napkins and two pairs of silk pyjamas she had washed that morning.

"You see?" said Maurice politely to the grey face, "She spins webs all day and all night for people's washing. She's so busy she hardly has a minute to herself." And as he watched fascinated, the spider ran around in circles, creating a marvellous web. Maudie at once hung up her washing on it and the spider scuttled off to her next customer. Umbraluna felt rather useless. What did he do?

"I can glimmer," he said hopefully.

"Really?" replied the moles. "Show us." He switched his eyes onto their brightest blue twinkle, and wafted up through the roof, vanishing for a moment, and then returned again to land beside them.

"You can become invisible when you want to, and make that bright blue light?"

"Yes," replied Umbraluna.

"Well that's doing something, isn't it, Maudie?"

"It is, and it's very useful I'm sure."

"Shall we have supper now, my dear?" asked Maurice, looking forward to eating the fat worm that was making a noise in the larder. At this Umbraluna decided to leave before he received an invitation to stay and join them.

"I hope to see you before I go," he told them, getting up quickly. "And, I do like your house," he added wistfully.

"If we move again you'll be the first to know," Maudie told him kindly. Umbraluna wafted off down one of the dark tunnels, the moles waving him goodbye as the spider frantically rushed past him on her busy way.

Tired and having spent a great deal of the day and night talking, Umbraluna wafted up out of the ground and along the woodland path towards Watermill Cottage.

Between the trees he caught sight of the partial circle of the moon. It was a glorious bright white light, and he felt a little surge of electricity glow over him. Perhaps Maudie was right, he should move round to the bright side and then he could look down onto the planet Earth, and twinkle at all his new friends.

He returned to the cottage, to the upper bedroom window that faced the trees, and glancing at the moon's three-quarter face, he slid inside the window frame and found himself a warm spot between Eddie's feet. Reflecting on his interesting day, he realised he had encountered yet again creatures wishing to kill and eat each other. It seemed to be so common here on Earth. Did they all eat somebody else? With this question unanswered but still worrying him, he gently fell off to sleep like Eddie, the boy he had come to Earth to talk to.

***

During the night a warm front of rain moved in from the west, and tried to push the cold air away. This had settled over the British Isles and had brought the frost, snow and freezing weather they had experienced for a while. Where the warm and cold air met and collided, a huge swirling storm was created, with strong winds and powerful forces at odds; hailstones, thunder, lightning and crashing gusts of fierce energy suddenly and terrifyingly lashed the south coast. Trees fell over like matchsticks in the path of the ferocious weather, telephone lines and electricity conductors toppled and swayed, the sea beat onto the shore, the waters tossed this way and that in the wild gales. Eventually huge cracks of thunder and swords of lightening woke the sleeping family. Ellie was frightened and crept into her parents' room.

"Mum? What's happening? I don't like it," she whispered in the dark.

Her parents woke immediately and Peter turned on the bedside light, only to find that it didn't work.

"Power cut. Must be the storm. Don't worry, Ellie, I'll get a torch and some candles from downstairs," and he got out of bed and gave her a quick hug. "You'll be alright, sit on the bed next to Mum until I come back."

Ellie shivered, she had never liked thunder and this was so loud and sounded so close it was just as if the roof was cracking open. Mary wrapped her in a dressing gown and together they listened to the rain battering on the window panes.

"It's a bad night now. I hope Irene and Sam arrived alright," and she yawned. Peter came back carrying his torch and some saucers, night lights and matches.

"Put these in some water on a saucer for safety, here you are, put them beside the bed, they'll look quite pretty, Ellie" he told her reassuringly. "The storm will be over soon. Don't be frightened you silly thing."

Ellie lit the nightlights, got some water from the bathroom, and set them on the saucers as she had been told. They gave a flickering soft light that made patterns on the ceiling and walls. Ellie loved them and jumped straight back into bed to watch them make their soothing shadows.

"OK, Ellie?" her mother called.

"Yes, fine thanks," she replied, snuggling down under her duvet. Then it was Eddie's turn to be woken up, as the south-westerly wind came roaring through the trees behind the house, snapping off a branch of the ash tree and toppling over several spindly rotten sycamores. The rain sheeted down the window pane, making a pattering noise on the glass.

Eddie opened his eyes to see the bright glare and flash of lightning through the curtains. He was still half asleep, and it made his heart beat very fast, not quite knowing what was happening. He heard the rush of the wind and the beat of the rain and saw yet another flash so bright that it startled him and made him jump. He was awake now, and pushing the warm covers aside, he got out of bed and padded over to the window, pulling the curtains open to see what was happening .Umbraluna waited as Eddie peered out into the darkness. He too was awake.

"Quite a storm," Eddie muttered to himself, leaning forward to look out. "Couple of trees must have blown over." He yawned and then shivered, pulling his dressing gown around him. He was cold and rubbed his hair.

"Better get back to bed," he told himself and tried to switch his bedside light on.Nothing.

"Blast! Power's off and I was going to read my fishing book for five minutes."

"I can help you with that," said a voice. Eddie stood very still. What had he heard? Umbraluna turned his blue lights on, very faintly at first. Eddie's heart beat fast as he watched it. What was that he could see? It seemed to be coming from the bedclothes. Gradually the light increased and then it slipped off the bed and made the shape of his shadow on the floor, outlined in blue. Eddie took a step and so did the shadow. He put his hand up to his mouth and the blue figure copied. The room was lit quite clearly by the strange blue brightness.

"Do not be frightened of me," said a voice exactly like Eddie's voice. It was as if he was talking to himself.

"I am Umbraluna. I have travelled from the dark side of the moon to visit you. You brought me here with your moon-coloured light and bright sparkles. I have been here on Earth for a little while to fulfil my dreams. I have only two days left and then I must return to my home."

Hearing his own voice, Eddie was confused and a bit frightened. He looked at the shadow of himself and slowly a grey face with eyes and a mouth were visible. Umbraluna continued, trying to reassure the boy further.

"For the next two days, whoever I shadow, I can assume their shape and voice; so now I want to be part of you."

Eddie's eyes opened just a little wider, and he remained silent.

"I know of your beautiful Moonmirror that brought me here. I have been watching you and your sister and your friend; I have learnt much about the Earth."

Eddie finally understood, although he could hardly believe it. This was the blue twinkle that had beamed at him, the bright light that had answered him, the same one that had broken his window, right here in his bedroom. Was it possible? He felt very excited.

I must get Ellie, she's got to see this! he thought.

"Wait a minute!" he told the shadow on the floor and went to open the door but the shadow followed. Eddie smiled, amused, and tiptoed across the landing to Ellie's door and opened it, seeing at once the flicker of the nightlights burning in the saucer. She had fallen asleep again.

"Ellie!" he whispered urgently. "Ellie!" and he saw his shadow on the floor.

"Can't you turn that light off for a minute? I don't want to frighten Ellie." Umbraluna obliged, fading gently back to a dim glow.

Ellie opened her eyes.

"Eddie? What is it?" She sat up, confused.

"Get out of bed and come with me," he whispered, pulling a throw off the chair. She wrapped the pink checked blanket around her and looking puzzled, got out of bed and followed Eddie back to his room. She could only just see.

"What's wrong?"

"Look," he said gently, guiding her towards his rocking chair. "We've got a visitor."

And as he pointed to the floor, Umbraluna obliged and turned up the light beam to reveal his shadow outlined in bluish light; it was a shadow of Eddie.

"A shadow!" she exclaimed.

"Yes! And it talks!"

Ellie looked horrified, watching as Eddie took a few steps across the room and the shadow followed. She could see the grey face now and the face wore a smile. It turned and spoke to her.

"I am Umbraluna from the dark side of the moon."

"But it's your voice!" Ellie gasped, trying to understand.

"Yes it is. Everything I shadow, I can take their shape and voice. I have been granted three days to communicate with the creatures of this planet. I came to see your Moonmirror light that beckoned me from my land of darkness. I have a strong beam of my own; it is greater than anything you have here on Earth. I have used it once to help you – to shine your light when there was no charge."

Eddie listened and remembered that day on the hilltop when he felt sure the Moonmirror would not work. "Was it you?" he asked, as the reality of it sank in.

"I have followed you many times and observed your earthly lives, but only now have I obtained the power of speech. I took three drops of a special elixir, the Fulfilment of Dreams. I mean to use it well. I have seen the colours and sights of many things, but am here now to make you my friends and to talk together. I have not found a suitable charging station and therefore I must not stay too long, for how would I return?"

Eddie wasn't listening. He was still thinking about the Moonmirror and how it had lost its charge that day, just when he wanted so badly to signal to his father on the ship. This strange thing had powered the signal; which meant that the discovery of the submarines had really been a joint effort between this Umbra thing and Sargasso. How long had he been here? Silently shadowing them, listening and watching?

Ellie sat quietly on the chair. It was hard to know what to make of it, but of course she had not seen the blue flashing beams from far away, answering to the hypnotic light of the Moonmirror.

Umbraluna decided to have some fun and switched suddenly from Eddie to Ellie, copying her every action as she sat in the chair.

"How do you like me now?" he asked her, only this time it was Ellie's voice. The two children laughed in delight and Ellie got up and did several twirls. The Moonglimmer copied her.

"Satisfied?" Eddie was enjoying himself now.

"What do you look like when you are not being a shadow?" she wanted to know.

"Like this." He shrank back from being a shadow to his usual star-shaped self. Due to the elixir he had a face and a mouth to speak with, and could be seen.

"I am a Moonglimmer; we live in the darkness of the unlit side of the moon, in a land called Obscuraluna. It is cold and grey and barren. The people live under the ground in linked tunnels. Coming here to Earth, seeing everything so bright and colourful makes me want to move into the light. That is how I saw your signal. I journeyed to the other side of the moon to see what was there."

Both the children yawned.

"You must return to sleep for that is how you charge your earthly power centre and refresh your body." And he glimmered in front of Ellie across the room, forcing her to follow him, pulling her from the chair, directing her to bed, sleepy and amused.

"Goodnight, Ellie," he whispered. Then he returned to Eddie.

"Can we visit your Moonmirror tomorrow? I would like to observe it closely," he asked, changing back to Eddie's shadow.

"Yes, of course, but it probably needs to be charged." said Eddie, thinking aloud.

"Leave that to me." Umbraluna twisted his grey mouth into a smile. "Now, into bed." Eddie jumped into the bedclothes. It occurred to him that the bad weather might obscure the moonlight, not full until the week after Christmas.

"There may not be enough moon yet," he said anxiously.

"Do not worry about that, there will be a way."

And with that, the little creature returned to his own shape and disappeared through the window out into the darkness.

Chapter Thirty-four
The visitor plays a few tricks

Outside, another heavy burst of rain arrived, and with it the wild winds whistling through the trees. Umbraluna had an idea and wafted up towards the top of the hill. The whole town had been plunged into darkness by the power cut; all the lamps had gone out and the streets were empty. Daylight was still a few hours away. Reaching the top of Gallants Bower, he located the Moonmirror fastened to the Great Ash Tree and by the time the thunder roared again, he was ready.

He connected one of his arms to the Moonmirror's battery and one rested on the ground. When the next flash of lightening came he switched his eyes on and the great jagged, cracking, brilliant source of power, with its blinding intensity, conducted itself through the Moonglimmer into the power centre in his back, through the Moonmirror's battery, and down to be lost in the earth as the energy disappeared. Everything crackled and flashed, but the power was so strong it charged up the Moonmirror and the Moonglimmer simultaneously. Perfect! Umbraluna smiled with satisfaction, and slipped down from the tree. The two problems solved in one. Now to fix the town.

He turned his speed up for travelling and shot off like a satellite crossing the heavens. Everything he touched resumed its power and his arms were busy re-connecting cables between buildings, lamp posts, the railway line, the hospital, the shops, and most exciting of all – the Christmas tree in the centre of town. Then he switched everything on, all at once. It looked very bright indeed. Unfortunately the Moonglimmer did not realise the extent of his power which was many times stronger than anything that can be produced on Earth and all the televisions, radios, video recorders, computers, lights, hearing aids and doorbells were all switched on as well. Music blared from hi fi's, in store music played, and the entire town woke up, wondering what had happened.

Umbraluna chuckled to himself, *Oooops!* as he realised what he had done, but he liked the bright lights on and left it as it was. People looking out of their windows saw a strange blue light crossing the sky, and several reported a UFO to the police.

Arriving back at Watermill Cottage, satisfied, the Moonglimmer dimmed and went back to bed, choosing the foot of Ellie's bed to sleep on this time. He couldn't wait for them all to wake up and be part of his new earthly family again.

***

Irene and Sam, now comfortably installed at the Old Bath House, did not see any reason to rush the move into Waterside Cottage.

"Of course, we'll have to check it all over and see what remains to be done," they told George and Bridget over a large breakfast, seated at the dining table overlooking the river.

"Now, I shall need the telephone number of a good hairdresser; and I really could do with a manicure," Irene told her old friend, looking disapprovingly at her nails. "This computer work doesn't help does it?"

"That reminds me, we'll need some connections put in for the computer workstations and a satellite dish for the television. Did you do that, Patrick?" Sam shot his question at his son who was becoming more and more anxious.

"Um… no, Dad. I don't think it was on the list."

"Right, let's make a new one then. Ready?" and Patrick went off to find his works clip board, rolling his eyes in frustration, as he wanted to be off somewhere with Eddie and Ellie. He sighed heavily. Why couldn't his parents be like everyone else's?

Bridget cleared away and she and George exchanged glances in the kitchen.

"Shall we open up a little earlier today?"

"Good idea. We can welcome our early birds with coffee and a mince pie, eh?"

They could hear Irene and Sam giving Patrick a whole load of instructions, and they shook their heads. "They haven't even looked at it yet," said George dryly.

"Oh well, I expect they will sometime today," his sister told him. Arrangements were made to meet Patrick at the cottage at 11 o'clock and Irene and Sam returned to their seats beside the river view and the log fire.

"This is lovely," smiled Irene, her hair appointment secured, manicure organised, and lunch table booked at the Castle Hotel.

"I really must buy some sailing clothes, something casual and suitable for Dartmouth," she added.

"Can I go now?" Patrick asked, wishing to escape.

"Yes, we'll see you at eleven then. Bye," and Sam returned to check the financial stock market in his newspaper. George, Bridget and Patrick all left the house together and said goodbye in the lane.

"I should leave them to it, lad. You go and enjoy yourself with your friends. Make this the last day at the cottage, eh?"

"I hope so." Patrick nodded, wholeheartedly agreeing. "But, in a way, they did it for *me*."

"Believe that if you like," grunted George. "Good investment I'd say."

"Now, now, George, let's go shall we?" and Bridget took his arm, "Goodbye dear," she told Patrick, smiling. "Don't forget to enjoy yourself just a little."

***

At Watermill Cottage, Mary and Peter had gone off to Totnes to do some Christmas shopping, surprised that Eddie and Ellie hadn't wanted to join them.

"We're going to see Patrick today, Mum, so we'll stay here, thanks." The two had waved them off from the window.

"Come on, wait till Patrick meets our new visitor, he'll be—"

"Over the moon!" chimed in Ellie, and they giggled hysterically, running back upstairs to where Ellie had hidden the Moonglimmer under her blanket. He heard her coming and appeared at once.

"Are we going to see your friend?" asked Umbraluna hopefully.

"Yes, we are," Ellie told him happily and he wafted up from the bed and placed himself at her feet, a soft grey outline ready to follow. Ellie kept tripping and bumping into things because she was constantly watching the shadow.

"Ready?" asked the impatient Eddie, and off they went, closing the kitchen door behind them. The three of them pranced down by the creek, zigzagging, waving their arms and twirling round, as the shadow changed from one to another to entertain them. They were at Patrick's cottage in two minutes and pulled on the small ships' bell hanging on a bracket by the door. They could see the lights were on by peering through the glass in the front door, which quickly opened to reveal dear old smiling Patrick.

"Come in." He welcomed them into the sparkling clean shiny new kitchen. Eddie winked at Ellie and saying nothing they stepped inside, Umbraluna following and transferring his shadow shape to Patrick's.

"I've just got a few phone calls to make for Dad, I'm afraid," he apologised.

"OK, we'll wait," as they watched the shadow moving around, following Patrick. He went to the phone, but before he had even dialled the number on the piece of paper, Umbraluna had read them and connected him.

"Yes?" said the phone to him. Rather surprised, Patrick told it what he wanted. "Very good, Mr McNab," the phone said, and hung up.

"How strange." said Patrick.

"When are your parents coming round?" asked Ellie timidly.

"11 o'clock."

"Do you have to be here?" Eddie asked impatiently "Can't we leave a note saying we've gone out or something?"

"Oh go on, Patrick," persuaded Ellie, "They might like to be on their own you know… get familiar with it and move things around a bit."

Patrick, used to obeying his parents in everything, found it hard to even think about not being there when they arrived, but he did desperately want to go off and do things with Eddie and Ellie.

"Do come with us, it will be fun," said a voice that sounded like his own. Patrick turned his head slowly from side to side, looking around. Eddie and Ellie went to look out of the window, almost bursting with stifled laughter. Patrick made no comment, thinking one of them was just being mischievous and copying his voice.

"Are you going to leave them a note, then?" continued Ellie, pressing him into making a decision. Patrick sighed heavily and bit his lip several times, thinking, torn between his sense of duty to his parents and his desire to go off and have fun.

"Oh blow it!" he said, "I'm coming with you!" his face blushing.

"Good for you," said Eddie. "Let's go."

So Ellie and Patrick composed the note and wrote it, leaving it on the table, a prominent place for Irene and Sam to see it. Patrick was torn with guilt. He was having second thoughts now.

"I should really stay here, you know." He sucked his teeth and looked guilty.

"Oh come on, stop that!" said Ellie. "You've done all their work for them." She grabbed his coat and scarf off the peg in the hallway and ushered him to the front door.

"Key?"

"Got it."

"Right, McNab, go!" as Ellie and Eddie shoved him out into the road, firmly closing the door firmly behind them.

"Where to?" Patrick asked, happy at last, his decision made for him.

"Let's go for a long walk round all the old places and then go to town for fish and chips," suggested Eddie.

"Good idea," agreed the others and they stepped the few metres to the creek.

"There's Sargasso," pointed out Ellie, "and he's got a friend with him." Sure enough the pretty female gull was by his side. Sargasso hopped over on his one leg to greet his friends. Umbraluna left Patrick and shadowed Sargasso at once.

"I am Umbraluna from the dark side of the moon. I am pleased to meet you at last, Sargasso. You brought tidings of the strange sea craft, did you not?" he cawed in seagull language.

Rather surprised, the gull replied. "Yes, are you the bright light that came from the sky? The one that broke the window?"

"Yes, I was brought by the light of the Moonmirror. I helped the boy to charge it up when there was no moon for a signal, on the day you brought the news of the sea craft."

"You helped us all and I thank you," said Sargasso warmly. "I have been their friend for a long time now, they are kind and good. I welcome you here on behalf of the Seafarers. How long will you stay?"

"I have the power of speech for only this and one more day. Then I am as an invisible shadow once more, left with only my bright eyes. I am merely a visitor from another planet for a short time, here to ease my curiosity about this place which I have found to be full of many wonders."

"Have you seen the sea and what lies beneath it?" asked Sargasso coyly.

"No." Umbraluna was puzzled. "I do not know how to enter it."

"I will show you if you like," offered the seagull. "Come back this afternoon when the tide is full and Seraphim and I will take you on a guided tour of the Seafarer's world."

"Thank you," replied Umbraluna gratefully, "I shall." And he left the shadow of the seagull and returned to Eddie's side.

The children had been watching the seagull cawing gently and had wondered if he was talking to their Moonglimmer. Patrick looked over the familiar green creek and found it hard to believe his luck at being back beside it again with perhaps the prospect of sailing the little green boat in the Easter holidays next year.

"Shall we go?" he urged and they trod the worn track around the creek, along the road to Sugary Cove and up to the top of the hill to the coastguards' cottages, the Moonglimmer shadowing them the way. The sun came out just when they reached the place where Eddie had seen the whales and the submarines that fateful day.

Patrick eventually noticed the shadow walking beside him, dark on the path's surface. Suddenly it was in front of him, keeping in perfect time with his step. The sun went in and it occurred to him that as the sun had disappeared, should there be any shadow at all? He stopped, but the dark shape kept walking and he felt compelled to follow its irresistible strength that was dragging him along.

"Hey, what's happening?" He looked back at Eddie who seemed to be laughing. By now Umbraluna was having fun. He picked Patrick up in his grey arms and flew him faster than the speed of sound to Start Point lighthouse, a blue flash in the sky, travelling so fast it was impossible to see.

"Wow! He hasn't done that before. Lucky Patrick!" Eddie stared after the rapidly disappearing flash of light.

"I wish I'd done that," complained Ellie, shielding her eyes to try to see, but it was impossible. Whizzing through the cold air Patrick was deposited on the very top rails of the lighthouse balcony and rather unsteadily found his feet; he was even more amazed when he heard a voice that was just like his own.

"I am Umbraluna from the dark side of the moon. I have come to visit the planet Earth. Wait here please."

Patrick, too scared and confused to move, stood on the highest viewing platform of the lonely and empty lighthouse. The

Moonglimmer shot back, and grabbing Eddie and Ellie, one in each hand, he whisked them off too, hurtling through the winter sky in seconds, a small blue blur in the heavens. They too landed, and wobbled on their feet beside the bewildered Patrick, who was very relieved to see them.

"We've been flying!" they both laughed, breathless from the incredible speed.

"Yes, but what's happened?" insisted Patrick, "And who is Umbra… thingy?"

"Oh that's Umbraluna, he's been shadowing you all day," laughed Ellie. "Didn't you hear him talking to you? He copies our voices when he becomes our shadow. He made your phone calls for you."

"He's the blue flashing light I told you about. He saw our Moonmirror from the moon, imagine that," Eddie added proudly.

"But I thought he said he came from the *dark* side of the moon," insisted Patrick, by now extremely confused.

"Oh I do!" chimed in the Moonglimmer. "But I journeyed round into the brightness out of curiosity. It's so dull and dreary in the grey shadows for all of your life," he continued in Patrick's voice.

"How long have you known about this shadow creature called Umber… lu… ny?" stammered Patrick accusingly.

"Umbraluna." He was corrected at once by Ellie. "He says he's been here for days, but he's only been able to talk for three. He's been following us."

"How *did* you find out how to talk?" asked Eddie, realising that something must have happened to him.

"I saw some little creatures called moles and I followed them to the Cornucopia tree in the woods. There are two birds that live there with many elixirs of life. One was called the Fulfilment of

Dreams and I had three drops, one for each day. I have been talking to many things, but you are the first humans. The seagull is taking me to see his world of the sea this afternoon."

"And we are taking you to see the Moonmirror tonight," added Eddie, not exactly understanding what he had been told about the elixirs. They stood on the top of the lighthouse and looked into the special light and the complicated reflective and magnifying lenses that made it shine so brightly.

"That looks a bit like our light, only much more powerful," Patrick observed.

"Is this the light I can see from the hilltop?" asked the Moonglimmer, interested.

"Yes, this is a lighthouse, to shine out to ships at sea; it saves them from crashing onto the rocks," Eddie explained.

"I can make it brighter," said Umbraluna at once and turned his eyes on to full blue beams and blasted a fierce dazzle onto the carefully arranged lenses. "That will be better tonight," he said with satisfaction.

The three stood watching in disbelief and then turned to the panoramic view all around them. It was a wonderful sight, watching the sea from such a vantage point as it rolled and swept across the bay.

"Are you ready to return to the hilltop?" asked Umbraluna, "I think we can all go together if you can hold on tightly enough .Take each others hands." They made a circle with the shadow's hands and with a sudden blast of blue light they spiralled up into the air and shot off at immense speed, to land a few seconds later back on the edge of the woodland.

"Phew! Now, I need some fish and chips after that," said Eddie breathlessly to Ellie and Patrick who were still speechless, trying to get their balance back. It had been amazing.

"May I go to visit the seagull now?" quietly asked the Moonglimmer, shrinking back to his star-shaped self, a little grey insignificant being.

"Yes, of course you must, it will be brilliant," insisted all the children together. "Thank you for the trip to the lighthouse."

"We'll see tonight if it was worth it," said the shadow of Umbraluna and he wafted away, soon becoming invisible to the curious observers he left behind. Patrick shook his head, trying to take in what had happened to him since stepping out of his cottage door.

"I'm after thinking that you two canna be real," he said, lapsing into broad Scottish. "What is it about you two?"

"But we didn't do anything," protested Eddie, "it was the Moonmirror's fault. That's what brought him here and as you helped to invent it then it's your fault too. So there!"

"Look how much help he was over the submarines," added Ellie. "Come on, you can't say it's a bad thing can you?"

"We didn't even know he was here. He broke my window, its lucky Dad wasn't here, he'd have made me pay for it out of my pocket money and I didn't do a single thing!"

"OK, I get it." Patrick held his hands up for peace.

"Let's get down to town for fish and chips now for goodness sake, I'm starving! Race ya!" and they skittered off, chasing down the hill, overtaking each other and grabbing each other by their scarves, to shouts of protest and laughter.

They reached the town puffed and hot and sniffed the smell of chips from the doorway of their favourite haunt, the Sea Shanty. They made their choices and hardly able to wait to unwrap the paper, hot and steamy, carried their precious parcels along the road to the town's Avenue Gardens. Passing the Castle Hotel, Ellie idly peered into the window of the smart Bristol Bar and to her horror saw Irene and Sam engrossed in conversation, lounging on a leather sofa, drinking huge glasses of red wine, an attentive waiter about to take their food order.

"Quick, look the other way! It's your mum and dad!" hissed Ellie frantically as both the boys' faces changed to looks of horror and they darted off across the road to the nearest empty seat in the park.

"Lucky they weren't sitting by the window or they'd have seen us for sure," breathed Ellie with a sigh of relief, tearing at the wrapping paper in haste to get at the chips. The two boys did the same, burning their mouths and fingers as they gobbled the scalding tasty morsels, Patrick keeping an eye on the front door of the hotel, just in case.

Chapter Thirty-five
The Moonglimmer meets the Seafarers

Down by the creekside Sargasso and his new companion Seraphim bobbed and waited on the incoming tide. Seraphim had been attacked by a spiteful cat when only a fledgling, due to the unsuitable site her parents had chosen for a nest. She had a torn wing, shorter than the other, which had never recovered. She had felt ugly and clumsy even though she could fly, until she met Sargasso. He with one leg, and she with one good wing, they made the perfect pair, their disabilities invisible to each other, their friendship growing and both gaining confidence. Sargasso felt the time was drawing near when he would have to reveal his exalted position and power amongst the Seafarers to her. She was already inquisitive about the mother of pearl shell he wore around his neck, but there was much more to tell her – so much more.

He required permission from the Spirit of the Sea to bring such an alien being as the Moonglimmer into their world.

"You may see strange things today Seraphim, I hope you will not be too afraid," he told her gently. "You need not accompany me if you wish, wait here by the lime kiln if you prefer."

She smiled back prettily at him, tilting her head to one side in an inquiring way.

"And why would I do that? I am as interested as the moon creature to see where you are going today. I am not brave like you, Sargasso, and have hardly travelled at all outside the town. It will be an adventure. When I am with you, I have so much more courage."

He was filled with pride to hear her words.

"Very well, I am pleased to have you with me. I wonder where he is, this Umbraluna from the dark side of the moon."

"I am here," came Sargasso's voice from a shadow of a bird, rippling and changing shape across the shiny aquamarine waters. "I can only speak to you if I assume your shape, but I still have my powers."

The two gulls stared at the dark shadow beside them.

"Very well, you are most welcome today, Umbraluna, but first I must seek permission from my lord, the Spirit of the Sea. He must have the final word. Let us see if we can find him." And he searched beneath his feathers for the pearl-covered beautiful spiral shell he wore around his neck.

"Listen," and he held the shell to the shadow, "come closer; put this to your ear." And the shadow left the side of the seagull to put the shell to his ear. He could hear the rise and fall of great waves, rhythmically echoing with its faraway foam breaking on distant shores. It was hypnotic and he felt he could listen to it forever.

"What can you hear?" asked Sargasso, breaking into the shadow's dreamlike state.

"I can hear the sound of a thousand oceans lulling me to sleep," replied Umbraluna softly.

"Good," replied the bird with satisfaction.

"Now you, Seraphim," and he passed the shell to the little gull who was eager to hear too.

Her eyes opened wider as she heard the reassuring sounds of seas she had never visited and shores she would never see, soothing and refreshing her mind.

"Wonderful!" she said, with a look of sheer pleasure on her face.

The gull took the shell back and called into it. "Spirit of the Sea, please reply to me. I have a visitor from another place, far away in the heavens, who wishes to see our world. He is not a Seafarer, but will respect our ways and hold fast to our secrets. He will swear an oath at the Caves of Astraeus, I am sure. I await your answer." He looked up at the shadow and the gull who were spellbound at his ability to converse with the great power of the sea.

Almost immediately there came a faint soft ringing of several notes from the shell, a gentle sound that seemed familiar to Seraphim. It was the haunting faraway song of the sea, of breezes blown from warm oceans where the water laps and sighs in the sun.

The shadow nodded; he too recognised the voice of the wind. He had heard it many times as he travelled across the expanse of space to reach Earth. This wind carried the voice of the Spirit of the Sea.

"It is he. He is answering us," the seagull told them. "Listen." He held the shell so they too could hear the voice, saying,

"You are welcome, traveller. We will satisfy your curiosity. The Seafarers will permit you to enter our world. I will open the deeps and the shallows to your eyes. When you reach the Caves of Astraeus you must make a pledge to never reveal the mysteries you will see. Take care not to venture over the cliffs, into the Graveyards of Caedus, as all the entrances to the Deep Places will be open. I shall send word of your visit ahead of you. That is all, Sargasso." Gradually the gentle noise stopped and silence fell.

Seraphim and Umbraluna were suitably impressed and watched as Sargasso tucked the shell away under his feathers.

"Let's go." He smiled at them and they followed, the two gulls swimming on the surface and the shadow following behind. They paddled to the black rocky edges and ducked head first in to the green unknown, where strands of browny black bladderwrack swayed in the moving water and translucent prawns pedalled furiously in large groups. Everything was silent; the noise of the world above closed off. Thin curtains of richly coloured tangles of red and russet weeds hung from the black rocks and small fish, blennies and butterfish, nosed out to look.

Umbraluna was enchanted. There was so much down here and the light refracting where it hit the water changed the colours to deep emeralds and turquoises; everything had a blue-green tinge. The birds popped up again and carried on swimming to the rugged rocks on which the castle fortifications were built. The river Dart met the sea here and the water was deeper and eddied and tugged in many different directions, sometimes splashing furiously against the rocks, gushing and foaming.

Down dived the birds again, followed by their shadow, to seek out dark crevices where unfriendly lobsters and crabs took refuge. These looked very fierce to Umbraluna, covered as they were in their shell armour plating, waving large terrifying claws with a deadly nip to them and thin feelers prying around to sense their presence. Many little eyes steadily watched the visitors, alert, claws ready to strike. The floor of the sea was littered with half-buried spars of old ships and rusted cannonballs eaten away by the salty ocean, remnants of history and old battles fought. The seagulls swam upwards, emerged and clambered onto the rocks to sit looking out to the horizon.

"We must fly now farther away from the land to the wide open sea if you are to see everything," Sargasso told them. "Many Seafarers are content to live by the rocky shores and some by the sandy beaches where food is plentiful and shelter close by, but our largest and most secret creatures do not come to the land. Even I have not seen them all. Are you ready for a long journey?"

"I am," replied Umbraluna eagerly. Brave little Seraphim nodded in agreement and touching wingtips the two birds took off, three shadows cast over the water in the afternoons' weak spell of sunlight. Out they went, wings beating, eyes watchful, steadily crossing the rippled ocean with its changing colours, over peaks and crests of the waves. Several miles from the shore Sargasso landed on the surface of the sea and rested. Almost at once Seraphim called to him, bobbing in the strong waves, "Look! Look! A shoal of fish," and Sargasso knew who it was, as the Silver Tinkling Shoals sent by the Spirit of the Sea surrounded them.

"We have come to direct your path, sent by our master, for you do not know the dangers of the Deep. You must stay close and follow. When we arrive you will be able to exist without breathing until we return," their tiny ringing voices explained, sounding like a hundred wind chimes.

"Are you prepared?" Sargasso asked the gull by his side.

"I hope so," replied Seraphim, a little unsure.

"I can't wait!" cawed the voice of Umbraluna imitating the seagull and at once the small silver fish began to circle around them, glinting and glistening, increasing in speed until they were whirling and spinning, creating a vortex in the water, into which they all spiralled downwards, disappearing beneath the surface into the funnel the fish had created. Soon they were deep in the ocean – dim and tranquil, silent and shadowy, with huge caverns and tall cliffs around them and sandy places in between.

"Come," tinkled the fish, and led them through a rocky entrance of cathedral-like proportions, where sea scorpions stood guard and sting fish patrolled, armed with their deadly poisoned spines. At once the scorpions all grunted angrily at the visitors, spines erect, but the fish stopped in front of them, lining the way, as the two uneasy gulls passed through.

"They mean you no harm," tinkled the Silver Shoals, "they are merely guardians."

Moon-shaped jellyfish began to float by and eyes appeared on the rock walls, staring at them. They were sucker fish stuck fast to the edges, waiting for small passing creatures to feed on.

"Look!" Umbraluna pointed excitedly and high above them a bright phosphorescence of ghostly light shone, illuminating the whole area, travelling slowly like a bright cloud. Eventually a large space opened out and the Silver Shoals stopped.

"Wait here," they ordered and the two birds stopped and rested, overawed by their mysterious journey. They seemed to be in a sort of garden with coloured sea anemones clustered around, their delicate petals of pink and white like pretty daisies gently swaying. Green sea cucumbers and purple starfish made patterns on the floor like a mosaic and sea urchins and sea lilies waved their red and green fingers on long stalks.

"How beautiful it is here!" Seraphim was delighted with the sea garden, as a large spotted turtle swam purposefully towards them.

"Sign here please." He stopped abruptly, holding out a book made of a large bi-valve shell.

"Repeat after me… I the undersigned, make a pledge of silence, that I shall never reveal the mysteries of the Caves of Astraeus as long as I swim in the Oceans of this Life."

Sargasso and Seraphim pressed their beaks into the soft interior of the shell-book, their marks preserved for ever.

"Now swear," instructed the old and patient turtle, and they repeated his words carefully, Umbraluna trying to keep up with them; their voices sounding like bubbles of air escaping. At last the turtle smiled and greeted them warmly.

"Thank you, we are grateful for your co-operation. Welcome to the Caves of Astraeus. The Great Kraken will see you very soon. We are having a feast in your honour ordered by the Spirit of the Sea – you must be highly thought of."

Slowly and gradually the space in the garden filled up with sea creatures drifting in. Small sand hoppers began to dart about carrying tables and preparing a meal. Sea ferns were dotted about to decorate the tables and piles of sea jellies and sea gooseberries appeared. Great platters of seaweeds decorated with laver and lichen were piled up and sea squirts were placed at every plate to drink from. Several octopuses slithered by, Umbraluna admiring their many legs. Two huge conger eels poked out from a dark crevice, smiling a ghastly grin with their razor sharp teeth.

"Good to see you!" they mouthed, "Coming for a meal?"

Sargasso and Seraphim were terrified in case they were the meal and they watched and waited in uncertainty as the area was transformed by the busy workers, the countless sand hoppers skipping backward and forward.

The cloud of phosphorescence above them, tiny pinpricks of light, was the only illumination and there was a blue-green ghostly look to everything. At last it was ready, the sand hoppers disappeared and huge spider crabs and sea spiders with small bodies and enormous legs came creeping in over the sand, followed by spiny lobsters in great numbers. The turtle reappeared with his white bi-valve shell which seemed to be open at a seating plan and he directed the crabs and lobsters to their place. Then he seated the octopuses, several small white squid that had floated in, and at last he beckoned to Sargasso and Seraphim and the grey shadow of Umbraluna who sat down on the piles of coiled rag worms obligingly provided. The two conger eels were directed to the largest table, one each side of a barnacle-encrusted throne, the moon jelly fish filled up the remaining spaces, and the turtle, satisfied, nodded and disappeared. Everyone sat quietly waiting. Who was coming to sit on the throne? Sargasso wondered. Would it be the Spirit of the Sea?

Then some green-gold sea mice appeared, each pulling a different seaweed rope, and a huge giant squid emerged from the dark, huffing and puffing, too fat to swim, rather ugly and menacing with large unwinking eyes. The twenty or so little sea mice had to drag him wherever he went and they heaved him in a slithering mass onto the throne where he sank down, arms flapping, his body constantly throbbing and pulsating, like a fat Buddha from the human world. His beady eyes travelled around the seated company and raising one of his many arms as a signal, a tube worm popped up and trumpeted the welcoming tune of the Seafarers' Song. When the worm had finished, one of the conger eels stood up and announced in a gravelly voice,

"Silence for our leader, the Great Kraken, the greatest secret on this planet!" and everyone clapped, hummed or whistled as they were able. The giant squid raised one of his arms to hush them and spoke in his oily, quiet voice.

"Welcome visitors, especially our Moon friend, – you will entertain us later. Eat now and throw everything you do not require onto the floor. Our scavengers will clean and clear during the banquet. Begin!"

Sargasso and Seraphim were startled and anxious at the Great Kraken's announcement. Entertainment? What did he mean?

Umbraluna whispered to them, "Leave it to me. Don't worry. Eat and enjoy the food."

The piles of food was consumed in minutes and the vegetation of the sea that was not eaten was collected from the sandy floor, by sea slaters and sea slugs who swept the debris up into the mouths of the waiting sea anemones, whose tentacles waved, grabbing the food.

The other conger eel stood up and said,

"We thank you Great Kraken for this feast and await your signal for the commencement of the rest of the evening."

The huge squid, who had gorged himself, wiped his mouth, burped loudly, and banged his many arms onto the table.

"Show us something entertaining, you creatures from the world above the sea, for I never leave this cave and am mighty bored. Orchestra, play!" and the whole floor was immediately pierced with tube worms with trumpets. Sargasso and Seraphim shook in fear, mesmerised by the hideous giant squid, who fixed his eyes on them menacingly, waiting... but Umbraluna was ready. He returned to his star-shaped self and as the music played he switched his eyes on and gave them the first laser light show the Caves of Astraeus had ever seen. His blue lights were shining and seeking out corners and crevices, reflecting off substances in the rocks, glinting on minerals and crystals, shifting and swirling as the sea creatures from the deep were fascinated.

"Enough!" called the voice of Kraken eventually. "We are blinded by your Moon display and impressed with your amazing entertainment, but I have seen enough and I need to rest. Take me back," he ordered rudely to his twenty sea mice, who began to wrestle him out of the throne and to drag him back to his chamber of rest. He did not turn to say goodbye, and disappeared from sight. The conger eels, embarrassed, stood up again.

"We thank you for your wonderful show and your visit. You have witnessed the existence of the Mighty Kraken, the only giant squid remaining on our planet Oceanus. All others are extinct and we are bound by the Spirit of the Sea to preserve and look after him. We are honoured to have met you, but, the banquet is now over."

At once the sea creatures began drifting away, vanishing as quickly as they had come, as the sand hoppers returned to clear up and soon the two gulls and the Moonglimmer were left in the sea garden quite alone.

"Well!" said Sargasso, quite relieved, "I'll be glad to go home, won't you?"

"Yes I will," agreed Seraphim. "It was an extraordinary day."

Umbraluna resumed his grey shape of the seagull and said in his seagull voice,

"I wouldn't like to live here in this strange cave. I long to see the light again."

Sargasso, eager to leave, called the Silver Tinkling Shoals, who had been waiting in the shadows rather uninterested, for they had seen the giant squid before and they willingly led them through the dim caverns, past the scorpions and the sting fish to the entrance with its great arched doorway where they could see, high above them, a grey light.

"That's the way." And the gulls followed the glinting shiny flecks in the ocean, passing steep gullies which descended into the unknown and skeletons scattered on the floor. The ghostly outline of a sunken galleon appeared lying on its side, where teredo worms, fat and lazy, gnawed their way into the rotting woodwork. Sargasso stopped and looked closely. It was the wreck of the *Fancy* lying at rest – the ship that Eddie's friend Captain Avery had sailed long ago. He shivered; it was all long gone, everything given up to the worms and the barnacles.

They swam on and on. As they neared their own shore, they passed crabs and lobsters imprisoned in cages, floating in the deep water.

"Help us!" they implored, faces pressed to the netting sides. "We are trapped!"

Sargasso and Seraphim looked at each other sadly and Umbraluna said, "Set them free, I beg you."

And so without a word the seagulls flipped the many doors open and the grateful crustaceans clambered out to freedom, crying out their thanks loudly, "We will not forget you, Sargasso!"

The Silver Tinkling Shoals were impatient and surrounded the gulls. "It is time to go, go, go. Please follow us, us, us!" they echoed.

The fish tinkled and swirled together, moving upwards, creating a water spout which broke the surface as a rotating pillar of water and mingled with the mist from a cloud above it to create a column of spray and water. The gulls were transported through the deep ocean to the sea's surface and the water spout travelled away from them, the fish disappearing in a distant silver flash, calling, "Goodbye!" in their tiny musical voices. "Goodbye!" And they faded away. The gulls felt the faint warmth of the winter sun and breathed in the cool fresh salt-laden air and were very glad to be out of the dark and oppressive deep of the ocean floor with its strange secrets.

"I have heard of sea monsters in legends and old tales but we are the only ones to have seen the Great Kraken, but I never want to see him again," resolved Sargasso, relieved to have escaped from the eerie place.

"No, I don't think we will miss his hideous body or ugly face, or… his very bad table manners!" laughed Seraphim.

"It only makes your world seem more beautiful to me," added Umbraluna, as they set off back to their quiet and lovely Warfleet Creek where they sat together happily in the dry cosy lime kiln and recalled everything that they had seen.

Chapter Thirty-six
Building family bridges

Heading back from their picnic in the park, Eddie, Ellie and Patrick were overtaken on the road by a large black car.

"It's Mum and Dad!" gasped Patrick. Then, "Oh no!" as the car abruptly braked, and stopped a little way in front of them. Sam's head popped out of the window.

"So this is what was so important, loafing around the town, up to no good, breaking your promise to us, my laddie. Get in the car." he called crossly to his son.

"I want to stay with Eddie and Ellie," Patrick replied mutinously. "I'll see you back at the cottage, I won't be long." Eddie and Ellie felt afraid for him; wouldn't he only make his father angrier? They shifted nervously from foot to foot.

"Very well."

And with a screech the black car and its furious occupants surprisingly sped off up the hill. Patrick looked at them both.

"Sorry about that, he can be a bit off sometimes."

He paused for a few moments as they continued walking in awkward silence.

"He'll have to get used to it. I'm not a child anymore and I'm not going to do everything he tells me. I'm not somebody at the bank he orders around, he'll have to lump it." He grinned mischievously. "I can't believe he drove off, I bet he wouldn't have if you two hadn't been with me."

"I hope he's not cross with us." Ellie was worried, she didn't like upsetting people.

"Oh, don't bother any more about it," said Eddie. "I'll get Dad to talk to him; they seem to get on alright, don't they?"

Soon the broad sweep of the little inlet appeared overlooked by the old Watermill which seemed to keep a friendly eye on the whole area. Ellie noticed the car in the driveway.

"Mum and Dad are back."

"I'd better go home, I suppose," sighed Patrick, not feeling so brave now and knowing he had to face his parents.

"Don't forget, tonight we're taking Umbraluna up to see the Moonmirror. Just say you're coming round to ours," Eddie told him.

"OK" Patrick wasn't so sure he'd be able to get out but he was determined to try. They parted company at the top of the creek and waved goodbye to each other.

"Poor Patrick," Ellie said anxiously, watching him go. She and Eddie walked around to the back door and straight into the kitchen. The smell of coffee was in the air and sitting in one of the rustic wooden chairs was Patrick's father, Sam, staring at them. Eddie stopped so suddenly that Ellie bumped straight into him with an "Ouch!" while he uttered a surprised and rather feeble "Oh!" His father, who was leaning with his back against the sink, arms folded, smiled and greeted them.

"Hi, terrors.Sam and I are just discussing the boat," he informed them cheerily. "Mum's gone down to have a coffee with Irene. Spent all your money?" He grinned at them.

"Um, not quite, we… we went for a long walk and then had fish and chips in town," confessed Ellie, remembering not to tell him about their flying visit to Start Point lighthouse, which had been the high spot of the day.

Sam sat quietly, staring at the children, wondering how one possibly got to know one's own children and to be relaxed and friendly to them as Peter was. He felt a hopeless failure as a parent. Patrick hated him and didn't want to spend any time at all with him. They were awkward and polite to each other and seemed to have nothing in common. All Patrick wanted to do was spend his time here at Watermill Cottage or in the Old Bath House, as far away from him and Irene as possible. He felt hurt and upset and unsure of what to do. All he had ever wanted was to help his son become a success. What was wrong with that?

"Do you like the cottage?" burst out Ellie, unable to contain herself, wishing she hadn't said it the moment the words came tumbling out of her mouth. Eddie grimaced. *Oh Ellie*, he groaned inwardly at her tactlessness, but she continued blundering on.

"Patrick's worked so hard you know, phoning and organising everything, and we've helped with the moving in and the furniture and the food and we've had all that snow, and they couldn't get the vans down. He's really tried to make it nice for you, and—"

"Please!" Sam held his hand up. "Please, Ellie... I think it's lovely and I feel terrible now putting it all on to him, he's only a kid."

"But that's the trouble." Ellie had both her hands out in front of her, palms upwards, trying to make him understand her. "Sometimes you treat him like a child and then sometimes you treat him like a grown-up and expect him to do far too much. It's not fair." she accused him bitterly.

Sam was lost for words; he looked blankly at them and then down at the floor, like a lost soul. "I want to make friends with my son now, that's all, before it's too late," he mumbled rather pathetically.

Peter nodded his head at his son and daughter indicating the door, and picking up his meaning at once, Eddie and Ellie went out and upstairs to escape. Peter poured Sam another coffee, thinking hard. He'd had an idea.

"I'm just going to give Mike Oswald a ring, I won't be a moment." He took the telephone book, found the number he wanted, and dialled.

"Hello Mike, its Peter here, got any fishing trips organised this week? Oh, that sounds just what we want. Yes, there's probably going to be five of us. You can? Great! Book us in then and we'll see you tomorrow at 10 o'clock, weather permitting. Yes, we'll bring a packed lunch with us. Bye." And he put the phone down with a satisfied click.

"That's good. Now Sam, what we need is a bonding exercise and I'm proposing a fishing trip. Mike Oswald is very experienced, he's got a big sturdy boat, the *Alice May*, and takes about twelve rods when he's full. There's a trip tomorrow, I think it's just the thing. The kids will love it. What about it?"

He looked at the man who knew everything about finance, banking, and the European money market, and nothing at all about his 13 year-old son. He wanted to help him.

"If you feel that's what we need then yes, it's a good idea and I'd like to come. But I haven't got any fishing gear," he added glumly.

"A perfect opportunity, then, to go shopping with Patrick. You'll enjoy it. The Tackle Box doesn't close until 6 o'clock; you've got plenty of time, Sam. Forget your computer, phone and fax machine for a bit. Go off and get to know your son. He's a great lad, still waters run deep in his case I think you'll find." And he smiled reassuringly at the man out of his depth in the real world. It was rather sad.

"Right. Of course you're right. That sounds like a good idea. Ellie told the truth – he has worked hard. We were just too busy and left it all to him. We thought it would be good for him, making decisions about the cottage he wanted so badly."

"I think perhaps they were decisions that you and Irene should have made, but it's too late now Sam, so just accept whatever he's done and leave it at that. He's tried hard and he has made the choices. He's done well. Heaven knows what Ellie and Eddie would have done –filled up the fridge with Mars Bars and crisps I expect, and left all the lights on." He laughed and Sam joined in. Maybe it would all work out in the end. Just maybe. Sam got up purposefully, ready to go home.

"We'll settle on a price for the boat then, when you find a replacement, yes?"

"That will be fine," agreed Peter, and he walked with him to the end of the driveway.

"See you tomorrow then, call up here when you're ready."

"Yes, I'm quite looking forward to it." He walked briskly down the creek. Peter returned to the cottage, spying the robin on the empty windowsill.

"Aha! Looking for lunch eh? So am I," and he found some biscuits crumbs and sprinkled them outside for him. Eddie and Ellie came running downstairs.

"Has he gone?" Ellie called, looking down over the banisters, hopefully, Eddie behind her.

"If you mean Mr McNab, yes he's gone," replied Peter. "You really will have to learn to control your tongue, Ellie," he told her firmly.

"Sorry, Dad, I couldn't help it. I don't think I like him very much, he's so horrible to Patrick."

"Well, I don't think you're helping the situation by bursting out like that," explained Peter. "Come on into the kitchen." He smiled at her downcast face. "I've got something to tell you." And they followed him, pushing each other to get through the door.

"I've booked a trip on the *Alice May* for tomorrow morning for all of us. We'll soon sort Sam out, get him onto the boat a few times and baptise him in seawater. He'll be alright, you see," he laughed. The two youngsters were relieved. Their father wasn't cross with them after all –well, not very. A day's fishing would be wonderful; they hadn't been out in a boat since their own little green Cornish shrimper had been brought out of the water. Would the weather hold? Eddie wondered.

"Shall I check the forecast, Dad?"

"If you like, but I think Mike would've told me if it was blowing up. He's got a good number of guests now, he seemed pleased, good little extra earner for him just before Christmas. Which reminds me, hadn't we better jump in the car and get a nice tree for Mum and pick up a few things in town? Can you be ready in five minutes?"

"Course we can." Ellie was pleased and excited. There was never a dull moment when Dad was around. Eddie was already browsing through Ceefax on the television for the shipping forecast.

"It's going to be fine tomorrow, winds moderate South West, force 3 to 4. Great!" he called out joyfully to his dad. Soon they had scribbled a note for Mary and were filling up the car with their lively fun and chatter as Peter drove off to town at high speed.

Ten minutes behind them, Patrick and Sam walked leisurely together along the same road, discussing the merits of spinners, feathers, and sand eels, already enjoying themselves in a newfound way, heading towards the Tackle Box.

Inside Waterside Cottage an amazed Irene had watched her husband and son set off on probably their first shopping trip together for many years.

"Well!" she said to Mary, "I can't believe my eyes."

"It will be a good day together," replied her new friend and confidante, "you'll have to make two packed lunches tonight, you know."

"What?" shrieked a horrified Irene.

"Oh yes, they get so hungry out in the fresh air."

"Oh," was the thoughtful reply.

"Let's see what's in your fridge." suggested Mary, as Irene heaved a sigh of relief, feeling help coming her way.

Chapter Thirty-seven
Tolivera's Christmas party

When Mary finally arrived home she found her family engrossed in putting up the Christmas tree, surrounded by a sea of mysterious carrier bags, rolls of Christmas paper, and an air of excitement throughout the house. Ellie, who was the only one who knew where anything was, ferried brown cardboard boxes from the loft, containing Christmas lights, baubles, tinsel, and all manner of decorations they had collected over the years – many of them made at school and much too precious to part with.

The four of them spent a truly happy afternoon, only fighting and squabbling over the assortment of fairies competing for the position at the top of the tree. Mary decorated the kitchen with holly and ivy, a string of fat angels, and to complete it, Peter had bought her a tiny Christmas tree for the kitchen table.

They sat down to supper together which Eddie and Peter had insisted on, a Chinese takeaway from Jimmy Lung Wong's in town.

"You're not going to cook tonight," Peter had told her firmly. "I'll do supper." But Eddie and Ellie knew at once what he meant. Eddie broached the subject of the trip to see the Moonmirror as the time drew near to set off.

"Do you mind, Dad, if we go up to the Moonmirror tonight? Patrick's probably coming with us. I thought I'd take the Crystal Signaller up too, ready for the full moon next week. It's so near Christmas now and I might not have time another day and it's going to be a dry night with no frost forecast." He waited nervously for his father's decision.

"Do you really want to go out tonight in the dark, Eddie? Are you going, Ellie?" He looked at his daughter's face, which betrayed nothing.

"I would quite like to go with them," she replied bravely, wondering at that moment where Umbraluna their guest was.

"Aren't you frightened to go in the woods when it's dark and spooky?" Mary asked them, wishing with all her heart they would give up this silly idea.

"No, we're not. We've grown up here and we know every inch of it, every root sticking out, every tree trunk, just as it's always been. Why would we be scared? We've got our torches."

"Do Sam and Irene know about this?"

Eddie avoided his father's eyes. "I'm sure he's asked them."

"I think I'll just give them a ring."

Peter got up from the table and went to the telephone, ready to challenge Eddie. He hoped his son was telling the truth. Everyone sat still and silent, listening to the conversation go backward and forward. Eventually Peter returned and he was smiling.

"That seems to be alright with Irene and Sam. Patrick's getting ready and will be here in ten minutes."

Eddie and Ellie realised at once that their father's telephone call had been instrumental in establishing Patrick's release for the evening's adventure. They both heaved great sighs of relief.

"Thanks, Dad," was all Eddie said, and Peter nodded, saying nothing.

Soon Patrick was knocking on the door, peering through the glass, hooded and zipped up against the chill night air.

"Come in." shouted Eddie getting up from the table, and before any more obstacles could be put in their way he and Ellie put on their outdoor clothes and found two bright torches, giving Patrick the Crystal Signaller from the bedroom to carry.

"Now," said Peter seriously, "let's establish a time for you all to return and then everybody will know where they are." He looked at his watch.

"It's 6.45pm now, shall we say 8.45pm?" glancing at their faces for a reaction. "I think that's plenty of time don't you? I expect after that both your mothers will start to worry." They all unanimously agreed.

"Yes, Dad, that's fine."

"All set for tomorrow, Patrick?" Peter enquired with a smile, clearing the dirty plates off the table.

"Oh yes, Dad and I have bought loads of fishing tackle, we had a great time looking at all the rods. Mum's even done us two packed lunches, they look great," he told them with gusto. Mary smiled a knowing smile to herself.

"Good, good, well, off you go, keep together, out of trouble and be back on time." Peter wagged his finger at them all.

"We will," replied Ellie, flashing him one of her most winning smiles.

"Where is Umbraluna?" hissed Eddie to Ellie.

"I don't know, the last time I saw him he was off with Sargasso on a tour of the sea. Perhaps he's down at the creek; we'd better go and look." So they walked down the creek, past Waterside Cottage where Patrick could see his parents in the kitchen as they went by. They had almost been normal parents today, he thought.

Sure enough, as they shone their torches into the darkness of the lime kiln, Sargasso and Seraphim were fast asleep, but the beams of the torches showed three shadows on the cave floor. The Moonglimmer was sleeping too, fatigued by his busy day in the world of the Seafarers. But he woke up at once and seeing the visitors, quietly jumped to become Eddie's shadow again.

"Let's go," he told them all in Eddie's voice. Sargasso cawed a sleepy goodbye and tucked his head under his wing again. He had had enough for one day.

They set off again along the creek edges, along the road, past the old hotel, the church and castle, and up the winding path at the top of Sugary Cove. They knew the route so well they could have walked it blindfolded.

***

As the three children escaped the cottage, Freddie had hopped down off the wall. He and Oliphant were going to Tolivera's Christmas party.

He flew up into the trees behind the house and tapped on Oliphant's door. After a pause it opened.

"Is it time to get up already?" yawned the little white owl sleepily.

"Yes, we don't want to be late do we?" replied the robin, hopping inside and glancing at the Dark Dwellers' clock. Its hands pointed to STAR RISE.

"Alright, alright, I'm coming, just looking for my bow tie," grumbled Oliphant, rummaging in the bark drawers set into the solid trunk. "Ah, here it is." He pulled out a length of springy twine with a purple bow on the end of it, made from the petals of large Devon violets.

"Very nice," agreed Freddie patiently, "I haven't got anything for a party, didn't think about it. He shook his head sadly.

"Well think about it now – help yourself and take what you want."

So Freddie peered into the untidy wooden drawer and pulled out a very fetching yellow, fluffy waistcoat, fashioned from mimosa's sweet-smelling flowers.

"That's perfect," nodded Oliphant encouragingly, "put it on, go on." So Freddie did and they looked a very fine pair, both dressed for the Christmas celebration.

"Right, close the window, lock the door, hide the key and let's go-o-o-o-o!" instructed Oliphant.

Flying outside, heading up the hill, their way was illuminated by glow worms on duty all along the steep path.

"Buzzard's orders," the owl explained to a surprised robin. One thing was bothering Freddie. Surely by now the Elixir of Humility would be getting so diluted in the Mists of Time that it would soon have no effect? What would happen when Tolivera returned to his former self? He voiced his worries to his friend on their flight up to the top of Gallants Bower.

"I see what you mean," replied the white owl thoughtfully, "Yes it could be very tricky. Do you know if the Underconstumbles are coming tonight?"

"Sure to be," was the confident answer, "they'll know what to do. Let's ask them, shall we, as soon as we arrive?"

"Good idea, my friend."

They both felt happier and were looking forward to the prospect of a splendid evening. It was an unfortunate coincidence that Tolivera's lavish get-together and Umbraluna's exploration of the finer points of the Moonmirror were going to clash. The little robin had seen his beloved Eddie and Ellie setting off in the opposite direction, towards the creek, and had not given it another thought.

Up at the Great Ash Tree a transformation was taking place, overseen by the Deputy Lord of the Woodland, Tolivera. A pair of woodpeckers had been assigned to turn two old and dried-out tree stumps into comfortable thrones for the buzzard and his consort, and the tap-tap-tapping of their concentrated efforts had been echoing around the woodland for several days. Bryony was woven in and out of the highest branches spreading subtle rosy rounds of light and the slugs had been given strict instructions to travel round and round the circle for dancing until they were almost dizzy. The slimy trail they left shone like a pearly rainbow when the light caught it.

Late the previous night an army of moths had carefully scattered dried toadstool spores and in the morning, smooth round seats had been magically provided – more than enough to seat the expected guests. Tolivera nodded in satisfaction as the entertainment and refreshment he had meticulously planned came to fruition. For, as he said himself, what was the point of power if you couldn't use it once or twice for your own pleasure?

The music was to be provided by the Nightingale Quartet, whose daily practising had charmed any walkers passing by. Tolivera knew that the three young Princes of the Woodland, now on the brink of adulthood, might be bored by the melodious tunes of the songsters, but he didn't care. They would get their chance when they became rulers of the woodland.

And the dancing? That was to be led by Walter and Winifred Wagtail who strutted and pirouetted in perfect time, their feet and tails a blur, moving so fast and with such precision. They really were the best sequence dancers the woodland had ever produced and were at that moment powdering and preening behind the scenes, smoothing their tail feathers to a glossy sheen.

The squirrels, who always organised the catering, were striving to complete the winter menu ordered by Tolivera and were putting the last-minute touches to the tasty supper. The time had arrived, the hour had come and the excited guests began to drift towards the Christmas event long awaited on the social calendar.

Maurice and Maudie had begun the climb to the secluded hilltop venue and were thrilled to find the steep path strewn with shining glow worms. Maudie carried a small parcel, tied up with string, containing a modest Christmas gift for the powerful Tolivera. As a pair of woodpigeons set off from the trees above them, Maurice politely thumbed a lift and they both gratefully climbed onto the soft grey feathers of the obliging birds who were distant cousins of the woodland doctors.

"To the do-o-o-o-o?" they cooed, checking the mole's destination.

"Yes please!" Maurice replied, and clinging on tightly, they were gently air lifted to the summit of Gallants Bower, now lit up and welcoming, where they were set down, arriving in perfect time.

"Thank you very much," puffed Maurice, helping Maudie find her feet as she carefully made sure she still had her parcel. It contained a valerian and camomile pillow to promote restful sleep, neatly stitched by hand. Tolivera's name had been carefully embroidered on the front with the pale gossamer threads of wild clematis. It was a work of art.

The woodpeckers put the final touches to the two armchairs by covering the seats with soft cushions of moss, and stood back to admire their work.

"Hurry up, hurry up, no time to waste!" chittered the squirrels irritably, anxious for the birds to finish and get out of their way, rolling their eyes at each other at the stupidity of people who just didn't understand the pressures of catering for large numbers.

Maurice and Maudie blinked behind their crystal raindrop glasses, looking around, admiring the transformation and enjoying the party atmosphere the decorations had created. It was all so very exciting for the quiet, shy couple.

Belvedere and Boadicea flittered in from their home in the bell tower of St Petrox church. Freddie and Oliphant greeted them warmly and they sat together exchanging news of the woodland.

Gradually guests arrived in twos and threes, part of a select group handpicked by the great Tolivera who was nowhere to be seen – yet. Dr Dew and Dr Yew Underconstumble arrived hand in hand carrying a small covered basket, each wearing a shiny scarf, one of silver and one of gold, with a long, fringed, tasselled edge. The silver one was woven from filmy threads tinged by the silvery light of a winter's dawn, and the gold one from fine threads caught from the golden light of a summer sunset; each was able to shine its captured rays for a short while in the dark and was only worn for extremely special occasions such as this.

The blue tits had laid a new winter rug in front of the two wooden thrones made from soft coloured feathers gleaned from the Skywingers and wool from the moulting sheep that grazed on the hilltop. Everything was ready, the toadstool seats were occupied, there were soft lights shining and soon the sweet music would begin.

The buzzard and his consort strolled in from the Citadel, choosing to walk through the woods, glimpsing the starry lights in the distance. The three princes followed, unimpressed, wishing they could stay at home and continue their astronomy studies lying in bed staring at the sky. The two reigning birds had put on their royal robes for the occasion, long russet cloaks with ermine linings, warm and luxurious. The young princes wore grey fur mufflers; they were too young and vigorous to feel the cold. At Tolivera's request the squirrels had built a fire in the centre, unlit but prepared in case of a frosty night. He had thought of everything.

As the buzzard family arrived everyone became quiet and watched as they took their seats graciously, admiring the craftsmanship of the smooth chairs and acknowledging the nervously waiting woodpeckers with a smile and a nod. They liked them! The two birds were thrilled – at last they could relax and enjoy themselves. Everyone looked around for Tolivera. Where was he?

Oliphant, realising something was amiss, flew up to the back door of the Great Ash Tree and quietly tiptoed inside. Lying under the warm coverlet, glass in hand, was Tolivera, his feathery chest rising and falling in gentle slumber.

"Wake up Tolly, wake up!" whispered the little owl, quietly disturbing his sleeping cousin.

"What? What's going on?" Gradually Tolivera struggled back to consciousness.

"You'll be late for the party, everyone's waiting," spoke Oliphant urgently, shaking him gently.

"Oh, yes… must wake up!" and groggily trying to focus his thoughts, sitting up abruptly, the room swimming before him.

"Cousin, is it you? Nice to see you. Help me up, boy, there's a good chap." Obediently the little white owl helped the great tawny owl to his feet.

"Had a few glasses of the Mists of Time to prepare myself for this evening. Must have dozed off. I'll be down in a minute. I'll be alright now. You can go. Start the music and give everyone a drink. Off you go!" and he waved Oliphant out of the door. Reluctant to go, Oliphant didn't move but Tolivera wasn't having any of it.

"Off you go, I said." he repeated loudly, so Oliphant tiptoed out of the back door and slipped quietly down the Great Tree trunk. He whispered to the head squirrel to serve the drinks and to the songsters to begin.

At once the air was filled with the sweetest music and the squirrels spread out amongst the enthralled guests, dispensing glasses of fizzing elderflower champagne and crunchy toasted beech nuts.

Freddie edged closer to Dr Dew and Dr Yew who turned and spoke to him in united voices before he could say a word.

"We know what you are going to say, indeed we do-o-o-o-o-o. We have brought some remedies with us in case we need to calm a few-ew-ew-ew."

The robin heaved a sigh of relief. "Thank you. What would we do without you?"

The pigeons patted the covered basket reassuringly. "We want to enjoy the party too-oo-oo-oo!"

Soon there was a sea of happy faces, laughter and conversation as the whole crowd of assorted Woodlanders began to enjoy themselves. The party was in full swing. Everyone forgot Tolivera's absence for a moment; everyone except Oliphant and of course the exalted buzzard, who missed nothing.

Chapter Thirty-eight
Humans join the woodland party

Making their way upwards through the woods from Sugary Cove, Ellie thought she heard birds singing. Then Patrick turned and said to her,

"Can you hear birds singing?"

"Yes I can, I heard them a minute ago."

"That seems very odd, I don't know any birds that sing in the dark, do you?"

Eddie stopped walking and stood still.

"Are you serious? I can't hear anything and I'm sure I…" His voice trailed off into silence as the haunting notes of a nightingale chorus clearly pierced their ears. They all looked at one another.

"What do you think it is?" whispered Ellie. "Why would they be singing in the dark?"

"Well there's only one way to find out," said Eddie firmly, "but let's just take it a little slower and be prepared to hide ourselves."

The others agreed and mouthed OK to him. Keeping alert and watchful they tried to shine the torches at their feet to avoid crunching on fallen twigs and frightening the birds away. Umbraluna kept quiet and just watched and followed. This was getting exciting.

At the edge of the earthworks, which long ago had been the fortifications piled up to defend Dartmouth from attack, the trees thinned out and the whole area became a grassy tussocky hillside looking across to the hills beyond. Ahead they could see lights flickering in reds and greens and hear faint high-pitched voices beneath the melodious birdsong. The lights were coming from the huge ash tree where the Moonmirror was fixed. It was all very puzzling and certainly Eddie, Ellie and Patrick had no idea what was going on. They listened, and shrugging their shoulders at each other stopped again, uncertain whether to proceed. Crouching down, they whispered breathlessly to each other.

"What do you think?"

"Shall we go on?"

"Should we circle round and have a look?"

"We can't reach the Moonmirror!"

"Who do you think it is?"

They couldn't agree on what was best.

"Let me go," offered Umbraluna suddenly, the others having forgotten his presence for a moment. "I can make myself invisible and see everything. Then I can come back and tell you, and you can decide .Will you let me go?"

"What do you think?" Eddie asked.

"I reckon it's a lot easier if we know exactly what's going on up there. I'm just worried about the Moonmirror, that's all," announced Patrick after careful thought.

"I agree with Patrick," whispered Ellie.

"Alright, you go first and report back to us," decided Eddie, nodding to the shadow that disappeared at once from sight, silently and without a word.

"Got anything to eat?" asked Eddie gloomily as they settled down on the side of the uncomfortable pathway to wait. They were almost at the top of the Bower. Everything was dark around them, just the halo of light coming from the direction of the large ash tree and the black sea rippling far below them, shining gently as it travelled backward and forward. Occasionally there was a chill wind and they all shivered. Patrick found some old sticky sweets in his coat pocket and they ate them gratefully, passing the time thinking of various reasons for the strange scene at the hilltop. Stars peeped out of the endless black sky and a half moon, white and shadowy, appeared now and again between the thick clumps of clouds. It was rather comforting.

The Moonglimmer wafted his way towards the lighted arena, unprepared for what he saw when he rounded the top of the steep banks. A party – a crowd of happy animals, birds and insects, dancing, drinking, and eating, to the music of a Nightingale Quartet who were singing their hearts out. He saw the buzzard he had shadowed resting on a carved seat, his wife beside him and three sons close by, gobbling up food offered by a band of squirrels in red waistcoats and long white aprons. Perched on a circle of toadstools he recognised Freddie, the robin from Watermill Cottage, and next to him were the two pigeons he had received the elixir from, their faces full of happiness and enjoyment. Other birds and the two moles he had visited were seated too, all tapping to the music, cast in the rosy light of the glowing berries woven into the tree above.

Undiscovered and unseen, the box containing the Moonmirror still hung on the tree. The whole circle in front of it was illuminated by a pearly rainbow of dull sheen, created by the endless circling of the slugs.

What should he do? At first the Moonglimmer did not know, but he watched in rapture at the enchanting scene below him; more and more of what he saw on Earth of the animal and human worlds amazed and delighted him.

He focused his eyes on Dr Dew and Dr Yew and he knew that at once that they could feel his presence. Both looked in his direction, and he began steadily to glimmer towards them, seating himself beside them.

"I would like my human friends to join us, to share in this unique gathering. Is it possible?" he asked. "They might frighten the animals, however. They are so big."

"Indeed they are, so we must make them smaller. Help is at hand, nothing is impossible. We have an elixir for everything; we only wait to be asked. Every wish can come true-o-o-o." Dr Dew and Dr Yew delved into their basket and removed a small corked bottle marked the Elixir of Wishes, and reaching for an acorn cup, put a few drops into it.

"Make them drink this. When they see the party, they will want to join in and will long to be smaller. Then, it will happen, all in good time. Carry it carefully, spill not a drop. Go, Umbraluna. Enjoy your last day on Earth with the voice that you yearned for, and be satisfied."

The Moonglimmer was grateful, and thanking the pigeons in their own cooing voice, he returned to his invisible star-like shape and carried the precious cup through the darkness so carefully in his clumsy arms in case he spilt it. He reached the spot where the three sat together and tipped several drops onto the lips of each person. Eddie, Ellie and Patrick felt an unfamiliar sweetness, moist and syrupy, that tasted of the scent of lilac flowers, and licked their lips.

"Those sweets were delicious weren't they?" they remarked to each other. "I can still taste them," as they swallowed the Elixir of Wishes.

Umbraluna became a grey shadow shape again and told Eddie what he had seen.

"I am here beside you. There is a Christmas party for the woodland going on beneath the ash tree. All are assembled. If you creep closer you will be able to see it. I think you will not have seen anything like it before. Come." Rather surprised, but eager to see, the three youngsters stood up and the shadow led the way along the path.

"Turn off your torches," he told them, "you will be able to see." And they followed the shadow, which was now pale blue and gently lighting the way. Ellie giggled.

"Here we go," she whispered to Patrick happily, "I can feel one of our happenings coming on."

Patrick was thrilled, he so wanted to be part of them and of the exciting and mysterious things that they always seemed to find, or that found them. Crawling over the edge of the high ridge with Umbraluna beside them, they peered cautiously over the edge.

Ellie's eyes opened wide as she took in the prettily decorated woodland secret revealed before them. Rose-tinted lights glowed from the berried trails, the pearly shimmer of the rainbow circle shone, and the Nightingale Quartet sang their haunting tunes. A lavish buffet exuding delicious smells was spread out exquisitely and the animals normally so shy and withdrawn were bedecked and bedazzled in their finest clothes, relaxed and chatting in groups all around, just like humans. She admired the toadstool seats and the large carved chairs, and watched the buzzard strutting in his russet robes. He, who she had only watched from afar, wheeling and spiralling in the skies above them, a dull brown elusive bird, seemed to be the most important person.

Eddie and Patrick were agog. All this going on and they hadn't known about it? *Is this what animals do when we can't see them?* Eddie wondered, and then he caught sight of Freddie, sporting his mimosa waistcoat, next to a white owl with a large violet bow tie. *Good old Freddie!* He smiled to himself. There were pigeons and blackbirds, owls and skylarks, squirrels and moles, bats, slugs and snails, and a rather fine pair of buzzards.

"Don't you wish you could join them?" asked Patrick, highly amused, and surprised at what he saw.

"Oh, I wish we could!" whispered Ellie back. She turned to Eddie, "Don't you? I can see Freddie, and he's dressed to kill!" and she nudged him. Eddie nodded, smiling, and breathed deeply.

The doctors were right, and the next minute all three of them collapsed like a pack of cards, their skin, hair and clothes folding up, until they stood no more than nine inches tall! Shocked and feeling rather odd, they looked around them and realised they had become the same size as the Woodlanders.

Umbraluna was at their side. "Now you can join the party too," he told them. "Go on," and he urged them on over the hill top.

Why not? They looked at themselves and then began to creep around the back of the ash tree which had assumed gigantic proportions, and Eddie tapped Freddie on the shoulder lightly as he reached his side. The robin almost fell off his toadstool in surprise.

"Eddie, what's happened to you?" he asked, and then saw Ellie and Patrick behind him.

"I'm not really sure, but we wished we could join you, and it happened. We don't want to intrude but we came up to use the Moonmirror. We have a guest with us from the dark side of the moon who wanted to see it. He's here, he's our shadow," and Umbraluna obligingly danced out to show himself to Freddie, who at once thought of the shock the humans might be to the animal party guests. Wishing to keep everything peaceful he tactfully suggested, "I'd better just introduce you to the buzzard, he's the Lord of the Woodland you know, and make sure it's OK with him. We've got to observe all the correct proceedings up here at a formal gathering," and he hopped off to approach the buzzard, hoping for the best.

Dr Dew and Dr Yew took over the three new bewildered guests.

"How do you do-o-o-o?" they said quietly together. Eddie, Ellie and Patrick stood, trying to take it all in and feeling, well, rather small.

"Hello, it's very nice to meet you," replied Eddie nervously.

"You wanted to join the party too-o-o-o-?" they asked, cooing gently.

"Oh yes, it looks such fun."

"We shall see, but watch out, there may be a hullabaloo-oo-oo, stay with us, do-o-o." warned the quiet grey pigeons, one of which clutched a covered basket, close to his wing.

"Where do you live?" asked Patrick, curious to know about everyone.

"Why at the Cornucopia tree, in the heart of the wood, high out of view-oo-oo," they cooed together.

"Oh," replied Patrick, not really understanding, but remembering the name to discuss with Eddie later.

Freddie had found the buzzard, who was starting his third elderflower champagne and feeling warm and benevolent to all his gathered subjects. He was having a great evening.

"Ah, Freddie, having a good time?"…

"Yes indeed, my lord. I have some… er… unexpected guests, Sire, you may be rather surprised but I hope they will be welcome. I think rather unusual events have occurred to bring them here, but I felt I needed to seek your permission to allow them to join us this evening—"

But the buzzard, bathed in the pink glory of the heady mixture of champagne, good food, music and company, silenced him.

"Nonsense, nonsense dear fellow, they are most welcome of course, let them be entertained by the Woodlanders and enjoy the hospitality of so great a friend as Tolivera. I say, Freddie, where is old Tolly? I don't recall seeing him. It has quite slipped my mind. Yes indeed, go and sort it out will you? And don't worry any more about a few extra guests. Off you go!" But his wife sitting nearby slipped away, having heard everything and wondering who the new arrivals were.

Freddie hopped off back to Eddie's side as the buzzard went to join his three sons, who sat adoringly, bewitched by the subtle charm of the Nightingale Sisters.

Oliphant joined him, becoming so overheated and anxious about his cousin that the violet bow tie he was wearing had begun to wilt.

"I've been up to see Tolly but he was asleep. I'm afraid he's been sampling the Mists of Time. That must mean a fresh brew is ready and you know what could happen." He gave a very meaningful look to Freddie, who caught his message at once.

"Ah, yes… Oh dear. I see what you mean."

They both looked rather scared and looked at Dr Dew and Dr Yew, who nodded their heads and cooed kindly.

"We understand very well, but we know what to do-oo-oo, we are prepared, don't get in a stew-oo-oo."And both patted the covered basket, in a knowing way.

"Have you brought something? Something to help?" questioned the quick-witted, black eyed robin, as sharp as ever. The pigeons nodded confidently and patted their basket again, to reassure him.

The female buzzard had been scanning the assembly to try to spot the newcomers and was transfixed in pure amazement when she saw three little miniature humans seated beside the Doctor

Underconstumbles, Freddie and Oliphant. They seemed deep in conversation.

There's always been something about that robin," she thought to herself, *wait until my lord sees them.* She glided away to be nosy and see what the squirrels were conjuring up for desserts. It had been simple country food so far but they had done it well, in her opinion. The reigning buzzards wouldn't have to stay much longer and she was keen to get the boys home and out from under the seductive brown eyes of those wretched Nightingales, who she knew were flirting shamelessly with her sons.

She found the squirrels lining up large bowlfuls of rosehip jellies with nectar topping. It was one of her favourites and she nodded and smiled at the busy gang.

Suddenly the door in the Great Ash Tree opened, and Tolivera appeared in a red hat and smoking jacket of finest velvet, his face like thunder and his eyes on fire.

"What is going on?" he screamed in rage over the whole assembly, as he struggled to keep his balance.

"Who gave permission for this Tramps and Trollops Extravaganza to take place? Here, in front of MY house? You must be mad to think I would allow such bedlam here! Eh? Speak up somebody! Somebody is responsible for this and I'll find out who it is, if it's the last thing I do!" and he brandished his pipe at the lot of them. The Nightingales stopped singing, the squirrels froze on the spot, and the children were petrified. Ellie clutched onto Eddie and Patrick's arms.

"Who's he?" she whispered to Freddie anxiously.

"That's Tolivera, the Deputy, he organised this whole party, but I don't think he's feeling too… very…well." He turned quickly away from her.

"The elixir's run out!" he hissed to an almost fainting Oliphant.

"What shall we do?" gasped the white owl frantically, but Dr Dew and Dr Yew acted at once, opening their basket quickly and calling out in whispers, "Shadow from the dark side of the moon, we need you *now*!"

Instantly Umbraluna was there.

"Take this elixir and place two drops on his beak at once. Hurry, as fast as you can! Then put a drop in each of the desserts, – be careful, we don't want to give anyone a clue-o-o-o-o! Go now, do-o-o-o-o-!" was the pigeons' urgent command.

The Moonglimmer tried to take hold of the bottle being offered to him but before he could grasp it, Tolivera saw the three children gathered by the toadstool seats and his eyes opened ever wider in rage. Anger glinted in them. He recognised them; they were his enemies.

"Those interfering humans again! Aha! They are just the right size now!" and he took off from the ash tree and flew down, talons open wide, everyone watching in horror as Ellie was caught in his grip and lifted off her feet, high into the air. Horrified gasps were heard from the onlookers but Umbraluna was ready and shot off after him, chasing and zigzagging around the woodland at high speed, following him in and out of the trees, weaving and turning in pursuit, finally cornering him by the Citadel and stunning him with a blast from his eyes. He immediately dropped two globules of the potent liquid, the Elixir of Friendship, onto his beak. Ellie was petrified with fear but as yet unharmed and as the elixir took hold of Tolivera his mood changed and he looked in astonishment at the little human creature he found himself holding, rather tightly.

Freddie and Oliphant caught up with him and as the dizzy tawny owl perched on the pine tree to recover, they closed in, one on each side of him, forcing him to release his grip on the poor shaking girl. She turned at once to the robin she loved.

"It's alright, Ellie, you've had a bit of an adventure that's all, Tolivera just wanted to take you for a spin round the woodland. Don't cry." The robin enfolded her and comforted her as she wept into his soft warm feathers.

"It was so frightening!" she sobbed, "I thought he was going to eat me!"

Meanwhile Umbraluna arced back through the air to the food tables and did as he had been instructed by the pigeons and put a drop in each rosehip jelly. He returned the bottle to the doctors, watched by the distraught Eddie and Patrick. Dr Dew reached into the basket again.

"Just for good measure," they told him, and held out yet another bottle, labelled the Elixir of Distant Memories.

"We think this will help you-o-o-o-o," and Umbraluna exchanged bottles and returned to the desserts and the dandelion coffee, liberally dosing them both to be quite, quite sure. The party would not be ruined after all.

"Now, my little maid, shall we return to the party?" Tolivera asked Ellie kindly. "You have seen where the buzzards live and we don't want to miss the desserts, do we? I'd like to meet your other human friends. Coming along with me again for a ride?" Freddie assured her it would be quite safe and encouraged her to go. Gently Tolivera picked her up, closely followed by a shocked and worried Oliphant and the good, kind Freddie. Ellie was returned to her brother and Patrick who both hugged her, thankful for her safe return.

The buzzard, piecing it all together, realised that the three very small humans were the ones from Watermill Cottage – those nurtured and guarded by Freddie the robin, and hated by Tolivera. He didn't quite know how they had got here, but felt one of his special speeches was in order, perhaps after he had eaten the alluring rose hip jelly with its tantalising nectar topping. Yes, that would do, after dessert he would speak.

Trying to ignore what had happened, the buzzards and Tolivera were invited to be first to the buffet table by the trembling squirrels, who were now in fear of the old tawny owl, but he was all smiles and good cheer and soon everyone was enjoying the dainty puddings. Dr Dew and Dr Yew looked after the three rather shy and quiet humans, encouraging them to eat and drink. The Nightingale Sisters were persuaded to sing again and a semblance of normality returned to the woodland as the Elixir of Distant Memories miraculously worked its magic. Tolivera's outburst was forgotten.

Now it was the highlight of the evening – the performance by Walter and Winifred Wagtail. However, the buzzard wanted to speak first. He tapped on the table with his wooden goblet and gradually the voices were hushed.

"My friends, tonight we are grateful to the Honourable Tolivera for his generosity in holding this splendid party and we are particularly pleased to receive some special guests who have come to us in rather reduced circumstances, but it is a step forward and good for our inter-woodland relations. Therefore we welcome you!"

"Does he mean us?" Eddie whispered to Ellie and Patrick, uncertain of what to do.

"Just bow," advised Freddie, so they did. Tolivera sat beaming having eaten three jellies and feeling warm and full of kind thoughts, although he couldn't quite remember what they were.

"And now…" The buzzard hesitated, what was he going to say? Oh yes, "Now for the dancing. Please welcome… um, let me see… ah yes, the Wagtails!"

There was great applause as the smiling couple stepped into the limelight. He, dapper in black and white tails, a bow tie and patent shoes and she in lemon-and-black striped chiffon, yellow stockings and high-heeled black shoes. How they danced! Their feet entwined, their heads tossed, they simpered and smiled at every turn, the smiles becoming fixed, giving a faint snarl to their beaks as they threw superior glances over their shoulders.

Ellie felt the giggles coming on but Patrick restrained her; he didn't want any more unpleasant mishaps. They were offered jellies with nectar topping by the discreet squirrels in attendance and ate happily, watching the show. Dandelion coffee was served and soon the yawns began. Maudie and Maurice were the first to give their thanks and slip away. Ellie suddenly noticed them leaving.

"Are they our two lovely moles? The ones we saved?" she asked Freddie.

"Indeed they are. They're rather shy and quiet and it's been a long evening for them." He excused their early exit politely. Ellie beamed with joy, so glad she had stood up to her father that day. The dancing ended to rapturous applause and bows and the Wagtails posed for autographs and interviews.

"What shall we do about the Moonmirror?" Eddie asked. "We're too small to even reach it."

"It's not important now," replied Umbraluna, sitting in Eddie's shadow. "I was curious to see how your lights travelled so far and admired the brightness and colour, but I know now it is of human engineering and I could never reproduce its workings. We have advanced a great deal and our own ways are best for us. Let us leave our lights a mystery to each other, for therein lies its fascination – everything is the better for not understanding it." The three youngsters knew he was right.

"How will we become ourselves again?" Patrick was worried, but the two wise pigeons were listening.

"You have only to dream of being yourselves and wish for it and you will be," advised Dr Dew and Dr Yew together. "The party is almost over. You have seen much and glimpsed the world of the Woodlanders, an honour granted to only a few-o-o-o-o-o."

Tired now, they did as the pigeons advised and gathered up by Umbraluna in his five outstretched arms, invisibly and quietly they were whisked away over the trees and down the dark valley each to their own homes not a minute late, where they climbed into bed, sighed and snuggled down.

Their disappearance was not even noticed by the buzzards or Tolivera, who were also falling asleep, and one by one the little creatures crept home to a slumber induced by the elixirs and the party became just a distant memory for the entire assembly of assorted Woodlanders.

Chapter Thirty-nine
A memorable fishing trip

At 9 o'clock the following morning Peter woke his two sleeping fishermen.

"Wakey wakey, shake a leg!" he yelled into their rooms as Ellie and Eddie both groaned and told him to go away. Eddie opened his eyes.

"Oh no, got to get up… fishing trip today, isn't it?" He focused on the ceiling and tried to wake up.

"Downstairs in fifteen minutes," threatened Peter, "or no breakfast." That did it. They struggled out of bed, washed and dressed begrudgingly and went downstairs yawning, wishing their father wasn't quite so jolly first thing in the morning.

"Any toast, Mum?"

"You know where the toaster is Ellie; it's hardly Cordon Bleu cookery is it?"

"Patrick and Sam will be here soon and we've got to put the stuff in the car. You'll give us a lift down to the quay won't you, dear?" Peter addressed his wife with a cheeky grin.

"Why yes, sir, I've nothing else to do today except run around after you lot. Glad to get rid of you."

"Mum," said Eddie in a hurt voice, "surely not?" and then burst out laughing.

Full up with toast, they explored the fridge for three packed lunches and put it all into a waterproof sailing bag. Eddie collected the rods from the garage, hooks and reels and rolls of line, disgorger, sharp knife and a few plastic bags.

"I'm off to give the church a good polish and cut the greenery for the Christmas flowers," Mary told them. "I may see you from the river's edge on my way. Have a lovely time, won't you?" she added kindly, glad they were all going off together.

Sam appeared round the corner followed by a bleary eyed Patrick, looking half asleep and not at his best.

"Good morning to you. This is a great idea, everyone ready?" He was excited at the prospect. The three youngsters raised their eyebrows at each other and got into the car, quiet for once, and concentrated on waking up. Sam and Peter squeezed in somehow and Mary drove them down to the quayside where the *Alice May* was quietly rocking on her mooring lines, impatient to be free.

"Mornin." A bright and breezy Mike Oswald peered out from the bridge window, a mug of tea in his hand.

"Goin' to be a nice one," and he looked up at the sky. It was dry and bright with a thin covering of cloud. The river was flat and calm and the wind light. It was perfect for fishing. Eddie, Ellie and Patrick stood yawning on the quayside, their brains not really working as their dads chivvied them up and tried to inspire them into action. Eddie and Ellie kissed their mother and she drove off with a wave, anxious to begin her own busy day.

"Come aboard," Mike instructed them, and helped transport all their precious equipment from the quayside. Mike's wife Lillian busied herself in the galley and produced a tray of teas and coffees and bacon sandwiches. Life appeared back in the three tired souls and soon they were sitting round the highly polished chart table, munching happily.

"We're just waiting for three more guests," explained Mike, "and then we'll be off. I'd be very grateful for your discretion, as they are on a private visit to Dartmouth – but you'll understand Peter, being in the Navy, so I didn't mind your lot joining us."

"Of course," Peter replied at once. Sam nodded, wondering what he was talking about, but knew that Dartmouth attracted the rich and famous for a quiet retreat.

A black car with tinted windows drew up, driven by a uniformed driver, who halted opposite the boat. A man, a lady and a young man in his late twenties got out. The chauffeur then opened the boot and produced a large hamper, rugs and waterproof clothes. Lillian wiped her hands nervously, tidied her hair and looked at Mike. They both left the cockpit to greet the guests and help them on board. They shook hands with the visitors who clambered over the side, the hamper, rugs and waterproofs following, the driver assisting in the operation.

"Thank you Dobson, we'll ring you when we want you. Don't get into those dreadful dens of iniquity in Dartmouth, and stay away from the local cider." The man wagged his finger at the smiling face grinning from the quayside.

"I'll try, my lord!" was his reply, as Lord James Beverly, his wife Elsa and his son Sacramento ducked and joined everyone in the bridge cabin with the enticing smell of bacon and coffee. Sam, having watched their arrival with interest, and realising this was someone of importance, was rather taken aback.

"Good morning, everyone!" beamed Lord James, "How nice to see you again, what a wonderful surprise," looking at Eddie, Ellie and Patrick, who were halfway through their bacon sandwiches, but stopped, mouths open.

"Lord Beverley!" they all said together, "Hello!" and smiled in recognition.

"Elsa my dear, meet the three young people I told you about – the real heroes that helped the Navy out of a tight spot, eh?"

His wife greeted them warmly. "Don't shake hands." she laughed as they put their greasy sandwiches down.

"And meet Sacramento, this is our son," Lord Beverley continued, proudly introducing the tanned handsome young man to the children.

"Hi there, how are ya doing?" A faintly American accent was detectable. "Well done you."

Sam was totally confused. How could such an important person know the children? Especially Patrick? And why didn't he know about it? Did he hear somebody say Lord Beverley? It was all very strange.

Patrick was overjoyed. What was his father going to say now? Peter came to the rescue seeing the confusion on Sam's face.

"Lord Beverley, Lady Beverley, may I introduce Sam McNab, Patrick's father from Edinburgh, who wasn't in Dartmouth at the time the Russian submarines were discovered and doesn't know anything about Patrick's role in the well-kept secret. The boys have taken your security warning very seriously, haven't you, boys?" They all nodded furiously and Lillian brought three more bacon sandwiches, fresh coffee and croissants to the table and invited the new guests to join in. Patrick was looking very embarrassed as gradually the story unfolded, told by Peter, Lord James, Eddie and Ellie, and the odd addition by Patrick when Eddie nudged him.

Sam just couldn't believe it. It didn't seem possible, but when Lord James proudly told him about the lunch and the medals it finally sank in. He was utterly lost for words and kept shaking his head and saying, "Unbelievable! I canna take it in! My wee lad!" lapsing into his childhood Scottish and seeing his son with quite new eyes.

Mike and Lillian, who were now sworn to secrecy, started the engine and began to get their guests organised for the fishing trip. Ellie couldn't stop staring at Sacramento who told them he made wildlife documentaries for television. She blushed whenever he spoke to her. He really was just like a film star.

They motored out of the river enjoying the peace and fresh air, getting lines exactly right, bait and hooks together and exploring the boat down below. Soon everyone felt a swell lifting them up and down as the river met the sea at the castle.

"Look for Mum," remembered Ellie and they went to the guard rails to have a quick scan along the river's edge for her. There she was, visible in her red jacket, brown hair blowing in the wind, waving to them for all she was worth. They waved back, pleased they had seen her, then she disappeared, probably back into the church.

As they crossed the bay and looked ahead to Start Point, they could see a strange glow in the sky.

"What is that?" Lord James pointed towards the lighthouse, where the brightness seemed to pool on the water.

"I'm not sure." Mike was puzzled. He and Lillian, who were used to crossing this stretch of water almost daily, were unable to reach any firm conclusions, never having seen anything like it before. Eddie and Patrick, however, had their suspicions, and as their eyes met they knew they were thinking the same thing – *Umbraluna*. What had he done to the lighthouse beam? They had been there yesterday, hadn't they? Oh no!

Soon Mike advised them to try casting their lines and they all found their own spots around the boat and began to try their luck. Sacramento and Elsa told them of how they had been fishing off the coast of California hoping to catch marlin and of the enormous rods and special seats required to pull in the huge fish. Eddie listened with interest.

Ellie and Patrick looked over the side and saw swirls and shoals of many fish simply cruising in the water, hardly swimming at all, and they seemed to be facing the strange light from the very top of the lighthouse. They ran to the other side of the boat where clusters of jellyfish, eels and strange spiny fish also floated, almost suspended in the water.

"Look! Look!" they called out to the others, "Come and see all these fish!"

Everyone stopped fishing because it became quite obvious that the fish were not interested in feeding in their dreamlike trance, idly swimming slowly through the water seemingly towards the light.

"Why is the lighthouse switched on at this time?" asked Lord James. "It should be on a special timing device. I think I'll ring the coastguards. It must be the reason for the fish appearing on the surface. Can you arrange that for me, Mike, on your VHF radio?"

"Certainly, sir." And off he went to call them up. The light was faintly blue-tinged with an alluring brightness, not dissimilar to the moon against a black sky. The children knew at once it was most definitely the work of Umbraluna who they had left snoozing in Patrick's bed. He had not wished to see the capture of the fish creatures he had so admired for their beauty.

"Ready to take your call, sir? Brixham coastguards replying now," Mike called out from the cockpit and Lord James Beverley, Admiral of the Fleet, dressed in a yellow and white sailing jacket and a red baseball cap, took hold of the phone and explained the situation.

"Yes I know it shouldn't be like it, and I appreciate there's a failsafe device, but it's not working. Do you hear me? Yes, I think you'd better send somebody straight away. Thank you. Goodbye." He took a deep breath in frustration.

In the office at Brixham, Fred Hannaford rolled his eyes and whistled at his colleague.

"Some nutter on the VHS, Bill, did you hear him? Says the lighthouse is shining a weird bright light and it's disturbing the fish! Did you ever? Wants us to go and have a look at it! Fat chance! I nearly told him to stop disturbing me with his fairy tales! Been on the gin I'd say! Posh twit!" and he chuckled with the crew on duty in the ops room.

The fish, drawn by the artificial moonlight, forced by the pull of the divine light that controls the cycles of all creatures on Earth, automatically began their journey to the surface of the water which was thick with every species of fish relentlessly moving towards the light that was irresistible to them.

"Cut the engine, Mike," called Peter, "we're going to slice them up with the prop soon, there's so many of them."

They reached the jutting point of land where the lighthouse stood.

"Do you think they're dying?" asked Eddie anxiously, leaning over the side.

"Somehow, I don't," answered Sacramento, taking pictures with his camera. "This is a natural phenomenon. You see the failure of the light to switch off is drawing the fish to the surface, but somehow the light is different. It's much stronger and a different colour. I think the fish think it's the moon casting its light and of course lots of creatures reproduce at a full moon."

Mike and Lillian gave everyone the binoculars they had on board and Sam, who had them first, noticed a strange flat mass floating far away.

"Something unusual over there I think. Can you see?" and Lord James who had the other pair looked carefully, scanning the sea until he spotted it. "Yes, I've got it; it's a dark shape floating on the water. Looks a bit like an oil spill to me."

They waited together for the object to reach them and as they drifted nearer to the light the object became clearer. They all asked Sacramento what it was. He took the binoculars and said nothing for a long time.

"It's not possible, but it's here in front of our eyes. It's supposed to be extinct, but I'm pretty sure it's a species of giant squid."

"Really?"

"What? Surely not."

"Quite impossible!"

"It does *look* like it." The whole crew on the *Alice May* were the first to witness this strange and vast sea creature for over a hundred years. Drawn from the deep by the power of the lunar influence the giant squid, the Great Kraken, urged by a force he could not resist, hurried his great bulk out of the Caves of Astraeus. He began a momentous journey through the deepest parts of the ocean. Willed on, straining his weak and unused muscles, knowing it would probably be his last and fatal journey, he was unable to repel the constant pull of the light that at first he could not even see. The Seafarers were all under the influence of the pearly brightness.

***

Back at Waterside Cottage, the Moonglimmer had woken up alone. He felt a little sluggish, wondering if he had enough energy left inside him to make his journey back home. He felt a strange sensation, and sensitive to the thought vibrations sent to him, he knew that Eddie, Ellie, and Patrick were thinking about him and wanted him urgently. Gradually their thoughts became stronger.

"I'd better go and find them," he told himself, and wafted out of the window into the fresh air, switching on his navigation system as all his sensory terminals became alert. He moved over the hillside to face the open sea, spotting the faint rays from the lighthouse. He whisked himself off at the speed of light, found the *Alice May*, and hovered above her surveying the scene. He saw the small figures on deck, the sea engorged with fish of all kinds, and to his horror, the Great Kraken. The giant squid had struggled from his dark retreat in the ocean, the eerie Caves of Astraeus, and now lay motionless on the surface; his great body and huge legs a mass of pulp, spreading a dark stain over the sea. Blinded by the light, his body was disintegrating slowly. He was dying.

Umbraluna realised that when he had beamed new light into the circular lantern of the lighthouse he had charged it with moonlight, more intense and brighter than the Earth had ever seen, and consequently it had much, much, more power. Its effect upon the sea creatures had been great indeed.

Umbraluna went immediately to turn off the light and he re-absorbed the energy he had sent it. It charged his centre up at once and as the power was transferred from one to the other, the beam was extinguished. The Moonglimmer was full of remorse for the floundering and pathetic mound of jelly that the Great Kraken had been reduced to. He went at once to his side and asked him if he wished to return to the darkness of the ocean. The reply surprised him.

"I have been in perfect bliss this last hour. To see the light again from the eternal heavens has brought such happiness to me. I long to die now in its shadow, for I have lived too long. Let me go, Umbraluna, now I have glimpsed the light once more. Let me go. I cannot return to the darkness. I am become fat and bloated and discontented. Let me drift away to freedom. The Spirit of the Sea will understand for he knows all things. Let me go!" and because of his pleading, Umbraluna agreed sadly and the giant from the unknown floated away in peace, his eyes closed and his body still.

Sacramento was now frantic with excitement and was snapping away with his camera to record the sensational discovery.

"We ought to tow it to land, to let the Maritime Museum see it, don't you think, Pa?" he asked his father, looking for his advice. Suddenly everyone saw the brightness fade and disappear. Gradually the fish seemed to move a little more, fins flapped and one or two tails broke the surface; they had begun to disperse. Mike felt it safe to switch on the engine once more.

Lord James studied the floating mass as it began to shrivel and break up, the exposure to moonlight and then daylight too much for it.

"I'm sorry, Son, but I don't think there's going to be much left for the scientists, do you?" and they both watched the disintegration in front of their eyes.

"What a shame," sighed the children together, "It was huge, wasn't it?"

Eddie kept looking around. He knew the Moonglimmer could not be far away and he took himself off to the far end of the boat, where at once he saw his own grey shadow appear on the deck. Then he heard his own voice,

"It is I, Umbraluna, Eddie. I am sorry I interfered with the light. It has forced the fish in the ocean to come to the surface to look at the moon. I have caused the death of the Great Kraken too, the Secret of the Deep."

"Do you mean you knew about the giant squid?" asked an astonished Eddie.

"Yes, I saw him on my visit with Sargasso in the underwater caves, but he was a Seafarers' secret. We swore an oath of silence which I had to obey. I also have news for you that I hope you will understand. This is my last day with a voice, my last day on your beautiful Earth, and I must depart before I lose all my strength. Today I must return." Umbraluna told him sadly.

"But the moon is not full yet, not until next week," desperately whispered Eddie, unprepared for this blow.

"I know and if I wait any longer I will have no power left. I have exchanged energy with the lighthouse for today, but I have a long journey to make. I will wait at the Moonmirror tonight, if you all wish to say goodbye."

"We'll be there! We've got to be there!" agreed the disappointed boy, holding his sadness back inside his heart. He watched his own shadow wave goodbye to him and disappears. Patrick and Ellie joined him, excited by the dispersal of the fish.

"They aren't dead, Eddie, they must have been sort of hypnotised by the moonlight. Is Umbraluna here? He must have turned the light off," said Patrick.

"He was here but he's gone now. He says he saw that giant squid on his visit under the sea with Sargasso, he knew about it all the time but had to swear to secrecy."

"Is it dead now?" asked Ellie, "because it must have been very old, Sacramento thinks they've been extinct for years. Nobody's ever seen one – we're lucky to have been here."

"It looks pretty dead," agreed Patrick. "Maybe it came to look at the light and couldn't get back."

The three looked over the side watching the huge mass getting darker and disappearing in clumps, drifting out to sea. A slight breeze increased and the surface rippled, helping to move the dead squid away. Gradually as Mike increased the speed they left the scene and moved out of sight, Sacramento staring sadly at the fading remnants of an extraordinary discovery.

"It's such a damn shame; it ought to have been saved for research. Who's going to believe us?" He shook his head, disappointed and depressed. "Photos aren't real evidence, they can be faked."

"Never mind, son," consoled his father, "perhaps pieces of it will reach the shore. We can always alert Professor Palmer from the laboratory in Plymouth. Geoff was at the experimental unit in Gosport with me. Let's give him a call just in case."

Sacramento cheered at the prospect and they began to use Lord James's special mobile telephone to contact him, just in case any remains of the giant squid were washed ashore.

"Lunch?" called Lillian.

"What, already?" replied Elsa and the three youngsters together.

"It's half-past twelve," she told them. Where had the morning gone? Elsa helped Lillian unpack the hamper she had brought, disclosing crusty pies, boxes of salads and warm French bread. By the time hot sausages, sandwiches and a hearty vegetable broth had been added, the table was completely covered. Eddie looked as if his eyes might pop out of his head!

"What a fabulous feast," he remarked, as Lord James opened a bottle of champagne.

They tried to forget about the morning of strange occurrences and began to enjoy the superb lunch. Somehow the interest in fishing had waned. Mike, sensing everyone's feelings, suggested he take them further round the coast on a sightseeing trip.

"Good idea, Mike," agreed Peter, and gathering up Ellie and Eddie he chose a sheltered spot out of the wind to sit with them. Patrick and Sam took turns at the wheel and Lillian and Elsa sat drinking coffee in the warm. Lord James and Sacramento wanted to take photographs of the birds, and it proved to be an interesting afternoon. The boys polished off all the packed lunches.

"I can't possibly take the first one she has ever made me home," laughed Patrick munching. As darkness fell so early in the winter, Mike was watchful and returned to the local waters by 4.30pm. The boys trailed feathers on the way home and caught some whiting and mackerel; they were very satisfied and it had proved to be rather a special day.

Eddie, not wishing to get Patrick into any trouble at home and knowing Ellie would not want to go out in the cold and dark again, told no one of his intended visit to the ash tree. He would have to go to bed and get up later; it was the only way. Consequently he was quiet and thoughtful on the journey home. Tying up alongside, Eddie hoped Lord James would not remember the Moonmirror he had asked about at their previous meeting, but then horror of horrors, Peter remembered.

"Excuse me, Lord James, have you time to come and see Eddie's Moonmirror?" Eddie closed his eyes in despair.

"Well, I don't know," he replied thoughtfully. "Elsa, how are we doing for time? What's on this evening? Any chance of squeezing it in?"

His wife smiled and left Lillian's warm wheelhouse. "Have you forgotten, dear? We're dining at the Imperial Theatre and then watching the Strasbourg Ballet Company. We haven't got a lot of time, I'm afraid to say." She looked apologetically at them all. "Perhaps next time we visit we could see your fascinating invention; it sounds so marvellous," she added kindly.

"Right, dear, I see," replied her husband, and turning to Peter he shook his head.

"Sorry, Peter, not possible I'm afraid, but we'll make a definite date for next time."

"I'll send you kids some photos of the squid, yes?" asked Sacramento. "I'm dying to get these developed."

In the end they all stood on the quayside, Dobson arrived and fond farewells were exchanged. The two men and the three children walked leisurely back home, carrying their fishing tackle and empty picnic bags, as the lights of Dartmouth were turned on and darkness made its silent entry. Eddie looked anxiously at the sky. Was there any chance of a clear night ahead?

Sam talked quietly to Peter. He couldn't wait to get home to tell Irene that he had met Lord James Beverley, Admiral of the Fleet no less, and of Patrick's involvement in the discovery of the Russian submarines. It had not escaped him that had the submarines not been located, the outcome for them all could have been so very different.

"I never would have believed it of him," he told Peter confidentially.

"We never really know what our children are capable of," replied his companion. "Often we can only see their faults and we expect them to be like us and think like us, but of course they turn out to be so different – and you know, Sam, they are allowed to be different, they are not us and why should we expect them to be? Patrick is a very sensible boy and a thinking person. Let him go his own way. He'll make good by himself, you wait and see. He and Eddie are good for each other; they seem to spark when they get together. That's an incredible thing they've invented, you know."

"I'd like to see it," Sam agreed enthusiastically. "Do you think they would show it to me?"

"Well ask them!" laughed Peter, looking up and searching the navy blue star-speckled sky for signs of heavy cloud. It seemed fairly clear.

Sam caught up with the boys and Ellie as they rounded the corner at Warfleet and the creek waters came into view, shining shady and sheeny under the cover of darkness.

"Patrick?" he called out, and at once they stopped walking and turned around.

"Yes Dad?"

"I've got something to ask you and Eddie." He hesitated, not wanting a refusal. "Do you think I could see your Moonmirror? Maybe tonight? There's three-quarters of a moon I'm sure, will it do? I mean, is that enough moonlight?" He felt stupid asking the question.

Eddie and Patrick looked at each other, unable to discuss this in private, put on the spot by Sam. There was only one possible answer, as Peter caught up with them all. Eddie felt as if his heart had sunk all the way down his legs to his ankles, and his feet felt heavy and rooted to the spot. What should he do? …But it wasn't his decision; Sam had asked Patrick and he had no choice.

"Of course," they both replied together, not looking at each other's face.

"That'd be great, son," replied a grateful Sam, as the boys then flashed meaningful glances.

"Don't think I'm going out in the cold again," complained Ellie.

"You don't have to," replied Eddie at once. "Stay in with Mum and wrap up all my Christmas presents!"

"You cheeky thing!" she laughed, but she was determined to have a hot bath and stay by the fire. They dispersed, the two men making arrangements, agreeing to telephone last-minute plans while Eddie's mind was working frantically. Umbraluna. What should he do? He just couldn't think; it was all going horribly wrong. Where was he? He never knew from minute to minute.

***

The Moonglimmer was not at home. He was down in the lime kiln with Sargasso and Seraphim, discussing the day's events and explaining the death of the Great Kraken. Sargasso listened quietly, taking in the astounding news.

"Do not be upset, Umbraluna. The Great Kraken has proved to be a liability and a burden for the Seafarers over the past five years. His exceptional status of age and rarity meant the Spirit of the Sea had to protect and care for him, but he was very difficult and increasingly aggressive and bad tempered – his great age I fear. It is a kind of blessing, for now his faithful carers will be set free and the Caves of Astraeus can be cleaned out and repaired and opened up to everyone who seeks a dark and secluded resting place. I do not fear the anger of the Great Spirit: he will say that fate has run its course, I am sure. I will await his message, for he is certain to have received the news."

Seraphim was quiet, but reassured by the seagull's words. Umbraluna too, had listened, glad that he had not been the means of destroying something very precious to them all. It seemed they had all been ready to let the ancient unhappy giant squid go.

"Thank you, Sargasso," he cawed, dancing and fluttering his wings as he took the shape of the pale blue-lighted shadow of his friend, the seagull. "I will hope that you hear forgiving words from the Spirit of the Sea."

The three of them sat in companionable silence, safe and warm in the lime kiln, watching the fascinating lights playing on the smooth water beside them. Umbraluna, knowing that it was probably the last time he would share an evening with these good friends, felt sad.

Chapter Forty
Tolivera goes too far.

In the woods, sunset came and went and a chilly twilight was indicated on the Dark Dwellers' clock. All remembered only being at a party, but the details and events were merely a distant memory, blurred forever, just as the elixir had promised. Tolivera was therefore puzzled by the dainty herb pillow to promote peaceful slumber he had found, beautifully embroidered with his name. It had obviously worked, he thought to himself, as he had enjoyed one of the best night's sleeps that he could remember.

"Such a tasteful gift." He looked at it again and saw a faint *MM* worked in the corner.

"Hmm." He mused. "I wonder who?"

The buzzard and his wife had also no recollection of their sons' obvious delight with the Nightingale Sisters and consequently there were no post-party rows or recriminations, which was just as well. The last remaining evidence of the party was removed by the exhausted squirrel gang, who packed everything away, then gradually crept into their cosy drays and curled up for a well-earned winter sleep, thankful it was all over.

Up in the Cornucopia tree, Dr Dew and Dr Yew were on duty as usual, always ready to coo and do their best for any unfortunate Woodlander. A light burnt continuously in the ivy-covered window, lit to guide the ill and needy to their door.

Oliphant and Freddie had become great friends now, sharing many secrets and exchanging tales. Sometimes the little robin forsook his cold and damp wall under the shrubs below Eddie's bedroom to stay in Oliphant's tree trunk home, sheltered and dry.

"I think you are just the person to take over from Tolivera… that is…, when he retires." Freddie told him carefully, not wanting to offend him by suggesting his cousin was inadequate in any way. "By the way, did you eat any dessert or have any coffee last night?" asked the robin.

"I don't think I did." Oliphant tried to remember. "I was too anxious about that poor girl, Ellie…"

"And I was too busy," added Freddie, "but, that means we may be the only ones to remember everything, because the doctors gave the Elixir of Distant Memories to Umbraluna and he put it into everything."

"Really? Well, we could go and look and see if it's all recorded in the Mists of Time, couldn't we?" Oliphant was getting rather excited now at his own idea.

"I don't know if anyone is going to like what we see, do you?" frowned Freddie, remembering the aggressive and hateful outburst by the doddery old owl. "Though it's likely everyone will be having an early night and with any luck we can go down the fluepipe again and have a look. What do you say? Shall we, Olly?"

"Yes indeed. Count me in, just don't let me fall into that vat again old chap, took me days to get my feathers straight after that, you know."

"OK, I'll try, I promise," reassured the bright-eyed robin, ready for another adventure.

Under the cover of darkness the two birds flew up through the woods and managed to locate the flue pipe again once they had reached the Great Ash Tree. This led directly to the huge vat.

"Let me go first," offered the robin, "And I *will* catch you at the bottom."

Oliphant looked doubtful; he was much bigger than Freddie.

"It will be alright, I'll find something to stop you with," encouraged Freddie, "Come on." And with a whee of delight,

Freddie disappeared over the edge of the pipe and into the dark beyond. Oliphant put his ear to the hole and heard a faint splash at the bottom. Then, silence. He waited anxiously as the robin, down below, spluttered out of the vat, shook himself dry, and finding a piece of wood, struggled to carry it to the pipe end and propped it there like a makeshift slide for the small white owl.

"Ready?" he called up the pipe, and his voice echoed up to the outside, to the rather frantic owl. With great relief that his friend had not drowned, he squeezed into the opening, looked all around quickly, and slid into the void, where, diverted by the makeshift slide, he hit the floor with a thud.

"Oh, well done!" said the robin in a satisfied way. It was, however, very dark, very dark indeed, and they searched for candles and strikers to see, knowing there must be some form of lighting. Finding the small metal rods and the attached strikers, they sparked the strips of beeswax into life and a flickering glow grew into a flame, illuminating everything.

"That's better," pronounced Oliphant happily, "and now for the evidence. Shall we?" and he indicated the silver dish which stood upon an old, heavily carved table. The Under Root Room was as they remembered, with shiny pipes and taps, measures and gauges, and loud plops and gurgles coming from them all the time.

"Which one is it?" asked the robin. No one else had ever viewed the Mists of Time before. It was only the buzzards and Tolivera who had ever seen the amazing liquid.

"It must be this one, next to the silver dish, I reckon," reasoned Oliphant, studying a polished brass tap sunk into the largest tree root.

Everything was captured in vision from the tips of every branch above ground and the sap ran down into the roots and was stored. To view any happenings, the tap was turned, and the coloured striped liquid flowed into the large silver dish where it pooled into pictures, moving and silent, and ran away into storage barrels.

Tolivera was in charge of the processing of the Mists of Time and was a surveillance specialist; very little happened in the woodland that he did not know about.

They chose the tap, dragged the table bearing the dish underneath it, and looking at each other for reassurance, said, "Shall we?"

There was a pause, then, both agreeing, they turned the tap slowly, and gradually out poured the amazing stripy liquid. It spread over the surface of the dish and the two birds could see everything. In the floor was a collecting drain and as the liquid spilled over the lip of the dish, it was funnelled away by pipe for storage.

"He clearly hasn't looked at this for a few days," remarked Freddie.

"Probably can't remember much about it," agreed Oliphant as he watched, fascinated by the pictures, the party revealing itself, and eventually Tolivera's frightening outburst and snatching of Ellie was replayed to them.

"There it is!" pointed Freddie, "Just look at his evil face! It's obvious he intended to hurt her. He's quite mad."

"He looks pretty nasty," agreed the owl, knowing the unhappy events just witnessed were the evidence they wanted.

"Seen enough?"

"Quite enough, thank you," was the grim reply. "He's certainly due to be removed from office now. I shall make a formal complaint to the buzzard, our Lord of the Woodland himself, and he can decide."

"Good." Freddie was satisfied. "Shall we go?"

"Yes, I've had enough of that creature's tantrums for one night."

They turned off the tap and returned the dish and the table to their correct place. It had all been very satisfactory. Blowing out the candle, they prepared themselves for their return up through the pipe.

"You'd better go first this time Olly, and I'll put the wood back," decided the sensible robin, and so the white owl squeezed himself into the pipe, and taking a deep breath, launched himself upwards, feathers compressed flat to his body. His head hit something hard at the top.

"Ouch!" called the surprised and frightened owl, and pushing once or twice upwards found he was unable to escape. He was forced to let himself slide back down, to where Freddie had carefully removed the wood, and he fell splashing into the black vat. Freddie was shocked and helped to drag the stunned owl out of the liquid history.

"Whatever happened?"

"Pipe's blocked! Can't get out! Hit my head!" gasped Oliphant, wet and dishevelled.

Freddie felt very scared.

"Somebody must have seen us, it's the only answer. But who can it be?"

"We're trapped now!" The not-so-white owl shook his feathers as Freddie used a striker once more to light a candle

It was an unbelievable stroke of bad luck. One of the young princes had sneaked out of the royal residence, lovesick for a particular songbird, and spotting activity with his intensely powerful eyes had remained still and silent, watching, amused and intrigued. He was now sitting over the venting pipe, deciding whether to tell Tolivera of the cheeky antics of the audacious pair.

They're obviously up to no good, he decided. *This pipe must surely lead to the secret Underground Root Workings. What can they be doing?* His youth and inexperience did not equip him with sufficient knowledge to piece together the reasons for the birds' strange behaviour, luckily, but his youthful arrogance and royal position meant he chose to exercise his power over them. It was irresistible to him. He was going to get someone into trouble. Not being the brightest of the three sons, he left the pipe to go and rouse Tolivera, making his way around to the other side of the tree to the main door.

Down in the Root Store things were not any better.

"Let me go and try," bravely suggested the robin as the two birds sat together, very worried indeed. Before Oliphant could protest, Freddie took a deep breath and shot up the flue pipe, only to pop out of the other end with a mighty whoosh! He turned and shouted down the pipe.

"Come on Olly! Hurry!" Hastily putting the candle out, the wet, cold owl made a huge effort and closing his eyes and pushing upwards with all his might he shot out of the other end like a cork from a bottle.

"Whew! We made it! Let's go before anyone sees us!" he begged the robin, who was keen to see who or what had blocked the pipe. They heard the voice of Tolivera talking to someone and he sounded pretty annoyed.

"What do you mean, you young whippersnapper? Waking me up? What d'ya say, someone in my Root Store? I don't believe it! Not one word! An owl and a robin? I don't think so, they wouldn't dare! And, what do you know about the Root Store, you nosy little begger? Eh? Now if you know what's good for you, you'll go away at once and stop poking your nose into my affairs! Be off with you!"

But the young prince tried to protest. "But, I saw them and—"

Tolivera pushed him off the branch angrily. "Leave me alone you little pest or I'll strip the feathers off your back. Do you hear me?" he screeched, brandishing his yellow talons at him. The young prince, who had landed uncomfortably at the bottom of the tree in the damp grass, was furious and frightened.

"You wrinkled old rat-catcher!" he shouted up to him, "I'll see you starve next winter, wait and see!" And he shot off home feeling humiliated and angry, as Tolivera slammed his door.

The robin and the owl, who had heard everything and now knew who the spy had been, sat huddled in a nearby sloe bush. What should they do about the prince who had seen them? As they contemplated this problem, cold and ready to go home, they heard voices in the woods behind them and turned anxiously to see who it was.

***

Eddie, Patrick, Sam and Peter quietly trekked up the hillside, hoping the sky would remain clear and that the visible portion of the moon would stay.

"Tell me again what happened," asked an incredulous Sam, having heard the story once and almost unable to believe it. "You actually signalled with this gadget to your father's ship and he knew it was you?"

"Yes, and we knew where the submarines were, we'd seen them." replied Eddie modestly. Sam was too out of breath for further conversation, as the hill was steep and he was not used to it, but eventually they reached the grassy summit of Gallants Bower where the panorama spread out, dark and eerie, hardly any lights visible.

Eddie found the Moonmirror and Patrick the Crystal Signaller and they pulled them from the makeshift hiding place. The moon was a few days from full, but well risen in the winter's darkest sky.

The group were recognised with relief by the robin and the owl concealed in the bushes. They decided to stay to observe even though they were cold and tired. Freddie was pleased to see Eddie and Ellie and enjoyed seeing the marvellous Moonmirror. Looking to their left, they saw a large bird approaching. The buzzard was on his way to the Great Ash Tree too, having been alerted to the intruders by his outraged youngest son. The buzzard liked neither particularly; the robin was too big for his boots, always hobnobbing with the humans, and the owl was too timid and shy, only good for carrying out orders, with not a single idea of his own in his head. First they had to be identified as the intruders.

Umbraluna was also on course for the Great Ash Tree, having parted from the shore-loving seagulls, wafting his invisible body upwards through the trees. As he caught sight of the mysterious white light of his home planet he felt a new faint longing to return. He had made up his mind that in the future he would lead a group from the linked tunnels on the dark side into the brightness and light of the other side. He would become a pioneer and set up a new colony, where he could look at Earth whenever he wanted to. Yes, he was ready to return, there was much to do. He sent a message via his integral personal transmitter to his fellow creatures, announcing his departure from planet Earth. His journey would begin very soon, and he hoped they might venture to the edge of darkness to look for him.

So it was that the Moonglimmer, the buzzard, the men and the boys all reached the ash tree at the same time. Freddie and Oliphant were hidden spectators, unable to move. Umbraluna sadly had only a few minutes left of the three-day human voice granted to him by the Dr Underconstumbles. The Elixir of Dreams was fading fast; time was running out.

Eddie knew the Moonmirror was fully charged, thanks to Umbraluna, and switched it on, wondering where his friend from space was. At once a creamy piercing light shone out, making a glittering pathway across the sea and joining with the reflection already provided by the moon itself. The effect was dazzling and everyone shielded their eyes. The buzzard, blinded, halted at once and took refuge in the nearest tree. Patrick switched on the Crystal Signaller and the rainbow gleams danced up and down the spectrum, sending sparkling rich colours of light twinkling across the night sky. Umbraluna reached Eddie's side, becoming the boy's shadow on the ground for the last time, and whispered in his ear.

"I must leave you now, Eddie. I am returning to my home but I shall signal to you and you to me, whenever you can. Say goodbye from me to little Ellie. Perhaps we may never meet again, but who knows in the future where our paths in the universe may lead? I have learnt much about the Earth, and one day you might visit me, our beams may yet cross again…" He faltered sadly, choking, "I am leaving you now. Shine your light on me forever…" and then his voice was gone, fading away softly into the night.

A message had been received far, far away, thousands of miles up into the black sky, where an excited group left their tunnels, switched on their brilliant blue eyes and travelled to the edge of darkness to look for the brave Umbraluna who had left his home to seek the strange signal from Earth. They directed their beams towards him and several intense flashing blue lights were visible, emitted from the unseen dark side of the moon.

"Look! Look!" called Sam excitedly. "What's that?"

Oliphant and Freddie were frightened by the brightness in the sky.

Peter was unsure of what he could see but suddenly, before he could understand it, a blue flash rose up from close by them and descended towards the sea. It began to follow the reflection of the moon, travelling along the moonlit pathway, a moving blue dazzle on the white watery road. At the horizon, where the light met the darkness, it arced up towards the sky, moving fast, outlined against the black, and in seconds it could no longer be seen.

The Moonglimmer was travelling at the speed of light, guided by his inbuilt navigation system, and glimpsing the blue twinkles above him knew he was going home. He turned once to watch the Earth spinning round, a last lingering glance at all he had loved, and then shot off on his chosen course.

Eddie and Patrick whispered, "He's found the way," to each other, silently saying goodbye to the Moonglimmer, knowing he had made his last journey from Earth.

Sam didn't know what was going on, and Peter was sure it was tricks of the light and mirrors sending multiple reflections between them.

Tolivera, above them in the tree, was disturbed by the bright beams and opened his door and screeched at the figures he saw outside. Humans again, was there to be no peace?

Sam was petrified and shone his torch beam into Tolivera's face, which only made him angry and screech more.

"Oh no! He's in one of his rages!" whispered Oliphant as the robin looked on, terrified fixed to the spot. The enraged owl jumped out, talons spread and landed on Sam's head, pecking and shrieking. At once, Peter grabbed a large branch of wood from the ground and hit the owl with it and down he fell, knocked out.

"Dad, Dad, what have you done?" yelled Eddie, as a stunned Sam, with blood running down his face, staggered and sat down, holding his head.

"Have you killed it?" asked Patrick calmly, looking down at the spreading wings of the very still owl. Peter, who had acted instinctively, was rather sorry and knelt beside the bird, pronouncing him merely stunned, no blood spilt and very much alive. Tolivera began to flap and move, suddenly springing to his feet and disappeared into the darkness. Oliphant felt faint, but Freddie was furious. What was the buzzard going to do?

The buzzard was aghast. He had seen everything, but it had all happened so fast he had been unable to intervene. Tolivera had proved by his behaviour what he had suspected for some time – it was definitely time for retirement. He had broken the Woodlander's Code and attacked a human. Maybe the Freedom Gate was the answer, but it did seem a rather severe punishment. Once escorted to the Gate, the offender was banished forever, expelled from the protection of the woodland and left to fend for themselves. Often they didn't survive. It would be the end of the reign of surveillance and gossip; no more veiled threats, insinuations and intimidations, which were some of the tactics the cunning, scheming Tolivera resorted to.

Perhaps I have let him get away with too much for too long, thought the Lord of the Woodland, feeling guilty. *He's grown too powerful; I should have curbed his vicious nature long before this. Now look what's happened,* as he uncomfortably surveyed the scene before him.

Patrick sat dabbing his father's head with a tissue. Sam was shocked and upset that the large owl had chosen to attack him. Peter felt extremely guilty for hitting out at the bird, a wild creature whose territory they had trespassed into, and the two boys were cross with Peter for hurting him. They felt sad and disappointed that Umbraluna had left them so quickly, not perhaps understanding that it was the best way to leave. The robin and the owl watched helplessly.

Hearing the commotion not too far away, Dr Dew and Dr Yew got up quickly, and picking up a small drawstring bag made from fine calico, left the Cornucopia tree to assess the situation. They flew quietly into the darkness, spotting at once the fading light still issuing from the Moonglimmer, and perched themselves above the huddle of humans to observe.

"Dear, dear, what a to-do-o-o-o-o!" cooed one to the other, shaking their heads.

Tolivera was groggily falling in and out of sleep under a thick gorse bush, unseen in the dark shadows. He was nursing a bit of a headache, but otherwise unharmed.

"Shall I?" cooed Dr Dew, and nodding, Dr Yew helped to open the bag, and calling "Renew! Renew! Some help for you-o-o-o-o!" they shook the contents out over the whole area and Heavenly Healing Flakes fluttered down all around them, white and pure and perfect.

"It's beginning to snow," said Peter, rather wondering how, as the sky was clear and he could see the stars. "How strange!" and he held both his hands out to feel the cold soft flakes reaching their destination.

Quietly satisfied the situation would now return to normal, the two pigeons left the tree and went back home. "That will do-o-o-o-o," they agreed confidently.

The boys were beginning to pack up their two light inventions which they then stored away in the tree. Sam and Peter felt better as the Healing Flakes covered them, and yawning suddenly, everyone felt tired and longed for bed. It had been a very eventful night. Gradually the flakes stopped falling; each person had been sprinkled by enough to influence them, including Tolivera, as a few filtering through the gorse bush onto him, healing him.

"Are you OK, Sam?" Peter asked, and he nodded in reply. The four began to head for home, leaving the woodland in its natural darkness, silent and peaceful.

The Moonglimmer was still travelling on and on through space, past orbiting satellites, unknown planets, shooting stars and sun showers, speeding on his way to his home on the dark side of the moon. He was recalling his experiences on Earth and trying to picture all the things he had discovered living on the bright and colourful planet, grateful for the enlightening experience.

The robin and the owl flew back down the hill, wondering what would happen now.

"Poor old Tolly," commented Oliphant, feeling sorry for his uncle.

"Nonsense!" spluttered Freddie, "He'd have had it in for us. We're just lucky he didn't believe the young buzzard." He was tired and irritable, and went home with Oliphant to his cosy tree house in the second ash tree on the right, to a warm bed and a good sleep.

The other subdued group reached Warfleet Creek and their homes, some pleased and some disappointed with the evening.

Only the buzzard remained awake and alert, staring into the night, unsure of his next actions, but knowing something would have to be done. This evening could not be ignored.

Chapter Forty-one
Difficult decisions

The next day was Christmas Eve, and last-minute preparations were underway in the households at Warfleet Creek and at the Old Bath House. The café at the castle was of course open as usual, all the regulars relying on its warm comfort, good food, and cheery staff. Everyone went into Dartmouth for last-minute Christmas shopping where it was full of atmosphere, with various charity groups selling chestnuts and mince pies, singing carols and collecting money for less fortunate individuals. Queues grew in the supermarkets and the cafés and tea shops were thronged with weary shoppers, reviving and refreshing themselves.

Eddie, Ellie and Patrick wandered around just drinking in the atmosphere, enjoying the hustle and bustle of Christmas. The fishing boats tied up for the last time and the crews looked forward to a few days' rest at home to relax and have a good time with their families.

Down at the creek edge, away from the excitement, Sargasso and Seraphim, who now seemed to go everywhere together, pecked in the muddy oozes of the beach at low tide, talking to a pair of oystercatchers, searching for tasty morsels in the mud. The weather was dry but cloudy and dull with a little wind – just how they liked it. The water, still and smooth, was a dark green sheet broken only by tiny ripples.

Sargasso heard a faint roar in the silvered pearl shell he wore around his neck, and looked up, concerned. A message was crossing the ocean, finding him over miles of water, travelling like the wind.

"Hear me, Sargasso. Greetings from the Spirit of the Sea. We are indebted to the creature from the dark side of the moon. The Great Kraken had lived too long in the Caves of Astraeus, and many of my subjects toiled willingly to provide his every need. Now the caves will be cleansed and restored and opened to all who seek a restful place once more. You have served me well, Sargasso the Seagull, friend of Seafarer, Skywinger and Woodlander, and as a reward I have decided to grant you the Gift of All Transcending Language so you may continue to nurture good relations with all our fellow creatures. To welcome the stranger from the dark side of the moon is much to your credit, and to have shown him life under the sea in my domain has pleased me well. I shall inform the Skywingers and Woodlanders of my decision and they will acknowledge you for this honour. That is all. Use this special gift wisely, as I know you will." And the roaring began to diminish as if the water was receding like a spring tide on a shore.

Sargasso was filled with emotion, and could hardly grasp the enormity of this rarely awarded honour – the gift of universal language, the ability to talk to everyone in their own tongue, even humans. He was utterly thrilled and sat very still, thinking deeply about Eddie and Ellie. He could talk to them whenever he wanted to. Seraphim who knew he had received a message, but could not hear it, waited patiently.

Eventually, Sargasso spoke. "Come, my dear Seraphim, let us find some tasty morsels and bring them back to the lime kiln. I cannot wait to tell you." Soon they sat together in the shelter while he told her the wonderful news. Afterwards, he gazed earnestly into her eyes, and touching her wingtip said,

"Sweet Seraphim, on this special day I ask you to please be my life's partner, if you wish it. To make our home here at

Warfleet Creek and perhaps to raise a family close to all that I cherish most. What do you say? Tell me at once!" he urged her hopefully, gazing at the pretty, wise and kind gull. She fluttered her wings and raised her beak a few times before replying.

"I am honoured, Sargasso, that you have chosen me. I think it will be a good partnership. I like this creek, undiscovered from prying eyes, with its gentle waters and rocky shore. I will willingly become your wife." And she looked at him proudly with her large devoted eyes.

"That's settled then," replied Sargasso, offering her a tasty morsel from his beak. Soon they would exchange the Seafarers vows quietly, just the two of them, and afterwards they would begin their new life together, united as one.

***

Very early that morning the buzzard, unable to rest or sleep, had sought the advice of the Dr Underconstumbles who he thought owed him some of their wisdom; after all it was he who had invited them here and found them their unique home high in the ivy-clad branches. He pulled the bell-rope, heard the jangling conker shells far away, and the door swung open. He hopped up the spiral staircase adorned with neatly labelled jars, phials and glass containers held in cases all around the walls.

Dr Dew and Dr Yew sat at the large partners' desk, pen in hand, writing in a huge ledger, crystal spectacles perched on the end of their beaks. The air was lightly perfumed with that unmistakable heady mixture of wild flowers.

A small white dove appeared and curtsied to him. "My lord, come this way," and she led him to a window seat and brought him valerian tea and clover cakes.

"You will be seen in a very short time, my lord," Verity told him, curtsying again and vanishing into a side room. The buzzard relaxed in the peaceful scented atmosphere and drank the warm pink-tinged tea. It was strangely enjoyable and the clover cakes were sweet and mouth-melting. He sat back feeling tired and overwhelmingly sleepy. Verity peeped in through a window in the door and as Dr Dew nodded to her, she tiptoed in and guided the buzzard, now almost asleep, into the side room where the most exquisitely comfortable soft bed was waiting, and laid him down, soothing him with her gentle cooing. He did not resist and was soon asleep, covered by a plump feather quilt of the finest down.

"He's fast asleep, Doctors."

"Good," said Dr Dew and Dr Yew together. "We've been expecting him. He's in a bit of a stew-o-o-o-o-o, but we know what to do-o-o-o-o-o!"

Dr Yew got up from the desk and went to the large dispensing cupboard, took a gold key from a hook and went to a special case on the wall marked EMERGENCY REMEDIES. He removed a green bottle marked Elixir of Necessary Decisions. This was not a popular elixir but nevertheless it helped make life a great deal easier to those in high authority. It reduced guilt and self-reproach after making important decisions that affected many people's lives, for some decisions were unpleasant and some painful. A few drops were placed on a cotton wool pad which was carried carefully to the sleeping buzzard, where it was placed over his nose to breathe in gently as he dozed. The bottle was resealed and locked away carefully, the key replaced on its hook.

"It's up to him now, we shall have to wait. When he wakes he will accept what is true-o-o-o-o and know what to do-o-o-o-o," the doctors agreed and went to write the dose they had administered to the Lord of the Woodland in the large ledger.

The buzzard slept on, many dreams flashing before him: trees and houses, forests and mountains; he seemed to be on a journey of endless flight. He saw a craggy hilltop with pine trees, a fire burning on the slopes, smoke and flames; a lake of black water, dark and deep; a group of frightened animals and birds, fleeing this place; and then he knew – it was a forest fire on Dartmoor. An eagle had been trapped and injured, the whole area was evacuated and in disarray. It was terrible. The pictures came and went. Eventually re-growth appeared, as the forest began to recover; but very slowly. He could see a little gathering of birds and animals; they were looking for a new leader, now that their eagle was injured and helpless, but there was no one.

The buzzard woke up. He knew what he should do. He stretched and lay back on the comfortable Cloud of Ease, feeling alive and refreshed. It would be done. He looked around the room with its grey and white cloud-strewn walls and thanked the day he had invited the two quietly dedicated doctors to the woodland. He got up, pushed open the door and entered the empty room before him. He knew the way out and left stealthily, tiptoeing down the staircase and out into the new woodland morning waiting for him. The pigeons and the dove had retired to another room, not wishing their ruler and lord to be embarrassed at his previous helpless and confused state.

Immediately, the buzzard made his way to the Great Ash Tree and hammered on the door.

"Enter, my lord," drawled the voice of Tolivera. "To what do I owe this visit?" he enquired arrogantly.

"We're going to look at the Mists of Time, Tolly. The New Year will be with us soon and a fresh batch will be started. Shall we go down?" he said to the surprised owl with authority.

"As you wish my lord." Tolivera led the way down to the root system, deep in the underground room. The taps, dials and wheels were all familiar to them both and the silver dish on the elaborate carved table was put in place. They both looked at the dates which clicked round over the large vat.

"Have you checked this recently?" demanded the buzzard.

"Umm no, my lord, not that I recall. Very little happens at this time of the year, what with hibernators asleep and the dark days."

"But the date is almost today's, this must have been looked at by someone?" the buzzard quizzed him, remembering the information his youngest son had given him and the possibility of intruders. Tolivera said absolutely nothing. He was confused. Was it possible? That young prince had woken him one night… surely not! A faint wave of fear shivered over him.

The buzzard recalled the Mists of Time in the vats for the previous month, by turning the wheel backward, and the dates reversed. He sat down beside the large owl and waited. Then he turned the brass tap and out poured the coloured liquid to pool into pictures in the silver dish.

What revealed itself to them both was shocking indeed. The party, now just a distant memory to them due to the elixir was quite clearly shown – Tolivera's non-appearance, then his outbursts, then his attack on Ellie. The three princes' adoration of the Nightingale Sisters showed up only too well. The appearance of three minute humans was a real shock. Everything was recalled to the buzzard. Everything. The striped liquid kept flowing into the dish. Next came the robin and the small white owl sneaking into the vent pipe; his son and Tolivera arguing, and later, worst of all, the vicious attack on Sam McNab. It was too late for Tolivera to deny it. The evidence was here before them, shocking and condemning.

"I see that you are not what I thought you were, Tolivera. You have misused your authority and broken many, if not all of our Woodlander codes. I am going to have to remove you from office, old fellow. This cannot continue."

Tolivera was broken. He could hardly believe it. He heaved great shuddering sobs and the buzzard let him. He remained silent. After a while Tolivera spoke.

"Where shall I go, lord? What shall I do? Am I to be shown to the Freedom Gate?" His voice was quavering and hoarse.

"I have an alternative for you, if you are willing to take the challenge," announced the buzzard gently.

"Anything, lord! Anything other than the Freedom Gate! I'm so afraid of…being out there…" He began to sob again.

"Come on, Tolly," urged his master, "It is not so bad, gather yourself and listen to me. There is nothing so hideous and depraved as the misuse of power. I will not tolerate it, but you can redeem yourself."

"Tell me how, lord, tell me!" cried out Tolivera, with a seed of hope now implanted.

The buzzard had got him where he wanted him: now he would obey him.

"There is a small woodland community on high Dartmoor who have suffered a great tragedy. Their Forest is damaged and their leader injured. I want you to go and help rebuild those shattered lives and you are to take my youngest son with you and teach him how to govern. The eagle is alive and will guide you, but you will be the one. All eyes will be on you. This is the challenge. I offer you the choice."

There *was* no choice as far as Tolivera was concerned, but he would have to be very careful, very careful indeed. It was his only chance.

"I will go, my lord and… I thank you, I will not fail you."

"You are to fly by the rising moon to your new position in the Forest, accompanied by Treen. I will instruct him, for he knows nothing of this yet."

The tawny owl nodded, thankful that he had been saved.

The Mists of Time with so many shameful actions on it was sent into the vats and distilled at once. The buzzard did not want them kept on view.

He left Tolivera to contemplate his fate and went back to the Citadel to confront his three sons, Een, Tween and Treen, and to tell his wife that one of her precious brood was leaving, and very soon. It all had to be done, just as his dream had revealed to him. He was well pleased with his monumental decision, and had already chosen the old tawny owl's successor.

Chapter Forty-two
Christmas preparations

Eddie, Ellie and Patrick completed their last Christmas trip to town with hot chocolate topped with whipped cream and far too many mince pies in the Sea Shanty café on the river front. Enid, the plump proprietor, adored these cheeky, cheerful children and always piled up their plates.

"They'll only go stale," she told them. "We're closed now for quite a few days." Putting a plateful of pies in front of them she said, "It's you or the seagulls!"

"Sargasso would love them," commented Eddie to his sister and friend.

"Isn't it a pity Umbraluna's gone now, he was such fun," complained Ellie, folding her hands under her chin and looking out of the window at the river gliding by.

"*And* I missed him leaving," she added, looking accusingly at the boys.

Eddie knew in his heart he had kept it a secret, but he had been his discovery and parting had been so sudden. Some things just cannot be shared.

"We didn't know, did we?" they both claimed together, defensively. "But it was pretty spectacular!" agreed Patrick, "Except when that owl attacked my dad – that wasn't so funny."

"He almost got us once, do you remember, Ellie?"

"Yes, it was awful. They're quite big close up to you, with big talons."

"Have we done everything?" Eddie asked, getting bored, picking up the parcels.

"Think so."

"Yes, got all I want now." So they reluctantly agreed it was, at last, time to go home.

"Mum's at the church doing the Christmas flowers, so maybe Dad will get fish and chips!"

"Hope so."

Paying Enid for their snacks the three started to walk back up the hill to Warfleet.

"We've had a really exciting time recently, haven't we?" Patrick said, thinking about the last couple of weeks.

"Yes, and George and Bridget are having a party tonight before we go to Midnight Communion at St Petrox."

"I hope I can stay up that late," said Ellie in a worried voice.

When they reached the creek, Eddie and Patrick went down to the beach to mess around and Ellie walked to the church to meet her mother. She wanted to see all the beautiful decorations and help clear up – she had neglected St Petrox since her pet mice had moved out and she felt guilty. Skipping along the road, she was suddenly full of the intense excitement of Christmas, which she loved, and looking forward to the family rituals peculiar only to them. Their father always made breakfast while Mother went to church, everyone dressed in their best clothes. Mother let them eat whatever they liked and as much as they liked for just one day! Presents to each other were always after the Queen's speech, but their "big" presents were there for them first thing in the morning. And so on.

She reached the large door, now adorned with a circlet of greenery and berries and went inside to the smell of newly cut fir, vanilla-scented candles and the elusive perfume of white lilies and red roses. Everything was in place, shiny apples and fir cones dressed each window shelf, beneath tall flower arrangements.

Her mother was putting the figures out for the Nativity scene just inside the doorway so that visiting children could see it clearly.

"Hello, Mum, this looks lovely," she told her admiringly.

"Hello dear…Yes, it's turned out well this year," she agreed modestly. Your Father always comes and does the tree and lights with me. It's all done.Going to help me with this? It's the last thing."

"I'd like to, Mum." Ellie reached into the cardboard box and began to carefully remove and unwrap the Wise Men. The familiar little scene unfolded – Mary, Joseph, and the Baby Jesus with the shepherds, an ox and a donkey, an angel and the Three Wise Men, all crowded into and around the tiny stable; moss was laid around the base and the tiny star fastened to the roof.

"There!" breathed Mary with satisfaction, "All done," as Ellie picked up the tall broom and began to sweep up and clear away. Mary emptied her flower buckets outside and suddenly a bird flew into the church and all around the inside. Ellie noticed it at once.

"Oh! How will he get out?"

"The same way he got in, silly!" replied her mother, coming down the steps. Ellie wondered if it was Freddie but couldn't see in the dimming light.

"Right, let's go," said her mother brightly. " I hope the Vicar likes it." And they turned to go.

"Shall we leave the door open for the bird?" Ellie asked anxiously.

"Yes dear, if you like. I expect the choirmaster will be coming with music and books, and somebody from the castle locks it up later anyway."

Hearing this, Ellie felt much better and they began the walk home, past the Old Bath House, where smoke was coming out of the chimney.

"Smoke's up! Somebody's home," remarked Mary, noting Sam's car parked in the bay.

"They're getting ready for the party tonight, I hope," said Ellie gleefully, "now what shall we wear, Mum?" and all the rest of the way home they discussed this, running through lists of the possibilities.

Arriving back at Watermill Cottage they found Eddie and Patrick, Sam and Peter in a state of high excitement, with various newspapers spread over the dining room table.

"Come and look, Mum!" Eddie ran excitedly to greet her. "There's some pictures and an article about the giant squid! Look! They must be Sacramento's photos!"

"Really?" Mary was intrigued and sure enough, Peter and Sam showed her on the front of the Dartmouth Post and in the Daily View, a national newspaper.

"Good heavens!" She read the headlines,

EXCITEMENT IN THE MARINE WORLD, and *GIANT SQUID REVEALED AFTER SUPPOSED EXTINCTION!* together with the photographs that Sacramento had taken on board the *Alice May*. There was also a picture of a Professor Palmer examining remains on a beach, and an article written by the young wildlife photographer himself.

"Well, well, well," laughed Mary. "Isn't that amazing!"

Sam was so proud to have been there and to have witnessed this strange phenomenon. He was very impressed. Eddie looked closely at the photo taken on the beach. There seemed to be a grey shadow on the ground beside the remains of the giant squid. Yes, Professor Palmer had two shadows, Eddie was sure of it.

Could it be? Was it possible? Had Umbraluna gone to investigate the death of the giant squid? He sat and wondered. He would never really know, but he was determined to try and keep in touch with the visitor from the dark side of the moon just as he had pledged - to signal for ever.

"Any one for fish and chips?" asked Peter hopefully, interrupting Eddie's thoughts.

"Oh yes, Dad, yes please," was the united reply and Peter and Sam went off in the car to fetch lunch for everyone, just as Irene arrived on the doorstep.

"Where is everybody?" she complained, stepping inside. She too was shown the newspaper headlines and the story was retold for her benefit.

"How interesting," was her reaction, as she carefully read the newspaper articles.

"Fancy you being there with that admiral's son, things certainly seem to happen round here," said Irene, surprised.

Patrick, Ellie, and Eddie glanced at each other and smiled their special secret smiles. *They certainly do,* each one of them silently agreed. If only you knew!

Irene had discovered she didn't like being alone. During her busy working life, lecturing and touring America, attending seminars and writing articles, she had imagined that to work in the peace and quiet of Waterside Cottage would be perfect, but it had proved to be otherwise. Not being interested in cooking, homemaking or children, if she wasn't working, there only seemed to be the same old shopping and Dartmouth had proved too small to have enough scope for her. After the few days of the Christmas celebrations, she knew she would be bored and restless. Sam surprisingly seemed to be much more occupied and

335

enjoying himself. However tonight, there was a party to look forward to.

"Mary, I want you to help me choose gifts for George and Bridget, I've bought quite a few and need a little expert advice. Would you?" she asked her. Mary, who was rather tired from cutting masses of greenery, planning, fetching and carrying and then standing around on the cold stone floor of the church, just wanted to sit down for a while.

"Can I come down a bit later, Irene? It's been a busy day," she told her. "What if I pop in on the way to George and Bridget's?"

"I suppose that will do," sniffed Irene ungraciously, accepting an offer from Ellie of a cup of coffee and settling down in a comfortable armchair. Mary sighed inwardly. She was here to stay. They sat together drinking coffee, waiting for the fish and chips to arrive. Although Irene didn't want it for herself, she enjoyed other peoples' domestic lives and was content to join in for a while.

The men arrived back, lunch was eaten and there were mysterious goings on afterwards; cars ferried backward and forward, buckets, whisperings, bags, and trips to the garage and to Blackpool Sands; the children were intrigued.

"Don't spoil it," Mary told them anxiously, "your father has got a real surprise for you. Just wait until tomorrow."

Reluctantly, they stopped trying to figure out what was going on, and wandered up to Eddie's bedroom. The three sat around, talking over their latest exploits, looking at the newspapers and discussing the Moonglimmer.

"Do you know, I think he was the one who broke my window?"

"No surely not! How could he have done it?"

"With the light, stupid! When he turned it on it was so incredibly strong, don't you remember?"

Ellie flicked through the local paper, not entering into the discussion of Umbraluna.

"Look here, someone's written about a strange blue light visible over the sea one night, they reckon it was a UFO and are warning of a possible invasion," she laughed.

"A nutter, of course." Patrick said wisely, nodding. "Totally impossible as we know. Visitors from outer space? Whatever next!"

"I don't know where they dream these things up from, do you?" added Eddie, and they all laughed and laughed in hysterical amusement.

***

Later that evening, joining together in the brilliantly lit riverside drawing room of the Old Bath House, they ate delicious tasty snacks made by Bridget and drank grape juices and fizzy drinks. Everyone was looking their best, smiling and chatting, mingling with the few neighbours from along the road who had been invited; a retired Commander and his wife, a local nurseryman, his young wife and new twins, and a widow who lived alone and wrote gardening books. They were a very merry group and the Christmas tree lights twinkled over the river and the fresh red poinsettias in pots along the windowsills carefully placed by Bridget, looked festive and welcoming.

At 11.30pm, drawn by the insistent church bells, the churchgoers left and wrapping up warmly, walked the short distance to St Petrox: Eddie, Ellie and Patrick, Mary and Peter,

Irene and Sam, and finally, George and Bridget. As they reached the doorway, candlelight spilled out onto the ground and the scent of flowers, greenery and Christmas trees greeted them. Andrew the Vicar welcomed them warmly.

"Good evening and welcome to you all." as the sound of organ music reached their ears. Sitting in the shadowy church, candles flickering around them, with so many other people who had made the journey from Dartmouth town, there was a real sense of belonging, as the magic of Christmas and all it meant touched them all. Singing the familiar carols in this beautiful setting, it became an intensely meaningful experience; each in their own way was glad they had made the effort to come here on this special night.

High up on a stone lintel a robin sang out thankfully, unnoticed by anyone, and the bat family, awoken by the bells, listened to the music of the human race that was being repeated all over the world.

Higher up in the dark woods of Gallants Bower, a tawny owl and a young buzzard said a sad goodbye to a small family group and winged over the valley, past the church, hearing the faint strains of music as they left for the distant peaks of Dartmoor; setting out on a journey of repentance and discovery, one to comfort the other.

Down in the second ash tree on the right in the trees above Watermill Cottage a small white owl prepared an acceptance speech for his new position, worrying and fretting that he would not be equal to the task before him.

Far, far away, across the miles of the everlasting mystery of space, a small blue light flickered in the black night sky. He was home!

Learned astronomers who were now keenly observing the unusual light being emitted periodically from the moon, noted the date and time: midnight on 24th December, 1988, and wondered…

Could this be a new beginning?

THE END